BENEATH THE DARKNESS

ARCHIE OLIVER

World Castle Publishing, LLC
Pensacola, Florida
Copyright © Archie Oliver 2015
Paperback ISBN: 9781629893303
eBook ISBN: 9781629893310
First Edition World Castle Publishing, LLC, December 14, 2015
http://www.worldcastlepublishing.com

Licensing Notes

Cover: Karen Fuller
Editor: Maxine Bringenberg

PROLOGUE

Iridescent blue-black eyes blinked twice and then slowly closed. Ten heartbeats later, the lids opened to a slit again and stayed open. She watched in intervals like this while she napped. Her breathing sounded ragged and forced. Several days ago, she had been in a fight with another meat-eater over the remains of some less fortunate animal. She had won the rancid flesh, but suffered severe bite marks that still pained her. The ripped skin around her left nostril would probably never close. At the end of each breath, a gravely *sneeert* sound issued from one of her nostrils. Ragged edges of a terrible tear vibrated and flapped. Each breath would be a constant reminder of the encounter. *Shhh…sneeert*, over and over again.

***

Mother observed and recorded the large animal from about twelve feet directly above it. Mother was a time traveler from another world whose people had discovered this planet many years earlier. They had the capacity to not only visit other solar systems, but to voyage through the past…forbidden to change anything, but recording everything. This was Mother's favorite creature in this time period. The animals were slightly similar to her people's evolutionary tale. They were admittedly more primitive than any of her ancestors, but there was a small connection to their appearance and sense of family.

Although she was not supposed to be here now, she was concerned enough that she felt the voyage necessary. Her people had moved on to a later time in the planet's progression to start new observations, and would be furious if they knew she had disobeyed them. Her request for one last look had been expressly denied. She and several others were due to meet up with the main body of observers sometime in the next three rotations of the sun.

Mother had slipped away from the other observers for a last look at Sneert before her own birthing pains became too much to ignore. She thought she had at least two more days before it would be necessary to begin seriously thinking about the birth of her child.

She had sentimentally nicknamed the large beast Sneert, because of the sound of her frayed breathing. Mother wished she could reach out and heal the big animal — she had the capabilities and was sorely tempted — but the damage had already been documented and she could not interfere, even though it would be such a simple thing to do.

It would be pointless, in any event. This planet was about to go through abrupt and pronounced changes. Everything would change, and death was inevitable. Very few of this planet's species would survive if the future was to be as it should. She often wrestled with this no-interference philosophy. It would be so very easy to step in and keep everything as it was. They had the technology to do exactly that. This was not a planet they intended to use for anything except research. Why not let the current species survive, and damn the next evolutions?

Mother and the other observers had been studying this particular planet for many years. Several of the other scientists were in the near future, observing the animals who eventually would inherit this planet from the current masters. They had started with its origin and worked through its demise, recording all that happened. Their first scan was primary, an overview with no real details. Now they were working on the specifics. Her specialty was this particular era, and she had been doing it long enough to become emotionally attached to some of the animals, even though logic dictated against it.

She had a real fondness for the large beast in front of her. Sneert seemed to register something familiar in temperament and her nurturing behavior. Mother realized that once her own child came, it would be a long time before she could visit the large beast again, if ever. She would be reassigned to another timeline after her birthing, and this may be the last opportunity to see her old friend. Her next assignment would be to observe and record the small surviving animals that endured and subsisted in the small places of a soon to be ravaged world.

These small creatures, as far as she could tell, were not very inspirational and would test her attention span. They lived in the mud, filth, and dirty holes of the world, scabbing out their diminutive existences, snarling and tearing at each other in the back shadows of desolate places, where once stood monumental forests, rivers, and plains. These were only the backs of animals over which a new species would evolve that might achieve some prominence and significance worth chronicling.

Mother's mind was filled with the bleak despair of leaving her beloved animals. She realized through observation that these large beings only killed to survive. They were not vindictive, nor the malevolent executioners she had once thought them to be. Instead, they prized life. Often tender and gentle with their own, they were furiously protective of their family and would sacrifice themselves if necessary.

Mother's vehicle was soundless and invisible to any animal below. Remaining overhead, she cautiously maneuvered a little in front of the large animal, closer to Sneert's face. She reached out and lightly dragged the back of her hand across the viewing screen, which was filled with Sneert's face. Emotions of love, respect, and reverence flowed over her. She patted the screen, knowing that Sneert had no idea that Mother and her ship were now within touching distance. Sneert had remarkable senses, but none detected that she was not alone.

***

Sneert was forty feet in length, and when she stood was a little over fifteen feet in height. At the moment, she was balanced on her two feet and tail, leaning forward on a large dead tree that had fallen long ago. Her two useless arms hung in front of her with her thick, muscular neck resting on the tree, barely hanging over its edge. This was her favorite place to rest. It was dangerous for her to try and lie down because of the difficulty in getting six tons back on her feet, even with her immense tail to counterbalance the large head and chest. Leaning on the tree gave her a comfortable position and allowed her to stand quickly if needed.

Flies and other insects were entangled together, swarming in clouds around her mouth, each trying to taste the pale yellow pus that leaked from the corner of her left eye, or the left over pieces of rotting meat that hid between her six-inch serrated teeth…morsels left over from her last meal. Sneert belched and shook her head, scattering the insect clouds.

Sneert looked over the edge of the tree and confirmed that her two young nippers were where they were supposed to be. They were about six weeks old and resting in a scratched out nest of compost and mud that Sneert had commandeered from another, much smaller animal, which had surrendered the nest with no fight. It was a well-protected haven. A severe cliff with a long drop into water framed the background behind the nest, allowing for no attack from that direction.

She began to softly rumble deep in her throat, a sign that she was comfortable, content, and safe. Urine, dark yellow and brown, began to run in steaming rivulets from beneath her feet and tail. Sneert propelled a miasma of fetid gas and slightly changed positions. Several hours passed. Midday gave way to approaching darkness.

***

Unseen by either Mother or Sneert, another set of eyes peeked out from behind brush held back with clawed fingers. The eyes were black, fringed with red, set above a brownish orange mandible. About eight feet in length and about two hundred pounds, the animal clenched its claws and nodded in anticipation and desire. Sneert was far too big and dangerous to even think about, but her offspring…they would do just fine.

His kind hunted in packs, and this one was no exception. It silently backed out of the bush, hunkered down, and went to find the rest of his deadly little friends. The pack soon surrounded the sleeping mother and her children, hiding in the dense brush but staying well down wind. The problem that needed to be worked out was a diversion. It was impossible to attack Sneert or her sprogs directly. To confuse and briefly disturb Sneert's attention, two of them positioned themselves away from the pack and began to make scrabbling noises in the foliage…not really aggressive, but just loud enough to get Sneert's attention.

***

The large beast contentedly half slept, only vaguely registering the noise. Her eyelids slowly parted to thin slits, and she almost imperceptibly swiveled her head just enough to look in the direction of the noise. As of yet, it was only a noise and not a threat. She softly inhaled air, trying to identify the sound. Nothing. She again closed her eyes, but kept alert.

***

The pack separated into two groups. One group drew as close as possible to the sleeping young while still staying downwind. They quietly settled in the brush, every head pointed in the direction of their quarry. The other group went in the opposite direction, positioning themselves behind and to the side of Sneert. Instinctively they all knew they would have to be a little bolder if they wanted to pull Sneert's attention away from her young.

***

Mother was oblivious to everything except her own thoughts and feelings for the large animal in front of her. She continued to zoom in on Sneert's face and think about how she would miss all of this. Her instruments registered everything, mutely acknowledging the nearby scene and its players, giving no audible resonance or suggestion of what was about to happen.

***

The divided pack was in position. Those closest to the great beast skulked even nearer to the ground and made their way forward, exposing themselves ever so slightly out of the brush. They held their breath, bunching their muscles, ready to spring forward. In a synchronized moment, they leapt out of concealment and growled their challenge. They boldly snarled and gnashed their teeth in quick mock attacks, moving at Sneert and then backing off, challenging the much larger animal to attack them, hoping she would think them enough of a threat to respond. While this was happening, the rest of the pack watched, ready to rip the young animals' throats out. Given the opportunity, they would kill and carry them off in less than ten heartbeats.

***

Sneert immediately responded. As she struggled to quickly gain her feet her head shot up and hit hard against something she could not see. Undeterred, she bowed her head and with all of her strength, threw her head up again. This time, whatever she hit gave way and she struggled to her feet. In a fast spin she turned on the intruders, her mind black with rage. The seemingly gentle giant thundered her fury in a deep rumbling roar that stopped the pack in their respective tracks. Her teeth chewed the air, shaking large globules of saliva as she converged on the smaller predators.

***

Mother was thrown backwards hard and to the floor of her vehicle as Sneert's head came up. Before she could regain her feet, Sneert again hammered the ship, this time upending it momentarily. Mother, now on her knees, was sent sprawling again. Still on the floor, she reached up for the maneuvering wand, jerking it violently in an attempt to pull herself up. The vessel spun backwards and to the left. In an instant, her ship slammed into a large tree, pushing it over enough to expose the roots.

Sneert turned to the sound of this new menace, but saw nothing, so she spun around to face the pack again. By this time they had separated, and were all trying to get to her litter while avoiding those vicious teeth. Counterbalancing her spin, Sneert's massive tail smashed into Mother's ship.

Still trying to gain her feet, Mother pulled again on the maneuvering wand. In a spin of her own, she collided with Sneert, and both went over the edge of the cliff. Sneert gave voice to her anguish as she hit the small ledge about half her body length down, and bellowed in pain. One of her legs broke from the sudden enormous weight and angle of the fall, the bone protruding through the meat of the leg in an angry wound that pumped blood onto the ledge.

Mother's ship hit the bottom and sprayed a fountain of water into the air.

The pack, always the opportunists, moved as one toward Sneert's offspring. There was no hurry now. Once they had crippled the young beasts, they ate at their leisure, killing their quarry one bite at a time.

Mother, knowing her ship was damaged and going down, reached for the timeline control and pushed it forward in a blind attempt to reach her friends. She knew the bottom of the chasm was coming up. There was no time for an accurate line, just a push and a hope. She hit hard and darkness swallowed her.

***

Sneert writhed on the small ledge, unable to regain her feet. She smelled the stench of her own blood and feces, and knew she was dying. The desperate sounds of her children tormented her soul. She screamed her rage and impotently thrashed her legs, causing the blood to flow faster. It took most of the night for her to die. Long after her children's cries had quieted, Sneert lay helpless in her sorrow.

***

When the pack was sure the large beast was dead, they spent most of eight days eating her. Her bones, bleached white in the sun, were scattered by scavengers and became buried in the mud run offs from above.

***

Mother awoke in the dark. A haze filled the air, making it difficult to see. Only a few thin beads of blue lights blinked here and there. She could smell the working fluids of the ship, and debris was everywhere. Attempting to stand on the tilted floor, she had to grab makeshift handles wherever she could. She dragged herself to the controls, where everything was silent and black. A choked gasp of despair issued from her lips when she ran her hands over the screens and nothing responded. She ranted against her stupid decision to share one more moment with her beloved creature, because she had told no one where she was going or when. In desperation she pounded her fist against the blank view screen, hoping to jar it back to life. She could not tell where she had landed, or more importantly, when. The chance that she had pushed the timeline controls to a time when her friends could find her was bleak. There had been no time to be specific, and now, looking at the controls, she knew it was too late.

Sitting down to think, she physically took inventory of herself. She was in pain, but no visible wounds could be seen. As her eyes became accustomed to the gloom, they came to rest on a compartment housing emergency supplies.

Mother crawled over to the manual handle and spun it to the left. A hiss sounded as air escaped the compartment and it opened,

11

revealing three bundles. She knew what all of them were, because it was mandatory that she did. Each of these packets held vital supplies to heal, give light, and provide sustenance. She pulled the parcels out of the cubicle, as well as the weapon stored below the packets, which would also be prudent to take.

Assuming the atmosphere on this planet was respectable, she might still survive. Mother pushed in the code for the emergency opening to her ship. There was a whisper of sound from the skin of the ship parting, and almost immediately, water surged in, pushing Mother to her back. There had been no way to check the outside, and as her luck would have it, the ship had crashed in a ravine with deep water at the bottom. She grappled for her packets, but the water was too strong. Losing her breath and with the inside filling with water, Mother fought her way through the opening. Being in water was not an experience she had ever had, but, frightened for her life, she instinctively struggled upwards, finally reaching the surface. Gulping great mouthfuls of air, Mother flogged her way to shore.

One of the bundles leaked a stream of orange powder that floated to the surface and danced in a path toward the deep water's edge. The bulk of the powder came to rest against a large rock. It congealed and rubbed against the bank as an eddy of water softly swelled back and forth. An orange residue began to scab on the gray surface of the rock.

Mother made it to the closest shore and pulled herself onto the wet sand. Anguish spread across her like the red wind of fire as she sobbed for breath, gulping air in great mouthfuls. Rolling over on her back, she mentally checked for damage. Something was wrong...terribly wrong. Just below her sternum, pain began to tear at her in earnest. Bones were definitely broken and organs damaged. How bad, she could not yet tell. When she tried to come to her knees, the pain screamed no, so she gingerly lay back on the sand and took in more air.

Mother looked around her. The deep ravine that she had landed in did not look that much different than it had earlier that day, when she was in the past with Sneert. But there were differences. There was now a more pronounced cave further ashore. How far into the future she had come she did not know. Mother was not optimistic that she would ever be found, and being rescued was probably a desperate hope. Her wrecked vessel was unreachable and full of water. The present was her reality. She beat both of her fists down on the sand in frustration and gave voice to a deep, "Ooooruh."

Immediately the pain ratcheted up, threatening to make her lose consciousness. Mother closed her eyes and tried to think. The pain subsided into a throbbing ache that was tolerable. Some of her ribs were undoubtedly shattered and probably had pierced her organs. She moved her head right and left, looking for the first aid bundle. It might have popped to the surface and floated ashore. She saw nothing, and a new bit of panic picked at her. She closed her eyes again.

A stream of soothing wind began to wash over her as the sky darkened. As the night enveloped her, her perception of the world grayed and then there was nothing when she lost consciousness and slept. Like a shadowy, damp cocoon, the night protected her. No animals disturbed her.

Mother opened her eyes and could tell where the sun's influence colored the top of the ravine gold. It was midmorning, she told herself. She flexed her waist. Yes, the pain was still there. She could hear the broken edges of bones grating against each other. It wasn't as excruciating as it had been last night, and that alarmed her. The damage was still there, but the pain had dulled. Mother knew she was going into shock. She leaned her head toward the sand and threw up blood and bile, then passed out again. This time the memory of Sneert and her children played against a backdrop of dread. Logically, she knew that the large beast was now nothing but a few shards of petrified rock. Mother's mind cried for Sneert, her children, herself, and the unborn infant that she instinctively knew was about to be born.

When Mother became conscious again, she knew that she had given birth. The squirming infant was lying across her legs intuitively slurping up some of the blood that had pooled. She reached out and lovingly patted her child. They laid together for most of the day. Sometime just before darkness shrouded the ravine, Mother died.

***

The male child squirmed in tighter to his mother's flesh, trying to find the warmth that was quickly waning. Instinctively he began to

13

chew the meat around her breast, sucking the juices from the pulp. Mother's body nourished him for the next several days until it became rancid and unpalatable. He grew fast, reacting to the stimulus of the forest and the small creatures around him. Although he was frightened, lonely, and unsure of how to survive, he began to adapt to his environment. He eventually asserted his dominance, causing the smaller animals of the immediate forest to flee and fear him. The larger animals would soon learn to do the same.

***

The American hemisphere saw nothing of the slow, distressful evolution of man. The man-apes in all their uncouth variety never set foot there. The brownskin people were the first form to enter the area. They came from the rain-soaked lowland jungles north and northwest of the Guatemalan highlands. Moving slightly north and west out of the Yucatan Peninsula, they settled in the lower area of what would eventually be known as Mexico, and claimed a high rise overlooking a lush valley of forest, wildlife, and water. Fifteen hundred years later this site would be known as *Palenque* and be one of the most valuable sources of early man's history. *(Current Time line: 800 BC)*

Chapter 1

Lethal Transgressions

The bruised and tattered edge of darkness slid with ever increasing speed downward, pressing heavily on a small sliver of luminous blue-gray resting on the horizon. The forest seemed to hold its collective breath. And then, in a slow blink, the sun's last bit of dominion was gone. Night had come. It was time to feed.

The small nub of hoary flesh that had once been a tail quivered with excitement. Sparse body hair became erect across his back as his eyes narrowed and became fully dilated. His senses were on full alert although he felt no immediate danger. In fact, he had never felt real fear in the two-hundred plus years of his life. There was no animal in the forest that could match his strength, speed, or killing capacity. He had dominated his world as chief predator since he was born.

Having no real language or anyone to share it with, his thoughts were in images that flowed across his synapses. He was capable of abstract thought; he just lacked the words to express them. His world was one of shape, color, touch, taste, sound, and above all, a piercing loneliness. The animals of his forest all had some type of companionship; he had none. He was uniquely singular. What he felt now was the excitement of discovery. Something new had entered his domain; something never before seen.

It was dusk when his senses had first scanned their presence. Three animals, bipedal by nature with similar though inferior characteristics to his own, had invaded his domain. It appeared that their skin was a smooth brown from this distance of about five hundred strides. He raised his muzzle to the air in an attempt to use

15

his considerable olfactory talents. Just a hint of their smell was available, enough to say this was something he had never encountered. Heavily muscled legs lifted over the dense undergrowth with almost no sound. He sinuously flowed over the ground toward the new animals, using every available cover to conceal his presence. He settled in motionlessly in a thicket of fronds a hundred strides from his quarry.

Patiently he watched the intruders as they camped. He had seen fire before but had instinctively avoided the phenomenon. The animals were crouched before the flames eating flesh from sticks they had cut earlier and placed above the flames. His heightened senses could now smell and taste the air currents that wafted toward him. An image of a small pig came to him. This was apparently what they were eating. He could detect the clump of bushes near which the pig had been cleaned. Small scavengers were even now scurrying away with small morsels left over from the butchering. He was neither repulsed nor interested in the meat. His sole source of nourishment came from the blood of his prey.

His muzzle jutted out from beneath black, intelligent eyes. Triangular teeth with serrated edges filled his mouth. At the back were three large molars on each side, above and below, for masticating juice from meat. Two fanglike canines dominated the top. These were equipped with special evolutionary tubes that could siphon blood in a forceful flow that eventually slid down the back of the esophagus, piercing the dorsal aorta.

All of his life he had been ruled by two basic and driving needs…to feed and to find another being similar to him. Now in front of him were the closest examples he had ever found to being like him. Yet they were so alien at the same time. Where he had plates of hard bone, they had an almost hairless, frail looking brown skin. Their muscles were weak looking and they moved erratically, with no real grace or economy of movement. Their flat faces seemed intelligent, though, as if they too understood the forest as he did.

Curiosity overcame him. He moved closer and was incredulous that at this short distance they still seemed oblivious to his presence. There was a musk about him that other animals smelled, and their reaction was always quick and unmistakably born of fear. These beings did nothing. They did not even look in his direction, but rather continued the sounds that were rhythmical and pleasant to listen to. The large animal moved closer, to where he could be among them in half a heartbeat if the need arose.

Time passed quietly as he continued to watch. One of the brownskins got up and headed toward him. *Amazement.* The brownskin loosened and lifted a flap of red color and urinated in a steaming flow not ten feet from him. He, too, urinated in a similar fashion, but never had to uncover himself first. Confused, he tilted his head in concentration. Heat radiated from the brownskin. The blood just beneath the skin of this frail newcomer to the forest pulsated faintly. More importantly, he could smell the nourishment just beneath the skin. Over a day had passed since his last feeding, and he was beginning to feel the pangs of hunger.

Mother's child was still curious about these new beings, knowing they were may be distant kin, but different. But the closeness of so much sweet blood was too much to resist. Closing his eyes and raising his head, he inhaled the brownskin's scent. Instinct took over. In one smooth and deadly rush he was on his prey. A savage bite and a wrench at the base of the brownskin's neck severed the spinal cord. Blood roared into the creature's maw, and he gulped greedily as he pulled the meat closer.

The sound of his dying prey alerted the other two, as he knew it would. They jumped from their sitting position with spears already in their hands. Surprisingly, they rushed *at* him instead of away. These were indeed strange creatures.

***

Thinking their comrade had encountered a large cat of some kind, they ran to the sounds. They were not prepared for what they met. Their friend was obviously dead. His head leaned at an impossible angle to his torso, attached by meager shreds of muscle. The campfire illuminated black eyes that peered at them above a gore splattered mouth still holding a large chunk of their friend's spine. The rest of the creature's body was still hidden by the darkness. If this was a cat, it was the biggest they had ever seen. Surely it must be standing on something.

Their spears instinctively were out in front of them. In a jabbing motion, they pushed forward with all their strength, hoping to hit a vital spot in this nightmare of the dark. Obsidian points broke on dense plates of bone, and shaft wood splintered half way back from the tips. With no time for them to react further, he was on top of them. Razor like claws ploughed furrows through the chest of his nearest attacker, going to the bone and breaking the sternum. The remaining brownskin tripped as he dodged to his left. It saved his life as a powerful arm razed the space his head had just occupied. The brownskin rolled to his feet and ran, never looking back, and was allowed to escape.

***

There was plenty of blood to sate his needs. He was not angered over their token resistance, but rather disturbed by how little effort it had taken to dispatch them. It should not have been so easy. He tore a large portion of flesh from just under the rib cage of one of his victims and chewed the meat into a visceral pulp, extracting all traces of the blood juice. He spat out the gray, tasteless mass without swallowing any, needing only the life juices of his prey. Tearing off another hunk, he chewed as he recalled the events of the night.

A hundred questions raised their curious little heads and demanded answers. *What are these new creatures? Are there more? If so, where are they? Why have I never encountered them before?* Further thought was required. Contentedly, he leaned against a tree and drank more from the meat.

***

Ahau was just fifteen cycles and already considered a man by his tribe's standards. Only recently had his band of tribesmen migrated out of the forests of his people. They were the first people to inhabit these forests. About six hundred men, women, and children had fled a tyrannical ruler three moons before. They were in search of new land and opportunities for their families, where they would not have to submit the best of their farming and hunting efforts to appease a king whose only interest was his own. It was an old story. Overcrowding, disease, and lack of food had made several bands of the people leave and seek new lands.

Ahau was part of a group of men who had volunteered to explore and report to the tribe if game, water, and farming ground were

18

available in front of the tribe's march. This smaller group steadily roamed the forest, observing everything and always checking for suitable land. Ahau had been pleased. His brother and uncle had asked him to splinter off with them for a couple of days to explore a low lying area different from the rest of the forest they had passed through. As they headed down, the undergrowth was much thicker and the trees seemed even more ancient than those above. They had descended into this unnatural, primordial bowl, cautiously checking for threats. So far, the going had been rough, but uneventful. There was game for the taking and they hunted when it was convenient without losing sight of each other.

With night nearing, they had camped. They were not afraid of what they could see and hear, but they suspected they were being watched by hidden eyes. Some of these, they suspected, were spirits they needed to assure and placate with offerings as the first fire was made in three days. A wild pig had been speared by his uncle, and they had offered the entrails to the ghost beings they were sure were watching them.

The rest of what happened that night was a blur. They had been eating and talking about the strange depression they were exploring when the darkness had exploded with blood, teeth, and claws. His uncle and brother were dead, but by what they had been killed he did not know. The animal that had attacked them was something horribly unfamiliar. It may have been a cat, but he did not really think so. The creature was just too big and it had been upright when it attacked. The darkness had hidden too much for him to be sure of anything.

Ahau kept rolling the events around in his mind. He thought he would meet up with the rest of the group sometime that morning, and knew they would want a clear report of what had transpired. He tried to formulate a story in his mind, but the facts just kept rebuking his sense of reality. The creature that had attacked them seemed almost human in form, but was so animal-like at the same time. It had to have been some kind of demon that habituated this area, and they had angered it somehow…probably by trespassing. Ahau decided he would just tell what he could remember and let the priest fill the blanks. The old man always had an answer.

***

Ahau's demon feared none of the scavengers that the rank smell of death summoned to the killing site. Not wanting to be disturbed, he took his leave, dragging one of the lifeless husks behind him. He sat with his back to a tree and pondered what he held in his hands. He turned the remains of the brownskin over and over, trying to evaluate what it had been. Attempting to dredge up past memories of such an animal was useless. Mother, who had died giving birth, was the closest creature resembling himself he could remember. She had been bipedal with a dense hide and a similar body to his. Great mats of hair had covered portions of her body, where he had none. Both of their hands had four fingers that ended in curved, thick claws with an opposing thumb. All this he remembered clearly. Instinctively he had crawled up to her breasts to suckle and had drawn his first taste of blood. Chew-sucking her flesh for days before the body began to fall apart in his hands, the large beast had hung what was left in a tree for no real reason he could fathom. It had just seemed right. The smell of her taste came back to him. He grunted his pleasure.

The remains of the brownskin had similar hands to his only much smaller, with weak, pathetic nails that pulled out of the gristle with ease. The teeth seemed of almost no use in a fight. *How has this creature survived? Was disease involved in its weakness?* The blood had smelled and tasted healthy enough. The muscles obviously were weak in comparison to almost any other animal in the forest. *Have they lived in stealth as scavengers? Why have they wrapped strange red leaves around themselves?* The coverings were from no tree he had encountered. They smelled strange and pulled apart differently than other leaves.

It had been a very long time since his curiosity had been aroused as it now was. The forest had become so predictable he had been bored, and hadn't really realized it until now. The brownskins needed to be found again, but for now dawn was coming, and he intensely disliked the bright light and that hateful round orb that seemed to spread it everywhere. The light hurt his eyes and made his head ache if he stayed in it for more than a few moments. This prevented him from much movement during the day. Sunlight was now beginning to filter its way down through the thick leafy umbrella overhead and make spotted, irregular patterns on the forest floor. He needed to find shelter. A thick canopy of leaves from a low set of bushes would provide refuge. He picked up the wet skin, slung it over his shoulder, and set out to find just such a place.

***

The explorers were not expecting contact with the three men who had gone into the large depression for two more days. They were moving with a speed only people born to the forest could achieve. They saw everything and marked trails as they went. The land was rich in wild life and fertile soil. It would take many days to clear areas large enough to accommodate six hundred people, but it could be everything they sought. Already they had passed through long stretches of virgin forest still intact with abundant prey and fresh water.

Large carnivores were in evidence, but they had not seen anything close. Even spread out as they were, enough noise was being made to alert the animals of their approach. Only those sent out to specifically hunt meat for the evening meal ever met the large cats.

Nothing to suggest other people had ever been here was found. This indeed was good land. It was just setting there for the taking, and they were ready to take it. Camp was made near the river they had been following to try the fishing and give the men a rest. They planned to be there for two days to allow Comal, Campeche, and Ahau time to return from exploring the unnaturally deep basin. Everyone was lighthearted with the prospect of spending the rest of their lives here in this new land. They were already making living decisions for their families.

***

An exhausted Ahau crested a rise and searched with hands above his eyes for any sign of the others. He was not worried about finding them. He had come across their trail sometime before and deduced they were about half a day ahead of him. Their passage was as clear as the iridescent markings on the butterfly crossing to his left. To the trained eye, evidence that a large group of men had hurriedly traversed the terrain was there to see. Bruised leaves and broken stems were only now beginning to turn brown. Plant juices had seeped and almost dried along their inevitable path downwards. Ahau saw all of this and more. Trees had been marked with a heavy horizontal slash. These were placed for others to see and follow. Ahau broke over the ridge and headed down into the dense stand of conifers.

***

Tikal was alert in his tree and scanning what he could see of the horizon. He and four others had been prudently assigned as lookouts for any danger that might come through the forest. From his vantage point near the top of a gentle rise, he could see Ahau making his way toward the camp. Tikal and he were good friends of about the same age, and had been through the rites of passage together as brothers. The tattoos on their ankles signified as much. Tikal shouted down that Ahau was near and the direction he was coming from. Several men grabbed their spears and loped out to meet him. Amid shouted questions and claps on his back, he tried to explain why he was alone. Taken to a central part of the camp, Ahau told his story to a hushed crowd for the third time. He was going slowly, trying not to forget anything. His eyes looked up at the old man in front of him.

***

The hymen, who was a sorcerer, a medicine man, and a holy priest, narrowed his eyes and gave the impression of grave concern and contemplation. He knew his opinion would be asked. An explanation would have to be given and a course of action recommended. The priest closed his eyes and made tiny sucking noises on his pipe. He grunted as if he understood and took another deep breath of the hot, bitter smoke. Red embers stirred the bowl and sent smoke spiraling upwards to mix with the cloud already hanging above their heads.

Pochotl had lived fifty-two seasons. His deeply wrinkled face was mottled with firelight. Swiveling his head, he eyed each man. Finally, Pochotl took the easiest route by pinning his gaze on Ahau. In a deep, commanding voice, he pronounced his conclusion of the events. "We have lost two of our brethren. They rest in death, but their spirits will always be with us. Comal, Campeche, and Ahau, while exploring the depression, have obviously met a guardian of the abyss and have been punished for their transgressions."

What these transgressions had been was a little vague, but for sure the blame was squarely fixed on the three and not him. He had made the initial suggestion that the deep depression should be explored, but that had only been common sense. That Ahau had escaped only confirmed that the guardian wanted the rest of the people to know the land there was sacred and should never be again entered. This was a place of dangerous spirits. He expressed all of this to the people.

***

The men all seemed to accept what Pochotl said. His words were wise and made sense. That there were many strange gods and demons in the forest was a known fact. It was decided that in the morning, half the men would be sent back to the people to help lead them to this fertile land they now considered theirs. The deep crater would be avoided, and its importance explained. They all shook their heads and murmured how wise the hymen was, as surely it must be as he said. Ahau shivered, remembering the creature and his narrow escape. He, for one, was not convinced this had been a spirit confined to the limits of the bowl. Real or imagined, the memory of this horror was going to be with him for a long time.

CHAPTER 2

OBSESSION

No important event could ever happen in the people's culture without religious rituals to give thanks to the deities or to ask for the wisdom necessary to decide a course of action. Pochotl proclaimed the need to have just such a ceremony. Thanks for the new land and the necessary wisdom to proceed should be asked for. Itzamna, patron of esoteric knowledge, would be consulted for his approval. Pochotl, as hymen, was principal acolyte in these affairs, and by nature was ruthless, sadistic, and self-serving, taking every opportunity to use the sacrosanctity of his office to satisfy his lusts or increase his status. He liked to think of the people as his children, and himself as their all knowing father. He could do no wrong.

A carefully wrapped bundle containing a ceramic bottle stoppered with rawhide was brought before Pochotl. Only he could administer the sacred balche, a ritual hallucinatory drink with anesthetic properties. Each man came forward, kneeled before the priest, and received a swallow of the potent, amber liquid, along with a blessing for his sacrifice. Blood was the mortar of ancient ritual life, and Pochotl liked a lot of mortar. In a state of subjugation, the men spread their blankets in a circle around the hymen. Each man had in his personal pouch sharp edged oyster shells, as well as stingray and sea urchin spines. These were placed carefully on the blanket near their left side when the men lay prone, awaiting the priest. Pochotl's eyes were glassy from the balche and the power he possessed. The men around him were willing to give their life's blood and pain for Itzamna and any other god he could think of.

25

From a pocket attached to his leather belt, he drew out several obsidian lancets and knelt down over the first man. These small pieces of volcanic glass were extremely sharp. He had been practicing for thirty years and was a master of the cut. In the early days before he learned to control his zeal, Pochotl had bled several young men and women to death. Under the tutelage of his father, he had obtained knowledge of the locations of nerves, tendons, muscle, and vital organs. The cut did not need to be deep or long to achieve the desired pain and blood, if one knew where to lance.

Pochotl pinched the tender skin of the inner thigh of the first man, high up near the crotch, between his thumb and forefinger. Picking up one of the sea urchin spines, he slowly pierced the skin until it poked through the opposite side, then left the spine in. The man squirmed, made a short, hitched moan, and held his breath. This pain was for his people, after all. Pochotl moved to the other thigh and again used a sea urchin spine, and smiled tightly at the agony in the man's face. Blood seeped between his pinched fingers and ran in two directions down the man's thigh.

Wiping his hand in the grass, he laid the lancets on the man's chest. Pochotl liked his supplicants to see the instruments he was going to use. Using the smallest lancet, he made a series of eight cuts under each inserted spine to form the symbol of Itzamna. This blood he collected in the oyster shells, to be used later.

The man was visibly quivering now because of the pain. With his eyes closed, small piteous sounds escaped his firmly closed lips. Pochotl thought the man's lips were a bit too firmly closed. Taking one stingray spine, he pierced the skin under the bottom lip till it came out between the gum line and teeth. He continued to push until the spine's length was balanced on both sides of the lip. Now the audible signs of his work were to Pochotl's liking.

Gingerly, the priest took hold of the skin just above the man's left nipple. Using the two remaining stingray spines, he pierced the outer skin in a sewing motion until each had entered and come out on the other side. The barest trace of a smile crossed Pochotl's face as he surveyed his handiwork. His own breathing became more rapid now. He was becoming aroused.

Pochotl had started with this man because he was beside Ahau.

Ahau was the only living link to what had happened with the demon of the abysses. Pochotl's credibility would suffer if the young man remembered anything that would make the official synopsis and explanation of the event inaccurate. That would never do. The priest went the other direction, away from Ahau, making Ahau last. The young man could then see and hear the other men's suffering and build a solemn awareness of what awaited him. Special attention would be given to young Ahau.

***

Man to man he went, performing the same ritual with a variation here and there just to keep it interesting. Ahau waited his turn, almost sick to his stomach, wishing it was over. He realized the importance of the honor bestowed on him and the rest of the men. Their sacrifice would make this place both sacred and safe for their people. He also trusted the hymen explicitly. He was one of the priests that had presided over countless ceremonies for all of his young life. This was his first time as participant instead of a spectator, however. He held onto this trust and clenched the blanket tightly in his fists. Pochotl approached.

***

The priest's arousal was hurting him now. He looked down on the young body. Ahau's eyes were screwed tightly shut and his hands were clenched in white knots. While obviously trying to hold as still as he could, a tremble was still visible.

Pochotl said in a whisper, "Ahau, relax my child. Trust in Itzamna's wisdom, and know in your heart that what we do today will be of lasting importance." His words seemed to have an effect as the young man's hands unclenched slightly. He only fingered the blanket now. "I am your priest and have only your welfare and the good of our people in my heart. Look me in the eyes!"

Oh yes, this is going to be exhilarating. Such a beautiful young body.

He went to work. When he finally finished he had spent twice the time on young Ahau as the other men. Ahau lay unconscious, his blanket soaking up small pools of blood. The hymen had soothed the young man through each scream, feining just the right amount of sympathy and assuring him that all of this was necessary. Pochotl hoped he had not gone too far. Ahau's death would be damaging to

27

the trust the people had in him. The peoples' confidence and faith were crucial to Pochotl's plans. He bent closer to the young man's face and listened intently to the pained breathing. With the back of his hand he lightly caressed Ahau's forehead, making sure the others saw his concern. He thought the young man would probably live. Standing up, he noticed that his arousal was gone, replaced with a twinge of guilt.

The spines were removed from the men, and poultices derived from plants and mud were applied to the wounds to stop the bleeding and alleviate some of the pain. Another swallow of the balche was administered. Several men tended to young Ahau, following the hymen's advice. Though speaking of dizziness and obviously experiencing great agony, the young man apparently would live.

The blood filled oysters were placed in a crescent on a flat rock appropriated for this stage of the ritual. Pochotl stood before the shells looking solemn, with no trace of the blood lust that had filled him earlier. He lanced the flesh of his inner arm and added his blood to each vessel. He wanted the men to realize that he also shared in the sacrifice. A finely ground yellow powder, pulled from one of the priest's pouches, was sprinkled heavily on the coagulating surfaces of blood. Bits of dried grass were added until each container was covered. Pochotl took a hot ember from the campfire and ignited each offering. Rank coppery fumes permeated the air. The men began to chant from kneeling positions, with their heads and hands lifted upwards. It had been a good ritual.

Night descended.

***

Even before he awoke, his senses browsed the surroundings. Ants had found the now stiff rag of flesh he had pulled into his makeshift lair. They had carried off what they could in six distinct lines radiating from the decaying mush. Flies were trying to lay their eggs in the little remaining flesh, but bothered him not because of his dense hide. He pushed his senses out further. In front of the entrance to his dark refuge, a turtle made its way to safety under a dead log thick with termites. The tip of his tongue flicked and caught the minute, earthy aroma of deer mouse defecation piled up in an abandoned hole two strides to his left. Birds settled in among the luxuriant leaves far above him, cawing their displeasure that a serpent had chosen a limb in their tree in which to lie. His hearing brought visual images to his mind. Without opening his eyes he could see that all was as it should be. No threat or situation demanded his immediate attention.

He stretched his arms forward and raked the ground in front of him as he arched his back. A low rumble issued from his curled lips, breaking a bubble of pink froth. It was time to wake up. The putrefaction partially lying under him brought last night's memories flooding back. The brownskin who had gotten away would have to be found. The answers to his many questions would be puzzled out one way or another. Bounding out of hiding with a sense of purpose, he was as content as he had ever been.

Reaching the killing area in moments, he headed up and out of the deep overgrown crater, following the trail left by the brownskin. The brownskin's sugary smell of fear was still sweet to his memory. His highly developed smelling pheromones craved more. This creature he might play with before he killed it.

Long before he reached the camp he knew he had found an answer to one of his questions. *There are more brownskins!* They were not far away now, and apparently bedded down for the night. Reaching the vicinity of the campsite, his senses found the four sentries, all in trees along the periphery. With a fluid grace, he unobtrusively entered the nearest tree and worked toward the middle of the camp. The sentries never had an inkling they had been invaded. Mingled smells were sorted out until he identified the one he had followed. Lightning hitting a tree with a jaguar in it years ago provided the memory of cooked flesh and burnt blood. A similar smell seemed to be in the very trees he traversed.

Only the moonlight was quieter than his approach to a low hanging limb the size of his thigh. He settled in just above the young brownskin, who trembled and jerked in his sleep. The creature above him could only guess, but he hoped the brownskin dreamed of him. He liked the idea of chasing the brownskin in dark visions full of rent flesh and screams. Involuntarily he reached out toward the brownskin with a gleaming, hard edged index claw, and slowly scribed a line across the young brownskin's chest through the air. The young man, still deep in the arms of troubled sleep, brushed an arm down his breast almost in unison to the creature's stroke, as if warding off images of teeth gnashing at his soul.

Powerful muscles changed position as he dropped to the ground near the base of the tree. Still cloaked in the deepest shadows, the eyes seemed to burn with a malevolent blue black light. He knelt down and peered at the wounds up and down the young man's chest and legs. The patterns puzzled him. *How and why were these made?* He sniffed the remains of one poultice still clinging to Ahau's chest. *Mud! These are strange animals.* Leaning in closer, he smelled the brownskin's breath. *Foul smelling, like stagnated pools of clotted filth.* A hooked claw delicately lifted a lock of hair hanging over the brownskin's ear. Remembrance triggered in his mind. *Mother had such hair, only much shorter!* The beast suddenly felt affection for the small form at his feet. The feeling was new and unpleasant in its strangeness. Confused, he again knelt closer and very lightly touched one of the wounds on the brownskin's chest with his tongue, tasting old and new blood mixed. The desire to dig into the soft flesh and shred from the meat the warm nourishment he knew was there conflicted with his ache to be with his mother. The thought of her had not invaded his thoughts for years. It was hard to identify the emotion. *How can this pitiful shape beneath me possibly be related? Yet, there is something!*

***

Ahau's eyes snapped open. He had felt the creature's hot fetid breath and raspy tongue on his chest. He could see his reflection in the inky blackness of eyes four inches from his own. Both froze. Terror welled up in Ahau's breast. Within the space of a blink, Ahau's demon disappeared. Like a thin stream of campfire smoke, the creature vanished upwards.

Trying to scream, Ahau could only manage a hoarse, "It's here! IT'S HERE!"

***

Tikal, only three body lengths away, quickly crawled to his friend. He cradled Ahau's head and assured him nothing was there. A nightmare was all it had been. Tikal felt deep pity for his young friend. The priest had almost seemed vicious in his handling of poor Ahau. It would be days before the young man would be able to do anything but lie on his blanket. Tikal pulled his own blanket closer to Ahau's. He draped a protective arm around his friend and drifted off to sleep, muttering something about it would all be all right in the morning.

***

Ahau tried to find solace in the arms of his friend, but remained awake for hours. His eyes, open and unblinking, agitated from the stink of the shadowy illusion, were slow to close. Only it had been nothing as simple as a dream gone wrong. *This nightmare was real. The demon was here. I still feel its tongue and see death promised.*

***

Pochotl was also awake and slow to sleep. He had witnessed the entire scene, but had been too afraid to scream a warning. Pochotl had been lying on his side, not quite asleep, when the beast had dropped out of the tree. The description the young man had given of the demon fit this monstrosity completely, confirming in his mind that he had heard the truth from Ahau. *Why did the demon flee when Ahau awoke? Why did he not simply kill and silence the young man?*

Even now the demon was only forty strides away from him in a tree. It had been astonishing how fast the creature moved. Just the barest glint of bluegreen scales could be seen below the head. The mouth fit a chin that jutted out like that of a large predator. Its nostrils were significant slits in a human-like nose, only flattened. A chest, swelled one and a half times that of a normal man, glistened in the moonlight as if oiled. The eyes were the most impressive feature; large, black orbs outlined with bony ridges across the top and outside edges glowed from within. The pupil's blackness reflected the available light like beacons. Small, upside down v-shaped protrusions lying close to the sides of the creature's head served as its ears. Muscles rippled and armored the beast entirely. It was standing upright, high in the foliage, most of it camouflaged by a thick collection of leaves.

In the brief time Pochotl had to study the creature before it secreted into its present location, he noticed several things. It had been almost human in the way it knelt over Ahau, belying the creature's frightening appearance. The delicate touching and other gestures seemed to demonstrate tenderness. A thought crossed Pochotl's mind. *What if the demon is angry with me for abusing the young*

31

man? Perhaps I should rethink my position concerning Ahau. The way the demon had tilted his head as he peered at the young man with attentive eyes suggested a strong intelligence. *What did it want?* It did not seem a threat at the moment, but that could change in a heartbeat. He had seen its speed. All the men in the camp might not be enough to deter the beast.

A thought clicked. In all of his life he had never seen a real sign of the deities. He believed in them just enough to convince the people, but he had always had his doubts. Most of what he did in the many rituals was more for show than for any real direct line between him and the gods. The religious rituals were necessary to hold sway over the people and to give them purpose of life and hope in the dark times of misfortune; of this he was convinced. This beast, however, was something else again. He had never heard of such an animal. If it was part of a species, he was pretty sure his people would have encountered one before now. It had to be singular, a very special singularity; a product of genetic chaos. Pochotl continued to watch with his eyes opened the barest fraction in a hope to feign sleep. Instinct told him this was one creature who did not want to be seen. *I will call him Bela De Oxhutz, He Who Owns the Darkness.*

***

Standing on a limb not far from his primary target, Bela watched the camp. The brownskin opening his eyes had been unfortunate. It would be prudent to study it further without alarming any of the herd. He was also aware that the old one below knew of his presence, and was even now intently watching. This was of no concern as long as he remained quiet. This one he would kill first if an alarm was raised. Bela watched as the young brownskin was quieted by another. The other stroked his hair and head and whispered rhythmical sounds. One particular sound he had heard repeatedly; *Ahhuu. Ahhuu, Ahhuu.* His vocal cords could mimic most sounds in the forest. His tongue rubbed over the sound; *Ahhuu, Ahhuu.* Yes. This sounded right. The beast would refer to this brownskin from now on as *Ahhuu.* Words were becoming thought.

***

The old man vaguely registered that the creature was leaving. One moment Bela was there and the next he was not. The great beast had melted out of the tree into another and hit the ground running. Pochotl lay awake contemplating everything he had seen. For several moments longer, he allowed the images to run around the edges of his mind, trying to accommodate things he had never had to think of before.

***

It was time to feed. Bela had decided not to harvest from this herd at the moment. He did not want to alarm them or cause them to move. He would be back later to observe further. There were even more questions now to be answered.

The subtropical forest was Bela's private smorgasbord. Redolent juices seeped from the corners of his mouth, which was salivating as he went through the menu. Tonight, within a couple of hundred strides, several kinds of tree dwellers, from monkey to squirrel, were available. A lone sloth, piglets suckling their mother, small marsupials, and a large cat were all images that flickered through his mind one by one as his senses picked them out. There were more, but these would supply the most blood with the least effort. He chose the jaguar.

***

The jaguar had been stalking the sloth for the last several heartbeats and was working her way up on its left side for a position from which to spring. Her tail became very still as her muscles bunched and tensed. In her mind she saw herself vaulting onto the sloth. Pushing her claws deep into the back, she would penetrate the base of the skull with her canines, severing the spinal cord. Her ears went flat when she was ready to leap. But something was wrong. Musk assailed her from above, and she had just enough time to recognize her own death.

***

Bela slammed down on top of the big cat, breaking its spine and opening a five-inch wide gash across its belly. The cat's eyes filmed over as its entrails spilled out onto the ground. It kicked once, twice, and then was still. The sloth never knew how close its death had been.

A flash in the sky accompanied by an echoing boom made Bela hurry. The jaguar's life blood was nearly consumed anyway, and he did not want to miss the rain. Using one of his claw-knives, he cut a rough rectangular patch of fur from the cat's left side. This he folded inwards from all four sides, careful to wrap the wet side down. When he had a pad of fur to his liking, he scrambled to a clearing to await the rain.

Bela sat on a large boulder that had tumbled away from a nearby rock cropping. He thought the rain was perhaps close, but would hold off awhile from the smell and taste of the air. Fireflies twitched their lanterns on and off, disturbed by his passing. He playfully swatted at them, not really trying to harm them. Looking down, Bela saw pugmarks in the earth made earlier by the jaguar, and felt a sudden sense of loss. They reminded him of the large, light brown cats that used to be in the forest. Much earlier in his life, they had ranged over a lot of the same area he did. They had been his favorite animals.

Finding an onza asleep in a tree had been great entertainment. He would sneak into the tree upwind of the big cat and toss pieces of dead monkey at it. When a monkey or some other small animal was not readily available, Bela would stand well above the big cat and urinate rank fluids on it. Either method got a quick response. When the onza reacted, Bela would taunt the cat into chasing him. He would let the big cat get close, then sprint out of reach again and again, causing the onza to become so agitated it would literally be whining its anger. Eventually he would allow the cat to catch him, but it never had a chance. Bela's strength and speed were just too great.

He had killed the onzas by degrees. He would circle the cat, dart in making a quick cut, circle again, slash, circle, and slash until the cat collapsed. A bite to the onza's spine usually ended the game. He would consume what he needed of the cat and leave the rest. Unfortunately, after a few years all of the onzas disappeared, either killed or driven off. He still searched for them from time to time in hopes of finding one.

The ever-raucous forest chatter lapsed into a parenthesis of silence, and the rain came. Snapping out of his revelry, Bela stood on the rock with his face to the sky. When he was thoroughly wet, he began to use the fur pad to wipe himself clean as the warm rain continued, soaking everything. When it did eventually end, Bela, feeling cleansed at last, tossed the rag and waited to dry.

He reached under his left arm pit into the only patch of thick hair he had. The hair was reddish-brown in color and about the length of his finger. Hidden behind the moist hair was a membranous pocket, from which he pulled out a thick tube-like appendage about a hand span in length. He massaged the flaccid tube until it became blood engorged. Using a milking motion, Bela filled the palm of his right hand with a dark, oily secretion, then worked this into the skin on his chest and abdomen. He continued to milk and wipe the lubricating secretions all over his body. Every seven to eight days, Bela did this to help rejuvenate his skin. When rain was not available, he used his private pool at home. Bela liked to be clean and took special pride in the black iridescence of his hide.

Now that the rain had abated, the forest night life began to talk again, giving voice to the night. Under his feet, Bela heard a small rustling sound a short distance down. He jabbed his claws into the ground on both sides of the sound and brought up the dark earth. Among the lumps of wet dirt sat a small mammal, squeaking its fear. It tried to jump from the terrible claws, but Bela prevented it from escaping and brought it closer to his face. Peering at the small creature and listening to the pitiful sounds of abject fear, he decided to keep it awhile. Loosely clutching the small mouse, he headed home. All thoughts of the brownskins were gone for the moment.

Bela's home was deep in the depression the brownskins had discovered earlier. At the bottom of the now lush forest bowl was a natural well. Rock had been broken out, exposing a deep shaft that ran down to the water table. This particular cenote had a cave well above the water line that ran back for several yards before going left and right another hundred feet. This was Bela's home.

A short time later, Bela stood high above the cenote at the beginning of his hidden entrance. It was the only readily accessible path down. Everywhere else was made of vertical rock, most of it loose. He scanned the area, searching for anything out of the ordinary. He had lived here for so long that the usual sounds and smells had been hardwired into his memory, and he found nothing out of place now. Sitting down on his haunches, he slid down the smooth path seventy meters to level ground. The path was so well worn that the descent was uneventful.

Just at the cave's edge, a plant growth which could be seen from several strides away glowed orange. A large tree's roots tangled down through the soil above and snaked along a side of the rocky surface of a massive boulder shoved into the limestone walls some violent event long ago. The strange, orange fungi grew between the snarled patterns of the roots against the stone. Bela hooked a finger in the fungi and brought it to his mouth. He craved the taste but instinctively never ate much. Almost immediately, his blood seemed to rush into his ears. A feeling of euphoria smoothed his features and half-lidded his eyes. It was the only substance besides blood that he ever ingested. Many cycles ago, when he had first discovered the curious anomaly, he had smelt and then tasted the fungous growth, and it had become addictive. At least once every fifteen to twenty days he consumed some of it.

Still clutching the small mouse, Bela entered the darkness of his cave. He placed the little animal on a ledge and piled rocks on top of each other until a cage was formed. The mouse squealed and skirted to the back as far from Bela as it could get. On the same ledge were trophied onza skulls picked clean by the small scavengers of the cave. There were fast scuttles as beetles tumbled in and out of the empty eye sockets. In three days, they would have another meal. Other bones lay in piles and by themselves littering one side of the cave. Every so often, Bela threw the broken, skeletal reminders of past meals into the water and watched them slide side to side before sinking.

Very little light penetrated this far down, so Bela could sleep and wander his lair at will. A thick pallet of leaves had been brought in and situated near the back of a passageway. Here he occasionally slept, never feeling chilled or over heated in this underworld haven. His metabolic furnace kept internal heat at a constant. Large fruit bats and the occasional snake shared his domain, but never intruded in his personal part of the cave.

Bela stayed in the immediate area for several weeks, rarely going out to feed. The brownskins were not entirely forgotten…he just had other things on his mind. He was shedding his skin.

***

In two year intervals, Bela would shed his outer skin much like a reptile. His armor of muscle, layered to an impressive thickness,

36

began to loosen. The outside exoskeleton-like keratin regenerated pebbled skin from the inside out. The middle layer, made up of smaller convex plates of bone, separated ever so slightly in key positions. The real marvel of Bela's skin was the inner layer. Made up of especially thick strong bone girders arranged in a collapsible configuration, this inner layer gave Bela exceptional strength and flexibility. Every two years, the three layers softened, allowing for Bela's continuing growth. The outer layer of skin sloughed off in sections over a period of several days. The new skin took almost fifteen more days to harden back to the original toughness. This was when Bela was most vulnerable. The only animals he fed on were those whose own defenses were weak enough to overcome without danger to him.

***

Drinking copious amounts of water from the pool, Bela subsided on monkeys, small burrowing mammals, large birds, and the occasional weak reptile. Bela's mood was foul. For four days now he had been waiting for his new skin to harden to its original toughness. He itched furiously.

His thoughts turned to *Ahhuu* again. He recognized the rhymical sounds the brownskins made as communication. If these were sounds he could make, perhaps he could convey thoughts or at least transfer something intangible in the way of an idea. He still thought of them as food, but the need to find others like himself still drove him. These brownskins were the closest creature to himself that he had found in two hundred years. He would try.

Chapter 3

New Beginnings

Most of the night was spent finding them. Bela knew from the trails and debris that a great number of the brownskins were in front of him. Three-hundred plus souls now occupied an area much farther west of where Bela had first discovered them. Finding them at last, Bela was astounded at their behavior. In the thirty days Bela had spent near his lair, the brownskins had made great strides in reforming the land for their habitation. For three light and dark cycles he watched their progress from a small cave-like opening amid rocks overgrown with vegetation less than five-hundred strides from the central core of their camp. During the day, Bela watched from the deepest shadows of his hiding place. Even from there the bright light made his eyelids close every few seconds. He would wait a moment, and then open his eyes again. In this method he watched all day, patiently waiting for the night.

He found himself confused, irritated, resentful, and envious...sometimes all at once. These were no ordinary animals. They cleared trees from large tracts of ground and dug straight lines in the earth. Shelter was made from pieces of those same felled trees. Cutting tools were made of large ropes of obsidian inlaid in black wood and tapered to an ax-like edge, enabling the brownskins to deliver heavy blows to the trees. When they became dull, they were sharpened on the spot. Their methods of food gathering and rerouting water were remarkable. Teams of men and women, armed with baskets, gathered fruit, roots, herbs, and nuts from the bounty of the surrounding forest. Enormous ceramic vessels were placed on high mounds of earth. These caught the rain water which fell almost every day. Ingenious clay pipes were connected to these vessels and traveled downwards to a central common reservoir shared by everyone. It was evident that these brownskins communicated, cooperated, and worked together as a group; that any of this was possible made Bela marvel. Strength and speed had always equaled a certain ecological arrogance in the subtropical forest until now. For the first time he had to doubt his own superiority. Here was an ingenious, weak-skinned animal of possibly greater intelligence than his own. Awe-inspired hatred began to seed and grow.

During the night, Bela three times took some of his hostility and aggression out on the brownskins. While clandestinely examining the brownskins' work more closely, Bela methodically and quietly attacked lone individuals when he came across their path. With a speed born from his desire to demonstrate superiority, he slashed from their right temple downwards diagonally, effectively taking their faces off. His left hand tore out their throat a split second later. Each died gurgling his life out noiselessly in a broken heap at Bela's feet. Dragging the meat behind him, Bela concealed his kills away from the people's encampment. In a quiet place the victims were torn apart piece by piece amid snarls and savage grunts of pleasure. The bones he snapped and crushed in his hands. Remaining flesh around the skull was ripped and torn at until all that remained was an unrecognizable broken shell of bone. That this had been a brownskin was now hard to imagine. The heart and liver he ravaged blood from, throwing all else away. In Bela's already long life, he had never killed in hatred before. This was new. This was good. This he would do again.

Intuitively he knew it was best not to let the brownskins know he was feeding on them. He buried the remains each time in shallow clawed-up graves. *Surely these three will never be missed. The herd is large.* He was wrong.

***

Although the remains of the men were never found, families of the slain victims missed their loved ones immediately. The killing sites looked as if a large cat had attacked them and dragged off the bodies to feed in private. The tracks were confusing and made little

40

sense. But death was something they understood and had lived with all of their lives. The forest was a dangerous place.

Only Ahau and Pochotl suspected that perhaps it was not a jaguar carrying off the men. Precautions were taken. Sentries were posted in groups of two every so often around the temporary shelters. Large fires were built in the center of the enclosure and at intervals between the sentries. No one ventured out at night alone if it could be helped.

Two guards died that first night. They saw and heard nothing. In the morning there was only congealed, bloody mud where they had been. Tracks indicated a large animal had been there, but little else. If it was a cat, it was abnormally large. The prints were just too unclear to be sure. Warriors were sent out to hunt down the beast. They fanned out in nervous groups, radiating in several directions from the camp. With spears and grim determination they began to scour the forest, looking for revenge. They moved slowly, looking at and in everything.

***

Bela was napping in the small cave he had been using for the last several days when his hearing caught the unusual sounds being made by the warriors as they looked for him. Instantly awake and alert, he peered out of the mouth of the cave. He could see brownskins making their way up the slope where his hiding place was located. *Click!* His nictating membranes closed over his eyes. He squeezed them shut and waited, then opened them again. They were closer. *Click!* When he could see again, they were within fifteen feet of the opening and still coming. The brownskins had their spears held at the ready with both hands as they approached the dark opening in the rocks in case the cat was there. Crouched over, they were trying to look into the cave without getting too close.

Bela screamed a challenge and burst out of the darkness directly at them. *Click!* Blinded, he thrust his right arm high in the air and swiped down at where he thought the closest brownskin was. *Pain!* He had caught one of the obsidian spears between the index and middle finger. The momentum of his swing forced the sharp blade to cut through two fingers and most of the last. Bela howled in agony. His eyes opened. Ignoring the pain, he tore channels through the

41

brownskins' torsos. *Click!* Bela stumbled over one of the bodies and lay sprawled on the thick vegetation in front of the cave. A few moments later, thinking he had killed both the brownskins, Bela crawled back to the only darkness nearby on hands and knees. Back to the cave. The pain was excruciating. He huddled back into the farthest reaches of the tiny cave and waited. *Click!*

***

Within forty-five heart beats of the first screams, warriors racing through the forest came to the bodies of their two companions. In a dying gesture, one of the warriors pointed to the cave and choked out his last breath. Staying well away from the entrance of the cave, the men hunkered down and peered in. Two large illuminated eyes blinked and went out. A shuffling sound amid deep, growling rumbles from inside the cave confirmed their suspicions. Thinking the large cat must be in the cave, they began to roll large nearby rocks into the opening. Others arrived, and within moments they had the small entrance closed.

***

Bela watched all of this, not caring if they sealed out the hated light. Since they did not come in, he felt unchallenged. No animal in the forest had ever inflicted damage on him before. There were so many of the hated brownskins out there. Looking down at his hand, he cried out in anguish. Two fingers were gone from his right hand, and one dangled from a few slivers of muscle. He tore the final shred of connective fascia away and threw the finger against the wall. Again he howled, feeling fear for the first time in his life.

The people began to throw burning grass, branches, and chunks of wood into the small openings between the rocks and the top of the opening to the cave. The burning debris began to accumulate, causing a sizeable fire to catch inside the small cave. Bela squenched tighter to the back. Detecting a small air passage near the top, he closed his eyes and pressed his face as close to it as he could get. Heat from the fire was building as more wood was tossed in, and the fire was now almost within reach of him. He did the only thing he could do. He endured and waited it out.

***

Smoke was leaking out in several places around the rocks in tiny

42

streams. The brownskins made sure there were no openings big enough for anything to get out of. They had not seen Bela directly and still thought of him as a large cat trapped in a small cave. That they were killing him, they were sure. Revenge for their lost relatives and companions was being exacted. There was much celebrating. Warriors waved their spears and shouted their victory. Women and children added their voices to the clamor and tossed rocks at the cave. They gleefully shoved bits of wood and grass in where they could.

So many brownskins had now come to see the killing that all signs of the initial struggle were stamped out. Only the blood remained on the torn and trampled earth to signify death had occurred. The limp and broken bodies had been carried away.

Ahau and Pochotl were among those who had come to see. A silent, knowing look was exchanged between them.

The village spent the next several hours celebrating or mourning, depending on how close the victims had been. The cat was surely dead now and everything would be back to normal. Many, however, looked on from the outside with grim contentious expressions, wishing they could personally contribute to the cat's death. It had been their relatives the cat had killed. Eventually, people began to drift away. They had no idea how dangerous this part of the forest had just become. There was still much work to do and time was precious. The rainy season would come soon and they had to be prepared. Soon, everyone had left the smoking rocks completely. In the morning, when the fire had died out, they would roll the rocks away and pull the carcass out for the village to see.

***

Two heavily clawed fingers lay where they had been kicked under the grass during the confusion. A crow landed a short distance away. Cocking its head, it spied the dead flesh and hopped nearer. Grabbing one claw in its mouth, the crow flew the morsel to its nest, where it dropped it in a recession between two dead limbs of a high tree. Three hungry chicks tore loudly at it with their beaks. The mother flew back for the other finger. The scales and claw prevented the birds from shredding the flesh, but with persistence, some sustenance was gained from the meat around and in the torn area of the finger.

Later, it was very quiet in the nest. All four birds were dead. They had died convulsing in throes of transmogrifying pain. Their distended and mutated bodies were never disturbed. They rotted where they'd fallen.

***

Sometime during the late throes of the night, the fire died. Luminous eyes peered out from a space between the rocks. Still coughing from the smoke and feeling the pain of three missing fingers and a scorched side, Bela rolled the large rocks out of the way and sniffed the air. The brownskins were not close. He bolted from the hole and into the forest, cradling his injured hand as he headed home.

Chapter 4

The Discovery

Ahau's uncle had taken him in two years earlier after his parents had drowned in a canoe mishap. Since his uncle's death, Ahau had continued to live with and help his uncle's bride's family. They had accepted Ahau with open arms and had made him one of theirs.

The young man drooled in his sleep, making his cheek sticky. He babbled in low tones as he raced through the forest with the demon chasing him, always closer every time Ahau turned to look. His legs scrabbled urgently in the dark in an attempt for more speed. A stream of blood replaced the drooling saliva and trickled out of the corner of Ahau's mouth. He had bit the edge of his tongue, sleep-running against the blackness of the forest.

Tikal came to Ahau sometime just before dawn. Four other young men of about the same age stood behind him.

"Ahau, wake up! Come on, wake up. We have to go now if we want to be first!" whispered Tikal as he shook his friend.

All six of the young men had been at the killing site the day before when the large cat had been fired in the small cave. They wanted to be the ones to tear the rocks away and drag the carcass back to camp. They were sure to be noticed by the young women in the village. Ahau had agreed to come along, but with real misgivings. He still had serious doubts about the jaguar. The horrible visage of his demon haunted his thoughts. This latest series of killings was just too close to the sighting of the large beast for Ahau to believe *it* was not the real instrument of death.

With the rest of the young men quietly urging him on, Ahau rolled off his mat and came to his feet. He grabbed his spear from the corner of the lean-to and exited in a trot, catching up to his friends. It was still dark and seeing was difficult. The sun would not appear for at least a while yet. One of the men lit a torch while passing a fire.

They stayed close to each other as they approached the cave, talking about how they hoped the jaguar was not dead and they could be the ones who finished it off. Much glory could be had this morning. Of course, all this talk was just bravado. They had to appear brave to each other. None of them really wanted anything to do with a wounded jaguar that had already killed several men in their village; men much older than themselves.

No smoke was visible, but the smell of a recent fire was strong. When they reached the cave's entrance, they froze as one. Someone had been there before them. They could see the dark maw of the cave where rocks should have been. They moved closer. With spears in front of them, they held the torch in the opening and looked in, and could almost see to the back of the small enclosure. No jaguar. Only the ash and burnt remnants of the fire were evident.

Tikal and Ahau crowded in with the torch. There was not room for more. Those outside waited their turn, constantly turning, trying to see into the darkness. The jaguar might still be around.

Ahau bent down and stirred the ashes with the butt of his spear. He could just make out the outline of something that shouldn't be there, near the outside edge of the ash. Reaching down, he retrieved Bela's blackened little finger. Holding it lightly, he shook it and blew the ash off.

Ahau held the blackened flesh near the torch so Tikal could see. Both of them crowded in close.

"What is it? What did you find?" Tikal said. "This is not from any jaguar or any other animal I know of. What do you think left it? What was in this cave? You know, don't you?"

Ahau thought he did know, but kept his real thoughts to himself. Instead he said, "We've got to take this to Pochotl. He will know what it means."

"Should we tell the others?" said Tikal, meaning their friends just outside the cave.

Ahau looked over the shoulder of his friend, trying to see the others. Keeping his voice to a whisper, Ahau gestured with his palm down in a quick left to right motion and said, "No."

He stuck the finger in his pouch and stepped out. The rest took their turn with the torch and entered the cave. Once everyone had their look, the young men headed back to camp. Speculations were rampant. Either the jaguar had somehow pushed the rocks aside and escaped, which did not seem likely, or another group had already dragged the carcass out. They could think of no other explanation. Those rocks were much too heavy for one man to have moved by himself. Tikal and Ahau said nothing, letting the others talk among themselves.

One third of the way back to camp, they could see a tight scattering of torches coming to meet them. The young men feared no retribution for checking the cave first. They were members of the hunting clan, *Ah Cacaw*, and were within their rights…at least they thought they were.

Pochotl, dressed in ceremonial garb, led the approaching group, with a torch bearer escorting him on either side. His headdress was of red spoonbill feathers with a quetzal feather device set on top and trailing down the back. Each of his arms was wrapped in a two-inch gold band inset with jade. Gold and jade ear plugs also adorned the lobes of his ears. His bottom lip sagged with the weight of an ornate jade device that fitted over the pulpy flesh from the front and behind. Ocelot skins wrapped his waist and feet. His right hand was filled with reed stalks that he sent in motion when he spoke, lending an air of distinction. He was indeed an imposing figure.

The two groups stopped within three strides of each other. Ahau spoke for his group. "The jaguar is gone. There is nothing there."

The hymen pointed in the direction of the cave in a sweeping motion with his reed stalks. The older men shouted curses and ran toward the cave. Pochotl continued looking at Ahau, trying to pierce the young man's thoughts.

"We must talk. You and me," he said. He flicked the back of his hand in a wave at the rest of the young men, indicating for them to leave.

"I know. Tikal and I were coming to find you. We found something," Ahau replied.

In a whisper, Pochotl asked, "Your creature?"

"I think it might be," said Ahau.

With an almost imperceptible glance with his eyes, Pochotl gestured back toward the camp.

The two of them headed to Pochotl's shelter. Each composed his thoughts; each wondered how much to say. Pochotl swept his arm toward the door, indicating for Ahau to enter first.

No man entered a priest's dwelling without feeling trepidation, for it was holy ground. A small fire sputtered an angry greeting at Ahau as he entered, throwing high shadows against the walls. Because of Pochotl's stature, this temporary dwelling had been the first to be built. Trees had been carefully chosen for their uniformity in diameter and straightness. The upright timbers had been embedded side by side in four feet of soil. Small wooden poles had been lashed together in a crisscross method to support the thatched roof. Mud and thatch filled the spaces. A large wooden table dominated one side of the single room, covered with clay vessels of varying shapes and sizes. Other unguessable holy items kept company beside the vessels, while a bench of simple construction rested in front of the table. An informal, though comfortable looking, mat of woven reed covered a leaf pallet bed nestled near the fire. An opening in the roof above the flames allowed the smoke an escape route. Three shelves were pegged into one wall. A large bowl of a copal resin sat on the top shelf. It smoked a hazy trail across the room, giving off a sharp aroma that made the eyes water.

The shadows and dim light did not allow Ahau to see much more. Objects hung on the walls and sat in corners, but their details were draped in darkness. His imagination wondered if any of the dark shapes were alive. He blocked that thought quickly.

Pochotl pulled the door shut, making the room seem even darker and definitely smaller. He brushed by Ahau.

"Come!" he said.

Pochotl sat on his pallet and motioned for Ahau to sit opposite him, with the fire between. Both sat cross legged, trying to see the other. Ahau could not see Pochotl's face clearly. The glow from the fire was inadequate, and smoke rose in small swirls from the burning embers. Ahau could just make out the priest's intricate tattoo illustrating the thirteen gods of the upper world that made an intertwining circle across his chest. The tattoos seemed alive as the firelight flickered rhythmically across the pattern.

***

Using both hands, Pochotl carefully took the ornate two-piece conch dress from his head and laid it to one side. He hoped this informal gesture would help the young man in front of him relax. It was a very visible symbol of his position and power. Taking it off meant that what was about to be said was between the two of them alone. He could see Ahau's wide eyes as they followed the headdress to the floor. A slight tremble at the corner of Ahau's mouth betrayed the young man's calmness.

Pochotl grunted and said, "So it begins. Show me what you have found."

Ahau pulled the blackened claw from his pouch and handed it to Pochotl. The old priest gingerly rolled the blackened finger across his left hand with the index finger of his right hand. He tried to feel every texture, every crevice. The fire had done little damage other than shriveling it up. It must not have been entirely in the fire. The black fleshy pad under the claw still felt resilient. He pushed on it and the claw extended even farther. The pebbled skin was still intact, though starting to turn on the edges. He drew his obsidian knife and tested the skin's worth. The knife may as well have been trying to cut stone. The significance of this one finger was considerable.

He closed his eyes and carefully measured his thoughts. Several minutes passed. *This finger means that Bela is definitely alive and more dangerous than ever. Wounded animals always are. We should expect more attacks. Bela can be hurt...and if he can be hurt, then he can be killed. But why is Bela here in the first place? What does Ahau mean to the beast? Could any of this be used to my advantage?*

"Tell me exactly how and where this was found," he finally said.

A few minutes later, when Ahau had finished, the priest nodded. Questions swirled in the dark ponds of the old man's mind. He needed to know if he could trust this young man to tell him everything. He tested the young man's truthfulness. He had seen the creature's assent from the trees that night weeks ago when it had visited Ahau. He had told no one.

"Ahau, have you seen the creature since the night it killed Comal and Campeche? Think carefully before you answer," said Pochotl.

49

Ahau visibly blanched. He whispered hoarsely with his head down, "Yes."

"Tell me about it," commanded the hymen.

Ahau sighed, took a breath, and began. "The creature came to me the next night after it killed my uncle and Comal. I woke up and it was just there, over the top of me. I could see into its eyes and smell its breath. It was horrible. I remember trying to shout, and then it was gone. It was just gone. One moment it was there and the next it wasn't. Tikal came to me and said it was just a nightmare, but I'm sure...I'm sure the creature was there. It was looking at me. It was almost like it knew I had been with Comal and Campeche. Why would it come and then not kill me?"

Several heartbeats went by in silence. Neither man spoke till Ahau continued. "I never saw it again, but I think it has been killing our people. I also think it was the same beast in the cave yesterday. There was never any jaguar. I think somehow it was injured and that finger is the result. But how could that be? You said it was the Guardian of the Abyss. Can a god be harmed?" Anger tinged his voice now. "I thought you said it would stay in the area where we found it!"

If Ahau could have seen Pochotl's eyes clearly, he would have seen the quick flash of anger and known he had said too much. He had questioned the hymen's word, and that was always dangerous ground. The old priest gripped his reed stalks and glared at the young man, waiting to see if he had more to say. Again several heartbeats passed in ominous silence.

***

Pochotl reached across the fire and slapped the young man full in the face as hard as he could with the reeds. Ahau fell backwards in complete surprise. His left cheek felt hot where the reeds had caught him. He stayed where he fell.

"Get up and listen, you sniveling little mouse turd," shouted the priest.

Ahau lifted himself up from the dirt floor and sat back down across from the old man. A series of red welts rose across the left side of his face. Ahau's mind raced. *What made the hymen so mad?* He wanted to rub his left eye where part of the reed had slapped it. It was

50

watering badly, but he didn't dare. He looked for the priest. The old man was not across from him but somewhere to his left...he could hear shuffling over by the table. Trying to pierce the darkness with his eyes, he could just see the outline of Pochotl wrestling something on the floor. The hymen laboriously dragged an object almost his own height to the fire. Pochotl could see it was covered in a red cloth as it got closer. Obviously heavy, it left a furrow in the dirt as the priest pulled it to the center of the room.

Pochotl stood the object up near the fire and pulled the cloth off. Ahau fell back with a gasp, both hands up in front, warding off the sight. It was the face of his demon in stone. The image was meticulously worked in low relief on the four sides of the stela, as clear and emphatic as a thunderclap. Under one side, (the side facing Ahau) were glyphs indicating the first encounter with the beast and its name: *Bela De Oxhutz, He Who Owns the Darkness*.

Ahau tentatively reached over and ran his finger across the name in stone, saying it aloud. "Bela...."

Ahau looked up at the priest hoping for an explanation, afraid to ask for one.

"I, too, have seen the demon," said Pochotl. "The night he visited you, I watched him. He obviously has some unknown interest in you."

The young man paled at the thought of this creature taking a special interest in him. The old priest gently patted the top of the stela.

"I have named him Bela. I think I know why he is here," said Pochotl. The wiley old priest continued. "We as a people have entered a part of the world that is so special that Itzamna demands we prove ourselves worthy. Bela was sent by the gods to test us. If we can overcome Bela, then we will have demonstrated our value. We are a great people and deserve this land. We will vanquish the forest of this demon and confirm our place in the new history about to be written."

The old priest was animated now. The reed stalk was back in his right hand and moving with the rhythm of his words. He continued to babble about the merits of the people, this fresh land, and their new adventure. Ahau tried to hold on to every sentence. He was still trying to discover the answers to his own questions.

***

51

Finding a break in Pochotl's words, Ahau quietly asked, "How?"

The hymen absently shook his head and stared at Ahau. "How, what?"

"How do we kill Bela? How do we overcome a demon sent by the gods?" asked Ahau again.

The question brought the priest back to the present. *Yes, just how are we going to overcome a demon?*

"Bela can be hurt. The finger tells us that," said Pochotl. "If he can be hurt, he can be killed. We just have to set a trap."

The old man walked over to Ahau as he spoke. He dragged the reed slowly across the top of the young man's head as he continued. "And you, Ahau, are the key! We know he is interested in you or you would be dead by now, torn up into little pieces."

Ahau held very still and looked straight ahead. The priest resumed.

"I am going to protect you, Ahau. From this moment on, this is where you will live." He made his arms wide, implying his small house. "I'm bestowing a great honor on you. You are going to become my apprentice. You will be near me day and night, and assist me as I need you. You will learn many things, and maybe, just maybe, one of these days you will rise to priesthood; although with your dim intellect, I wouldn't count on it."

At that moment a small thump trembled the wall behind them. Pochotl continued to talk to Ahau about how things were going to be while edging toward the window. With a swift motion, the old priest threw open the wooden shutters covering the window, reached down, and grabbed a fist full of hair, then pulled it upwards. Tikal followed. Before the hymen could speak, Tikal was stammering out an apology.

Pochotl's eyes were boring holes through the young man. The idea of the young man eavesdropping was a violation of protocol so vile it was punishable by death if the priest wished it. Jerking the young man's face close to his own, he said in a very clipped and restrained voice, "How much have you heard? And *you will not* lie to me!"

"I've been here since Ahau first went in. Honest, Your Holiness, I meant no disrespect. Ahau is my friend and I thought he might be in real trouble over the finger. I just wanted to —"

52

Pochotl cut Tikal's explanation short. "Shut-up and get your valueless skin in here." Pochotl gave Tikal's hair an extra jerk to add emphasis to the demand.

Tikal, still sputtering an explanation, entered the holy man's domain and went directly to stand behind Ahau. Pochotl scowled at them both, then went to Tikal. With the reed stalks, he began beating the young man. Tikal knew better than to try and ward off the blows…it would only make the old priest angrier if he tried to cover himself. He bent his head and endured the punishment. To his credit, he never flinched or took a step backwards anytime during the thirty to forty blows.

Pochotl finally ended the beating, his arm tired and some of his anger abated. As he caught his breath, he poked the butt end of his reed stalks into Tikal's chest and said, "Now, Tikal, you too will become my apprentice. If I can't control your curiosity, I can at least control your waking hours. You will be very sorry you were ever outside that wall, young man. This very morning, you will both move your meager belongings in here. Now leave! Both of you! I have to prepare for a meeting with the elders. Be back as soon as you can."

A smile flickered across Pochotl's face as the two young men left. Everything was falling into place. He had been planning to apprentice Tikal in any event. Tikal was too close to Ahau to leave unattended. Apprenticing Tikal would also help ally himself with the young man's father, Ah Tok, a very influential elder. It was a special honor to have a priest take a son to become an apprentice. Priests were, after all, the real backbone of any true society, or so Pochotl thought.

The hymen allowed himself to ruminate as he prepared to meet with the elders. Pochotl had known that he would never rise past the office of *Au Kin*, a lowly, ordinary priest, as long as he stayed in the city of his birth. The *Ah Kin Mai*, superior high priest, had regarded him as an embarrassment to the office. Pochotl's character had been called to task many times. Only Pochotl's family wealth and social status had kept him from being cast out of the priesthood. Pochotl's mind quickly skimmed over this last train of thought. He did not like to dwell on his failures.

It had been over a year ago that he had first approached the thirteen influential men of nobility about leaving the large community and striking out on their own. These same thirteen men now made up the Elder's Council in this new land. Pochotl had succeeded in getting them this far. The Halach Uinic's unpopularity had been the vehicle he needed to persuade the men to join him.

They had left a city of over seven thousand to build anew with only three hundred men, women, and children. The thirteen heads of wealthy families had in turn persuaded stone masons, men of the warrior class, farmers, artisans, hunters, carpenters, and skilled craftsmen of every walk of life to join in the adventure. Slaves had even been brought to help with the enormity of the task. Some of these same slaves would eventually be absorbed into the community. Some would not. It was from these that human sacrifices were chosen. Before today ended, in fact, one of the enslaved men would be honored with an extremely painful death for the glory and good of the whole.

Bela! If only this deadly intruder had not made an appearance, all would be perfect. If Pichotl planned right, though, even this minor irritant could be turned to his advantage. He had made the stela to convince the elders he knew the beast and its significance. More importantly, he would persuade them he knew how to defeat it. Only then would he have the chance to prove the leadership he so craved.

He had been going to the smoking cave earlier this morning in hope of seeing the Bela problem resolved. He didn't really think it would be that easy. He had seen the creature and knew of its deadly strength and speed. That a few warriors could have trapped Bela in a small cave was just too unlikely to pin much hope on. The fact that it *had* been Bela in the cave was serious news. It meant two immediate things. Bela was now injured and at large, more dangerous than before. Also, the finger found in the cave said he could be hurt and killed, maybe even captured. *Wouldn't that be a prize?*

Naming the creature Bela and acknowledging him as a demon sent by the gods to test them had been pure genius. Again the smile flickered. Pochotl's thoughts went to the two new apprentices. Pochotl's instincts told him that Tikal and Ahau would somehow be instrumental in killing the great beast. The entire plan still needed some thought, but the bones were there. More needed to be learned about the beast. Surely if he put his mind to it, he could think of a way to study Bela. His real evaluation of Bela was that the creature was only a mutation of nature and nothing more. Time would tell, he thought.

Pochotl finished mashing plant residues into pastes of blue, black, and white. From specular hematite, he made a rich red. To each of these he added a plant oil residue and water, creating body paints. He applied the blue with a small cotton cloth to the entirety of his arms, hands, and legs. Using a polished iron pyrite stone as a mirror, Pochotl carefully painted the top half of his face from the bridge of the nose up. From the ceramic dish of red, he drew a line the thickness of his finger horizontally across his face at the bottom of the blue. Under this, he applied the black to the rest of his face and neck. Skeleton-like teeth marks were painted in white across closed lips and chin. His hair draped over each shoulder to the collar bones. Turning his head this way and that, he looked at his reflection approvingly. It was the people's belief that after death, the soul undertook a dangerous journey through the underworld, which was ruled by nine specific gods and their pet demons. Some of these underworld gods were depicted as part beast and part man. It was this image Pochotl was trying to create. The world was a big place, full of the unknown, and the people listened most carefully to the prescribed gods to help them make sense of it all. Pochotl covered his torso with two ocelot skins sewn together with holes cut out for the arms, legs, and neck. The clawed feet were still intact and hung impressively. Bela's finger was tied off in a rawhide strip and suspended in the small of the hymen's neck. His head dressings, sandals, and jade jewelry were the same as before. He was ready.

Pochotl stepped outside his dwelling and blew mightily on a conch shell three times, signifying that it was time for the meeting of the elders. Shortly after the signal, the men had assembled on the new foundation of the Sun Temple. Only the floor had been constructed so far. Stone blocks, the thickness of a man's head, interlocked with mortar made of volcanic tuff, had been placed in a rectangle about fifty strides in each direction. These had been laboriously cut out of sandstone with harder stone implements and carried over half a day's distance to the present site. The floor was level and flat with the long sides oriented east and west, following the daily path of the sun.

Wooden benches were placed in a semi-circle near the center of the makeshift pavilion for the thirteen members of the Elder's Council.

***

Ah Tok, the wealthiest and most influential nobleman of the group, had been working with stone masons and slaves on his new house. He was not happy to be taken away from such important work.

He leaned in to the men seated nearest to him and grumbled, "The hymen had better have a good reason for calling us together. I, for one, am much to busy to listen to him prattle on about his opinions."

Ah Tok was not culled by Pochotl's presence or position. The nobleman had uprooted his family and vacated substantial holdings for reasons of his own. The old priest had given him a course of action that had fit his own desires, so he added his weight to the others and left the city of his birth, Kohunlich. If the right circumstances were to happen and he had the support, he could be named supreme ruler and his descendants forever after him. Of course, it would never do to openly admit such a plan. These things had to be subtly done, and timing was crucial.

Ah Tok shook his head at the thought of Pochotl's posturing. Before he had left Kohunlich, friends of consequence had told him stories about the old priest. They had described him as pretentious and self-serving. Ah Tok was now inclined to believe them.

***

The rest of the village went on with their work, ignoring the business of the elders and the village priest. The meeting was of no consequence to them and they treated it as such. To show interest in such affairs often invited unwanted attention by the hymen during blood-letting rituals. It had happened often enough before. The Elder's Council was, for all practical purposes, completely alone.

***

In an attempt to make an inspiring entrance, Pochotl now made his way to the council via a slow walk accompanied by the cadence of a drumbeat. Close behind him, two villagers pressed into service carried the stela on its side over two poles. A drummer trailed several steps behind. The old priest was very solemn and deliberate in his

56

approach. He wanted the council to be impressed with his bearing and realize his and the meeting's importance. All eyes watched him as he walked across the floor and came to the center area.

Pochotl pointed to where he wanted the stela stood up. The bearers did as he directed and left quickly. They wanted nothing to do with the council or the priest. The stela, still covered with the red cloth, sat before them, demanding their curiosity. Pochotl straightened himself as tall as possible, lifted his arms to the heavens, and commenced.

"We have been guided by the gods to this favored land. Here, we can build our monuments to the divine entities, farm our fields, harvest from the surrounding forest, and raise our families as we want. No longer are we held accountable to anyone but ourselves. No longer do we need to give a large share of the bounty we work so hard for to a ruler who becomes greedier every year."

Pochotl hesitated to see if he had their attention. He could see heads nodding in assention. The priest continued.

"We have made great strides in making this land our own. We sit now on the beginnings of a Sun Temple. Years from now, when it is completed, it will be a glorious tribute to Itzamna. Soon we will begin work on other temples. Our houses will rival anything we left in Kohunlich. Ours will be a magnificent city that will put all others in its shadow. We will reign supreme in this land. Our people will prosper and flourish." The old priest could actually feel the heat of his words and was becoming more energized as he spoke.

"Our children and their children's children will forever hold this land as their own. We have done well in our beginnings, but we must do more. We must prove ourselves worthy of such a future," Pochotl said as he ripped the red cloth from the stela.

The council, including Ah Tok, sucked in their breath. Almost as one they made noises of astonishment. The image fairly leapt out at them. Pochotl had an amazing talent of working with stone. It was something he took great pride in and labored exhaustingly at. His uncles had both been stone masons, and as a young boy, Pochotl had been allowed occasionally to work under their guidance. He easily could have chosen the work of an artist instead of the priesthood. His lusts had made the choice for him.

"This is *Bela De Oxhutz. He Who Owns the Darkness*. It is he who has been slaughtering our people. It is he who even now judges us and tests our resolve. There is no jaguar; there never was. Bela is a demon sent by Itzamna, and I have seen him."

Pochotl paused to let these words sink in before he went on. The council was dead quiet and listening to his every word.

Pochotl lowered his voice and said, "I have personally seen this great beast and can attest to its strength and speed. It is the same demon that met Comal, Compeche, and Ahau. Comal and Compeche are dead and only Ahau survived. Bela is here, somewhere in the jungle near us...."

The men looked around as if Bela might actually be in the nearby trees that very moment.

"And was sent as a test; a test that we must pass if we are to prove ourselves worthy of this new land."

The council accepted Pochotl's words as truth. Priests would know about such things. Even Ah Tok realized that this was indeed a matter of considerable importance. The old priest went on.

"Itzamna spoke to me in a vision two nights ago," Pochotl lied. "He has sent Bela as a trial to insure that our heritage and intentions are strong. If we can defeat Bela, then all we dream of, all we hope for, will be ours. In my vision I also was told how this could be done."

He lifted the finger off his chest and held it forward for all to see. The council seemed to take in a collective breath. They could see immediately that this was no ordinary animal's claw.

"This finger came from the great beast. Its claw is stone-hard. I have tested it with a knife."

Pochotl drew his knife and slid it across the pebbled skin for them to see. "To attack Bela head-on is not possible. He must be overwhelmed by many warriors at once for us to have any chance at all of defeating him. This finger was severed, I think, by accident. Near the connecting joint, the flesh is softer and a spear's edge or knife inadvertently sliced through. We cannot assume such an accident will happen again."

The old priest explained how the clawed finger had been found and came into his possession. He held it out for Ah Tok to touch with a warning only the nobleman could hear.

"Feel the texture of the skin and claw if you dare. But be warned Ah Tok...I can not tell you what will happen if you touch it. It is the finger of a demon and great power lies still within it. It may be that only my holy training allows me to do so."

***

Ah Tok pulled his hand back quickly. It was not that he was really afraid...*but why take the chance?* he thought. He locked eyes with the old priest and saw a contemptuous smile just behind the level glare. His hand was just barely out of reach of the finger. Ah Tok took the dare. He lifted the finger deftly from the priest's grasp, his eyes never leaving Pochotl's. He could see real disappointment register in the priest's face.

Ah Tok stroked his thumb across the claw, weighing the finger in his mind. This had been a formidable weapon. He would hate to be at the receiving end of it and its brothers. He solemnly handed the finger back to Pochotl. Whatever the priest had in mind, he would probably back him up. Even if this was not the finger of a demon, its presence spoke volumes. A dangerous beast did most certainly block their progress, and he was not going to allow that. It was important for the others to know he was supporting Pochotl. To openly defy a priest was not good politics. Using a tone of voice brimming with concern, he asked the question that was on everyone's mind. "How do we precede, Your Holiness?"

The priest outlined his plan.

CHAPTER 5

RIGHTEOUS WRATH

Bela, still cradling his right hand, sought the canopy of the nearby forest. Deep into the interior he ran, occasionally wailing from his pain and frustration. In his mind he nurtured pictures of himself ripping the brownskins into pieces until they were all dead. He drank their life juices and held his gore-spattered arms to the sky, screaming his victory. A low branch painfully breaking against his scorched side brought him back to the present. He slowed down to an easy lope.

Spying a boa constrictor sliding through the undergrowth, Bela wrapped his left hand around it and jerked it to him. The constrictor reacted immediately, and struck at Bela's injured left side near the middle of his thigh. The constrictor's fangs slid off the hardened skin, but the impact made Bela lose his grip. He dropped the snake and gave voice to a deafening howl. His good left hand went to his injured thigh. He could see no damage, but the ache was real.

Bela looked down at the constrictor. The snake opened its jaws as wide as it could and tried to lock its fangs into Bela's ankle but the fangs kept slipping off the indurate hide, so the snake wrapped its coils around the nearest leg. Bela stepped hard on one of the coils with his free foot, pinning it to the ground. He then thrust the claws of his left hand into the snake's body, creating an explosion of blood from the pressure. Bela dug deeper until he wrapped his hand completely around the snake's spine, then twisted his fist, snapping the bones and severing the nerves. The snake rolled and writhed as it hissed its death spasms, finally lying in a slow moving, coiled heap at Bela's feet. A thin river of viscous black blood trickled between his feet, cutting a path through the dirt, momentarily resting like a red rope before soaking in.

He draped the huge snake over his shoulder and began feeding as he walked. The snake had done no serious harm, but he realized how incapacitated he really was. His side ached incessantly and his right hand throbbed with every step. It was nearing darkness and still a significant distance lay between Bela and his home. He holed up in especially thick vegetation under a stone escarpment and resumed his feeding.

Sometime during the early morning of the next day, Bela's acute hearing picked up the sound of two heavy animals coming in his direction. His olfactory glands completed the picture. With the pairing of these two extraordinary senses, his mind pictured the wolves, their heads down, searching for food. Bela fervently hoped that they would not come anywhere near his dark refuge…he did not want to be disturbed. He continued to doze with his eyes closed, tracking the animals.

***

The wolves came nearer, sniffing and whining at the unfamiliar scent hidden from their immediate view. The congealed blood and musk of the boa constrictor were smells they knew, but something else was mixed with them and the smell excited their curiosity. They snuffled through the undergrowth, tracking the scent closer and closer to its source, and were actually wagging their tails in anticipation. They knew it was just in front of them.

The wolves' noses told them that what they sought was somewhere in the thick plant growth in front of them. They growled a deep reverberating challenge, but heard no response so they rumbled again. Again, only silence met their efforts. After a few more attempts to lure a response, the wolves started whining in frustration. The male wolf knew it was time to take action and hesitantly entered a few feet into the vegetation, where he found the tail of the boa constrictor. The snake felt and smelled dead. He cautiously picked up the snake's tail in his mouth and treaded backwards, but the snake was suddenly wrenched from the wolf's mouth and taken back into the interior of the inky, pitch-darkness. Both wolves yelped in surprise, their feet pawing the ground. They were almost never rebuked in their pursuits for food.

The male wolf felt the need to demonstrate his dominance, and he rumbled a challenge and charged in. A shrill, short cry was cut short...the male never came out.

The whimpering female made a hard decision. She left, making intermittent, plaintive cries for her lost companion. She had always hunted and fought by her mate's side. It was difficult to leave, but whatever had killed him, she knew, was more than a match for her alone.

Bela was happy with the kill. He rarely harvested in the daylight hours, but providence had smiled on him. The male wolf had been foolishly curious and had paid the price. Between naps, Bela supped on the meat, chew-sucking the wolf into lumps of unrecognizable gray mush.

The forest became dark. The sun had finally finished its course across the sky and descended out of view. Bela licked his wounded right hand, stretched his injured side, and left his hole. Discovering he needed to vacate his bowels, he squatted in the open. Finished, he scratched dirt over the cords of red-black excretion. Out of habit, he voided his bladder on top of the dirt mound, marking the area as part of his domain. He pressed on, anxious to get home. It would take time to heal, but the fingers would eventually regenerate and his side would slough off the injured skin, revealing new growth. Then the brownskins would be dealt with one at a time. Again the pictures of killing reeled in his head as he ran through the subtropical forest. It began to rain.

CHAPTER 6

JADED CHOICES

Pochotl's plan made sense to Ah Tok and the rest of the council. Because of the religious significance of the number thirteen, each member of the council chose a warrior of renowned abilities. These thirteen warriors would be accompanied by Chan Chel, the village's best tracker and hunter. It was Pochotl's contention that Bela's lair was in the deep forested bowl where Comal and Compeche had died. That first deadly encounter had probably been near Bela's home. The warriors would hunt the demon down, and in mass, attack it. Thirteen warriors were easily a match for any one beast. That night, in preparation for the hunt, they would hold a Ceremony of the Innocent. This ritual of human sacrifice would ensure that the thirteen choices were wise ones and that their endeavor went well.

The economy in Kohunlich and other similar cities was built on the trading of commodities, the bartering of services, and the green gemstone, jade. Jade was the most precious material available to the people's economy. Ah Tok and a few other families had for generations mined jade from secret stream beds near Kohunlich. Their large caches of jade had paid for the best stone masons. Immense temple-like abodes were built that housed many relatives at once. Only Kohunlich's Halach Uinic could boast of housing bigger and richer than Ah Tok's. Intelligent politics had kept Ah Tok from building more.

When he left the great city to strike out on his own, he had sold his impressive edifices for far less than they were worth. The secret jade beds he'd deeded to the Halach Uinic. It was primarily his sacrifices that had convinced the ruler to allow the large group to leave. The Halach Uinic had relished Ah Tok's jade mines for years. Even so, Ah Tok retained wealth enough to bring thirty-two slaves, eighteen relatives, and twenty-two employees with him. The other twelve members of the council had made similar sacrifices, though not as large. They too had brought employees, relatives, and slaves. It was from this collective pool of slaves that the human sacrifice would be chosen.

Round, finger-thick ceramic rods, painted with the colors and symbols of each of the thirteen houses, were placed in a polychromatic clay bowl. A small leather cape with a slit large enough to accept a hand was tied over the top. The priest ceremoniously reached in and pulled one out. Keeping the rod enclosed in his fist, Pochotl moved to the council and formally displayed his choice. Ah Tok was not surprised the human sacrifice would come from his stock. He had expected it. If anything went wrong with the mission, Pochotl could then place part of the blame at Ah Tok's feet. He would have to choose his slave well.

The council nodded its acceptance and disbanded in twos and threes. Runners were sent out with the news of the ritual. Within a hand span of light, the whole community was aware that tonight someone would die for the common good of all. News of Bela traveled faster.

Ah Tok caught up to the old priest as Pochotl headed back to his home. He had heard about Tikal's and Ahau's apprenticeship. He was not against his son becoming a priest…in fact, it might be the best avenue for young Tikal to follow. Should he ascend to the throne of Halach Uinic, his lineage would follow. Tikal, as priest king, would be very formidable, almost mystical. His powers would be godlike.

Warily grabbing the hymen's elbow, Ah Tok said, "Great Priest, I would speak with you. I seek…," the nobleman sighed his distaste, "your wisdom."

"What can an old priest do for one of your worth, Ah Tok?" Pochotl asked.

The nobleman decided to handle the priest tactfully. "My son, Tikal, has told me of his excellent fortune. He said you had chosen him and Ahau to become your apprentices."

Pochotl nodded. "They have exhibited signs of having special talents. With the right training and several years of diligent hard work, they could become priests our community would be proud of."

"Your wisdom in such matters is unchallenged. I am very fond of my son and his close friend, Ahau. I only want what is best for them and the community. Your reputation as a great priest is well known. I will abide by your judgment," Ah Tok said.

"Your faith in my judgment is flattering. I am glad you and I see things together," said Pochotl.

Ah Tok gripped the hymen's elbow a bit tighter. "Know this, priest...my anger would be boundless if any harm were to befall either of those two. I feel safe knowing you will shield them from anything injurious or detrimental." He narrowed his eyes and brought his face closer to the priest. "I will keep in close contact with you, checking on their progress."

***

Pochotl recognized the barely veiled threat. "Your son and his friend can become great priests only after rigorous training. Some of this training is necessarily dangerous. I, of course, will do all I can to protect them. Their final fates, however, are in the hands of the gods. Only they can dictate what will and what will not happen to our precious young men."

Pochotl jerked his elbow out of Ah Tok's grasp and turned his back on the nobleman, continuing on his path home. He understood his relationship with Ah Tok was tenuous at best. He would have to change that. For his plans to succeed, he needed to put the nobleman under his control.

As he got closer to home, he could see the two young men sitting among their meager belongings outside his door. Tikal and Ahau were instructed to take their things inside and throw them against the only bare wall. There was no time to put things away or bring bedding in. Pochotl explained about the ceremony and the urgency to help him prepare for it. They were soon off and running to do his bidding.

Excitement eventually changed to chagrin. It seemed the priest's list of things to do would never end. Everything they did was either not right or too slow. Pochotl berated, beat, and blamed them for every minor hindrance to his ceremonial preparations. Plants, roots, and even special reptiles had to be gathered. Other members of the tribe, as per Pochotl's instructions, cut and buried upright, large wooden poles in prescribed places against the Sun Temple floor. Wooden benches, ropes, firewood, and a seemingly endless list of other requirements had to be accumulated.

***

A very real sense of duty made the enslaved honor bound to do service for their captors. They had been won in battle and were obliged to perform for years the work required of them. Involuntary servitude was an accepted part of the people's culture. Guards were always on hand but rarely needed. Dignity and a relegated attitude to obeisance allowed few the nerve to run, but occasionally they managed to slip off the yoke of servility. By acts of bravery, sacrifices, and even marriage they sometimes were made a true member of the community. When word of the ceremony came, they knew one of their numbers would be glorified. That was just the way of things. One of them would be chosen as the sacrifice. It was an honor seldom sought.

***

Zac Kuk had been with Ah Tok for most of his life. Over ten years ago he and other members of his tribe had lost a territorial battle with the citizens of Kohunlich. His life had been spared and he was taken captive. Eventually, he had been sold by the king to the nobleman to work his jade fields.

Life with Ah Tok had been good. Quite by accident, Zac Kuk found he was very adept at stone carving, helping a stone mason make a lintel for a doorway. Ever since, he had worked stone for the nobleman and been treated with respect. A good stone mason was hard to find. By almost every standard, Zac Kuk had assimilated into the community...he thought.

When a crowd of guards came to take him, he was incredulous that he had been chosen for the sacrifice. This state of unbelieving soon turned into grim reality. His breathing became rapid and his face hot as his eyes searched everywhere for help. He kept calling Ah Tok's name in an increasingly loud voice. Surely the nobleman would clear up this obvious misunderstanding if they would only get him. Urine ran freely down the front of his legs.

The guards supported his arms and began to lead him to a sweat lodge, where he would be bathed and the impurities purged from his system. All the other slaves kept their heads down and concentrated on their work. The relief they felt was immense. It wasn't them...but it was a friend. They could only hope he died bravely. There was nothing else they could do.

Much later, cleaned and groomed by women, Zac Kuk had accepted that there had been no mistake. Ah Tok, for whatever reason, had given him to the community as an offering to Itzamna. There was no escape. In typical stoic fashion, the enslaved man embraced his fate, determined to succumb courageously to death. Great honor would be his if he kept his resolve. He sat straight as the women continued to comb his hair and rub palm oil over his body. In soothing tones, they sung to him about heroes past and his place in the list of reverence. Zac Kuk was almost at peace. He drank more from the balche.

***

Ah Tok's conscience troubled him greatly. He sat in a darkened room staring out the window, his eyes seeing nothing. *Did I do the right thing? There are several slaves to choose from. I even like Zac Kuk. If only I hadn't caught Zac Kuk eyeing my daughter, Jada. She is just beginning to blossom into a beautiful woman. It is hard not to notice the new curves and rounding out of enticing flesh. If she wasn't my daughter....* He felt immediately guilty for thinking such thoughts. *But when Zac Kuk notices, well, that's too much. The slave definitely overstepped his bounds. Besides, it's much too late to change my decision. The Ceremony of the Innocent demands that the sacrificial flesh be chosen by reasons of purity, not vindictive vengeance. What evil have I wrought? What will come of this? This surely will end badly.*

***

The village overlooked, from a high rise, a rich valley abundant with forest and wildlife. Pochotl stepped out of his dwelling and looked to the west. The sun balanced momentarily on the horizon, streaking the tops of the trees crimson. A slight breeze set the leaves in motion, giving the illusion of blood red waves washing towards the village. It was time.

Pochotl blew a sustained blast on his conch shell, signaling for the people to come together. The preparations for the ceremony had been

69

complete for some time now. Like fireflies, kindled blazes flared up all around the village, turning back the darkness. Drums were starting to beat a monotonous slow cadence. In honor of the sacrifice, the men of the village commenced to sing with the pounding of the drum. "Zac Kuk, Zac Kuk, Zac Kuk," was repeated over and over in unison. The women, in high falsetto, sang "Ahee" between the beats. The combination of the three sounds was eerily exhilarating.

***

Ahau and Tikal had never seen this ceremony and were not sure what to expect. Nor had anyone in the crowd witnessed this particular ceremony. Pochotl, as the people's priest, had assured the elders it was necessary. A few of them had voiced their doubt, but kept their thoughts to themselves. It wouldn't be very smart to rebuke the priest in front of anyone. The hymen, after all, was the supreme leader of all of their religious endeavors. He surely knew what was best for the people. As a mass, they trusted him. As a mass, they had to.

The Sun Temple floor was in readiness for Zac Kuk's gift of life. In the center, Pochotl stood over a stone table, examining cutting tools and various clay containers and their contents. He was dressed much the same as he had been earlier in the day. Tikal and Ahau were painted completely in blue with red cloths binding their loins. Their hair was dyed red and tightly braided to hang down both sides of their chests. At each end of the table they kneeled, head down, awaiting any instructions. They did not expect to be included in much of the actual ceremony…they were just part of the props, just the old priest's new apprentices. Their eyes briefly met.

The people pushed and jostled for positions to see. They stood around the Sun Temple's floor, never touching the holy stone. All sound stopped. The crowd parted at the east end as Zac Kuk was brought in on a litter born high on the backs of four men. His head wore a crown of purple flowers. He stared straight ahead, his eyes glassy. Only those up close could see the tremor in his hands, held together at his lap. The bearers laid Zac Kuk on the cold stone on his back, his face skyward. They spread his arms and legs as wide as they could and tied each with a sisal rope. From the other end of the rope, they pulled Zac Kuk tight. The song began anew.

70

***

Exquisite pain and prolonged suffering were just as important as the actual shedding of blood to the people's belief. To give of one's self in this way was the ultimate sacrifice to the gods. Pochotl was determined that Itzamna would be pleased with his efforts. Zac Kuk's death would be long in coming and tremendously painful. The old priest had learned from the Ah Kin Mai that the nerves in the human body could be enhanced greatly through the use of a slimy liquid secreted behind the eyes of a rare toad. Tikal and Ahau had spent over two hours with the hymen trying to find the small gray toad in the broken rocks north of the village. They had found three.

The priest raised his hands and as one, the voices ceased. "We give thanks and honor the spirit of Zac Kuk, housed in the body before us. By releasing his spirit, we reveal our commitment to this new land. We, as children of the infinite god Itzamna, must display our sincerity. With pain and blood, we manifest our desires and ask for the wisdom to defeat our enemy. The evil life source that is Bela de Oxhutz shall be vanquished. His vicious, malevolent soul will no longer feed on Itzamna's children. The people alone shall walk this fresh earth as rulers of all that is visible."

CHAPTER 7

HIDDEN AGENDAS

The song began again. Tikal and Ahau were instructed to hold the man's head still. The apprentices wrapped a wide leather strap across Zac Kuk's chin, sat down and braced their feet against his shoulders, and pulled the strap tight. Pochotl wanted most of his victim's senses dead...except the ability to feel pain. Using sinew, he sewed the man's lips shut in a crisscross pattern so he could not scream aloud. With almost delicate touches, the priest sewed Zac Kuk's eyelids shut...carefully, so as not to damage the eyes. Tikal and Ahau were hard pressed to hold the man's head still. Zac Kuk's muscles stood out in relief as he strained against the ropes holding his arms and legs.

Earlier, twigs, leaves, and pieces of bark had been minced and set on fire in a large open ceramic bowl. Pochotl had placed several long, small round sticks at angles around the inside of the bowl, resting the ends in the fire. He brought one of these burning brands near Zac Kuk's face, allowing the man to feel the heat.

The old priest brought his lips close to the man's ear and whispered, "Ahhh, Zac Kuk, how you must hurt, and we haven't even really begun yet." He brushed the brow of the slave tenderly and smiled at the two apprentices, who he knew were only able to hear a mumbled garb, and probably assumed the priest was comforting the slave.

"Such a brave face. You think your life ends for the good of the people. You think your courage will shield you from the pain. We will see if your beliefs make a difference. Let me tell you mine." The old man brought his lips closer to Zac Kuk's ear. "You die for nothing, slave. Your death and suffering are for my pleasure alone. All hope is lost to you and everything that could have been. It's not that I hate you...I just want to do this. I enjoy doing this. Are you hearing me, Zac Kuk? Itzamna does not know you exist. I promise you, Zac Kuk, I will keep you alive as long as possible. Embrace the pain as you would a lover." No one else heard.

Pochotl pushed and twirled the burning end of the fire brand into the man's ears just far enough to destroy his sense of hearing. The smell of burnt flesh reached the apprentices first before dispersing into the crowd. Tikal and Ahau were retching with revulsion. Pochotl, on the other hand, was exhilarated. He was compelled to defile the innocence of the man's flesh. A slick sheet of sweat reflected wet in the firelight off the priest's skin. His eyes were almost glowing in anticipation as he licked the splashed blood off his lips and savored the taste.

***

Ah Tok blanched at what he saw, the bile rising in his throat. *This man was my friend once. His suffering is because of my decision.* He wanted to turn his head and leave, but of course did not. Appearance was everything...he must seem strong.

***

Pochotl gripped a tukal hard in his right hand. With a hard over hand swing, he brought the smooth, hardwood club down on each of Zac Kuk's fingers, breaking the bones in pieces. In the logic of the ceremony Pochotl was removing the sense of touch, but in reality, the fingers were throbbing a message more intense than any the slave had likely ever experienced. For good measure, Pochotl brought the club down hard on the top of each foot across the arch, breaking the bones there also. Zac Kuk struggled in silent agony, and the men pulled tighter on the ropes.

Tikal and Ahau were signaled to go back to the stone table. They knelt in their original positions at the ends of the table, looking straight ahead yet trying to see all that was happening out of the corner of their eyes.

At Pochotl's command, the ropes were wrapped around the two poles in four places, two on each side. Grooves had been cut in the wood, high and low, to accommodate the rope. The men pulled Zac Kuk until he was suspended high, upside down, his feet and arms spread wide. The song became louder. People were swaying to the beat, their eyes glued to the victim and his macabre dance on the ends of the ropes. Balche was passed freely among them.

More men were called to help. Muscles tore, and ligaments and tendons snapped as the man's legs were pulled further apart, creating a tight-lined X. The ropes were tied off. The real fun was about to begin.

The crown of flowers dropped to the stones, and a light breeze blew the broken, purple petals across the temple floor. One of the fragile, dying pieces pushed gently against Ahau's calf. Ahau looked down at the broken symbol of Zac Kuk's glorified sacrifice and wept quietly to himself.

A muffled scream tried to push its way through the terribly swollen lips hanging at the middle of the X. The sinew held tight. Red drops caught in the light as they dripped to the floor, splattering like dropped rubies as they hit. Zac Kuk's head began to move faster and faster as he swung it first left, then right, and then back to the left. The movement became frenzied, and blood sprayed in random patterns, pelting everyone nearby.

As suddenly as it began, the motion stopped. The head hung dead center and was still. The singing stopped…everything stopped. Everyone was hushed.

The old priest glared at the hanging meat. *The man's heart could not have given out. Surely Zac Kuk would not dare to die now…not when the real work is yet to be done.* Pochotl went in close to check for a heartbeat, then barked an order at Ahau to bring him one of the small ceramic vials from the stone table.

Ahau did not appear to hear at first. Pochotl quietly repeated his demand. The young apprentice left his knees and brought the required vial. Unstopping it, the priest passed it over Zac Kuk's nose. The ammonia-like smell brought back consciousness, and the slave once again began to tremble…the only movement the ropes would allow. Excretion and urine mixed and slid down his back and stomach, eventually pooling on the stone beneath his head.

Pochotl told Tikal to bring the sack of toads. One at a time, the priest rubbed a secretion from the toads all over the victim's body. Just behind the eyes of the toads was a gland that, when pushed, spurted a sticky liquid that was extremely foul tasting to its attackers. Placed on human skin, however, the result was different. It began to burn, making the nerve endings just below the surface of the skin more sensitive — more attune to pain. Zac Kuk's skin quivered as new spasms of agony washed over him.

The song began again sometime during the toad-rubbing. Hoarse voices kept the chant going. Excited once again, the priest skewered Zac Kuk's body with slivers of sharpened wood. When he had finished, the porcupined-meat dripped blood from over fifty places. Each wood piece had been inserted just enough to tear under the skin and into the muscle, but never deep enough to be a mortal wound by itself. Pochotl knew the human body. He knew where the nerve ganglia hid beneath the flesh and where they were most sensitive. It was in these areas the skin was made to accept the piercing shafts.

Pochotl stilled Zac Kuk's head with his hands. Getting on his knees, the priest aligned his eyes with the slave's, trying to peer into the blood clotted slits between the sinews. No good…nothing could be seen. He made a mental note to next time use a looser stitch so that he could see into the pain-stoked furnaces of his victim's eyes. Pochotl picked at the blood clots near the corner of Zac Kuk's mouth. The swollen tissue and dried blood made it hard to get hold of the sinew. Finally getting a purchase, in a single jerk the priest ripped the cord through the tender flesh, releasing the lips. Immediately a shriek built in momentum and shattered through the background noise of the song. Everyone stilled.

Zac Kuk gathered a second breath and began again. Pochotl made Tikal and Ahau hold the man's head still. The priest began screwing a sharpened stick between the teeth, effectively opening the mouth and holding it in that position. The hymen reached in with a thin obsidian lancet and neatly sliced through the tongue. Tikal and Ahau released the head. The shriek now had turned into a bubbly, wet moan. Pochotl had wanted Zac Kuk to give voice to his pain, but had found the sound distracting. He carefully placed the tongue in his pouch. He would make a necklace out of it later. Having a souvenir of the occasion would be comforting.

Pochotl placed his mouth close to the slave's damaged, unhearing ear. In a wet whisper he said, "I give you release."

The old priest moved fast now. In a quick left to right motion, he severed Zac Kuk's genitals. These too went in his pouch. The victim's pain levels were red-lining now as he began the short slide into terminal shock. Instructing Tikal and Ahau to hold special bowls under the man's head, Pochotl slit the carotid artery.

Catching the blood from so much pressure was not easy. The first burst of sacred fluid seemed to catch Ahau by surprise. A full arm span from the source, blood arched, striking the young apprentice in the chest, then cascading down his waist and covering his thighs before he got control of the forceful flow. With Tikal's help, two bowls brimmed with the black-red claret. At Pochotl's command, the blood-filled vessels were placed on the stone table. Some of the blood was added to pom, strong incense made by the priest. The mixture would be allowed to dry, and in the following days, the incense would be fired, pungent wisps of smoke spiraling upward, carrying the people's prayers to the realm of the supernatural.

The hymen nimbly avoided the thicker, red-black, turbid pools at his feet. Slipping the blade of an obsidian knife through the stomach wall near the sternum, the priest carved from left to right. He jumped back as ropes of steaming intestines tumbled to the floor. Clouds of mosquitoes and flies flew up as the tubular invasion interrupted their feeding.

Pochotl reached down into what had been Zac Kuk's chest. With the blade, he severed the heart from its connecting tissues and pulled the sacred organ out into the night air, then held it high above his head and turned in a slow circle so everyone could see his prize. Blood ran in rivulets down his wrists and arms. The priest took the fist-sized piece of meat and placed it in a bowl on the stone table.

The saviors chosen by the elders came forward. Behind the stone table, Pochotl stood in readiness, awaiting the thirteen. His arms were above his head, his hands pressed together in supplication. Pochotl was trying for a trance-like state of consciousness. The selected warriors lined up shoulder to shoulder three strides from the table, facing the priest. Moments turned into agitated expectancy, waiting for the priest to finish.

Pochotl was silently chanting, his eyes closed, waiting for just the right moment. Everyone assumed he was conversing with the gods. The hushed, noiseless backdrop was perfect for the dramatic attention he craved. Finally deciding the time was right, Pochotl ended his exaggerated private conversation. He opened his eyes and nodded his head. The two apprentices recognized the signal. They began slicing the heart into bite-sized chunks.

In a loud voice, Pochotl thundered, "Zac Kuk will live in our memories forever. His ultimate sacrifice has greatly pleased Itzamna." He held one of the blood filled vessels up for all to see.

"This sacred essence of Zac Kuk's courage we now give to these warriors so they may be empowered with the blessings of the gods."

Pochotl held the bowl in both hands and tipped the edge to each man in turn so that they could sip from the blood. He unblinkingly looked into each man's eyes, insuring they knew the seriousness of what they did. Tikal handed the priest another bowl. This one was full of heart chunks. Pochotl again held the bowl high for all to see.

"The soul is found deep within the breast of our people. Zac Kuk's released spirit shall live forever in the warm embrace of Itzamna. His glory and bravery are symbolized in the heart he left behind. By eating a piece, each of our valorous warriors shall be imbibed with the strength and courage to contend with the demon. Bela de Oxhutz will forever be vanquished from this earth. Make no mistake. The destinies of the creature and ourselves are intertwined. We must prevail. I charge each warrior with the fate of our people."

Again Pochotl searched the eyes of each man as he watched them eat a portion of the heavily fibered meat. It was obviously hard to chew. Most chose just to swallow it whole. The crowd erupted in a thunderous noise of happiness as the priest fed the last of the meat to the men. The Ceremony of the Innocent was complete, and it had been a success. Bela's demise was assured and the future of the people was full of promised integrity. Pochotl dismissed the crowd by turning his back on them and turning to his apprentices.

***

After everyone had left, Tikal and Ahau were instructed by the old priest to dispose of the body and clean up the mess. The young men reverently lowered the tortured meat to the floor. The head clunked and lay to the side. Lips, puffy and caked with dried blood, parted abruptly with a rubbery smack. Ahau's imagination heard exquisite pain spiraling up and up into a stretched thin crimson scream that seemed to echo in the still air. He gently closed the skewed lips and compassionately smoothed Zac Kuk's hair from his face. He wondered if the dead man still felt anything, but was afraid to know. He hoped he would never know.

Zac Kuk's remains were buried near the west side of the Sun Temple floor. A stela, telling of his sacrifice for the people, would eventually be placed over the grave. The floor was meticulously scrubbed with water and sand. Deep in the texture of the stone, Zac Kuk's blood would forever stain the spot a rusty red.

CHAPTER 8

THE HEALING

Deep within the unnatural forested bowl were areas so dense with vegetation a man could not penetrate it without cutting his way in. Very little light found its way through the uppermost branchy coverings. The crowded growth was ancient here. Dead evidence of plant predecessors was several hands thick, slowly rotting back to compost. Termites, bacteria, and fungi had decomposed the dead plant droppings into a brown mat.

Further down, the soft loam was home to many varieties of worms. They crawled through their little tunnels oblivious to what went on above them, rarely visiting the surface. It was here in the darkness that black eyes stared out watching a bear crunch her way through a coppice of shrubbery and dead trees. Even though it was midday, absence of the hated light allowed Bela to hunt. The giant bear infuriated him. He considered all bears ignorant, clumsy animals. This one not only had ignored his warning scent piles, but had brought its cub into his private forest. The little one was just now coming over a fallen log, squealing for its stupid mother. Bela moved adjacent to the bears' path. No wind breathed his presence. They continued on, unaware of him and his deadly intent.

A ravine running parallel to the grizzly made for a perfect hunting blind. Bela's eyes narrowed. Saliva dripped on the fronds as he pushed his way through. The bear and her cub heard and smelled nothing. Almost there. Death was just a whisper away.

A sudden noise swiveled all three heads to the north.

Brownskins! Bela's pliable lips wrinkled in a silent scream. The bears would have to wait. They were inconsequential at the moment.

81

***

The warriors, led by Chan Chel, had found the area Ahau, Comal, and Campeche had camped in when the first deadly encounter with Bela occurred. It had taken several days, but here they finally were. Remains of the scattered campfire were still visible. The tracker roamed the site in ever increasingly larger circles. A third pass found a scrap of red cloth pushed into a bush of thorns. It had been his excited exclamation of discovery Bela had heard. Little else was found. The scavengers of the forest and recent rains had done their work. It was decided that this place of first encounter was as good as any to set up a base of sorts. From all of the information given to them from Ahau and the priest, Bela attacked mostly at night, and they still had several hours before nightfall. There was plenty of time to clear a killing field and set a few traps. Let the beast come to them.

***

A very low, very bass "*Ooooruh*" issued from the powerful form as it strode purposely, full of menace, toward the warriors. Bela believed the voices to be at the far north end of the bowl, about a thousand strides from his present position. Coming out of the dense undergrowth, the darkness ended like a curtain being lifted. The sunlight became stronger as it filtered through the less congested coverings of branches. Shafts of the abominable electromagnetic radiation reflected millions of dust motes spinning in the air. Bela would have to wait. His left hand clenched in frustration. A silent scream through wrinkled lips again rent his internal soul. Visions of blood flowing and wrecked brownskins reeled through his imagination.

Impeded by the light, Bela went back to the swarthy gloom of his private dark domain. He would not make mistakes twice with these animals. He would kill in his own time, on his own turf. He was learning patience and control of his monstrous rage. *How dare they come here? Here where I live...here where I have marked all as mine alone!*

His right hand had begun to heal. The wounds had closed and small bony protuberances appeared where new fingers and claws would grow. In two weeks the fingers would be functional; in four they would again be lethal. His side had sloughed the damaged skin and healed already. Aside from itching, it was as indurate as it had

82

always been. It was his pride and sense of arrogant superiority that had actually been wounded. Slaughtering these hateful animals would be the real healing process.

Bela followed a pitchy trail leading to his cave. Calmness enveloped him now, and he began to plan. *They have come here hunting me. Yes, that is the way of it. The brownskins would be hard to surprise. If they come anywhere near the cave, I'll be able to hear and leave. They trapped me once in a hole. No more mistakes. Late this night the advantage will be mine. Then we will see.*

Upon entering his cave, Bela went to the back. He took a piece of meat lying on a rock ledge where he had left it and brushed the tiny scavengers off. The great beast lay down near the front entrance and began to gnaw the meat, sucking its juices, and continued to plan.

***

At the far end of the bowl, Chan Chel and the men feverishly fortified their position. A bulwark of sharpened wood staves buried at different angles away from the interior of the camp was emplaced. A camouflaged pit with wooden pikes at the bottom awaited Bela once he entered the single point of entry left open. The men spread themselves out strategically. Each had two flint spears, a knife, and a tukal at his disposal. Three campfires were made ready to illuminate the approaching dark. They settled in for the long night.

Chan Chel stationed himself high in the lone tree within the enclosure to warn of any approach by the demon. Long black hair snaked in a braid down his back. Occasionally he pulled the braid over his shoulder and sucked at it unconsciously. While slapping at the mosquitoes and scratching new bites, he silently wished more of the smoke from the campfires would drift his way. Changing positions yet again, Chan Chel rubbed the back of his aching thighs. The tree was uncomfortable.

The hunter looked down at the men silhouetted by the campfire. A cough and low voices from his left identified the positions of the rest. *At least they are all still awake and in a state of readiness.* Other than the crackling of the fires and the occasional soft voice, all was quiet. Almost too quiet. This place had an evil taint to it. The usual night animal noises were not present; they had never been. Even the insects were unnaturally silent. Chan Chel kept his eyes off the fires and adjusted them to the darkness. He needed to give the men as much

83

advance warning as possible. The death threat represented by Bela was serious.

***

On silent clawed feet, malevolence slow danced through the brush. Heavily muscled arms gently pushed foliage out of the way. Getting close now, the creature lay down. Liquid black eyes carefully observed all. Bela sniffed the air. His lips wrinkled up, revealing perilous teeth that snapped with a hushed click. *The brownskins have been busy!*

The soft-skinned creatures were waiting for him. He could see the light reflecting off their spears. The fires were bright, but of no real consequence. The red-orange light did not travel far. Bela melded into a nearby tree. In a slow, deliberate crawl, he moved out onto one of the limbs. Jumping was the only way to the tree inside the enclosure.

Bunched muscles silently sprang forward to a large limb in Chan Chel's tree. Only the slight creak from the increased weight and the click of Bela's clawed feet on wood could be heard. It was enough.

***

Chan Chel looked down from his higher position, amazed at what he saw. *The creature is here!* Less than a body's length from him he looked into the face of evil and saw it staring back at him. For the first time in his life, the hunter froze. He simply could not move, not even to warn the men below. Being frightened had never been an option before. Now it was the only option. In a second he could see they had made a fateful error. The trap they had set was now their death. There was nowhere to run. Spears wielded by puny humans were no match for the beast that faced them now.

The creature actually looked surprised to find someone in the tree where he landed. But at that very moment, one of the men below looked up in time to see the huge black form in the tree. With a cry of alarm, he sailed his spear at the main bulk of the creature. The spear was deflected by a branch and rattled harmlessly off Bela's side. Other spears pin cushioned into the tree. None were effective. Bela jumped to the ground, hitting two of the brownskins on the way down. Both were dead before they slammed into the soft earth. Deep channels rent their flesh from the neck down.

With every wave of Bela's claws, red rain fell. The warriors tried to defend themselves with their knives and spears, but to no avail. One warrior, with courage bordering on reckless self-sacrifice, jumped on Bela from behind, stabbing with his knife. The glass knife broke on the first impact, making no entry. Not realizing only a blunt handle remained in his hand, the man stabbed three more times before he died from a savage bite to his throat. A few small ineffectual puncture wounds were all the combined efforts of the warriors accomplished. From beginning to end the slaughter had taken less than sixty heartbeats.

In his blood lust, Bela had apparently forgotten the brownskin first seen in the tree. It was well he had. Chan Chel, still frozen in fear, had watched it all. He knew there was nothing he could do. Now, from his high position, he watched the great beast savagely tear the warriors into unrecognizable pieces. These he threw in the pit until it could hold no more.

Chan Chel watched in horror as Bela, on all fours, drank blood from his friends' mangled bodies. The wet, gluttonous gulps sounded abominably like the purring of a satisfied baby at its mother's breast. Chan Chel had never felt so afraid for his life. He silently mouthed prayers to every god he could think of. *Please do not let the creature look up!*

***

Bela's skin reflected dark red in the firelight as he gathered up the severed and torn heads of all the warriors. Blood-suffused eyeballs protruded from some of the sockets like bird eggs sticking out of a nest. The pressures behind them must have been enormous. Bela could not carry them all and so he had to make choices. He placed them in a group and with guttural cries of pleasure picked three he liked...trophies for his cave. Still not aware of the hunter, Bela edged around the grotesque pile of broken flesh and left the enclosure with the three heads cradled in one arm, his fingers tangled in the mass of black hair.

***

Chan Chel trembled uncontrollably. His face ashen, he constantly switched positions, trying to see into the dark forest. Red blotched, cramped fingers grabbed and held tight the rough bark of the tree limbs in front of him. Finally convinced the beast was not going to reappear, his breathing slowed and his grip relaxed on the tree. All was quiet. The fires were dying with no one to tend them. They crackled out their last enigmatic messages to each other and winked out almost as one.

It took very little time for the first wolf to slink his presence into the enclosure. On padded feet, five more arrived. They made none of the competitive snarling noises wolves usually did. They seemed to sense that there was more than enough for them all, so they gorged themselves. The soppy sounds of dead meat going down greedy throats made Chan Chel sick to his stomach, but as before, he did nothing. He shut his eyes and covered his ears with his hands. Occasionally, crunching sounds from bones breaking between powerful jaws still found its way through Chan Chel's protected ears and into his anguished soul. He sobbed his remorse, realizing his cowardice.

***

Faint sunlight filtered through the canopy. The wolves had left long ago. Botflies crawled over the dead flesh that littered the ground and spewed out their eggs. Soon, maggots would burrow under the skin, embed themselves with hooks, and weeks later emerge as fat larvae. Black feathered vultures surfed high on the updraft of prevailing winds. A few of the braver birds squawked their delight at finding such a ready meal and hopped on and around the piles of sundered flesh.

***

Morning had arrived and gone. It was almost midday when Chan Chel woke up. He was incredulous that he had been asleep at all, considering the circumstances. Stiffly, he crawled down from his perch. Sometime during the night he had made up his mind on a course of action. There was no hesitation now in his actions.

Grabbing a broken branch, Chan Chel shooed the birds away. They were reluctant to leave. Solemnly, he picked up every scrap of bone and meat he could find and placed it in the pit. When he finished, the pile was depressingly small; the wolves had eaten well. Chan Chel threw as much loose wood on top as he could find and fired the funeral pyre. During his gruesome gatherings, he had found one unbroken spear and another with its shaft sheared halfway up its

86

length. With these, he moved at a lope to the spot he had last seen Bela enter the dense darkness of the forest.

Chan Chel knew he had limited options. Going back to the village as the only survivor was not one of them. He had made a pact with his people to succeed or die trying. To go back now went against everything he held sacred. There was nothing in Kohunlich worth going back to either. His family was in the new village. Kohunlich was a coward's choice. His only real course of action was to trail Bela and make the kill if he could. His sense of worth had deteriorated to the point he was no longer afraid. All of his life, he had been marked for his extraordinary talents as a tracker and hunter. Though challenged by events, his courage had never before been questioned. Now he felt deeply ashamed of his inaction, even though logically he knew all he could have done was die with the rest of them. He would not have made a difference then, but perhaps now he could. Not just his physical life but his spiritual being demanded that he at least try. He could lose everything...or maybe, just maybe, redeem his self respect.

Bela had left the killing area and entered the forest, where trailing mosses and spreading ferns made a tangled understory beneath immense, broad-branched trees. Almost immediately the light source was cut in half. Thousands of species of insects, plants, vertebrates, and fungi lived there. The melancholy hooting of chattering gibbons gave evidence that they knew of Chan Chel's presence. The dim forest floor seemed darker every hundred steps into the interior. Puffball mushrooms, springing up among mosses carpeting a huge stump, were pimpled with droplets of blood left by Bela's passing. They launched clouds of spores as the hunter slid a leg over and dropped to the other side. He was still on track. Any dead organic material that had been moved, broken, or turned over read like a road map.

Much later, Chan Chel penetrated a region of the forest where the competition for light and space had been decided long ago. He had never been in a more ancient seeming place. He marveled at the age of some of the larger trees. Nothing moved. The landscape, so full of dead and living trees, seemed strangely empty of wildlife. Eerie, primordial stillness hung heavy with humidity. Once luxuriant growth hung intertwined in the mosses of enormous branched trees so high above, their tops appeared to be an indistinguishable black. Dipterocarps, that looked as if they had been fully grown for hundreds of years, made a canopy that effectively blocked out most of the light. Midday transformed into a morbid, brown-green twilight. Bela's trail was harder to follow now. Chan Chel hoped the heads still dripped.

Like a huge maze, sinuous buttresses of trunks angled out from the massive trees. Most the tracker could climb over; some were so high he could not see over them. The silence here was deafening. Every sound he made seemed like the thunder of drums. Bela could be anywhere. He could be around the next trunk or hidden in the thorny underbrush to his left. Chan Chel knew his only chance was surprise. *Not much of a chance.*

Giant flying squirrels the size of small cats lurked in the trees, occasionally sailing across the branches high above his head. His heart stopped every time he heard the smack of the rodents landing. The sound seemed unusually loud when what he needed most was complete silence. Several leeches in the damp forest litter found his ankles and attached themselves to the soft flesh by suction pads on both ends of their bodies. Three sharp teeth, under the heads of each, pierced the skin and found blood, and they began to feed. Later, being sated, they dropped off, bloated from their work.

A large, iridescent-winged blue morpho butterfly caught his attention. Its being here in such dull, drab, monochromatic surroundings was such an incongruity his eyes followed it like a light blazing across a dark sky. It hovered, skirted trunks, and flew three feet above the brown, dead carpet of the forest floor into a low patch of darkness carved out of a wall of vegetation. If the butterfly had not entered, Chan Chel would have missed the ingress entirely. The hunter followed the dim traces of the trail leading into blackness. He could feel it as he went in. *Bela is near.*

His pupils needed to acclimate to the near absence of light. The hunter squeezed his eyes shut, waited, and opened them slowly. The path could be seen but not clearly. The walls of old vegetation closed thickly around him…visibility was, at most, one body length in any direction. Chan Chel knew he needed every forest skill he had to survive. His every step was a lying down of weight as gently as possible. He pushed soft-toed sandals under the dried-up leaves rather than stepping on them directly, trying to mask his passage. Sound here could kill.

He stopped every four steps and listened several moments to his surroundings before he moved on. He tried to observe and understand everything. A mistake now could be his very last one. The butterfly he had seen earlier fluttered briefly against his cheek as it sought its way back out. It was apparently just lost and not the beacon of empathy he had hoped. Chan Chel continued to carefully step his way down the trail. That this was the right path, the hunter had no doubt. He could feel the malevolence Bela had transuded by his passing.

Without preamble, the vegetation parted. Chan Chel nearly fell headfirst into the deep void that opened up in front of him. He went down on his knees and quietly let his eyes and ears discern what they could just over the precipice. The light here was somewhat better, but still miserably obscure. The dark of night was beginning to take dominance. *Water!* He could hear it gently burbling downwards diagonally from him. The deep hole at the bottom accepted the water as it ran over the edge. *Rocks!* He could see the diluted outlines of them all around him and down the sides of the cavity, presumably all the way to the bottom. *This is a cenote! This is Bela's lair. It has to be! Everything fits. The beast is probably at the bottom at this very moment in some kind of rocky enclosure.*

Chan Chel could feel anxiety generating heat in his face and ears. There was no turning back now. Somehow, he had to get down the face of this cenote without being seen or heard. *Is this Bela's private path, and is he near enough to see me? Maybe there is a better, quieter way down.* The hunter knew with absolute certainty any miscalculation spelled his death.

He crawled to the edge and peered down, but there was nothing to see. It was too dangerous to attempt descending here. He decided to go back and try traveling either left or right, and backed away from the edge as quietly as possible. Thirty strides back on the trail, Chan Chel went to his knees and quietly pushed into the vegetation. Moving slowly, he inched his way left of where he had been, circling the cenote another fifty body lengths. Finding the jagged edge, the hunter leaned over and looked down. He could see about half the distance down before the light gave out. It looked promising from here. Small stones, loose from the top soil and rock he was leaning on, fell into the void, making small noises as they bounced from the vertical sides of the cliff. The small conversation of pebbles was lost as they tumbled to their ultimate end. The hunter could only hope they had not alerted Bela to his presence. He scooted back from the edge and stood up.

Chan Chel tied the broken spear tightly to his leg with a vine. It was short enough not to be in the way and still accessible if he should need it. The unbroken spear was more of a problem. He dared not leave it behind. The hunter tied vines to the middle and top of the long weapon, and in a sling method draped it over his shoulder. The spear rested uncomfortably on his back, point up. It was time. He took a deep breath and started down. More pebbles dislodged and echoed his descent.

***

Bela was lying near the front of his cave, contentedly dropping bones into the water, watching them quick-dart to the side before plunging end-over-end to the piles below, when he first became aware of the hunter. The brownskins continued to amaze him. Like termites, they never gave up. He sniffed the air but only detected the one. The brownskin noisily crawled back into the vegetation. Bela could hear him rummaging to the side. *Ahh...there it is. It's coming down! So very clumsy. Unbelievable! It's looking for me!* Excited, Bela decided to stay where he was and just watch for the moment.

***

Chan Chel was having difficulty negotiating the rock. Some of it was loose to the touch and probably would not support his weight for long. It was necessary to go to the side at times to find solid footing. To his ears, the going so far had been very quiet. He was confident surprise was still an ally. Indefinite, long moments of grueling concentration had gotten him close to halfway down. Sweat pooled into large drops that ran down in rivulets into his eyes. The hunter stopped at a foot hold of high confidence to rest momentarily, and reconnoitered what lay below. He swiped the sweat from his face and readjusted the sling.

Looking down, he realized at his current rate it would be quite

90

awhile yet before he touched down. Chan Chel dropped his right foot another three hand lengths and searched with his toes for a suitable purchase. He found what he needed and shifted weight from his left to his right. He came to a small landing and sat back against the rock to gain his breath and look around. The warrior/hunter closed his eyes for a moment and hitched a few deep breaths. The sky was getting darker and he still had quite a ways to negotiate before he reached the bottom. He adjusted the spear over his back and looked for the best way to continue.

Just visible was a strange rock that almost seemed to be looking at him. Curious, Chan Chel leaned closer. He blanched at the now recognizable shape of a large beast's head. Empty eye sockets glared at him with rows of teeth grimacing just below. Panic ripped through him and he almost gave voice to his alarm when he realized that the beast was long dead and could not harm him. He had seen similar rock-like bones before.

**

Sneert was only a pitiful reminder of what she had once been. Her bones had been scattered long ago by the scavengers of the world. Now all that was left were a few minor bones and her head. Her empty eye sockets stared at nothing, and her primordial teeth had long since ceased their gnashing. There was no evidence of her children or the emotional pain that had tormented her to her last breath.

**

Without any warning, three mastiff bats swirled out of a small crevice near the beast's head, emitting bursts of angry, staccato cries. Chan Chel threw his hand up to ward them off and to protect his face. He instantly realized his mistake. The weight-shift caused him to lose already precarious footing. Falling back and down, he grabbed at the rock. Unfortunately, his fingertips found no purchase. Guano, recent and old, gave him no traction. The hunter windmilled down the rocky embankment, landing in a crumpled heap. A blinding flash filled his brain, then all went black.

**

Bela cocked his head, disbelieving. He wasn't sure what he had just seen. *Did the brownskin actually fall off the side of the rocky wall?*

Could anything be that inept? Bela was up quickly to investigate. Moments later, he was standing over the twisted form of Chan Chel. The hunter was badly mangled. Bela toed the brownskin in the side, eliciting an unconscious groan in response. A finger length of bone was sticking through the tissue midway up the lower right leg, and one arm twisted at an impossible angle.

Bela leaned over and touched the broken splinter of bone. Each time he did so a hitching moan came from the swollen lips of the hunter. The question now was what to do with the battered, near death brownskin. The great beast licked the warm blood off his fingers as he thought. He would finish killing the awkward intruder later. Hunger was not a consideration at the moment, and warm blood was always more enjoyable than cold. As Bela picked up his meat, he noticed the two spears lying nearby where they had fallen. These too he gathered up as he headed to his cave. The brownskin, slung over the beast's shoulder, continued to moan insensibly. The splintered bone grated against Bela's waist with every step.

***

Nauseating pain greeted Chan Chel hours later as he resumed consciousness. A hundred agonies assailed him in the near total darkness. He remembered falling. Hard resolve kept him from passing out as black brume thickened at the edges of his consciousness. Slowly the hunter moved his head. *Good. No broken neck.* Carefully he continued down his body, feeling for injuries. There was no need to wonder about his leg and arm. The sickening pain made it clear his right leg was badly broken. The elbow of his right arm throbbed a desperate message of wrongness. Swollen tissue around the joint probably indicated a severe dislocation. Chan Chel tried to move it slightly. Slivers of bone rubbed against each other near the very end of the joint. Panicked, he laid his head back down and fought down a need to scream. *I can't get back! A broken leg is sure death. I'm dead...even if Bela doesn't get me, I'm dead!*

Disoriented, Chan Chel tried to sit up enough to see more of his surroundings. Terror assailed him. *I'M IN THE CAVE! ITZAMNA HELP ME....* It was very difficult to see in the dark, but he could see the highlighted top of the cave, and beyond that the very wall he had fallen from some seventy to eighty strides away. His eyes came back to the ground around him. All around him were bones. *Bones of Bela's prey...they have to be!* They were in no order, just scattered where they had been thrown. Some bones were familiar; he, too, had killed such animals. Some skeleton structures, however, were strange to the hunter. Trying to puzzle the pieces back together in his mind brought impossible images of strange beasts. He took a deep breath and tried to calm down. His imagination was getting away from him. The sweet cloyed smell of decaying flesh wafted insistently in the air. It was not nearly as bad as he thought it should be considering the evidence.

Up above, just to his left, was an outcropping of rock ledges. It was here his eye found the grisly remains of his comrades. Like horrid trophies on a shelf, they stared back at him with occluded eyes. The faces were contorted and stretched as the rictus of death claimed the flesh. Mouths were open, shrieking their silent accusations. *It was your mission...your plan...your failure to warn us. Where were you?* Chan Chel closed his eyes and silently wept his guilt. How could he say sorry to a dead man?

He had been so confident of their plan to capture Bela within their little trap. Arrogantly, they had all assumed that thirteen armed hunters could kill any animal in the forest. Even if Bela was a demon, Pochotl had said the beast was flesh and blood. The cave finger had proven that. Again, the hunter wondered how everything had gone so wrong.

Hard scraping sounds somewhere to his right caused Chan Chel to swivel his head in that direction. *Where is Bela?* He could just make the outline of the great beast humped over something, dragging it back and forth across the rocky floor. It made a familiar noise, something he knew. Something important. He strained his eyes and ears.

Yes, I know that sound! Unaware he spoke aloud, Chan Chel whispered, "My spear."

Bela immediately turned toward the brownskin. Large luminous eyes glowed. In a deep guttural voice he mimicked the words, "Myyy speeer." He scuttled closer to the brownskin, dragging one of the spears with him. "Myyy speeer," he imitated again.

Chan Chel forgot his fear for the moment. He was incredulous. *Bela can speak. Or is he just parroting sounds?* Chan Chel tried something new. He patted his chest with his good hand and said, "Chan Chel." He motioned toward the hulking beast. "Bela."

A deep voice responded, "Myyy speeer...Chaaan Cheeel...Bail-la."

***

With this last syllable, as if to emphasize, Bela tapped the spear point against the jagged end of bone sticking out of Chan Chel's leg. The hunter, screaming through clenched teeth, gagged on the vile taste of stomach refuse and fell limp. He had passed out. Bela enjoyed seeing his enemy in pain. The brownskin's howling made the game more fun. He tried to make the high-pitched sound himself.

Using the spear again, Bela tried to prod the hunter back to consciousness. Unsuccessful at that, the beast bent over the broken leg and thumped the broken bone again; except for a small moan, nothing. Bela pushed and pulled on the bone until it accidentally plopped wetly back under the skin. Nothing...no response. He sat back on his haunches, sucked the blood from his fingers, and studied the brownskin.

Such strange animals. What did the sounds earlier mean? My speeer. Was the disgusting little creature trying to communicate? Bela rocked as he thought. *Chaaan Cheeel...Bail-la.* New thoughts stimulated the great beast. He prodded the brownskin once again. No longer was Bela thinking of the food Chan Chel's blood represented, but rather the tremendous possibilities real communication might mean. Bela had never before had another creature to speak to. That this frail, broken brownskin could be a part of what he had yearned for these past two-hundred years was astounding. He dragged the hunter further back into the cave. Suddenly hungry, he loped out of the cave in search of food, taking one last glance at the sundered form lying on his cave floor.

The great beast entered the cave with a great "Ooooruh!" He slapped two lifeless red uakari monkeys against the floor, hoping to impress upon the brownskin how successful he had been in such a short time. Chan Chel, however, was curled protectively around his injured arm and leg, his eyes closed. Bela dragged one of the monkeys across the hunter's face, hoping to elicit a response. Nothing. The great beast sat down near the brownskin with a dejected sigh and tore the throats out of both, slavishing the blood down his throat. Peeling the skin from one monkey, he chew-sucked the sticky meat, glancing furtively at the sleeping form of Chan Chel. The other he left for the brownskin, if it ever woke up. He licked the hunter's face and gently prodded his chest. Nothing. Bela went back to the front of the cave and continued to play with the spears. He would wait.

***

The hunter briefly regained consciousness, hitch-sobbed a whimpering groan, and slipped back into a dead-to-the-world sleep. He never heard Bela return. Sometime later, Chan Chel opened his eyes. Bela's voice echoed in his head, whispering, whispering, whispering. He lay listlessly, contemplating his death. The pain was still with him. It had abated somewhat, but was still a constant reminder that at least for a while he was alive. It was apparent he had been dragged to a back portion of the cave, meaning the opening was farther away than before. Chan Chel quietly retched bile down his chest. He was too weak to avoid the mess.

Bela's outline could be seen near the front of the cave, again scraping the spears on the stone. Every so often a spark jumped from the flint. The preternatural brightness released by the burning flakes of iron commanded complete attention in the otherwise dark gloom. The beast made a whooping noise every time it happened. Sounds of unintelligible low grunts and hoots, interspersed with "Myyy speeer, myyy speeer, myyy speeer," floated back to the hunter.

Chan Chel looked down at his leg to find that the bone was no longer sticking out. He tried to move it, but a red wave of nauseating pain rewarded his efforts. While there was a breath left, the hunter vowed not to give up. He reached down to where his knife should be. It was still there! A glimmer of hope surfaced. The small blade was probably useless as a direct weapon against Bela. *But if the beast comes close enough, maybe I can jam it to the hilt in an eye or a soft spot in the throat.*

Chan Chel knew his chances were small but not worth forgetting. He considered his surroundings again. He could feel a small breeze coming from somewhere back in the shadows. *It might be worth investigating. If it is a hole big enough to climb into and it reaches the surface, then just maybe....* His injuries brought back the reality of the situation. He was not climbing anywhere.

Near the ankle of his broken leg were two rock protrusions with opposing angles that stuck out of the floor. An idea occurred to the hunter. Chan Chel carefully lifted the ankle of the bad appendage into the area between the two protrusions, then laid the broken leg as straight as he could. Determined not to cry out, the hunter grit his teeth and pulled as hard and quickly as he could. He could both feel and hear the bone setting back into place, and against his will he screamed in agony. Breathing in quick bursts, he kept consciousness, but only barely.

Bela sprang to his side. Chan Chel reached for his knife when he realized the beast was on him, but quickly dismissed the idea. Bela was just out of reach, looking at the broken leg. The demon pushed on the knee. The cold kiss of Bela's claws tortured the hunter's already stretched-tight psyche. Chan Chel bit his bottom lip and held quiet. The beast moved up the leg.

With the back of his hand, Bela pressed against the hunter's waist and intoned, "Chaaan Cheel." He did this three times, looking the brownskin in the eyes, waiting for a response.

Chan Chel nodded his head in a slow up and down motion. He pointed to himself and said as distinctly as he could, "Chan Chel." He aimed a finger at the beast. "Bela. You are Bela."

The beast repeatedly said their names while jumping in circles from a crouched position. Spying the dead uakari he had left for the brownskin, he stopped his vocal antics and pulled it to him. He meticulously pulled the skin off and offered it to the hunter. "Chaaan Cheeel."

Realizing the significance, Chan Chel took the offering and ate large portions of the cold meat as Bela licked wetly from the underside portions of the hide. Blood and viscera marked the maw of the beast and slobbered down its neck. It was not hard for the hunter to envision the beast doing the same to him.

Making drinking motions with hands cupped to his mouth, Chan Chel asked for water. Bela was quick to understand. The beast grabbed a large discarded skull and left the cave briefly, but returned quickly. Water scooped from the pool brimmed to the jaw line of the skull, but was leaking fast. Chan Chel hastily gulped it down. It seemed the best water he had drunk in a long while. Time to think about thirst hadn't been available until now. He handed back the skull, and Bela refilled the makeshift goblet twice more.

His thirst sated, the hunter went back to work on his leg. He found two bones of the right girth and length lying nearby on the floor of the cave and secured them to the outsides of his leg. Rawhide strips from his sandals provided the binding. The leg was stationary, at least for the moment. The arm was another matter. It still spoke volumes of constant agony.

A fascinated Bela sat watching the entire process a short distance away, but his attention span was finite. Enough was enough! He wanted more speech from the brownskin but wasn't sure how to get it.   "Chaaan   Cheeel...Ooooruh!"

No reaction from the hunter made the beast furious. He grabbed Chan Chel by his injured arm and dragged him to the front of the cave. Fighting to stay conscious, Chan Chel's body quivered with pain. He pulled out his knife and tried to fend the creature off, but Bela swatted it away. It scuttled across the floor and came to rest against a wall well out of reach of the hunter. For several long moments, Bela made *Chaaan Cheeel* give sonance to his torment. Each time the hunter shrieked, Bela raised his head to the ceiling and echoed the sound. The piercing cries reverberated off the rock sides and sent any animal within hearing sprinting for safety.

CHAPTER 9

EMERALD RAIN

Tikal and Ahau were actually enjoying their new status. As apprentices to the hymen, the villagers treated them with a new respect. People took the time to speak, occasionally even asking an opinion. Their peers' attitudes fluctuated. At times they seemed envious and a little resentful of all of the new attention. Most of the time, though, Tikal and Ahau were treated as they always had been. The same group of young men who had checked out the cave still found time to get together late in the evenings to talk about the events of the day.

For awhile, at night, horrific nightmares had plagued both of the apprentices. They repeatedly relived the ceremony and their parts in it, but the dreams finally subsided. Death and torment were an integral part of life, and hiding from that fact was impossible. In any event, very little time for retrospection was available…Pochotl made sure that they had plenty to do.

The new Sun Temple had walls. It would be years yet before the temple was actually completed, but it was beginning to take shape. The ground floor was now divided up into four large areas. One of these new rooms was the future home of Pochotl, as befitted a high priest. He was already sleeping most nights in the new room, spending as much time as possible there, trying to make it his own.

It became Tikal and Ahau's responsibility to help the hymen prepare the new domain. All of the trappings and tools of the priesthood could not possibly have been carried from Kohunlich. New furniture was designed and being built of both stone and wood. Most of what Pochotl needed would have to come from the forest.

Plant, animal, and mineral extracts were gathered daily and treated according to the hymen's instructions.

The forest was like a giant marketplace. Children grew up knowing the names of most the plants and hundreds of uses for their stems, leaves, flowers, and roots. Tikal and Ahau already had a very good working knowledge of what the priest asked for. The sheer preponderance of things to do, build, assemble, harvest, and make ready was amazing. From the moment the two apprentices left their pallets, they were busy. They made the occasional mistake, but Pochotl was in too good a mood to let the little things bother him. All his plans were beginning to bear fruit. The Sun Temple was coming along fine. His new dwelling was going to be magnificent eventually. The villagers were happy and well, finding all they needed to build in this new location. Even the elders were seeing things his way. Ah Tok was, for the political moment, effectively out of the way.

The only real dilemma facing Pochotl was that the chosen warriors had not yet returned from dealing with the demon, Bela. Many of the villagers, especially the relatives of the warriors, expressed considerable distress. Speculation ran high as to what their failure to come back meant. Pochotl explained that there was no need for concern yet, and outlined several possible scenarios. The bottom line was that no news could be good news. After all, Bela had not returned either.

In truth, the priest was also concerned about the men; not for their sake, but for his. Even though he had not personally picked the warriors, it was his proposal that had sent them out. Their failure could end up being his. He kept telling himself that Bela, although formidable, was, after all, only one beast, and the warriors numbered thirteen.

It was in the middle of the leaf work after evacuating his bowels that the priest made the decision. He had been thinking about the problem off and on for days. *Two weeks overdue might mean some of the men were gravely injured and are recuperating before they head back. The survivors might all be injured. Maybe I should send out two or three men just to reconnoiter. Of course, no one will want to go this close to the celebrations, but I will not give them a choice. The elders will be aware that I am doing what must be done for the good of the people. Yes, this very day I will send out two hunters with considerable tracking skills.*

***

The fact that his best friend's little sister was suddenly not so little had not eluded Ahau. Jada and he had been friends for years, but now all that had subtly changed. A reason to be in her vicinity was found every chance he got. He fairly strutted in her presence, making sure she knew he was about on official priest business that just happened to take him near her. Much to Ahau's chagrin, many of the young men in the village were also newly aware of the enticing young Jada. From all directions, competition for her eye was substantial and persistent. Jada was well named.

***

She, too, had noticed the new physical changes in Ahau, and approved. Although she smiled inwardly at his dead seriousness, he was growing up to be quite handsome. He tried so very hard to impress her, but she feigned a polite indifference...never enough to deter him, just enough to torment the aspiring young priest. She did not want Ahau to know of *her* interest in *him* just yet. Jada did, however, make sure Ahau knew of his competition by flirting with several of the men in his presence.

***

Ahau's dreams no longer were of suffering and death. The memory of Zac Kuk's passing was buried beneath the hopes of enticing smells, pliable flesh, and the welcoming arms that now danced gloriously through his night time fantasies. The vivid illusions often haunted him after he woke.

***

Tikal knew of his friend's affliction, but offered no help either way. His sister would do as she wanted. She always had.

Her father, Ah Tok, was also mindful of all the attention his beautiful young daughter was receiving. He was especially aware of Ahau's designs for Jada. The young man's competence and general character were not in question, but his background was. At the moment, Ahau had nothing to offer his daughter. At least, not what Ah Tok considered important. Pochotl's young apprentice had no wealth, home, or family to consider. The wealthy nobleman wanted Jada to have the best the small village could offer in choices of a good life. Ahau, at present, was just not a consideration. He promised himself to keep a check on the two of them.

***

Black clouds towered over the tree canopies to the east, promising the eventual release of this year's wet blessings. Distant thunder rumbled and lightning flickered. Within the next few days, the rainy season would be upon them in earnest. Even now an undulating dark gray curtain stretched across the far horizon, kissing the land. It was a time of celebration; a time of showing gratitude to the gods. Rain represented a new cycle beginning, full of promise and hope.

The people began making preparations for the eminent festivities. Deer, monkeys, birds, turtles, heavy fleshed iguanas, and an array of other small animals were slaughtered and cooked over huge fire pits for the festivities. Smashed and squeezed vanilla pods had been placed in steam baskets ten days before to begin the fermentation process to give up their potent liquids. Other especially strong plant ingredients were added to this, and the result was a very strong concoction of liquor, capable of giving hallucinations to anyone foolish enough to drink very much of it. Waking up from a stupor with a dreadful headache for days was guaranteed. Only the very stalwart or those with masochistic tendencies drank from this source.

Buried pots of gentler liquor, prepared by the old females of the tribe, were also made ready. Weeks earlier, they had sat around a fire, gossiped, and masticated corn. When the kernels felt fully chewed, they spit the yellow-white mush into a common pot, and the saliva started the fermentation process. These pots were then covered and buried, and time did the rest. Unearthed, the stink was abominable to the uninitiated.

The young men and women were especially excited. For many, this would be their first real participation in the Courtship Dance and the Parade of Enticement. Numerous lifetime connubial relationships would result from these celebrations. The older people of the tribe would have a tremendously gratifying time watching and betting on the outcomes of these courtships. It was a time of great joy, a good time to be alive. The time of celebration was here. The rains were almost upon them.

Darkness finally came to the village. Since early afternoon, the young people had cleaned and primped themselves, anxiously waiting for the festivities. Nervously laughing at feeble jokes, they tried to mask their worried emotions as they waited for what could be one of the most important nights of their lives.

Slowly, the tribe began to gather near the centrally located large fires. None of the young people wanted to be first and seem overly eager. Separate lines of eligible unmarried men and women formed, waiting for the signal. After what already had seemed like an eternity, time for the Parade of Enticement finally came. A low, long draw of a shell horn started the procession. The two single file lines met and slow-stepped past each other, three strides apart. All eyes were straight ahead, seeing only with peripheral vision. At the end of the first pass, people in both lines excitedly switched places with others in front of or behind them, depending on where the chosen person was in the other line. Again they passed each other with solemn attitudes, always looking straight ahead and trying to keep their expressions neutral. Now straight across from each other and facing their intended target, the separate lines took their positions twenty strides apart, some of the men jostling for new choice positions.

The drums began. They provided a forceful, vigorous, background energy. Seedpod rattles, wrapped around the ankles and wrists of the young women, beat an insistent, repetitive beat as they danced in place side-by-side, their eyes down. The sound of the hard ripened ovules striking the skeins of the pods was designed to draw consideration to the slender, muscular legs and arms of the females. Sparse white cotton, wrapped to show off their best features, commanded attention. Bare midriffs with jeweled belly buttons bounced, swayed, and shoved clear messages of desire at the young men watching. Perspiration sparkled on their tawny skins, reflecting the light from several fires. Bone flutes rhythmic clapping and the deep resonant sing-song voices of the older men added significant composition to the music.

Across from the young women, the men vied for eye contact from the female they admired most, with paint streaked designs of yellow, white, blue, red, and black over their bodies. The people never decorated their skins with the mundane events and animals of reality. Their images came from the dream world. Eyelids blazed their young glory and advertised their needs in smudged colors. Warm mocha eyes flashed, blinked, and cajoled. Athletically, they moved to traditional patterns. Their steps, full of stealth, grace, and attacking behavior, symbolized hunting and war tactics. Over and over they killed unseen human enemies and stabbed at ferocious creatures of the forest, constantly looking up to see if the women watched. Suitably impressed by a young warrior/hunter, the females would make and hold full eye contact. If the contact broke, they were no longer interested and the men moved on to someone new.

***

Jada played the game well. She teased and prompted the many youthful suitors vying for her attention into a vigorous rivalry. Her eyes flashed up and down the men, giving some hope to some, but to most none. They counterpoised and bumped each other, trying to neutralize opponents.

Ah Tok watched from the side. He was relieved that no single young man had yet received the bulk of her attention. These were hard moments for the proud nobleman.

***

Ahau, dancing fiercely, also watched from his position. He had been gauging his chances and waiting for just the right moment to move in front of her. So far, no one had held her attention for more than a few seconds. Afraid of being rejected, he hesitated a while longer. Tikal, not really interested in signaling out any one of the eligible females, pushed his way to Ahau's side.

Breathlessly he whispered over the music, "What are you waiting for? The dancing is not going to last forever. You want someone else to beat you? Go!"

Ahau momentarily looked at his friend. *He's right! It's now or never. If I don't at least try, I'll never forgive myself.* He boldly jumped in front of two men already dancing for her. Immediately he was shoved and bumped from behind by older, more experienced bodies. Ahau lost his balance but held his position. Ignoring the stumble, he picked up the pace, staring straight into Jada's downcast beautiful dark brown eyes, trying to will her to see him. *Please look at me!* The betting on the sidelines picked up in intensity. Most gave the young apprentice no hope. Only a few of the older women had faith in the

104

young apprentice's chances.

Jada flicked her eyes up and down Ahau's dancing form, keeping her glances low. Ahau was losing hope. A full hundred heartbeats later, she slowly met his eyes and held. Electricity ran up and down Ahau's spine. She was the most ravishing female in the entire forest as far as he was concerned. *Please, please don't look away!* They looked into each other's eyes, feeling the heat and desire building as the rest of the world fell away. Ahau danced like his feet were suspended above the ground. Time seemed to hold still for them. In their eyes, nothing else in the universe mattered or existed except the two of them and the small space that separated their bodies. He had never been so esoterically happy in his life.

***

Ah Tok's mood was black, and he silently cursed. Standing up, hands clenched to his side, he skirted the sidelines and stood several steps behind Ahau, trying to catch his daughter's attention. A tight, bitter smile wrapped awkwardly around his face. His continence wavered but he managed to hold check. But others in the crowd noticed. New wagers relevant to young Ahau's chances with Jada flurried. Vehement disapproval shed furiously from Ah Tok's narrowed eyes. Balanced above a feigned smile, they appeared unmistakably menacing.

***

Jada glimpsed her father with a quick peripheral glance, but it was enough. She avoided direct eye contact with him...she had seen enough to know. Her stomach began to churn, and her mouth went dry. New heat, born of humiliation, burned her cheeks. She continued dancing and looking into Ahau's eyes, but she no longer really saw him. Tears threatened to well up.

Then suddenly, the music stopped. The Courtship Dance was over. Several of the young dancers walked off together in pairs to find a place they could be alone.

***

Ahau felt like a large hand had just pushed all of the breath out of him. It was hard to breathe. Everything had ended too soon. Jada simply walked away as if nothing had really happened. He watched her lithe figure from behind as she wound through the maze of people, all heading to private destinations. Ahau did not know what to think. Everything had been so wonderful moments before, and now…. *Do I follow after her? Did I anger her? What do I do?* He was truly confused by her actions. Frustrated by conflicting emotions, he watched her until she disappeared. Only once did she turn back in his direction. So far away and in the dark, he did not know whether she had been looking at him or someone else.

Tikal bounced to his side, almost bowling him over. "You did it, Ahau! When did you learn to dance like that? You were magnificent. My sister only had eyes for you, my friend. It's obvious that she has chosen." He clapped Ahau on the back, happy for his friend's good fortune.

Ahau angrily shrugged his friend off. "If she chose me, then who would know? She walked away as if I didn't exist. I hate myself for being such a fool. Jada will never be with me. I'm nothing in her eyes." He spat on the ground as if to emphasize his feelings.

***

Tikal tried to console his friend, using all of the obvious arguments. He had not seen his father stand behind Ahau during the dance, but he knew his sister. He believed that she was just headstrong and too full of pride. She wanted Ahau to run after her, exclaiming his love or some nonsense like that. Tikal knew his father would disapprove, but he would never say that. Answering that line of questioning would only hurt his friend more.

Ahau walked away mumbling to himself with his head down, ignoring Tikal's words, and headed for the area in back of the Sun Temple to be alone. Tikal let him go. There was nothing else he could do. These things would work themselves out. He was troubled by Ahau's reaction, but tonight was special. There was still a lot to experience and there was always tomorrow. He could check on his friend then. Tikal ran to catch up to other companions.

***

Possessions changed hands from the sidelines amidst much good-humored protesting. Those that had lost the most in gambling grumbled the loudest, though few people ever lost their temper betting on the Courtship Dance. It was a time for celebrating beginnings and giving thanks for blessings past. Food and drink were gathered up as families, friends, and couples found choice positions around the front of the largest fire. The storytellers were about to take center stage.

***

Ah Tok sat with his wife and anxiously searched with his eyes for Jada. He found her with four other young women at the food tables, excitedly talking about the dance and all of the participants. He smiled inwardly and grumped a sound of satisfaction. His daughter had done as he wanted. Ahau was nowhere in sight and more importantly, he was nowhere near Jada. He settled in and began to eat. The first storyteller was holding his hands up for quiet. He was ready to begin.

***

Jada chanced a hasty glance at her father. Seeing that he was busy, she piled more food on her ceramic plate and proceeded slowly and deliberately to the outer edges of the crowds.

Tikal had been watching her and knew her intentions. He caught up to her from behind, then confided in a low voice, "He's at the temple," and walked away.

He did not want to draw any unnecessary attention. If he had guessed right about his father, then it was important that his sister catch up to Ahau without prying eyes and the inevitable wagging tongues.

Jada nodded and thanked him with a grateful expression. She turned and headed in the direction of the temple.

***

Rheeeee, rheeeee, rheeeee.... Cicadas sang their tiresome song to each other in a seemingly never-ending pattern of monotonous tones as Jada walked silently around the new Sun Temple. Just beginning her second corner she heard a voice mumbling nonsense. She stayed on her side of the corner and tried to listen. It was hard to catch it all, but she got the gist.

"How could she do this to me? I may not be of noble birth, but I am going to be a priest. Isn't that good enough? I don't deserve...."

The rest was too low to hear, but she waited moments more. Backing up to give some distance, she called in a clear, urgent voice as if she did not know where he was.

107

"Ahau. Ahau, where are you?"

She kept calling to him as she rounded the corner, then saw him halfway down the length of the wall, sitting on his haunches with his back and head to the rock. His hands were in his lap. The clouds were briskly moving in and caused the shafts of illuminating moonlight to stutter. It was difficult to see clearly. Ahau immediately stood upon hearing her round the corner and swiped at his eyes. Another thirty steps and she was within an arm's span of him.

"I thought you might like something to eat. I brought extra so we could share."

Ahau's mind reeled. *What is she doing here now after shunning me in front of my friends earlier?* He held out his hands to take some of the food and guardedly said thanks. Mesmerized by her beauty and the fact that she was standing so close in front of him, he spoke his question.

"Jada, why are you here? Why would you care if I eat or not? Haven't you made your thoughts about me clear? I'm not a fool who needs —"

He would have gone on but Jada stopped him with a finger to his lips, then dropped the food and wrapped her arms around him. Their lips met and her tongue stabbed at his. For several seconds they kissed before a bewildered Ahau gently pushed Jada back and looked into her eyes. Deliciously warm breath rolled across Ahau's cheek, building shivers of pleasure that ended all too soon. Delicate light silvered her features, making the splendor that was she even more radiant.

"Answer me," he demanded. "I will not play games."

"Ahau, you have to know my father does not want us together. He could cause real problems if we give him reason. Of course I want to be with you, but we can't be like the others. Until we can figure a way around my father, we have no choice. Our pairing has to be secret and not in the open. Believe me, Ahau, I don't want it this way. It just is. Father would have me marry some nobleman from Kohunlich just for political reasons. To him, I'm just a tool to further his own ambitions. My happiness is only what he says it will be."

It was Ahau's turn to stop her. In answer, he gently stroked the contours of her face with both hands and drew her back into his arms, whispering, "I don't care about your father. I do love you! If in secret is the only way we can be together, then that's the way it will be."

As an afterthought, he added, "When I'm a priest, all will be different. Then your father can't say no."

More easily than he would have believed possible, he kissed her again, only this time slower, with the patience of a man who had all the time in the world. Ahau's soul intertwined with Jada's and danced on the promises of expectations.

Rheee, rhe...rheeeee. The cicadas took up their song again. This time, as the small insects called to one another, the sounds combined to resonate and enrich the night's backdrop of silence. The couple continued to hold each other, making the most of the few moments they had, exploring each other's bodies.

***

From nearby shadows, sepulchral eyes watched the two from the opposite corner of the new edifice from which Jada had first come. Tall red feathers topped a thin golden base, balanced above a hideously painted dark-green face. The rest of the body was covered with blue lightning bolts that zigged and zagged across a yellow-green background. Except for a red loin cloth, the otherwise naked priest continued to watch the amorously entwined couple from the impenetrable darkness of the shadows in which he stood. He felt envious. Aroused, the old man rubbed himself against the side of the building.

The two young people finally parted and walked back to the celebrations by different routes. He had seen and heard most of what had just occurred. Young Ahau's lust for Jada was no secret. That Ah Tok's buxomly young daughter felt the same way about Ahau...well, that was news; news that might later be worth knowing.

Pochotl readjusted his headgear and smoothed down his loincloth. It was time he made his way to the audience in waiting. He was the last of the storytellers. His was the most important story of all, the telling of Creation. While simultaneously filing away the information about Ahau's secret love, he was already thinking about and anticipating the raptured looks of his people. No matter how often he told the story, the people never tired of hearing it. Their gratitude was sweet nectar that clarified his desires and strengthened his resolve to be their ultimate leader, the Halach Uinic. He slapped his thigh with his ever present reed stalks. *By the gods, it is good to be alive.*

To a hushed audience, Pochotl's voice sing-songed the story of Creation. The world and then the animals had come into existence by the combined work of three gods. Itzamna, the supreme god of creation and lord of fire and earth, united with Ix Chel, the moon goddess and Kukulcan, the feathered serpent, god of the earth's rulers, to originate all that is. These gods labored for eons in efforts of love, dedicated to the tasks of consummated flawlessness. Man, in a complicated series of remakes, finally became the essence of perfection.

Pochotl was morbidly fascinating as he told of the frenzied destruction of early man and the reinvention of the people until they were as they existed today. Most of what he spoke came from word-of-mouth through the many generations of storytellers before him. The people recognized the story as an old one. Pochotl, however, was not prone to the absolute truth and embellished where he thought the story flagged. The gods, in his account, were still at work to make the world perfect. Revelations about the next temporal coming of Kukulcan seeded his account of a prosperous new future. Kukulcan, the god of the kings, would come back to the people as an Ah Kin Mai. This highest of priests would become Halach Uinic and embody the spirit of the holy god, Kukulcan. The people would greatly benefit from the vast knowledge, purity, and passion for goodness that only an Ah Kin Mai king could possess and bestow on his subjects.

Pochotl expressed this account humbly, as only a messenger. He confessed that in a drug induced trance two days before, he had been commanded by the spirits to let the people know of this eminent phenomenon. That he might be this new Ah Kin Mai, he never suggested. It was not advantageous to imply too much. Let the people make their own leaps of logic. He was also careful not to say exactly when or how. Planting the seeds of his aspirations was enough for now.

When he had finished, the people's silence was palpable. Through the whole story their hopes were soothed and coaxed by curiosity. *Could it be true? Is Kukulcan really coming?* These thoughts

110

suppressed all sounds to a hush. *Pochotl surely could not tell anything but the truth.* He was their paramount link from the mortal world to the spirits.

Pochotl scanned the faces of his audience. In the long ensuing silence, he thought he had perhaps gone too far. A smug perceptive expression met him from his immediate front. Ah Tok's thoughts pierced the priest with a smile confined to only his lips. The nobleman obviously recognized Pochotl's blatant deceit and evident ploy for power.

The green priest lifted his arms skyward and looked up. He closed his eyes and listened, his heart thumping rapidly. It was his best pose. Adrenalin pumped its chemistry through his veins, feeding on the fear generated by the grave mistake his arrogance may have wrought. It seemed the winds blew high above, murmuring to him alone their dark displeasure, whispering his downfall. Ominous clouds ran in packs, chased to the west, elevated from the diminutive concerns of humans. Time ticked by, chronicled only by the *rheeeee...rheeeee...rheeeee* of the ever present cicadas.

Then the night exploded with the cheers of the people. The sound was overwhelming. Thunderous clapping, stomping, and inarticulate yells of joy detonated the silence into a tumultuous confusion of noise. *I have them! They believe my every word!* Pochotl lowered only his eyes and met Ah Tok's stare of incredulous disbelief. The smile on Pochotl's face reached well beyond his lips. The people were his. He could feel the power, even if it hadn't been officially given.

***

The right corner of Ah Tok's mouth curled up like an angry dog defending food. An awful, empty coldness marbled the nobleman's eyes. Silent fury welled up in his breast and exploded red in his thoughts. *That fly-spit of a priest has gone too far, much too far. Now he is going to die, and the sooner the better.* It was a decision he made easily. The future of his people demanded it. He realized he would have to do it himself without the help of anyone. No one else should or would know. The more he thought about it, the more the idea pleased him. The curl relaxed into a genuine grin. The nobleman got to his feet, grabbed his wife, and shoved his way through the priest's adoring crowd.

The rest of the night was given over to revelry of every kind. Knowing about an assured future of prosperity augmented the soul as few other things could. Happiness was hard to come by in this new world, and any chance to express pleasure was seized. Until early morning, the fires witnessed spirited celebrating and the ground received the vomited offerings of the drunk.

***

Ahau and the rest of the young suitors were now commanded by tribal custom to live in a communal abode, separate from their families and especially from the females. Until the proper amenities of marriage were met, courtship without supervision was not tolerated. The proprieties of a man and woman uniting were strictly enforced.

Ahau's problems only intensified. With crystal-clear recollection, he repeatedly experienced Jada's warm lips and embrace. He ached to pull his new love into his arms. *How will we manage to meet in secret?* The cold, dark hours of the early morning or the chance meeting in a secluded spot in the forest could be dangerous. As he spent his first night in the new hut amid the snoring and nocturnal coughing of other young men, he contemplated his chances of a future with Jada. Anxiety was a poor substitute for sleep.

***

A still slightly inebriated Pochotl met the morning under the tangled arms of two women. He shuddered, heaved a sigh, and pulled himself slowly from the bed. Last night, large quantities of the green liquor had run smoothly down his greedy throat and warmed his insides. This morning his innards threatened to leave. His skull felt like it was going to burst into white hot pieces from the pressure.

Sometime during the night he had requested the company of the two women and had not been turned down. Living legends in the making rarely were. Pochotl could only remember brief snatches of what had occurred between them, but was sure they were sleeping satisfied. He prided himself on his abilities in bed. Roughly, the females were shaken awake and shooed out the door.

The priest stretched, yawned, and lay back on his arm, remembering the deafening sound of success last night. The expression on Ah Tok's face when the nobleman realized the power of a prophecy the people wanted to come true replayed in his mind.

112

Pochotl got up. Tikal and Ahau would soon be coming with his breakfast. Pulling the rough sisal curtain aside, he observed the sky and the dark banks of clouds dominating the close horizon. The weather looked like it might hold for most of the day before the wet season started in earnest.

***

Less than a thousand strides away, last night's nausea raised its ugly head and bit Ah Tok right between his red-rimmed eyes. He nestled deeper into the blankets and flung an arm across an empty mattress. He patted with the back of his hand, looking for the reassuring warmness of his wife. Realizing she was gone, he sighed and tried to sit up. Raw agony assailed him. He cradled his head from both sides and pushed himself to a sitting position. *What did I drink last night?* His breath brought his memory back. The throbbing ache in his head was justly deserved.

A thin, sultry rose-scented woman of about thirty cycles rounded the corner to the room. "Ah Tok, you're up! I thought we might not see you today. How do you feel?" She smoothed back the sweaty hair from his brow and handed him her herb tea.

Ah Tok grunted an approval. His hand snaked out and grabbed his wife's left buttock and pulled her to him, nestling in against her thigh. She continued stroking his hair, waiting for him to talk about last night if he wanted to. He had said some pretty weird things. He rarely drank anything stronger than the herb tea he had in his hand. She knew he saw weakness in those that did, and that's what had made last night so unusual.

"You are beautiful, Ix Cuy. You know that, don't you?"

She answered with a caress to his cheek that ended in a light pat. "Get up, old man, you'll feel better. Hungry? I can get you something."

"Unhhh, I think I'll just close my eyes for a few moments more." He sunk back against the feather filled bag.

Sun and shadow spilled through the small window, creating a subtle pattern of dark leaves against the wall. Ah Tok absently watched them sway back and forth as images of the old priest took center stage in his mind. Pochotl was smiling around a slightly dangerous, cynical split of a mouth. Ah Tok again argued with himself about exactly how the priest's accidental death would occur. Poison was the obvious choice. Should it be anonymously delivered by animal or secretly fed was the real uncertainty. A flickering thought far back in Ah Tok's eyes glinted the birth of a plan. *Tikal and Ahau prepare Pochotl's food. Soon, then. I just have to find what I need.*

CHAPTER 10
HARD WOOD

Soon after Pochotl had eaten and outlined their daily chores, Tikal and Ahau snuck off to be with their friends for a short while. Sporting events involving running, weapon prowess, and individual fighting skills were always going on somewhere in the village. These were poor substitutes for the ritual ball game usually played at this time of year, but there were no other alternatives. It would be at least two years before a proper stone court could be made. More spiritual than sport, the ball game served as the ultimate metaphor linking the movements of the heavenly bodies to the conflict between good and evil. The game was played with a large ball made from the rubber tree. The primary targets were stone rings set on opposite ends of the playing alley into which the ball must pass without the benefit of hands. The game was taken very seriously, and cities would play each other and bet huge sums of produce, property, jade, and even human sacrifices on the outcome. Until a real court could be produced, however, the new village contented itself with other less serious games.

During the bow and arrow competition Ahau had a revelation that would change his life forever. He had been watching the younger boys shoot at a tightly packed round grass target that rolled across the ground when an idea began to take form. For hundreds of years, the people had used the bow and arrow as a small game hunting tool. The arrows were made of thin cane shafts with sharpened split ends that pierced the target cleanly but without much force, spreading the cut points outward as it entered. The fletching was usually made from the tail feathers of a hawk. If used on any small animal, the arrow was usually proficient enough to kill. The cane was just too fragile to penetrate and quickly dispatch larger animals. The penetration was too shallow unless just the right spot was pierced, and shooting at a target over sixty feet away was usually ineffectual. A lucky shot was always the exception. As a rule, the bow and arrow was never taken seriously as a large game weapon, and never used in warfare except to launch ingenious hornet bombs. Easily deflected, it was hard to shoot in heavily forested areas. The bottom line was that the bow was not able to produce the energy needed to propel an arrow with substantial force to be reliable against a real enemy.

Ahau had used a bow for years and felt competent with the weapon. Numerous meals had been made possible because of his prowess. Now that he had reached manhood, though, he had switched to the spear as the weapon of choice. The shaft was much thicker and of fire-hardened wood. The obsidian or flint points made it very formidable indeed. It could be thrown with accuracy or wielded hand-to-hand very efficiently. It was a symbol of manhood. A warrior who brandished a spear was a serious threat. *But what if...?*

The idea was full blown now. He just needed to confirm a few suspicions. Pulling Tikal from the games was not easy. Tikal had just placed a wager on a runner and wanted to watch the outcome, but Ahau was not to be denied.

"I need you to come now! You can always find out who won later. I can't do this by myself. Get an axe, rope, your spear, and water. Meet me at the sacred Jaguar Stone as soon as you gather it all up. We'll leave from there. No. Don't ask questions now. I'll tell you all about it later. Just do it!"

Still not sure what was going on but always eager to share an adventure, an out of breath Tikal met Ahau at the appointed spot with everything he had been instructed to bring. Without a word, they entered the forest on the east side of the village. The two friends traveled silently for close to twenty stone throws before Tikal finally had to ask. Ahau would only say that they needed to find wood from the hardest tree in the forest. After they found it, he would explain why. He was still thinking about the possibilities and wanted a clearer picture of the design before he said anything to his friend. They did, however, speak of Jada and Tikal's father. Ahau confessed and expressed his love for the beautiful young woman, and almost embarrassed Tikal by revealing so much feeling aloud. Tikal felt for his friend and said as much. Ahau knew he could count on him to help whenever he could.

After much searching, they eventually found the tree Ahau wanted. The wood was extremely hard and arduous to cut. They skinned the bark from a selected section, revealing a very close veined, dark wood. While hacking several large staves from the center, Ahau revealed his plan.

The rains came.

The two apprentices were thoroughly drenched by the time they made it back to the village. Even though they were required to sleep at the bachelor's quarters now, they still had access to Pochotl's old house. The stone and wood abode would eventually be turned into something different, but for the moment it was empty and accessible. Excited, they lit a fire and laid the wood out before it. They had wrapped everything in large leaves when the rains first began, but the wood was still soaked in places. Once all the pieces were spaced out to dry around the flames, the two young men joined the rest of the village in the large communal square. By ritual law, everyone lanced themselves somewhere on their body and added their blood to the wet blessings that soaked the earth. They would do this every three nights before going to sleep while the rains lasted. The many small trickles of blood were their way of offering thanks to the gods for another year of life-giving moisture, and for the assurance that the forest would continue to provide for them.

Wiping the rain from his eyes, Ahau's fingers left clean tracks through the sweat plastered grime. Water misted up from the ground where, like tiny hammers, it beat incessantly to penetrate the earth and kiss-start new life. He moved under a nearby tree, and with the spiders watched the pools gather and deepen until foul mud sucked at his feet. A premonition, a worm of worry, chafed his thoughts. *Bela is still alive and looking for me.* He could feel the great beast's interest even from this distance. He shrugged the thoughts away and tried to dismiss them as strands of clinging paranoia. His sandals squelched in the mud and threatened to slide sideways as he headed to real shelter and friends. The breeze blew spider silk behind him.

CHAPTER 11

LUNATIC FRINGE

(Two Weeks Later)

Besh Po and Tarnae sat across from each other under the makeshift lean-to, listening to the clicking, roiling nests of insects that also sought refuge from the oppressive rain. It was bad luck that Pochotl had picked them to send on a fool's quest. The whole thing gnawed at their psyches. They had been torn away from the celebrations to find the missing fourteen. Besh pulled the blanket more snugly and spit into the fire. They had been sitting here, two days away from the village, for most of the day. They were soaked despite the shelter, and were developing ugly attitudes. Wistfully, they talked of women and their obvious lack of them.

They had no real intentions of hunting for the warriors. That was dangerous, stupid work. If fourteen of the best men the village had to offer had run into trouble, they wanted no part of it. Besides, where would they look? They could be anywhere by now. Besh and Tarnae had decided early that they would wait in the forest just long enough to make it appear they had tried. Then they were going home. Either the missing men would be back by then or they would use the old I-looked-everywhere-but-couldn't-find-them excuse. Bored, Tarnae suggested they spread out a blanket and gamble with carved monkey bones. It would help pass the time.

***

The whites of Chan Chel's eyes were no longer perceptible. Shallow, opaque skeins of blood swirled around the dark irises and even darker pupils. No light mirrored from the dull, colored surfaces.

119

For well over a week now he had been Bela's prisoner, pet, confidant, and mentor. The grievous wounds he had suffered from falling were mending slowly, but healing none the less. Occasionally, the crippled hunter mistakenly gave answer to a misunderstood question or simply didn't know what the demon wanted. It was at these times that Bela revealed his talent for a special, tender savagery. New lacerations and punctures were inflicted by Bela daily in his malevolent ache to comprehend. The hunter, with monumental, self-motivated effort, stayed alive.

Bela retained everything...and always wanted more. His thirst for knowledge was insatiable. The great beast was learning the people's language and their ways rapidly. It was amazing to the hunter that he rarely had to repeat his explanations or say a word twice, once Bela understood the meaning.

Chan Chel thought he was beginning to understand the beast as well. They were able to converse now in short limited speech, and Chan Chel believed that Bela's desperate loneliness must be immense. If he understood correctly, his new large companion never had a family...never had companionship of any kind. For his entire life, he had been alone in the forest. He shuddered to think what that must be like day after day, year after year. The beast was, by definition, horrifying and morbidly fascinating at the same time.

They settled into a daily routine. Early each day — or night...the hunter was never sure in Bela's lair — Bela would feed and water Chan Chel. After that, the hours passed with questions and answers. At first, the hunter pointed at things and drew in the dirt the ideas of speech. Later, Bela began asking questions in a halting, impossibly low voice that truly did give credence to the idea of him being a demon. As the weeks passed, the interrogations became more abstract in thought and more conversant. Chan Chel still feared for his life even though most of the physical abuse had ended. There were still times when he accidently made Bela angry. A predatory expression would materialize across Bela's face that twisted in Chan Chel roots of madness, tight as a feeding tick. At moments like these, the hunter made himself as unobtrusive as possible. He crawled close to the wall and curled around his injured arm.

***

Standing in the entrance of the cave and breathing deeply, seeking scents on the air currents, Bela slowly and intently separated the spoor scents of several animals in the near forest. He would identify them and their locations one at a time. Clouds, thunderhead black, moved rapidly to the west, pushed by howling, urgent winds. Lightning zippered from left to right, accompanied by the loud crack of a god's hand slapping the world. Further off, more bolts of energized fire chased each other from ground to low and turbulent sky. Like thin, white strands of spider silk, they wove intricate, flawed webs, lasting only portions of a second. Bela's eyes glittered dark as he trotted off to the northwest. He had caught a whiff of something he didn't like, something that demanded his immediate attention.

***

Besh Po again cursed his horrendously bad luck. He had lost everything he had with him except his weapons. Those he would not wager. They were discussing possible items left back in the village to gamble with when new rain began to fall against and into their temporary shelter.

Tarnae kicked more wood onto the fire. The smoke from the wet wood seemed to swirl everywhere but out of the tiny lean-to. Disgusted, he gained his feet, announcing the need to relieve himself. The rain was coming down now in a soft but steady stream. Tarnae was already soaked to the skin and paid no mind to the additional wetness. He wandered to a large tree forty strides from the shelter. In mid-stream, the hunter heard a tremulous whisper issue on the wind.

"Brownskin, why you heaeer? You come for meee? I glad you heaeer."

Tarnae could see nothing. He was now sure that the two of them had been here too long. He was starting to hear things in the wind. An active imagination could do funny things in the forest. Shaking his finish, Tarnae replaced the flap. Again a low whisper floated out of the darkness, seeming to come from above as the rain abruptly stopped. Stirred by curiosity, Tarnae looked up into the live, blowing shadows of the tree.

"Look heaeer. Meee show you."

Through the very tops of the trees a moonlit mist swirled high, cradling a bumpy edge of the moon against which clouds ran tightly.

121

Closer down, on a large branch, dark orbs reflected out of the foliage. Like rock flecked with mica lying on the bottom of a shadowy river, the circular shapes glowed fiercely from within. Tarnae's mind ran a quick inventory of possibilities. They were eyes, but of what animal? He was sure that anything that large didn't belong in a tree.

The dark mass surrounding the eyes began to move. Tarnae's feet involuntarily began to back up. A nightmare image flickered through his mind, ominous in its portent of imminent death. *Bela. By Itzamna, there really is a dem....*

Claws opened his skull and spilled the rest of the thought to the dirt below. The beast shivered from savage pleasure as it silently dropped from the tree and began to feed.

***

Besh Po stretched from his cramped position and called for his friend. Bela dragged his meat quickly to the other side of the tree and again climbed up.

"Tarnae, Tarnae, where are you? Let's do some hunting while the rain is stopped. Even frog legs would taste good right now."

Besh moved in the direction he had seen his friend going. The tree loomed large and silent to his left. Something was wrong. He could feel it to his core. Bad luck. He called again, but again received no answer. Turning toward the tree, he caught the bitter, rank, coppery smell of blood, too much blood, and his instincts took over...he began to run. After thirty strides, he chanced a look back and saw nothing. The rain began to mist down, just enough to make visibility strenuous.

Searing agony suddenly swiped across his right calf. Besh looked down and saw four evenly spaced, shallow slashes. Puzzlement gave way to panic as a thin, shrill, inhuman rumble sounded out of the darkness to his right. Running now with speed born of adrenalin fed fear, Besh frantically looked for a safe shelter. Again he felt something slice through his flesh. He spun, trying to see in all directions at once, and could faintly see a dark, wraith shape circle his backside, only a spear's throw away. Upright and huge, it spoke with a thick guttural sound from deep in the throat, sounding thoroughly inhuman.

"Run, brownskin. I seeee you!"

Besh, wide-mouthed and unbelieving, felt his bladder release wet, hot panic down his legs. He gripped his spear and sprinted. *Bela! It has to be. Nothing else fits. All the stories were true.* He and Tarnae had thought they were far from the crater-lair the fourteen had sought. They had picked this part of the forest to stay away from any possible demon. Bad luck.

***

Bela felt the same dark, savage thrill he had experienced chasing the onzas. This brownskin was slow and predictable, but if he was careful, the game could go on awhile yet. He tried to make his cuts shallow and never deadly. With dismaying agility, Bela continued to circle, slash, and castigate the poor hunter.

"Brownskin. Run. You can get awaaay. Run faaaster!"

***

Bela's vocal urgings were not needed. Besh Po ran. Wickedly thorned bushes loomed large in front of him. With no hesitation, he pushed his way through to the center, heedless of the hundreds of barbs tearing at his flesh. He stopped and hunkered down. There was no illusion of being safe. Besh could see the demon skitter the edges of the thorn bushes, tearing at them almost absently. Bela continued to furiously scold in a halting speech as he tossed in large rocks to prod the brownskin out. The thorns were no threat to his thick skin; he just seemed to be trying to flush Besh Po out. Besh Po got the impression that the beast was having fun.

Besh's breathing finally slowed enough to draw a breath that wasn't hot and ragged. He knew the beast would not stay outside his barbed haven for long. His mind raced for a safe direction to run. There had to be somewhere he could get to that would offer some protection. He pulled at some of the thorns embedded in his face. Another rock bounced through the thorns and thudded against his thigh. *Rocks!* He remembered an outcropping of rocks that had a floor fracture he might be able to squeeze down into. He and Tarnae had seen it only yesterday as they looked for a site to camp. *Where was it?* Besh stood up and tried to get his bearings as a rock sailed near his head. Bela was further into the bushes and still growling challenges. The hunter could see the beast clearly now. The image momentarily paralyzed him. No nightmare he had ever had prepared him for what he saw now.

123

Moonlight glistened through the scattered rain drops that now drizzled down. Softly thrumming wings betrayed the presence of an owl as it swooped near Bela's head. It was investigating what it did not know. Bad luck.

***

Ominous in the stillness, the soft whispers of feathers slashing the air startled the great beast and it ducked in reflex. Immediately realizing what it had been, Bela roared with injured pride. It infuriated and embarrassed him that a simple, rodent-eating owl had been able to spook him. Standing up, he turned towards the crouched brownskin. Thick saliva streamed from his mouth. The greater need for vengeance controlled him now. Powerfully, he began to push his way through the bushes. There was no mistaking his deadly intention. His eyes blazed feral bright. He was done playing.

***

Besh Po instantly found his feet and ran in the opposite direction. The thorns tore again at his skin. In the dim illumination provided by a cloud-sheathed moon, he could see what he thought were the rocks. With a renewed hope-fed burst of speed, he headed toward them, but risked a look back. The demon was still behind him, gaining fast. Besh Po's eyes searched for the fracture in the rock he and Tarnae had seen earlier. A darker shadow than the rest suddenly snaked out in front of him. Besh plunged feet first through the opening, heedless to what was below. The spear ricocheted out of his hand as his arm banged painfully back and forth off the unyielding sides of the rupture in the rocks. A scintillating blast of pain sprouted from his left ankle as it met rough stone below. He bit his tongue against the scream that threatened to expose him. He crouched as low as possible, twisting and pushing his back into the rock. Looking up, he could see only a thin sliver of the sky, about four arm lengths away. He hoped it was enough.

The little light that pooled around the edge of his hidey-hole suddenly blackened. Bela had found him. He wasn't sure the beast could see him that far down into the fissure and tried to still his slightly wheezy breathing. He was wrong.

"Ooooruh! Brownskin, why you in this hole?" Bela picked up the spear dropped by Besh and rattled it in the black cavity. "This hole belong to snaaake. You think you saaafe in hole?"

The hunter tried to squeeze to his left, out of the way of the spear. A new, quick pain assaulted his thigh. Again. Scratchy sounds at his feet confirmed his fear. Besh Po felt the snakes struggle over his wounded ankle and then all was quiet. Two eyelash vipers had sought the rocky solitude of warm darkness to mate. These same two snakes spent over ninety percent of their lives in the trees, but had picked this night and these rocks to copulate. Bad luck.

Within a hundred heartbeats, Besh Po's breathing became labored. He no longer cared about Bela. He knew the snakes had been venomous. He was also acutely aware that he was dying. He could feel the heat spread up around his ears. The numbness from the waist down became part of a peaceful illusion from which there was no escape. Tranquil and calm, he smiled and giggled hysterically. Looking up, he could no longer see the beast. He had beat Bela. At least he was not going to feel the beast's claws and teeth rip through his body. He tried to holler up at the beast but nothing came through his lips. He wanted to tell Bela he was not afraid. Unassociated images began to flicker rapidly through his mind and then there was nothing.

***

Bela, no longer anticipating tearing out the brownskin's throat, thought instead in terms of a special revenge. The brownskin stuck in the hole made him remember when he had once been trapped in a small cave, so he pushed large rocks over the entrance, sealing it up. From the lean-to, the beast brought back burning limbs of wood and shoved them in the small remaining openings above Besh Po's head. He added grass, plants, anything he could find, and shoved it all down the hole. Bela made three trips for the burning sticks.

***

Besh never felt his hair catch fire. Greasy hair snapped and popped as the fire seared the underlying flesh and began to crawl across his face, neck, and shoulders. He was beyond caring about anything. Rain gurgled down the hole in small individual rivulets. His luck, too late, had finally changed.

Bela stayed until the hole no longer smoked. He pushed one of the larger rocks aside and sniffed deeply of the smoke, death, and burnt flesh below. Patting the rock back into place, he left at a lope, back to the brownskin stashed behind the tree. Although the blood was cold and no longer flowed, he ravished the torn meat until his appetite was sated. Keening a shrill victory cry, he tore off a large, dripping chunk of Tarnae's thigh to bring back to Chan Chel. It never occurred to him that brownskins did not eat of their own. For over two-hundred years he had watched other creatures of the forest cannibalize themselves. Why would brownskins be any different?

***Ah Tok had searched the forest alone for many days. He harvested snakeroot, nightshade, and the potato-like tubers from the manihot esculenta plant. Only sixty steps from his front door, he found death cap mushrooms, and bloodroot. Now, back in the secrecy of his own room, he boiled and mashed all of the plants together, except for the bloodroot. The resulting mixture formed a green, vile smelling paste. Ah Tok sliced the bloodroot plant down its middle, releasing a rusty, milk-like substance that he added to the mix. He spread the abhorrent paste thin across the surface of a flat ceramic plate and allowed it to air dry. Later today he would grind the dried out remains into a powder.

It would take a while for the poison to affect the old priest, but that just made it more enjoyable. Pochotl would experience debilitating diarrhea, severe dehydration, and vomit until his guts retched dry. His corneas would cloud over and eye lesions would appear. If luck was with Ah Tok, the old priest would also experience grim abdominal pains that would make his dried up eyes cry sterile tears of burning anguish. Sometime during the next day, his liver and kidneys would degrade, causing gradual renal failure. Pochotl would be found dead within two days. No one would suspect anything other than time-worn age as the reason for his demise.

Tikal and Ahau almost always make the priest's nightly meal outside over a fire near the Sun Temple. If it is raining, they will be inside. Either way, I have to distract them long enough to hide the poison on the meat. It is lucky that they never eat with him. Being the superior piece of rat-dropping that he is, Pochotl always eats alone, preferring his own company to that of us lesser mortals. Well, we will see how he enjoys this!

Exhilarated, almost sanguine, Ah Tok left his abode to supervise the rock quarry where building materials for his new home were being cleaved from the sandstone cliffs overlooking the northern end of the valley below. Today's events would be the threshold steps to a better life for him and his family. *With Pochotl out of the way, well, who else could be Halach Uinic? I am the obvious choice. The people will prosper under my guidance. We will name the village in my honor. We will....* He continued to dream the fantasies of a supreme ruler all the way to the quarry.

***

Ahau and Tikal were sitting patiently on the floor in front of the old priest, listening to him explain the workings of the thirteen gods that ruled the upper world and the intricacies of negotiating with the nine underworld gods. They were constantly trying to stifle stale, weary yawns and hiding those that squeezed past their guard. More and more were slipping past their defenses. Inside the priest's quarters, it was muggy, hot, and dreary. No air seemed to circulate. They rolled their tired eyes at each other and made rude gestures at the old man when they thought they could get away with it. After several weeks of Pochotl's company, they no longer considered him the god-like mortal that they had at first. They still had a healthy respect for his office and the power he had over them specifically. They were just tired of his constant and vicious temperament and the strange and chilling stories he told of his childhood and his father. The same stories changed with every telling. They did not want to hear any more but knew they would. The priest was beginning to show what he really was; a lonely, dissatisfied old man who sought domination over others to camouflage his considerable weaknesses in character.

***

Pochotl was totally inebriated with the telling of his significant knowledge of the world. He shared his special insights and philosophies with energized enthusiasm. He paced up and down the floor, speaking the entire time. Lost in thought and without realizing it, Pochotl had a very narcissistic attraction to the pyrite mirrors that decorated all four walls. Often, he would pose in front of one of the polished pyrite slabs and prattle about life in general and his special place in the overall scheme of things. He stroked his hair, smoothed his eyebrows, and traced with his fingers the tattooed circle of god symbols on his chest. Sometimes he would stop in mid-sentence and scrape against one of the symbols in particular, never finishing the

127

thought, lost in reflection.

Now, admiring his reflection, he straightened up and studied his double from the side. Pochotl sucked in his breath slightly and tapped his knuckles on abdominal muscles still visible after all of these years. *How awed the two young men before me must be.*

***

Near midday the two apprentices were finally released from their holy instruction and allowed time on their own. For Ahau, this time was especially precious. He and Jada would conveniently find each other in their favorite private place in the woods, each arriving by a different route. Knowing that she would be waiting made it exceptionally hard to sit through Pochotl's tirade of old nonsense.

Alone, they observed most of the village's edicts concerning unmarried couples, but it was becoming increasingly difficult. They frequently sat for long periods, saying nothing, just holding each other and whispering promises with their eyes and the gentle exploratory touches of their hands across each other's bodies. People were beginning to notice their absences. Keeping their passion a secret was becoming impossible. It was their only time together, though, and they were not about to give it up. The gossip would just have to be ignored...at least until Ah Tok began to take notice. That was an entirely different situation. They had been cautioned. Knowing the time was coming, guilt flowed like tendrils of warning smoke across the back of their minds, waiting for the fire-storm Ah Tok's fury would unleash once he found out.

Today, a forlorn Ahau would make no discreet forage into the forest. Jada was with her mother and would be busy with chores all day. This happened more and more often lately. Ahau suspected Ix Cuy knew and was trying to stave off the inevitable.

At times like these, Ahau and Tikal usually worked on their new bows. Tikal and he had been shaving the black, hard wood into several flat and round forms using extremely sharp obsidian knives. The work was tedious and slow. Experimenting with new designs, they finally decided to adapt something in between extremes. The middle area of the bow would be rounded, giving it strength, and subtly flattened out toward the ends. They also used staves twice as long as the round, short traditional bow of the people. They reasoned correctly that the longer limbs would create more kinetic energy in releasing the arrows. Excitedly, they worked on their own bows, sharing ideas and failures. The failures outweighed the successes considerably, but they were still optimistic. Their goal was to create a weapon capable of bringing down large game or an enemy from a long distance, with full confidence in its ability to kill. The short, stubby bows his people had always used would seem puny and fragile against the innovative new weapon he painstakingly labored over now. Although he never mentioned it, privately he hoped the imaginative new bow would prove to be powerful enough to confront Bela's terrible arsenal of claws, teeth, strength, and speed. Just thinking about the alternative made Ahau work feverishly. He still believed deep in his soul that the great beast had a personal interest in him. Now he had Jada to live for.

**

Rain blustered its way down on soft breezes that made transparent sheets of water dance first from one side and then to the other. The people still gave nocturnal thanks for the wet blessings by adding their blood to the thousands of rivulets that ran through the foot sucking mud, but they were no longer invigorated by the ceremony. The rain was becoming old news. The problems it caused were real. Thankfully, they had chosen their village's location well, anticipating the vast amounts of water. The massive hill they sat atop, overlooking the valley, provided relief from the floods that came and went below. The daily lulls in the rain, however, never seemed long enough to get done what needed to be done. It became a common topic in the evenings, as families and friends ate their nightly meal. Work on the Sun Temple and other important buildings continued despite the hazards of working in the wet. So far no one had been seriously injured, but several reported cuts, abrasions, and broken bones from slippery mud and water-slicked rock. The women in the village were able to tend to these minor injuries by themselves. Occasionally Pochotl's advice was sought, but predominately the healing arts rested within the domain of the older women.

**

Light, streaked in hues of yellow and red, filtered faintly through the tops of the trees and lightly colored orange what it could touch.

Barely illuminated, the two apprentices watched their shadows lengthen steadily into the immense blackness stretching around them and spilling into the black valley below. The darkness would be complete in a very short time.

They fired wood. Ahau and Tikal were preparing Pochotl's nightly meal over meager flames just to the side of the Sun Temple. They had killed a small deer with Tikal's new bow, and were excitedly talking about the success of the weapons. Both bows had shot faster and farther than any they had ever used. The arrows, however, would have to be denser. Their flight had been somewhat erratic. The tail end, once released from the bow, traveled too far sideways before straightening out. Thinking about the perilous head of his spear, Ahau devised arrowheads with much the same shape. Pressure flaking flint into small, sharp, bottom heavy points like the much longer one on his spear was difficult. Binding it to the shaft with fish glue and sinew made the long darts look very formidable indeed. They deduced that a thicker shaft and longer fletching might make the desired difference. Three arrows had sought the deer's vitals before one of Tikal's found its mark. Ecstatic, they butchered and dragged the meat back to the village.

***

Tikal took a large portion of it to his family, as was his right. Ah Tok, feining an interest in the deer, came back to the meal fire and listened to the apprentices as they bragged about their new bows. The words blurred in his ears as white noise. He wasn't really listening. Hearing a chance to distract them, however, he asked if he could see the new weapons. As they were stored in Pochotl's old house, the young men ran for the chance to show them off.

Alone, Ah Tok turned back to the fire. The meat on the spit looked almost cooked. He sliced into it, revealing the brown flesh, and wiped a healthy portion of his special, powdered seasoning into the muscle fiber. The young men rounded the corner just as he finished. Ah Tok hid his actions by turning the spit, pretending to care about one side becoming over done. They showed him the new bows, talking over each other and pointing out new features and ideas about the shape of the wood. The nobleman created the impression he cared and congratulated them, even drawing back one of the bows. Later, if

130

asked, he would have no idea what made the bows different. His mind was on Pochotl chewing slowly and digesting venison and hopefully enjoying every bite. The nobleman's head felt tight, and his temples hot. Nervous energy coursed through his body as he anticipated the next few hours. Guilt never made an appearance.

***

Just to make sure they tasted no part of the tainted meat, Ah Tok entreated the young men to his house to eat. Recognizing an opportunity to see Jada, Ahau agreed for both of them before Ah Tok had finished the invitation. Leaving the priest's meal to his friend, Ahau raced to clean up.

Tikal entered the open door to Pochotl's holy abode, the ceramic bowl of meat, wild lettuce, and beans in his hands. The room was dark, the only illumination coming from a small fire. He could see the sitting, swaying form of the priest in the middle of the floor; small inarticulate sounds escaped the old man's lips. Tikal knew better than to disturb the old priest. He laid the plate down near the door and withdrew.

***

The priest squatted on the floor of his new quarters, stirring with his fingers the light dust that patinaed the dark, rusty spots in the stone. The stain on the floor was Zac Kuk's blood. It made a dripping pattern that pooled in the middle. Mushroom crumbs tumbled from his lips as he murmured the name under stagnant breath, his bloodshot eyes squinting from underneath droopy lids. His shoulders slouched and hung weakly over the top of his slightly swaying torso. Pochotl was hallucinating. Through a mushroom induced vision, he was reliving the slave's death. At times, he became both the audience and himself. He watched from the sidelines as he performed terrible cruelties, and took pleasure from the dark perversions. At other times, he saw and felt through the eyes of Zac Kuk and sobbed weakly, uncontrollably. Pochotl moaned for release and denied himself as he shoved a hungry mouth into his belly to taste the entrails that squirmed like snakes within.

The scene changed. Green-black, thick mist obscured his view. Slowly at first, and then gaining speed, Bela floated menacingly out of the green gloam. The beast reached for him with bared claws. Pochotl watched intently as a third person would from the sidelines. His vision had an unnatural clarity, different than the ones before. He tried to scream a warning. Just as the beast's claws started their slow motion descent towards the priest's face, white light exploded and Bela was gone.

A very pale, tall man replaced the horrible visage. Pochotl felt the thirteen gods, enshrined in black ink on his chest, lift in fiery pain and dance before his eyes on red jeweled pebbles. Dressed in ritual splendor, the man walked above the earth and blessed everything with his presence. The forest parted to allow his passage and then closed back, greener, lusher, and thicker than before. Luminescent fungi glimmered with a pale orange hue in the darkness as he passed. In a deep resonant voice, the Ah Kin Mai proclaimed the world as his with unrivaled arrogance. Immersed and tangled tight within the mushroom induced prophecy, an inspired Pochotl again wept. This time the tears were for a prophecy come true. He wept real tears as he interpreted himself as the new Ah Kin Mai.

Blackness, total and complete.

Later that night, when Pochotl finally awoke from a curled, fetal position on the floor, it took him a while to get his bearings. *Where am I?* Memory seeped through the insufferable pain playing against the inside walls of his head. *Ah Kin Mai! The vision revealed my destiny. I will be the Ah Kin Mai. Somehow, Bela, Zac Kuk, and my fates are all woven together, intertwined in the hard strands of fate.*

Tripoding himself with hands and butt, he slowly sat up. As his eyes adjusted to the absence of light, he looked down at the floor and noticed new blood soaking into the old, rusty spots. His blood. With hands that shook, he checked himself over, finding a chunk of lip chewed out. It had probably occurred while convulsing in the throes of ecstasy, reliving Zac Kuk's death. He trembled pleasurably thinking about it, momentarily seeing the scene once more.

His eyes still partially glazed from the mushrooms, Pochotl reached into his leather bag and withdrew the grizzled remains of Zac Kuk's severed tongue. It had shriveled and blackened, but still had gratifying weight. He held it up to better see it. The putrescent fetish had an eerie beauty to it, like a black pearl that hides in the pulpy pouch of its dark inception. He picked small pieces of grit off the curled surface and stuck it in his mouth. Moving it gently from side to side with his own tongue, he felt for the slightly bumpy texture. The flavor was bitter with a salty after taste. He pulled it out and tried to unfurl the twisted edges. His saliva had added enough moisture to do so. He stuck it back in his mouth and closed his eyes, maneuvering it tip to tip with his own tongue. Death was the sweetest thrill of all. He tried to taste Zac Kuk's last scream, and thought he could. It was a pleasant sensation. Resisting the urge to chew and swallow, he replaced the blackened morsel into the pouch. *Not yet. Not yet.*

Realizing he was hungry, Pochotl stood stiffly and went to his food. He dimly remembered one of the apprentices having brought it. Tendons flared along his neck. He had been on the floor a long time. Though cold, the meat still tasted good. Mushrooms always made him hungry.

Chewing deeply into the meat, the third bite extracted an acrid flavor his educated palate told him should not be there. Food expelled from pursed lips and hit the wall, nostrils flared, and his eyes went terrified-to-the-bone-wide. Acid tasting bile flooded his nasal cavities.

Fury born of fear exploded. Poison! He knew the taste. Pochotl tried to retch from his throat to eliminate all of the tainted meat. Spitting, spitting, spitting, his frightened brain deliberated for culpability. A dozen heartbeats later, he had the answer. *Ah Tok!* Tikal and Ahau he never suspected. They revered him far too much to be involved. They were innocent pawns in the nobleman's dreams of power.

He remembered Ah Tok's eyes the night he'd prophesied Ah Kin Mai. He should have heeded the threat mirrored in the nobleman's face. *How much of the poison went down? Did I swallow any?* Pochotl drank large amounts of water and scratched at the back of his throat to initiate regurgitation. The mushrooms, still sour in his stomach, made it easy. On his hands and knees, rocking and arching his back, the priest spasmed. Grey meat and other unguessable flotsam swam in the steamy pool that spewed forth. Pochotl used his index finger to push through the turbid puddle that sought its way in runnels between the stones. The priest wiped his chin with the back of his arm. *Tikal and Ahau will enjoy cleaning this up!* Only time would tell if enough of the poison had entered his system to cause alarm.

The old priest ascended the unfinished stairs from his room to the next floor above. Eventually the Sun Temple would be three stories high. Presently, only part of the walls was constructed for the middle section. When completed, stairs would open to all of the floors from various positions. Landings, such as the partial one Pochotl now stood on, would also open out onto walking ledges that traveled entirely around the temple.

The hymen looked grimly toward Ah Tok's house. From this vantage point, he could see it clearly. Murderous thoughts thrashed red in his mind. The need to act fast was vital. The nobleman would certainly try again. Sour-sweet spit blew from the priest's lips as he turned rapidly and went back down to his holy orifice.

Chapter 12
Sweet, Killing Edge

Chan Chel's chest was a groundwork of little hollows with pale skin stretched tight around the bone. Vivid and angry scars stood raised in stark relief against skin that had not seen sunlight for weeks. When open, his eyes were bruised and swollen. His chest expanded slightly, and then collapsed again. It repeated this process rapidly. Bruised ribs prevented Chan Chel from taking a normal breath. His ears heard the high pitched thrumming of leather wings displacing air as a bat shadowed through the cave, and he awoke. Pain, exhaustion, and blurred vision thwarted the hunter's attempt to locate Bela within the cave. He decided the beast must be gone. Bela was constantly leaving on strange errands that only made sense to him.

Chan Chel hobbled up. The broken leg was moveable, but only barely. It was time to explore the back of the cave and find the source of the moving air he had experienced that first day. Carefully, leaning on rock sides when he could, the hunter searched. He strained to hear should Bela appear. He found the sweet, wet forest smell on a cold, thin air current once again. Following it to one of the side channels in the cave, Chan Chel ran into a dead end with no hope for escape in that direction. The air filtered down from numerous crevices in tightly packed rock, high above his head. No way was he going to be able to get to the large rocks above and tear them down. His despair became almost tangible.

Chan Chel hitched and limped his way back to the front of the cave. Several times before he had sought a way out from this direction, but the high walls of the cliffs always made it impossible. His leg and badly healing arm made it futile. Frustrated, the hunter sat with his back to the wall and waited for Bela's return. Time passed and Chan Chel slipped into sleep. His body jerked on a frayed rope of spun madness. He limped through the corridors of his hopelessly lost mind, unable to scream his way out of the darkness.

Bela returned.

Chan Chel tried to shake the last shreds of a nightmare. He could smell the fresh kill, his stomach growling for a taste. As usual, the great beast peeled the hide off the meat before giving it to the hunter. He was grateful for the food. Bela allowed him a small fire to cook it on. Using the flint tip of the spear and the iron deposits in the stone floor, the hunter was able to ignite kindling.

***

A few days before, Bela had been astonished the first time Chan Chel had made fire. He too, tried to scrape fire from the stone but lacked the dexterity and patience. Frustrated, he gave up the attempt and left it to Chan Chel. As long as the fire remained small and stayed in the hunter's corner of the cave, there was no problem. Bela even brought him bits of old wood and grasses to use. Secretly, though he would never admit it to the brownskin, the ability to make fire was the single most impressive thing he had ever witnessed. Even though the great beast had no need for fire, he envied the hunter's skill to produce it. Fire was an element of the earth like water, wind, and forest. To control such things was power indeed.

Bela lay nearby, licking the underside of the hide he had stripped from Tarnae's thigh, and played with scorpions. Two large, black scorpions danced in front of the beast and alternately attacked each other and Bela's fingers. It was a game the beast knew well. He laid the hide over one of the scorpions and dueled with the stinger of the other. Bela's large clawed fingers jabbed, prodded, and stroked the large arthropod until it was seething to attack. It grabbed Bela's claw with pincers and thrust its tail at the finger, trying to insert the stinger into the flesh. The poison bulb glistened as venom seeped from its tip.

Chan Chel watched with both horror and hope written on his face. This was a scorpion whose venom could kill. Bela's impenetrable skin prevented any possible injection, however. He allowed the scorpion to run up his hand and onto his arm, where it again attacked. The great beast, with a delicate touch, lifted the scorpion by its tail and put it back to the stone floor. Tiring of the game, Bela pushed an index finger against the scorpion's fat body and slowly pulled the tail off. The arthropod squirmed for a few moments and then lay still. The one under the hide he allowed to escape toward the cave wall and into one of the thousands of dark holes.

Bela rubbed his belly. "Eat, Chaaan Cheeel. We taaalk!"

***

Chan Chel pulled a piece from the meat hanging over the fire and tested the taste. He wished for seasonings, especially salt, but overall savored the meat. He tugged another piece free and ate. The two of them talked about the rain, the forest, and whatever the strange mind of Bela brought up. When the meat was gone and his belly was full, Chan Chel conversationally asked Bela what the meat had been. He did not think he had tasted anything quite like it.

"Food from baaad brownskin."

Chan Chel, not sure what he had just heard, asked again.

"Meee find brownskins in forest…in meee plaaace. Meee kill baaad brownskins." He made a slashing motion with his claws to illustrate how he had done it.

Bela went on, telling the story of Tarnae and Besh Po, but Chan Chel didn't hear. Repulsed to his soul, he tried to dry-heave the offending meat out of his system. Convulsions seized him, but the meat would not make a second appearance. Ill, enervated, and weak with despair, Chan Chel wanted the nightmare to end. Sickness turned to rage. Rage turned to madness. Madness turned to stupidity.

***

Chan Chel made a half-despairing, half-rabid sound deep in his throat and lunged on a barely mended broken leg. With the broken spear, he meant to kill the great beast. Astounded, a startled Bela reacted out of reflex. Ruinous trenches across the hunter's left shoulder and chest opened. The second passage of Bela's claws ended through the stomach, spilling Chan Chel's intestines. The hunter fell, twitching like the scorpion, to the stone floor, silent in his pain.

Bela bent over the squirming brownskin. "Why? Why youuu come at meee? Chaaan Cheeel! Chaaan Cheeel!" The beast shook the moaning brownskin, trying to understand. "Youuu live. Youuu live. Youuu not diiie!" He shook harder, his hands covered with the hunter's blood.

***

Chan Chel, trying to hold his insides in, smiled painfully at Bela, knowing his dark release was finally near. Between the throbs of the severe pain, the hunter haltingly said, "Meat, uhhh, why would you? How could you do that? He was from my village. Can you understand what that means?" Chan Chel was starting to go into shock. His speech was hard to hear. "By Itzamna's love, I hope Pochotl spills your demon blood. I only wish I could live long enough to see it. We will never allow you to live in our forest. Do you understand me, Bela?"

The hunter sank limply into death, his eyes still accusing the great beast. Bela nudged him with his toe, but Chan Chel did not respond. His ordeal had finally ended.

***

Long after the hunter died in his hands, Bela puzzled through his last words. He knew who Pochotl was. Chan Chel had told many things about the priest and his imminent importance to the village. The hunter had spoken of how Bela De Oxhutz meant *he who owns the darkness*, and why the fourteen had come after him. Bela liked the name. Chan Chel had said so many, many strange things over the last few weeks. Still, he did not understand why the brownskins hated him so. They were the intruders here, not he. This was and always had been his forest. Pieces to the puzzle suddenly came together convolutely. He pushed them to fit around one image.

Bela said aloud to the stone above and below, "Ooooruh! Pochoootl! He tries to kill Belaaa!"

The great beast ate nothing from Chan Chel's body except what he licked from his fingers. He still liked the hunter, even though he did not understand why he had charged him. He decided that it must have been something the hunter had eaten. The great beast reverently stuffed Chan Chel's body, upright, into a crevice near the back of the cave. In the following days, the hunter began to smell horrible in the humidity and heat of the cave. But Bela patiently chased the beetles away, patted the top of the hunter's head, and tenderly licked the stiffening flesh of Chan Chel's face. He talked to the stiffening meat regularly; about his plans to visit the village soon, how he wanted to get to know Pochotl better, and oh, yes…he talked of getting into the priest's head and into his throat. Maybe play a little slash and mash with the old man. He told Chan Chel of his deep desire to lick the underside of Pochotl's skin.

***

Pochotl pressure-flaked his knife to a new edge…a killing edge. Sweet thoughts of Ah Tok's flesh opening around that black, perilous edge played in his mind. There was still a long time until the sun would make an appearance. More than enough time. Pochotl mixed some of his own blood with green paint and created tracings of madness on his chest, face, and arms. Sweat-soaked, the priest went out under the cover of night to murder. He approached Ah Tok's house from several directions, going quietly, trying to see everything. It would be very unfortunate to be seen by someone who couldn't sleep and just happened to be looking out of a window or doorway.

The moon skirmished with thin clouds, fighting to spread its dull, yellow-white blanket over the darkness. Waiting for the clouds to win, he silently climbed through one of the windows in Ah Tok's house, rupturing a large spider's web. Eight legs scurried the pregnant female to a corner. With her black eyes glaring, she did rapid pushups to show her fury at the intruder. Venom dripped in small, clear drops from her mandibles, sliding down her stomach. No one else saw him, or so he assumed.

He had never been in the nobleman's house before, and so with a quiet, slinking, deliberate method hunted his quarry. He could hear the long, slow, peaceful intake of breath that marked someone sleeping. He went through the doorway into another dark room. With eyes accustomed to the night, Pochotl saw the sleeping form of Jada. One perfect thigh peeked spectacularly out from under a cotton wrap. He could see that she was on her back, arms out flung, dark hair spreading gloriously in all directions. The priest delicately lifted the loose-woven, cotton cover and anxiously pulled it slowly down. Jada sighed and changed positions ever so slightly. Pochotl froze, with the cover still only part way down. He waited a few moments, and then continued to pull the flimsy cotton wrap down, revealing Jada completely. Pochotl's heart and breath quickened. Jada was exquisite. He explored her with his eyes for long moments more, wishing he had more time. Gently replacing the cover, he promised himself that sometime in the near future, he would find the time to get to know her better. Much better.

Pochotl left the room on silent, bare feet. His toes sought another room. Ix Cuy and Ah Tok were here...he could see them both. They lay side by side, both on their backs. Pochotl noticed that their hands lightly intertwined. *How touching!* He sniffed the air and caught the scent of lust spent earlier that night. The priest went to the nobleman's head and stood behind him. He brought the thin, black obsidian blade to his tongue and licked it, nicking his tongue, then mutely prayed to Itzamna to guide his hand.

He positioned the thin blade near Ah Tok's right ear. Available light twinkled off the obsidian as it moved expertly in Pochotl's hand. The old man took a deep breath, held it, and shoved it hard through the ear canal and into the brain. With his other hand, he clamped the nobleman's mouth and pressed with his elbow on the chest to prevent any sound. There was no thrashing, only a slight jerk, the kind of a jerk everyone makes during the normal course of a dreaming sleep. Ix Cuy never moved. Blood ran black-rope-thick out of Ah Tok's head and coagulated in a dark pool that spread wide and dark under him.

Pochotl went to the wife. The blade no longer sparkled. It dripped black. Positioning himself now above Ix Cuy, he waited for a reaction. Nothing. He waited a while longer. Still nothing. Curiously aroused, Pochotl lifted the cover from the top half of her body just enough to see under. Bending to peek, the priest's face registered real disappointment. He replaced it quickly. Pochotl sincerely hoped she at least had a charming personality. The old man left the building.

***

Ix Cuy wet her lips. The night air had dried them. Her eyes fluttered open to a slit, looking for the light she thought would be there. *Yes, it is morning.* She could see the soft dappling of shadow play against the wall in her immediate line of sight.

Shards of a dark dream pierced their way into her consciousness. Ix Cuy closed her eyes again, trying to remember the nightmare. The details were sketchy, as dreams often were. Pure evil, in the guise of a man-shape, had stood over her, vile in its intent, threatening in its potential. There was a hint of familiarity. She felt she knew the identity of the blasphemous presence if she could just get a glimpse of the face. The more she struggled to remember, the more the images resisted her. Ix Cuy was sure she had tried to flee but was paralyzed by the evil's power, and could not move until it had finished with her. She squeezed her eyes tighter, trying to draw the memory out. The evil selected her and then passed her by, leaving behind the smell of death and corruption. Ix Cuy couldn't pull the pieces together. It was gone. Like wisps of incense smoke, the dream's details disappeared.

Reopening her eyes, Ix Cuy started to stretch and realized strands of her hair were caught, like they were stuck to the feather-filled, cotton bag. Not overly concerned, she tried to turn her head toward her husband. The hair ripped up and out of the brown-black crust that had settled under it. Her first reaction was a question. *What is this?* Her hand went to her head, pulling some of the obscene material from the matted ropes of her hair. Looking past the hair and down, Ix Cuy's second reaction, after seeing the large pooled stain, was one of disbelief. *Where did this come from?* Her third reaction was panic. It was obviously blood from Ah Tok, and that much blood could only mean one thing.

She began to keen. A high-pitched wail vibrated low in her throat and built slowly into a full bodied, mournful scream of terror. On her knees, she tried to shake her husband awake, hoping she was still dreaming. His cold, rigid body rolled slightly, but would not turn. Ah Tok's occluded eyes were half rolled back with only a sliver of the irises showing. The whites looked dry, with small, almost imperceptible wrinkles starting to show. Ix Cuy's scream tailed off for a breath. When it resumed, it changed to a low throated moan. Her husband was dead. He had been killed; she could see that from the wound. She had to have been less than two feet from him when it had happened. The realization chilled her. *Who? Who would do such a thing?*

***

Jada was the first to reach her mother. As soon as she entered the room, she knew the reason for the scream. Shocked, bewildered, and unable to understand why she was seeing what she was seeing, Jada added her voice to the din. The women held each other, one standing and the other still on her knees. "How? Why? Who?" They both were shouting at once, neither hearing the other. The immediate neighbors began to press into the room with the word of what had happened spreading backwards and out faster than people got there. Ix Cuy's eyes rolled back silver-rimmed in her head and she collapsed in Jada's arms.

Pochotl looked out from his vantage point, high on the walking ledge on the second floor of the Sun Temple. He fought the impulse to smile. Giggles were harder to control. He went back in. People would be here soon. He must be ready. The news would be terrible, and he needed to practice his reaction—know what he was going to say. Violent crime was almost unheard of in the experiences of the villagers. Small infractions, offenses, and greater violations were handled directly by the Halach Uinic. In the absence of a supreme ruler, the priest would certainly be called upon to couple with the Elder's Council and help direct any investigations. He eagerly anticipated looking for Ah Tok's killer.

As expected, it was only a short time before the news was brought to him. Ah Tok was dead. He was killed in his sleep, probably with a knife. Poor Tikal had mournfully supplied the information. Ahau, with his arm around his friend, had added the part about the knife. The two of them left, commiserating together. Pochotl properly gave an abject reaction. Aghast that something like that could happen here, he assured them both that all would be done to bring the culprit to justice. He personally promised it so. Again, as expected, that same morning the elders asked for him to meet with them. Ah Tok had been an important man and justice needed to happen quickly.

The council met in the dead man's room. Fourteen men and a dead body made the room very crowded. Ill at ease, the noblemen crowded over the body, looking at the wound. They could tell by the sliced flesh that it was apparently made by a knife, entering at a slight angle through the ear. The knife must have entered the brain and traveled in a path that allowed it to cut the brain stem. Death was probably instantaneous. The pool of blood had crusted into a dark brown mat under Ah Tok. Flies crawled everywhere. The smell of so much blood spilt hours before was an abominable stench.

The noblemen talked quietly among themselves, in reverence for the dead. They offered possible explanations and theories that ranged from an angry wife to a friend of the dead slave, Zac Kuk. Bela was even mentioned, but quickly dismissed. The wound was not his making. If Bela had been here last night, the wounds would have been much more extensive and probably not confined to just Ah Tok. Through it all, Pochotl stood quietly to the side, arms folded. Eventually they would ask him his opinion. It was better to wait until they had gone through their obtuse theories and were ready to listen to what he felt really had happened.

Ah Kaba was the first to ask. "Pochotl, we are fortunate that you are here with us. Ah Tok was a friend of mine. He was a friend to us all. That something like this could happen here is unthinkable. I can not remember in my lifetime something like this ever occurring. We owe it to Ah Tok's family and the village to find out who did this. Do you have any ideas? Can you make any sense of this at all?"

Pochotl shook his head solemnly. "This truly is a terrible thing. Ah Tok and I had our differences, but we were also very close friends. His son, Tikal, whom I've become very attached to, is my apprentice. I am exceedingly sorry that the village has lost such a great man. Ah Tok's leadership and wisdom will be sorely missed. His considerable contributions to our society are now even more valuable and will never be forgotten."

He paused for effect. All of the elders nodded their approval of Pochotl's words. Everything he said was true.

***

Tikal and Jada, listening through the thin walls, their ears pushed to the small mud and volcanic tuff filled cracks between the stones, also nodded. Both wished that they could see into the room. Tikal, as Ah Tok's only son, would inherit his vast wealth and by right, be a part of the Council of Elders. For now, though, he was only Pochotl's apprentice and a grieving son.

Council business was not to be interfered with, even when it dealt directly with something so personal. His mother was in the home of good friends who tried to comfort her. He thought he could hear her grieving even from this distance. His heart went out to her. He hugged his sister tighter.

***

143

Pochotl began again. "I think of Tikal as my own son. I am very proud of his accomplishments. Someday he will make a great priest. Early this morning, he came to me with the horrible news. I could barely believe it. It was very hard for the young man to speak. Losing one's father in such a way is difficult to deal with. After he left, I became worried about his state of mind, and tried to find him. I thought he might be with my other apprentice, Ahau. They are good friends. I went to the communal hut where both of them sleep. No one there had seen them. I decided to wait at their mats on the chance that they would show up. I don't want to jump to any conclusions, but I found this."

An obsidian blade, about the length of a hand, rested in his palm. Thick as a thumb where it connected to the handle, the blade thinned and drew to a point. The elders all began to talk at once.

Pochotl continued. "I made two of these, one each for my apprentices. The twin blades were to be used in special ceremonial functions. I can tell by the ornate wrappings that this one belongs to Tikal. It has never been used. You can tell by close inspection of the blade and the absence of any stains on the leather binding. From the look of Ah Tok's wound, it would have been made by a long, thin blade such as this."

The elders were listening closely to Pochotl's words, trying to understand where he was going with his story. They could see the blade was new and in perfect condition. The priest pulled another blade from his pouch. This one was loosely sheathed in a palm leaf, identical in shape to the first. Pochotl unwrapped it and held it out for all of them to see. Bits of dried flesh and blood crusted almost its entire length.

"This blade is Ahau's. I recognize it by the blue bands at the bottom. As you can see, the two blades are a matched set. They were both made from the same large piece of obsidian. The only difference in the two is that Tikal's has red bands at the heel of his handle." He laid them side by side. "This one," he indicated the blue banded blade by hefting it into the air, "I found under Ahau's mat just as it is."

The council members all started talking at once. Pochotl made a small, thick noise in his throat and held up his hand to get their silence. Brother and sister could not believe what they were hearing.

144

Tikal crept to the door and sneaked an eye around the corner.

"I do not want to make hasty judgments. This may not even be the blade that killed Ah Tok. It is difficult to tell such things. I can, however, say for certain that Ah Tok did not want Jada in Ahau's company. The young man did not have the character, wealth, or position that he wanted for his daughter. Ah Tok spoke to me at long lengths about the matter. As a good friend, he asked if I would be interested in an arranged marriage with his daughter at the proper time. I was shocked at first, but Ah Tok sought only the best for Jada. He valued my many services to the village and knew that I would treat Jada with the same respect I have for all of you. I did not want to fault Ah Tok's logic and said that in time, young Jada would make a fine wife. A few days ago, Ahau, not knowing of Ah Tok's plans, came to me asking for advice. My apprentice was in considerable anguish over his love for Jada and her father's resulting anger." Pochotl shook his head sadly. "I, of course, told him that Ah Tok's wishes were to be respected. I did not tell young Ahau about Ah Tok's proposition. That was between him and me alone." Pochotl hesitated for effect.

"You need to understand that young Ahau is basically a good person. I think of him as I would my own son and only want the best for him. I told him that in the years to come, he would become a priest and then perhaps Ah Tok might change his mind. But Ahau is impatient, as young men often are. I hope... no, I pray that he has not done something drastic. His judgment might have been clouded by his thirst for Jada. I can only say that I did my best to guide him in the right direction. He might be able to explain why this bloody knife was under his mat. We owe him the chance. If you think there may be something to this, then I suggest we find him and bring him here." Pochotl looked grim as he laid the knife on Ah Tok's silent chest. Inwardly, he gloated. He had planned well. *The elders know about Jada and Ahau. The whole village does. They will accept the explanation of why young Ahau might murder Jada's father. Lust is a believable motive for a whole host of sins.*

***

Tikal was dizzy with disbelief. Jada, wide-eyed and heart pounding, had also heard the wild story Pochotl had related. Tikal let out his breath in a slow *whuff*. They knew that Ahau was being set up

145

to take the blame for their father's death. Together, they fled from the house in search of Ahau before the elders could send their runners. On their third stop, they found him in Pochotl's old hut, scraping on his bow.

Jada threw herself in his arms and tearfully told him of the preposterous story. Ahau's first reaction was anger. He wanted to immediately go in front of the elders and deny it all, tell them of his love for Jada and how he could never cause her such grief. He had never spoken to Pochotl or asked advice about Jada and her father's displeasure. Arguing vehemently against it, Tikal and Jada finally convinced Ahau that the trap Pochotl had laid was too well conceived. His best chance for survival would be to run and hide in the forest. Guilty or not, once the council had Ahau in their clutches, they would look no further. In all probability, he would be executed within hours. Long before the truth could be discovered, Ahau would be dead. Tikal assured his friend that he would find a way to twist Pochotl's words into the truth. He was now convinced that the old man had killed his father. Why else would Pochotl have a bloodied knife and say such crazy things about his father and Jada? He certainly had not found the knife under Ahau's mat.

Ahau gathered up his bow, arrows, spear, a few other meager supplies and left by the window closest to the forest. Tikal and Jada could bring him food and other things later. Right now, his main concern was to get away fast and unnoticed. He dropped to the ground and ran low into a thick stand of conifers. Without a look back, Ahau headed toward the secret place only he and Jada knew about. No one saw him leave.

Brother and sister walked back to their home hand in hand, back to where their dead father lay in a mat of dry blood, filling with corrupt gases in the gathering heat. Back to where Ah Tok's unseeing eyes dried and withered, the corners becoming receptacles for pregnant flies that left their small, white eggs by the hundreds; back to the misery of a life gone terribly wrong. Back to an existence that had lost all innocence.

Along the way, four men stopped them and asked if they had seen Ahau. They were carrying spears, and were not of good temper. Jada and Tikal did their best to steer the hunters in different

146

directions. Tikal said that he had not seen Ahau since early that morning, and that he was probably at the communal hut or hunting tonight's meal. He indicated a direction opposite of where his friend had entered the forest. The men left with a determined trot to where he had pointed. Tikal and Jada went home to their mother. That was what would be expected.

***

The rains began again. Like tears slowly leaking from a remorseful sky, the drops fell warm and slow, trickling through their hair and sliding down their faces to soak the already saturated ground below.

Pochotl sat down on a corner of the bed, careful to avoid the sticky brown areas of blood long dried. In places the puddles were thick, with black skins thinly veiling the redness below them. Flies congregated thickest in these spots. The priest shooed them away absently while thinking about Ahau. Over an hour had passed since the council had first sent out runners to bring the young man back. It was Pochotl's guess that his apprentice was long gone. Unfortunate. On one hand, Ahau's running obviously gave the appearance of guilt. On the other hand, justice would have to wait. It would be better if the whole thing ended quickly while the council was all of one mind.

The small, crowded room was stifling. Ah Tok was starting to heat up and the smell was cloying. Ah Kaba advised that they wait outside until Ahau was brought before them. One of the other council members suggested they adjourn completely. They all had important business elsewhere. Pochotl could summon them when Ahau was found. In agreement, they left Ah Tok's house.

***

Leaving, the men met Ix Cuy, Jada, and Tikal coming in. One by one they expressed their deepest sympathies, assuring them that Ahau would be brought to justice. Still in tears, Ix Cuy could only nod. At the moment, she just wanted to be alone with her family. She was glad the men were leaving.

Ah Tok was buried in a private ceremony by the family later that same day. Ix Cuy cleaned, groomed, and dressed her husband in his finest clothes. A few of his closest friends were asked by the family to be present as they lowered him into the earth. Pochotl was

147

conspicuously absent. As was the people's custom, Ah Tok was interred beneath the floor of his house. Maize balls, weapons, and jade were reverently placed around him for his journey through the underworld. Because Ah Tok's new house was stone floored but uncompleted, they chose a spot outside the house which would later be built over as additions to the main building were added.

Following the burial, Jada and Tikal asked Ix Cuy to come with them to a secluded spot where they could speak privately. They needed to get away from the house and the village for a while. The painful image of Ah Tok lying forever dead under their feet was too vivid. Only time would be able to lance the emotional boil the family shouldered.

They found a peaceful, cleared area near the forest where they could be alone. No one would interfere with them out of respect for their grief.

Tikal went first. He held Ix Cuy's small hand and peered into her eyes at close range. "Mother, by now you have heard all of the stories concerning Ahau and Father. None of them are true. Ahau loves Jada and would never do anything to hurt her or the family. That he could kill Father is unthinkable. It is true that Pochotl made those blades as a gift for us, but we never used them. We never had a chance. We've only had them for three days. Pochotl forbade us to use them for anything except ritualistic cutting. They were that special. Mother, I do not know how the blood came to be on Ahau's knife. I do not even know if it is Father's blood. I just know that Ahau did not do it. It is true that Father did not want Jada to become involved with Ahau, but that was only because he didn't really know him as I do."

Jada took over. "I love Ahau, Mother. He and I plan to be united when the time is right. I would never allow Father to arrange a marriage. I don't really think he ever spoke to Pochotl. It just doesn't sound straight. Can you imagine me married to that disgusting old man? Even if he is a priest, I would refuse. Ahau and I were ready to leave the village together if Father did not change his mind, but Ahau would never kill him. It's impossible! Ahau is not like that. He couldn't have!" Jada ended in tears.

"Children, I know in my heart that what you say is true. Young Ahau is an honorable man. Your father and I spoke of Jada's future many times. He was against you marrying Ahau only because he wanted you to marry into a house of wealth. Every father wants the best for his children. Your father was no different. I have always been on your side, Jada. I like Ahau and think he truly loves you. He would treat you well. I do not believe that he killed Ah Tok. What I do find suspicious is Pochotl so conveniently finding the knife. He and Ah Tok were not the good friends he wants people to believe. Something is definitely wrong here. The question is what to do about it. I suspect both of you know where Ahau is right now." She searched their eyes and saw that she was right.

"Wherever he is, don't tell me. Tell no one. If the council or Pochotl get their hands on him, he is dead. They would execute him for sure. We must have time to expose the truth. Like you, I suspect Pochotl is behind everything evil that has happened. I'm not sure why, but I feel it is so. This morning, just before I discovered your father dead, I was trying to remember a dream... a nightmare, really. I almost had it before it got away. I think whoever killed Ah Tok was in the dream. I will keep trying to remember. Perhaps it will come to me. Right now, we have to get Ahau help. Tonight, when all are asleep, Jada, you will take him food and let him know of our thoughts. Tikal, you will go with her. Take care that no one sees you leave."

Both Jada and Tikal hugged their mother and thanked her for being who she was. It was enough. They talked of their father and made a few tentative plans for the future. Tikal would have to move back into the house and assume the mantle of a nobleman. All that was Ah Tok's was now his. He must also assert himself on the council. Even if he was the youngest member of the committee, he was also now the wealthiest.

***

Ahau, flat against the ground, peeked out between the branches of the unusual tree he and Jada had found weeks ago. Numerous branches bent low, heavy with leaves, brushing the dirt. Concealment was complete. What made the tree special was the area under the branches. Smooth bark, barren of any branches for almost a body length up, allowed a person to stand comfortably under and behind great boughs of leaves. They had brushed all of the debris away and carved away a few errant twigs to make the area under the leafy umbrella comfortable. The tree sat up into the forest on a gentle slope that allowed Ahau to see anyone advancing from all directions. The forest was thick around him, so approaching the tree easily was only possible from two paths. He was intently watching both now.

Night had descended long ago. He knew Jada and Tikal would be coming soon. He had a hundred questions. Ah Tok's death was heinous enough; to be accused of it was a cruelty of undeserved fate. Ahau had not heard the entire story yet. His friends had told him just enough to convince him to run. Several times during the last few hours, he had been tempted to call to the warriors who hunted him. They had come close enough to see and hear him if he were to stand and step into view. He desperately wanted to confront those who accused him. His belief in his friends prevented him. If they thought running was the best course of action for now, then so be it. He stayed in his hidey-hole and waited.

Rain, for the most part, was shed before it reached the prone Ahau, but there were always a few holes that prevented him from being completely dry. He wanted to start a fire under the tree. He thought the heavy branches would filter the smoke enough that no would see. Now that it was dark, though, he thought the light might inadvertently give him away, so he suffered the damp and the chilled earth stoically.

***

"Ahau, Ahau. Are you there?" The soft voices came closer.

Ahau answered back. "Here, I'm here!"

Jada and Tikal, arms loaded with supplies, came quickly under the tree. In the dark, they could barely see one another. After some discussion, Tikal suggested they chance a small fire. Ahau scouted the perimeter to see if it was visible from different angles. It appeared safe. The light from the small fire could not be seen from outside of the tree. The branches and their bodies prevented the light from escaping.

Tikal and Jada noticed as Ahau hunkered over the small flames on his haunches, wolfing down the maize cakes and jerky, how haggard he looked. His hair stood out stiffly at different angles, with small twigs and pieces of leaves stuck tight in the oily strands. Dirt was ground into the creases of his palms, elbows, and neck. The

150

circles under his eyes made his pupils seem to recede. The small catch lights from the fire gave him a haunted look. He looked every bit the ragged fugitive that he was.

Jada went to him. She put her arm around his shoulders and pulled him toward her so that they leaned against each other, side by side. She picked the rubbish out of his hair and tried to smooth the errant tufts back into place.

Ahau listened while he ate, sipping from the water gourd. Tikal told him everything that had happened, including his suspicions. They talked until almost morning, looking at the situation from all angles, trying to make a plan that would put everything right. If Pochotl had done this horrible thing, if he had purposely placed the blame on Ahau, then perhaps they could turn the council's attention back to the priest. If evidence could not be found, maybe it could be manufactured. Tikal thought he had an idea. He knew of someone who might listen; someone of importance. Someone who was close to the family. In the meantime, it was not safe here. It was too close to the village to escape detection for much longer. Ahau would have to find a new place to hide...somewhere they could meet when necessary. Tikal left first, giving his sister and friend a chance to be alone. After what seemed a long time, he called to her.

"Jada, come on. Morning is coming. We have to go. We do not want anyone to see us coming back from this direction. Jada. Jada. Now!"

It was hard for the two to part. Ahau whispered his love and gently pushed her away. Jada, reluctant to leave, promised to see him in two days. She and Tikal left silently. Soon after they left, Ahau gathered up his supplies and weapons and abandoned his hide.

Chapter 13

Winds of Lust

Pochotl watched the morning arrive from his vantage point on the walking ledge. The sun was mostly obscured by dark clouds not ready to leave the area quite yet. The priest guessed that the rains would last at least another ten days. It was hard to tell. Chac, the rain god, was hard to predict. His wet blessings could fall for another thirty days if he thought it was necessary. Pochotl hoped that was not so. He, too, was tired of the rain. Pools of water were starting to appear too near the maize. That could prove to be disastrous. The welfare of the people depended upon the grain, not only as sustenance but also as a trading commodity. The many fields sparkled red and gold as the sun chose that moment to flit its light through a sliver in the gray sky.

Pochotl waxed compassionately as he watched the village awake. People were starting to leave their houses. His people, as he now thought of them, were a worthy race. They had created much out of the forest and would do even more under his guidance. The temples his people would produce would rival anything in Kohunlich.

Pochotl's gaze reached out toward the heavy foliage on his left. The sun, winning a wide path through the clouds, brilliantly illuminated the facing bark of the trees for several steps into the forest. Movement. The priest thought deer might be moving through the edges of the light, skirting the darkness of the forest the low sun could not reach. He watched intently, hoping to see the animals.

Tikal skulked out of the forest, paused, and then signaled for Jada to hurry up. Catching up to her brother, Jada grabbed his hand and they quickly covered the remaining distance to their home. Pochotl

153

was incensed. It was not hard to come up with a scenario as to why the two of them would be coming from the woods at this time of the morning. *They know where Ahau is. They have been with him and are just now returning.* It rankled the priest that the two of them obviously did not believe his explanation of Ah Tok's death. Jada he could almost understand. But Tikal was his apprentice. Tikal owed him much. Suddenly, Pochotl realized that he no longer could trust the young man and would have to be very wary of what he said and did around him. Tikal was the key to finding Ahau, a key he could twist and turn to his own designs. Pochotl went back inside and down the steps to his domicile.

Seeing Jada had given the old man licentious thoughts. Pochotl schemed, coveting her flesh. This was a good time of the year for the priest; a very good time. At the end of the rainy season, a sacrifice would be made to Chac and Itzamna for sanctifying the earth with life-giving water from the skies. A young, unmarried, chaste maiden would be chosen. She would be bound at the feet and hands and pulled over a round stone alter, bowing her back down and her chest up. The priest would deliver a swift, killing blow to the head with a tukal, and then rapidly slice the sometimes still beating heart out of the chest cavity. The young woman's heart would be cut into chunks and added to copal resin. Fired, the resin would burn hot enough to immolate the pieces of the heart and send skyward on wisps of fetid, black smoke…the people's sacrifice and appreciation for the god's gifts of life. Who was chosen was Pochotl's decision. Already this month he had saved four young maidens from such a fate by altering their vestal virtues. Late at night, at his suggestion, they would come to him, offering their bodies to his sanctification. When they left, they were no longer on his long list of virgin, young women to choose from for the sacrifice. He thought it was extremely considerate and generous on his part to offer such a service. *Perhaps young Jada could be persuaded to earn her name off the list. She might even be induced to marry me once she has tasted my many exceptional talents.*

***

Tikal quickly washed, changed his breechcloth, and went to the priest. Pochotl would be expecting him. There was no time for breakfast. He was close to being late as it was. Entering the door at the Sun Temple, he called out.

"Pochotl, my Ah Kin, I am here."

Tikal's eyes had not yet adjusted to the gloom inside the dwelling. It was hard to see if the priest was there. He stepped further in and again called out. Out of the darkness came Pochotl's voice.

"Ah, Tikal, you are unexpected. I thought you would be with your family today. Your father's death was such a tragedy. If you would rather stay with your mother and Jada today, I will understand. They may need you."

Tikal voiced his answer in the direction from which Pochotl had spoken. "I thank you for your concern. It is very kind of you to make such an offer, but I think being with you might help alleviate some of the terrible pain. Forgive me for saying this, but I often think of you as a second father." Tikal was glad the room was dark. If Pochotl could see his face, it would reveal that he was lying.

"Why Tikal, how nice of you to think so. I am also very fond of you. It is a shame Ahau's lust for your sister caused so much pain. I don't suppose you have seen him, have you?"

Tikal ignored the question and asked instead, "Pochotl, do you really think it is possible that Ahau did this terrible thing? I have seen the bloody knife, and it is his. I just can't understand my friend doing such a thing. Is there any other proof? Did anyone see Ahau enter or leave my father's home?"

Pochotl smiled grimly. "Son...you don't mind my calling you that, do you? I, too, am confused by Ahau's actions, but have seen what lust can do. Jada is a beautiful woman. Many men have been seduced into doing things they ordinarily would not for the sake of beautiful flesh. Ah Tok was right in his decision not to allow his daughter to marry beneath her status. I was reluctant to enter matrimony with your sister because of the age difference. Now, however, I would take Jada as my wife, making your father's fervent wishes come true and to protect her from Ahau. I owe it to Ah Tok.

"I ask again. Have you seen Ahau this day? We must find him. We will give him the opportunity to defend himself by answering our questions. The longer he stays in hiding, the guiltier he appears. I want to help the young man." Pochotl's voice turned sickeningly sweet with compassion. "Ahau has no family except for you and me. Together, we can help find the truth. If he really did this, maybe we

155

can find a way to satisfy justice besides execution. I might have the power to convince the council to exile him instead. If he is innocent, then perhaps we can help prove it. In either case, we must act together and find him. You can trust me, Tikal. If you know where he is, take me to him."

Tikal was not fooled. "I am thankful for your help, my Ah Kin. I knew I could depend on you. Jada and I have looked for Ahau but he is nowhere to be found. We think he may have left this area of the forest permanently. Jada is heartbroken. She believes Ahau is guiltless and he is hiding out of fear for his life. She is afraid that she may never see him again."

The old man was close enough now to read Tikal's face. Tikal struggled to keep his expressions neutral. Pochotl placed his arm around the young man in a fatherly gesture. Tikal could smell the heady aroma of unwashed sweat, copal resin, and a dozen other cloying smells whose sources he could only guess.

"We will find him, Tikal. Everything will work out, you will see. For now, maybe work is the best thing. Come sit by the fire. We will talk of other things."

Apprehensively, Tikal sat where the old man indicated with the fire in front of them. Pochotl offered a piece of jerky. They sat in silence, chewing the tough meat, each thinking personal thoughts.

The priest spoke first. "Very soon we will have the end of the rain ceremony." He chewed around the finish of the sentence. "We must properly satisfy Chac so that he will not withhold his gifts of life next year. According to our sacred calendar, the rains will end soon. We will have it then."

The old priest looked straight ahead as if in thought, still chewing the tough meat. His head began to nod like he had just made a decision. With a very neutral, measured voice, he said, "Tikal, I have been watching you carefully for many days now. You have progressed well. As the village grows, so do the many duties of the priesthood. It is time I share some of the responsibilities. I am going to make you a nacom."

Tikal visibly blanched. A nacom was an honored position within the priesthood. It was only they who were allowed to cut open the chests of the sacrificial victims and jerk out the beating hearts.

156

Pochotl was gratified to see Tikal's face pale. "As nacom, you must be prepared. The skills necessary for the office must be practiced. To kill with just one blow is not as easy as you might imagine. Then, as quickly as possible, tear the heart out while it still beats. We will prepare your skills on animals until you feel comfortable. The young woman we sacrifice must be shown our greatest respect for her offerings. It would never do to have you butcher the task by lack of rehearsal. We will start this morning."

All that morning, the priest and Tikal hunted and trapped the forest. They made many snares and dug camouflaged pits on trails where tracks of animals were found. It was long, hard work. By the end of the day, they had collected two fawns, an armadillo, and three small pigs. Just tying the live animals onto poles and transporting them back to the village was exhausting work.

That night, in the sanctity of the temple, Tikal learned to bless the animals whose lives he took. Before he delivered a killing blow to each animal, he repeated the sacred words of thanks for the life he was taking. The people atoned for all death, including the killing of an animal for meat. They shed their own blood and mixed it with the animal's blood on the forest floor as a token of reverence. At Pochotl's insistence, Tikal pierced his own tongue over each of the animals as he killed it, and reverently added his blood to theirs. The priest explained that the suffering Tikal experienced showed proper homage to a forest spirit killed for the sake of ceremony. One at a time, each animal was bludgeoned with a tukal and their chests parted by the sharp edges of Tikal's ceremonial knife. Each time, Tikal would puncture his tongue with a pine needle and draw it through to the other side. He was so very glad that Pochotl had decided to elevate his status.

He was also elated they had not caught more than they had. His tongue hurt so bad when he left he could only utter thickly as a parting farewell, "Tit was a goot ay. Ou taut me a lot. Ank ou Poctul... I ill see ou in the orning."

***

Ix Cuy and Jada met him in the doorway of their home. They had heard of his promotion earlier, not sure what to think about it. It was very early in Tikal's training for him to advance so quickly. Pochotl was not to be trusted and must have ulterior motives. They were sure that if Tikal's position was being raised within the priesthood, then somehow it benefited the old man.

They administered herbs and remorse in equal quantities. Tikal was wretched. His terribly swollen tongue needed moisture to help the salt and herbs to work.

Jada carried the family's ceramic jug to the community well. Pochotl was there ahead of her, filling a ceramic jug and stoppering it with leather as she walked up. She tried to politely ignore him. She waited to the side until he was done before she dipped into the well, hoping he would leave. Instead, he walked to her side of the cistern and wrapped a helping arm across her shoulders.

He tried charm. "Jada, you are as beautiful as the moon's light tonight."

She murmured a weak thanks and went on about her business. Still oozing charm, the priest moved in closer. He set his jug down and tried to help Jada with hers.

"Here, let me help you with that." He took the jug from her reluctant fingers. "I suppose you have heard about Tikal. You and your mother must be very proud of him. It isn't often that the priesthood is blessed with someone as dedicated as he is to the service of our people. He will make a fine nacom. His first ceremony will be the Ah Chac Colomche, in about four weeks, which brings me to a delicate but important subject."

Pochotl leaned in over Jada's back, arms still around her, posing as help with her water. In a soft, thick voice he said, "Jada, you know that for the first time, your name is on the list of those from which to choose. I am forced by our law to blindly reach into a container full of ceramic rods with the names of young, virgin, unmarried women. The person whose rod is picked will be sacrificed as thanks to Chac and Itzamna for their blessings. I do not want to pick yours. It would be a terrible thing for your mother to have her daughter taken from her so close to the death of her husband. Imagine what it would be like for your poor brother, to have to open such a beautiful chest and pull out the still beating heart of his own sister." He gently massaged the area over her heart to make his point.

Jada stiffened. She was deeply afraid now, recognizing the thinly veiled threat. She knew Pochotl had the power to do as he'd said. With closed eyes she tried to keep her voice from trembling and said, "Go on."

Brazenly, the priest continued. "Listen. Your father was a good friend of mine. I will cherish his memory. His leadership will be sorely missed. You may not know this, but it was his ardent wish that someday you and I would be married. Of that, we can talk later. The immediate future is more important. It is a sensitive question I must ask you now. Are you still a virgin?"

Jada hesitated before answering. She had to answer either yes or no, and she knew where he was going with his questioning. She had heard all of the stories from her friends. It was true that she and Ahau had been innocently chaste in their love for each other, but she balked at telling the priest. On the other hand, to admit not being a virgin and unmarried was against the tribe's law, and punishable by deep tattooing of her face for all to see for the rest of her life.

Her voice quavered. "Yes, I know I am on the list. I would be honored to serve my people. If I am chosen, then I will fulfill what is asked of me. My blood is the village's blood. I thank you for your concern. Now, I must be getting back. My mother and brother are waiting." She forcefully pulled the jug from his hands and walked out from under his heavy arms.

***

Pochotl watched her leave. Lust swelled in his loins. He would have to try a different approach. Next time he asked, she would say yes. He had in his possession certain drugs that would wave away her inhibitions. *Yes...next time I ask, she will literally bend over trying to please me.*

***

Bela had enjoyed the rains at first but, like the brownskins, was tiring of them. For weeks, the sky literally seemed to burst like a broken bladder. The rains would stop for brief periods of time, but never long enough to forget that the clouds that jostled, shoved, and extorted each other above would eventually moil collectively and pass their water to the earth below. Bela knew nothing about Chac, the god of moisture. Chan Chel had tried to explain to him the importance of the thirteen upper world gods and the nine underworld gods, but it was still confused in Bela's brain. He did not understand why the brownskins needed gods. The forest was as it was. There were no secret entities hiding behind the trees or underneath the rocks. The animals were just animals. Things happened in, above, and around the forest of their own accord. The brownskins were strange beings.

He still missed Chan Chel, and talked to him frequently, wishing the hunter could answer his questions. Bela stood in front of the decaying remains stuffed upright and tight into the rock crevice. Chan Chel's mouth was missing most of the lips. Beetles crawled out of the beast's way as he playfully pulled at what was left of the hunter's tongue. He waggled it up and down, trying to mimic Chan Chel's voice. "Bail-la, yooou giveee meee baaack my speeer. Why yooou killl meee? Meee tell Pochooootl!"

He deep growled a giggly sound. The great beast realized how foolish his actions were, but was bored and did it anyway. He thought it was about time to visit the brownskins again and pay his respects, to the priest in particular. There were many questions to ask the old man. From Chan Chel's earlier description, he shouldn't be hard to find.

The luminescent, orange fungi Bela had so long ago found near his cave's opening came unbidden to his mind. Suddenly he wanted, needed, to taste its bitter-sweet softness. It had been several days since he had last scraped its velvety flesh from the wall. He shaved soft fungi on to several of his claws and brought the orange mold to his lips, savoring the experience. His eyes rolled back and blood rushed hot in his ears, bringing him once again the feeling of euphoria he so craved. All was right with his world.

***

Pochotl met with Jada's brother again the next day, and once more they practiced the arts of the nacom. The old priest was inventive, if nothing else. For the sake of diversity, Tikal was ordered to pierce his cheeks using stingray barbs from one side through to the other as he killed each animal. Four rabbits and a squirrel were sent to their final resting places. The priest thought perhaps it was time to ask again.

"Tikal, we are still looking for Ahau. I don't suppose you have had any news about his whereabouts, have you? I thought that the

160

two of us could take a break from practicing nacom skills and find him. I still think I can help him through this disturbing ordeal. What do you say? Are you ready to take a break and help me find your friend?" Pochotl oozed sincerity.

Tikal wiped the blood from his chin and answered respectfully. "My Ah Kin, I would very much like to see Ahau. I know you want to help him, but I really have no idea where to find him."

"I see. Well, we have hunters looking for him, so I suppose our four eyes would not help much. We had better keep practicing. I had the hunters this morning bring us some larger animals. Tied in the yard out back are four wild pigs. I'll have them brought in. You know, your cheeks are looking rather sore. I loathe seeing you in pain. Let's start using the skin on your inner upper arms. I would hate for your mouth to become inflamed. That would never do."

They practiced through the day. Tikal was becoming quite good at it. He just hoped his body held up. He would like to tell the priest he was ill and needed to stay home for a few days, but knew that Pochotl, with benevolent compassion, would just try to heal him. The cure in all probability would be worse than the stinging pain he now suffered. He would just have to endure until the old man thought he had sufficiently learned the lesson.

That night, Tikal went to Ah Kaba. The nobleman had always been a friend to his family. Tikal had thought long and hard about what to do about Pochotl's accusations. He desperately wanted to help Ahau. It would be best if he could find some physical evidence that Pochotl had killed his father, but that had never been found. The wily old priest was too clever. Ah Kaba might listen, though. It was worth a try.

Tikal and the nobleman sat comfortably in Ah Kaba's house. The older man put his feet up against one of the walls and smoked his crusty, old ceramic pipe above folded arms. Every once in a while, he pulled on the stem with his lips and asked a question around it, testing Tikal's logic. When the young man had finished, Ah Kaba seemed impressed.

"Tikal, if what you say is true, then we have done a great injustice to Ahau. Still, it would be best to hear what your friend has to say. There are questions we need to ask. I realize that Pochotl is a man driven by dreams of power. That is one of the reasons we are all here. Remember, it was Pochotl who first suggested to our families to leave Kohunlich. His arguments of finding better, more comfortable lives for us and our children were very persuasive. Look around you, Tikal; we have accomplished much in these few months. Pochotl is at the center of all of that. If what you say is true, if your suspicions are confirmed, well, then we have a serious problem. A priest's words are inviolate. We must have faith in our religious leaders if we are to survive. To openly accuse Pochotl of this crime would tear our community apart. This is what I suggest…if you know where Ahau is and can get word to him, I will meet privately with him. I will bring no one. I give you my word that I will listen to all he has to say. If he convinces me that he is innocent, then he can come into the village under my protection and meet with the council. They will have their own questions. Pochotl will be there. You, too, will be there. As Ah Tok's son, you inherit his place on the council, though I advise you to stay silent until asked to speak. You must appear to be objective. The council will listen more kindly if your words are unprejudiced. Everyone knows how close you are to Ahau. The welfare of the people must seem to be your overriding concern."

Tikal was exhilarated. This was what he had been hoping for. If he could get the council on Ahau's side, then maybe the true killer could be ferreted out.

"Ah Kaba, I respect your wisdom. It was generous of you to listen to me. I will do as you say. I will get a message to Ahau and ask him to meet with you. As soon as I know when and where, I will tell you. I have taken enough of your time. I should be getting home."

***

Ah Kaba waited until he was sure Tikal had enough time to get home. Surreptitiously, he left his abode and went directly to the Sun Temple. He found Pochotl still awake. Behind stone walls they talked in whispers of vile perversions.

"It is as you thought. Tikal came to me tonight, asking for advice. I think you may have a real problem. The pitiful young man is very convincing. I thought he was going to cry right in front of me. Pathetic as his pleas are, if the little monkey slime is allowed to speak before the council, they may believe him. What he says makes sense. He speaks from the heart. Ahau's version might even be more damaging. Fortunately, I am to meet with him soon. I don't yet know where or when, but Tikal is arranging it," said Ah Kaba.

The priest was fitting a new jade ring to his big toe while he listened to the nobleman's report. A pile of dark mushrooms sat sinisterly beside him.

"You have done well, Ah Kaba. I thought he might come to you. He trusts you. Everyone trusts you. I guess they don't know you like I do."

Pochotl looked up at the nobleman with an expression that was hard to read. The tight smile that puckered the priest's lips was too small for his mouth. Ah Kaba couldn't tell if he was kidding him or not. He tried a brief chuckle, but it came out thin, fake, and nervous sounding. He cut it off immediately, cleared his throat, and tried to force a little dignity into his face.

***

Ignoring Ah Kaba's gargly voice, Pochotl locked eyes with the nobleman.

"This can work well for us both. As soon as you know when and where, let me know. We will organize a special reception. If Tikal is as persuasive as you think, then both young men may have to suffer an ill-fated accident. A pity, Ahau is just so much snot to be wiped on the tree of our choosing, but Tikal...well, that's a whole different story. His status requires a very special accident; one that no one will question. I will have to think longer about this."

To himself, he thought about Tikal's newly acquired wealth. *If the young man should suddenly die, by accident of course, then Jada would inherit. Her husband would have it all.*

Pochotl noisily ate of the mushrooms and offered one of the smaller black ones to Ah Kaba. The nobleman took it but feigned putting it into his mouth. Maybe Pochotl could eat them with immunity, but people had died eating these kinds of mushrooms.

The old priest dusted his hands together and said around and through the chunks of fleshy fungi, "Once this is all behind us, we can start convincing the people that I am the obvious choice for Halach Uinic. The prophecy of Ah Kin Mai will come to pass! Having you at my side as Batabob, head of the council and commander of our

163

warriors, makes me very pleased. I need someone like you to help share the many responsibilities leadership requires."

Pochotl dismissed the nobleman with a backward wave of his hand. "Go! Come to me when you have more information. Until then, speak of this to no one."

***

Deep in the forest a figure huddled within the enclosed embrace of three massive trees, whose trunks grew close enough to form a natural enclave. Ahau had stumbled across the extraordinary spot earlier in the day, quite by accident. Within an hour, he had dragged enough dead wood around the openings to make the sanctuary complete. At a glance, the area looked natural and gave no indication of the concealment within. Ahau thought that even with closer inspection, it was difficult to discern the large opening between the trees.

He'd nestled in long ago for the night, wishing he could chance a fire. He was wet, and cold to the bone. Under the protection of several leafy umbrellas torn from the forest, he slept nervously, slapping at the mosquitoes. The young man jerked in reflex to every cry, shriek, or snarly bark that came from the darkness around him. Even though he had spent all of his life in the forest, he had never been quite as alone as he was now. Ahau realized how much he had depended upon others for the security he had always felt. He had taken that sense of confident safety for granted. Logically, he could identify each and every one of the animals responsible for the menacing racket. But now, alone and hunted, the priest's apprentice heard every sound as threatening. Emotionally, they all seemed directed at him. His mind was irrationally rubbed by the fear of being alone and unprotected. In fragile sleep, dark dreams swirled their perilous threads through his subconscious. They created images of dangerous beasts with every new sound the forest offered up. In thin slumber he ran from moon-shadows, first left, then right, now turning, twisting, turning, seeing threats in all directions. He began to whimper in hitches, stabbing his dream-spear at the vigilant, glowing eyes that queried him from the darkness. The moon-shadows inquired of him his name and why he was afraid. Ahau tried to answer in challenge, but instead shrieked like a little boy, "I'm alone. I'm alone. Itzamna help me, I'm so alone."

164

Ahau aggressively shook himself awake, hitting his head on the back of one of the trees. He sat up, ashamed and angry. It was still a long time until dawn. He decided that anyone hunting him this far out into the forest was probably sleeping by now, so he built a small fire and sat rubbing his hands over it, thinking about Jada. She was never far from his thoughts. Tomorrow, at midday, Tikal would meet him halfway between where he was now and the special tree he and Jada had shared what seemed like a lifetime ago. At their last meeting, Tikal had pointed at a large swell in the forest with a runty, bald knoll running across the top of it. They would meet there. Ahau knew there was no use in trying to sleep again tonight. His overactive mind would not let him. He sat back comfortably against one of the trees, loosely gripping the spear across his lap, mesmerized by the night sounds of predators and the raw cries of their victims. In his mind, he tried to recreate the scenarios he was hearing. It was morning when he opened his eyes again.

He sputtered awake, astonished that he had slept. The fire had died out long ago and felt cool to the touch. He felt drier, more rested, and for the first time in a long time, more confident. He stood up, stretched, and massaged his growling stomach. It was time to eat.

The young man picked up his bow where it had slid down the side of a tree and swiped at the wet leaves that had stuck to its surface. Ahau rubbed the smooth length with his hands, drying it. He had wrapped a thin piece of leather around the handle and painted private designs below and above it in streaks of black. Near the fletching, his arrows were decorated with the same black swirls, riding high up against the long, snubbed hawk feathers. He had made a quiver from a tanned weasel skin turned inside out to dry and shaped by shoving into it a blunt, round length of wood. His ingenious use of small, spear-shaped tips of obsidian made the arrows particularly lethal. The weasel fur on the inside of his quiver kept the tips from noisily clinking together when he moved. The rattling clank of one's weapons never helped when hunting in the forest.

He slipped the handled quiver over one shoulder, resting it within easy reach over his back. Earlier in the night, he was sure that he had heard small deer tearing at the shrubs not far from where he was. He looked for tracks.

Ahau's tracking skills were incredibly reliable. He found the deer spoor right where he thought it might be, and trailed the deer for several minutes before he realized where they were going. The river was up ahead. Its swollen banks would prevent any crossing. They had probably eaten, drank water, and then bedded down not far from the river, using it as a protective back.

He checked the wind. No good. They would smell him long before he got close enough for a shot if he continued on from this direction. He would have to come from upwind. Ahau detoured in a large half circle and came at them from a northerly direction. First, he had to find them.

Crawling on his knees and scooting through bushes in the mud on his belly was long, exhausting work. There were several dense areas in front of him that they could be in. He waited in stillness for a sign. He needed movement to detect exactly where they were. After what felt longer than it probably was, Ahau brought his forearm up slowly to swipe away the sweat that had collected at his brow. The flies and mosquitoes had found him early and were making life almost intolerable. He just as slowly smeared several of the blood-bloated bodies off his legs and what he could reach of his exposed back. His eyes stayed alert and watchful, still hoping to see the movement that would tell him the deer were there.

Rain softly pattered down, giving him some relief. The moisture in the air fell increasingly harder, though not with the intensity it had at about this time yesterday. Ahau used the rain as cover to roll to his side and move closer. Movement! A deer, in complete camouflage, shook the wetness from around its head and shoulders. Its antlers were small....he could just see them as they peeked over the top of the bushes a little to his left. It amazed him that all of this time, he had been so close and yet did not perceive them.

He very slowly got to one knee and nocked an arrow. It was still a long shot, one he would not have tried a month ago. He hoped his new bow was up to the challenge. All he needed was a target. The deer was still lying down, under cover. He needed it to stand. Ahau looked around for something to throw. If he could alert the deer to a noise behind it, maybe it would stand to investigate before bolting. The real trouble was that bucks, this time of the year, seldom traveled without does, and these he could not see. They could be anywhere. Does alarmed much easier than the males. If they bolted, then the buck would quickly follow.

He found a sizeable chunk of bark and hefted it for weight. It was light but might travel far enough if he arched it high. In one motion, Ahau chucked the wood and drew back his bow once it had left his hand. The bark sailed tall overhead and landed well behind the buck, but there was no reaction...not even an ear flicker. The wood had landed softly in the leafy grasp of a bush, and very little sound had been made.

Bewildered, Ahau again searched the ground for something to throw. From where he was, he could find nothing else without making too much noise doing it. He decided to try a new approach. With his bow nocked, stretched and ready, he stood up and grumped low in his throat.

Immediately, four deer stood and stared at him with nervous, wide eyes that had never before seen a human. They were alarmed, but only mildly. Two of the does worked for a better position from which to see. They all lifted their noses into the wet air, trying to get a better smell of this strange, new animal.

Ahau saw all of this in the three heartbeats before he loosed his arrow. It struck the buck just below its throat with a satisfying thunk. It bellowed, spun, and ran less than twenty steps before it stopped abruptly, its skin trembling from its neck to its feet. It snorted large bubbles of blood and froth. Its lung had been blasted out near the heart. In a dying gesture, it tried to peer over its shoulder at Ahau with a look of puzzled pain. Finally, the buck collapsed in a pile and lay dead still. The does scattered. Two of them came back to the buck and sniffed suspiciously at his strange behavior. Smelling the blood, they bolted for good.

Ahau marveled at his shot. He stepped off thirty strides to where the deer had first stood. He had never shot at anything from such a distance. The new bow was, indeed, extraordinary. He had to work fast now. The dead deer would soon bring the unwanted attention of other predators and nasty groups of scavengers. Nothing ever died in the forest without it being known by a diverse party of hungry mouths.

Ahau took his hunting knife from its sheath and made a shallow cut across his forearm, then positioned the drops of blood so that they fell directly onto the deer. He said a quick prayer of penance and thanks for the life he had taken, and began cutting through the buck's belly. The steaming intestines tumbled out and he placed them to the side. Coyotes were already barking their impatience.

Ahau pulled out the liver and carefully laid it on a large rain-cleaned leaf. He cut and yanked the hide down and away from the shoulder area. With practiced speed, he sliced off a large slab of choice meat and added it to the liver. It was all he could carry and still make any speed. Regretfully, he had to leave the rest. There was not much from the deer that would not have proven useful to him had he the time to process the animal. People, if near and hunting him, would investigate what the coyotes were yipping so feverously about, and circling vultures pinpointed the spot.

Ahau said one more quick prayer and wrapped the meat up with more leaves, tied them off with vine, and scrambled to his feet. Less than a hundred steps away, he could no longer see where the deer lay, but he could hear the snarls, howls, and angry fighting over its flesh. He picked up his pace, recovered the spear he had left against a tree when he had gone to his belly, and headed deeper into the concealing vegetation.

Ahau ate most of the liver raw. It was wonderful. The sweet, blood enriched meat slid down his throat almost without chewing. Juices spilled over his lips and down his chest. He barely noticed. He hadn't realized how hungry he had been. He slow cooked the large chunk of deer shoulder over a small fire, careful to make sure the smoke filtered through the leaves above. The foliage should disperse the smoke enough that it would be invisible high in the air. He was tired of hiding like a sick dog under cover. Daylight, a successful hunt, and a full belly had done wonders for Ahau's psyche. *If anyone is around, let 'em come. With this bow, I can pick them off before they even know they're close to me.* Ahau realized it was foolish thinking to really believe that, but it felt good visualizing it just the same.

Envisioning his enemies going down from shots no other man could launch with his kind of accuracy made Ahau realize another possibility, one based in reality. *What if Tikal is followed? I should arrive early at the meeting place and set up some sort of blind. Something I can see from for a long ways and defend myself if necessary.* Actually, he thought his friend was very confident in the forest. If anyone tried to follow him, Tikal would know it. Yet, at the same time, why not? It would give him something to do, and being careful was never a bad idea. Ahau finished his meal, gathered up his supplies, and moved toward the bald knoll.

***

Bela made soft mewing noises as he dreamed of his mother. He hadn't thought of her in a long while. Once again he was at her breast, suckling the warm blood from her chilling body. She had died giving him birth, and only instinct had made him feed.

Bela had innately known her as his mother. He had never questioned this. He remembered hanging her limp flesh in the trees. Now, still under the influence of the orange fungus, she spoke to him for the first time in his life. That was the way things sometimes worked in dreams. The rules changed. She told him in a language he intuitively knew that the brownskins could never live in peace with him in the same forest. They would hunt him as they would any dangerous beast. He must treat them the same or move.

Bela wasn't going to move. The forest had been his for too long. It was all he knew. For over two hundred years he had been master of his domain. It also occurred to him that nowhere else in the forest did the orange fungi grow. Maybe that was more important than anything else. She spoke to him of Pochotl. Like tearing the head from a snake, he was the key to Bela's survival. She urged him not to wait too long. He soft-growled that he would not and tenderly hung her in the trees again. Sorrow worked at his heart and mind, making him wish once again for the impossible.

Much later, Bela vigorously pushed up from the cold stone floor of his cave. As usual, fungus-sleep left him feeling refreshed and robust. Time to move. Time to feed. Experience told him that the dark sky's clouds were about squeezed out. The rains were almost over. That thought preluded another.

When the wet season ended, the brownskins' presence in his forest would be no more. Dream residue rolled vividly through his mind. Mood swings often accompanied the use of too much of the

169

furry-orange smut. This one was a bad one. His right arm ripped through the air, claws extended, as he thought about the dream image of Pochotl. Brownskins fell by the dozens with the single blow. "Ooooruh!"

Bela's pantomime brought his eyes to the torn heads of Chan Chel's warriors. Now only dry skulls, the flesh long gone, they seemingly mocked him from the stone ledge. Their empty sockets screamed a soundless, hungry triumph. He angrily grabbed one of the bony vessels between his powerful hands and pushed his palms together, effortlessly pulverizing the skull into unrecognizable pieces. The rest he left where they sat. They reminded him of how weak the brownskins really were.

Still inflamed, Bela jumped from his cave and swiftly covered the ground to his private path up and out of the cenote. Viciously he marauded the forest floor and the trees above. Uncharacteristically, he savagely killed every large animal he came across for most of the night. All forest life became a luckless substitute for Pochotl. Rent and bleeding, the bodies lay undisturbed where he left them. No predator or scavenger dared come close to any of them. Ravished, he chew-sucked the blood from fourteen unfortunate victims, leaving the principal part of the meat and juices to the forest.

Bela fed until morning. His anger only grew. In his present mood, he felt the need to kill, to tear, to rend, to destroy. He blamed all of his miseries on the forest and its inhabitants. He had always hoped to find another companion, possibly a mate like himself. He was so terribly alone. False hope had been given by the brownskins. Their priest, Pochotl, plotted to kill him and had sent warriors to try. Even Chan Chel had betrayed him in the end. All of the brownskins were his enemies. He did not understand them. They would never be his equal.

Feelings of rejection, of being forsaken, isolated, and abandoned by the mother and father he'd never known coalesced into a hatred and fury that shook his sanity. Bela's anguish made his thoughts jump with unnerving rapidity. His reality was a frenzied jumble of emotions that threatened to drive him mad. Even the killings had only slightly softened the ragged edges of his rage. He lay on the stone floor of his cave and tried to hide in sleep. Whispers from his abused mind shifted eventually into soft, husky muttering. He could not understand the words, if that was what they were. But the message seemed to say everything would be once more as it once was and would ever be. *I need only myself...myself...myself...myself.* The muttering flowed in rhythm with his breathing, calming him. Slowly, his mind allowed him rest...his muscles relaxed and his eyes fell shut. He slumbered the fragile sleep of rotting wood and torn flesh, backdropped by blackened snarls of despair. Orange-swirled mood swings chased their own tails through his dreams, finally giving him the peace of deep sleep.

***

Ahau watched his friend climb the incline to the bald knoll, adjusting his course as the trees dictated. No one followed him. Ahau watched several long moments more before meeting Tikal near the top. Oily grass, thigh high, brushed against their sides. The two young men, feeling exposed and vulnerable, entered the forest to talk. Their meeting was necessarily brief.

Ahau was genuinely relieved that Tikal had gotten someone as important as Ah Kaba from the council to listen to his side of the accusations. He was surprised and concerned, though, that Pochotl had elevated his friend to nacom. He told him as much and asked him to be careful. The old priest never did anything without a motive. It was decided that Tikal would bring Ah Kaba to the same site tomorrow near the midday mark. No one else. Regretfully, it would be quite a while before Ahau would be able to see Jada again.

***

Almost as an afterthought, Tikal remarked as he left how much older Ahau appeared. It was as if his friend had aged ten years in the last few days. New self-confidence lined his face and reflected in his thoughts. Tikal had found himself capitulating, as he would to a much older, wiser man. It was unnerving. Ahau was no longer the restrained, timid youth he had known all of his life. The man in front of him was confident, capable, with the seasoned air of a weathered veteran. *How did this happen?* Tikal reflected on the metamorphism as he headed back to the village. Ahau had been through a lot in a relatively short time, he guessed. Much had changed since they had left Kohunlich. *I suppose it is possible. I just never really noticed before.*

171

Maybe its time I started taking my own responsibilities more seriously.
***

Ahau would have laughed if he could have heard Tikal's thoughts. Last night, he had almost teared like a baby because he had felt so alone. He had never before felt so hollow and utterly emotionally spent. It was true that killing the deer had shored up his confidence. Ahau knew he had the ability to survive the forced isolation. He did not, however, feel remotely more mature, just tired and anxious. If the meeting with Ah Kaba turned out well tomorrow, he could put all of this behind him and return to the village and his old life. Ahau knew he was innocent; he just had to convince the council. Ah Kaba was the first step and would know the truth when he heard it. He clutched tightly to that thought as he headed back to his three-tree sanctuary.

The night passed uneventfully. Ahau slept peacefully beside a small fire. Hunters still looked for the young man but were in a different part of the forest, far away. New hope had made the young man feel more at ease and less anxious. Ah Kaba would make the difference. Intuitively, he knew that tomorrow, when he met with the nobleman, his life would change.

The next day seemed to come quickly. Waking, Ahau ate a little of the meat cold and set off, chewing the last of the maize cakes. He wanted to be at the bald knoll well ahead of Tikal and Ah Kaba. As before, he thought it might prove prudent to be careful. He'd never let Tikal know about the hidden blind or observing his friend's approach, watching for any followers. It would have hurt his feelings. Ahau trusted Tikal, and knew his friend would never do anything purposely to hurt him. He also wanted to trust Ah Kaba.

Pochotl, however, had proven himself. *The devious old man could have them both followed without either knowing it if he thought they might be coming to meet with me.* It was this thought that made Ahau careful. That, and Jada. Having someone to live for was a new experience. If it were not for his love for her, he would have confronted the priest days ago, reckless of his own life. His parents had died while he had been very young. His brother and uncle had taken him in but he'd never felt close to either of them. Jada was everything. He would do his best to make sure he saw her again.

High in his blind, Ahau patiently waited for his friend and the nobleman. From the direction he watched, they should be coming at any time. The sun looked to be almost straight overhead. Thick, blue-black mud still heavily smeared the sky, threatening to release new sheets of rain. He hoped the rains would hold a while longer. The humidity, however, said the moisture would not be long in coming. Sweat ran down his forehead, stinging his eyes. He rubbed at the corners.

Yes...there! I see them. Two of them! Ahau and Ah Kaba were just coming out from the trees bordering the bald knoll. He watched them take several steps into the grass. Tikal called his name. Ahau started to answer then decided to wait a little longer. The two of them were almost at the center.

Sudden stealthy movement caught Ahau's eyes. Well behind the nobleman and his friend, Ahau could see at least two other figures in the trees, maybe more. The men were trying to move low and slow, flitting from tree to tree. They came to ground, working for positions near the edges of the trees on their bellies, much the way Ahau had stalked the deer yesterday. No, there were actually three of them. One had been farther back than the other two, and he also worked for position. They spread out with about four spear throws between them.

Ahau momentarily looked away, grimacing. He was sick to his stomach. There was no mistaking the three men's intentions. They were here for him. Light shimmered threateningly from the sharp tips of their spears. Ahau was not sure what to do. He still trusted Tikal and hoped against rational thinking that he could trust Ah Kaba. The nobleman was his chance to clear himself. If the three warriors were here because of Ah Kaba, then all was truly lost.

From his position high up in the dark canopy of the tree, Ahau knew he was next to invisible. The five men below him could not possibly see him from their locations and distances. He also knew he had to do something quickly. He could do one of three things. He could simply run, never looking back, and begin a new life somewhere else. Maybe even find another village further north, near the ocean, which would take him in. He could yell out to the men below where he was and come down, accepting the consequences, or—and this was the big one—he could attack first. He had never killed another man of his tribe before, but thought in his present state of mind he could. Betrayal was a great motivator.

Ahau slid noiselessly down a vine at the back of the tree, hidden from the others. He had pinpointed in his mind where the warriors had gone to ground. If he could pick them off one at a time, he could confront the nobleman afterwards. He broke left and turned in a tight circle toward the first one. They would never expect him to come at them from behind.

Ahau could see the first warrior right where he remembered him. The man was on his stomach, intently peering through the tall grass to where Ah Kaba and Tikal sat waiting. Ahau inched closer. He could see the man's spear lying close to his right hand. The warrior would have to stand to throw it with any force or accuracy.

Ahau felt guilt pulse rapidly just under his skin, making his face and ears burn hot. The mental anguish of what he was about to do was incredibly intense. Still, he nocked one of his black arrows and crawled closer. He would have to shoot the man where he lay…it would have to be an immediate kill. If the warrior cried out or even thrashed, the others would be warned. Ahau smiled grimly as he remembered something Pochotl had said. He aimed high on the back of the man's neck, just under the skull cap. Pochotl had said a knife thrust there would kill instantly. The sharp edges of his arrow's obsidian tip should cut very much like a knife.

He loosed his grip on the bow's string, sending the wooden shaft to the soft flesh waiting at the end of its flight. The resulting thunk was a wet, piercing, unpleasant sound. Ahau winced. The warrior fell immediately still, dead before his head plopped into the grass between his hands. Perversely, Ahau wondered if Pochotl would be proud that his lessons had not gone unheeded. He moved on, grateful that the warrior's face was hidden from view. He was sure that he probably knew the man. It was difficult not to know everyone in a small village.

The middle warrior was not on his stomach. He was crouched behind a thick, dead branch near the edge of the grass, his attention on Ah Kaba and Tikal. Apparently he had no idea that the man to his left was newly dead. The tattooed back was one Ahau recognized. His name was Kankin Mol, a despicable minion of Pochotl's. He and Tikal had seen the man several times in the priest's company speaking in low tones. The man's stink was an abomination. Ahau and Tikal had often made fun of the man's stench and apparent lack of social concerns. They wondered if he had a wife, and if so, what she must be like. What the man did for Pochotl was a secret Ahau had never learned. He was certain now that whatever it had been, it was malignantly evil. At least that was what Ahau told himself as he shot the man in the same soft flesh as the first.

Unfortunately, when Stinky dropped, he landed on a set of dead branches. Their loud crack alerted the last warrior. Ahau could see the man's head jerk in his direction. In an instant the warrior spotted Ahau and read the rest of what had just happened. He came to his feet and charged, meaning to spear the young man before he had a chance to react. Ahau's first instinct was to run, put some distance between them. His first step went wrong and his feet threatened to send him down, but he staggered for balance. An arrow appeared unbidden in his hand. He must have jerked it out of his quiver from habit after sending an arrow to Kankin Mol's back. Ahau nocked the shaft but fell before he could pull the bow.

The third warrior was almost upon him. Ahau issued a guttural growl from lips twisted in anger. The warrior turned his torso, shouldering the spear high above his head, poised to release it. Ahau rolled to his side and pulled the bow, the arrow still nocked. Both wooden shafts left at the same time in opposite directions. The larger shaft speared the earth next to Ahau's head, separating hair and the top part of an ear from the young man. The smaller shaft seemed to be growing from the other man's chest, sprouting a red bloom that widened around the hands that held it. Stunned disbelief registered on the warrior's face. Still on his feet, he pulled his knife and ploughed toward Ahau on wobbly feet. Ahau could do nothing. There was not time to draw another arrow or his own blade. He cringed with both hands splayed out in front of him. In the semblance of a downward thrust, the man fell face down on Ahau, his body finally giving over to the inevitable embrace of death. The blade found Ahau's shoulder, piercing it deeply, producing a red blossom of its own.

Ahau looked up to see Tikal and Ah Kaba staring down at him.

175

He pushed the warrior off him and came up to a sitting position, checking his wound. The knife slid out of the cut easily. It had missed the major artery but still bled considerably. Starting to stand, he found another problem. The arrow's wooden shaft had broken as the man fell on him, and the jagged end had punctured Ahau's right side, high up on the ribs. It, too, was bleeding well enough to require some attention. Tikal reached out to help him stand.

"Ahau, who are these men? I swear to you that I know nothing about them. I had no knowledge of being followed. I even backtracked earlier to make sure until Ah Kaba stopped me. He said we were wasting time."

Both young men, arms over shoulders, scrutinized the older man, looking for the guilt they thought might show in his eyes. Tikal, slightly supporting Ahau, spoke first.

"You know we respect you. That's why we chose you to listen to Ahau's side of my father's death. But, I have to ask. Did you know these men were here? Is that why you stopped me from going back to make sure we were not followed?"

Tikal brought his spear up slightly. It still pointed downward but was at a ready position. Ah Kaba's expression seemed to indicate that he understood the inference. His mind was probably going through possible explanations that might exonerate him.

"Tikal, Ahau. We have a real problem. But, I promise you, it is not of my making. Come. It is urgent that we talk about this. Let's get to a spot where we can be comfortable; somewhere away from so much death. Follow me!"

He turned his back on them and walked away, giving them no choice but to follow. Still bleeding, Ahau put pressure against his shoulder and side with both hands and traversed the knoll on his own power. Tikal came last. He was still watching the woods, like he expected more warriors to suddenly burst from cover and attack. Under different circumstances, his crouched, crab-like movements would have been comical. His spear was level out in front of him as he tried to walk sideways while looking back into the forest. Ahau was glad his friend protected his back. After what had just happened, he thought it very prudent. He tripped over a rough part of the ground, wincing as the wound in his shoulder sent spikes of pain radiating out from it. It was not much further to the other end of the knoll. His tree was just ahead.

***

Ah Kaba stopped under it and sat down. Both young men joined him. Tikal still glanced every few heartbeats back to the forest opposite of the knoll, looking for signs of movement. Ah Kaba, using the time it took to get to this spot, had furiously thought about how the three men might be explained. Pochotl had indeed sent the warriors to kill Ahau and then Tikal. Tikal's death would have been blamed on Ahau. Ahau's rage at his friend's insistence to give himself up and suffer the consequences of killing Ah Tok would be the only motive they needed to explain Tikal's death. Who would have guessed that the warriors would be the ones lying on their faces, dead in the mud? *How did Ahau manage it?*

"Ahau, this is difficult for me to explain. When Tikal came to me, I wanted to help. What he said made sense. I only want to see justice done. If you did not kill Ah Tok because of his reluctance to let you marry Jada, then we need to find out who did and why." He looked up to meet both of their eyes. This part was crucial.

"I discussed with no one what was said between Tikal and me. As you can see, I am unarmed. I wanted you, Ahau, to feel comfortable and unafraid when we talked. Here is where things get a little sticky. Both of you have to understand that I am an old man. If Ahau really did kill Ah Tok, then maybe his mind still suffers. I had no way of knowing for sure one way or the other. Those men were not here to attack you, Ahau. They were here to protect me."

***

Ahau's heart was racing. His hands shook as realization sunk in. He had killed three innocent men. Tikal and he exchanged wide-eyed looks that said both were thinking the same thing. Ah Kaba continued. "They would have stayed where they were unless I called for them or you threatened me in any way. Now, you have killed them. Do you see what this means? Whether or not you killed Ah Tok is no longer the question. You have killed three men today." Ah Kaba yelled, "You are guilty! I saw it all and so did Tikal. There is no way out of this, Ahau. Some of these men had families. How do I explain this to them? Why did you do it? Did any of them make a single threatening move toward you?"

Ah Kaba shook his head and made small noises with his lips pursed in feigned disgust. With his head down, he looked at them both under hooded eyes, as if to see if they were believing his accusations. It was easy to see they were. Ahau was as pale as the bird droppings on the tree he sat under. Tikal looked straight at the ground, his hands folded in his lap, no longer looking into the forest for potential danger.

***

Ahau's mind raced. It had all been so clear moments ago. Those three men were here to take him back or kill him here. Either way resulted the same. Now, he was being accused of killing innocent men. *Is this right? Is it possible? Am I guilty of shooting three men because I feared for my life for nothing?* He was convinced that it was so.

In a weak voice Ahau said, "Now what? What happens now?"

Ah Kaba had also thought about this. "Look me in the eyes, Ahau. I have one question for you, and I warn you now that I will know if you are lying. I have not lived this long or ascended to the council because I am a fool." He waited for Ahau to lift his eyes. "Did you kill Tikal's Father?"

"No." The small voice was hard to hear. "No, I would never do such a thing. I love Jada far too much to cause her so much pain."

"I believe you! Your eyes tell me that you are telling the truth. There is still the problem of the three men, though. I have thought about this. I think that you truly believed you were acting in self-defense. The men are dead, however, through no fault of their own. They were only here on my behalf. I will not lie to the council or their families about how they died. I'm suggesting that you do one of two things. Come back with me and offer yourself up to the village, or...." He hesitated to make sure Ahau was concentrating on what he said. "Leave this part of the forest forever. Exile yourself, Ahau. Personally, I hope this is what you choose. Your death solves nothing. Start a new life in one of the cities to the far north. Try to forget what happened here today and your old life. That includes Jada. It is not fair to her to ask her to leave her family and follow you into the forest to an unknown destination. Whatever you choose, you must be quick. The council will hunt you with a vengeance now."

Ahau knew that what the nobleman said was true. The council and the dead men's families would hunt him relentlessly. Only his death would satisfy them.

Ah Kaba stood. "Ahau, I am leaving. I cannot carry the dead back to the village by myself. Their families will want their bodies. I will bring men back to take them out. You can go with me now...." He paused for effect. "Or choose exile. There is no more time."

***

The nobleman made a show of leaving, stamping his feet to get the circulation going again. Ah Kaba walked hurriedly into the forest, only brusquely checking the dead men. It was a good idea to disappear quickly, while the getting was good. He had the two young men convinced Ahau had killed for all the wrong reasons. He couldn't help smiling to himself. Pochotl would be pleased. This was better than killing Ahau and then having to dispose of Tikal. Ahau was gone from the village for good. If Pochotl still believed Tikal a threat, then he could handle that problem himself. He walked even faster, a little hop in his stride, anticipating telling the old priest what had happened.

***

Ahau and Tikal watched him go. He stopped by each of the bodies before going on. They supposed he checked to make sure they were dead. Once Ah Kaba was out of sight, Tikal met Ahau's gaze. He let out his held breath in a sigh. Sorrow registered sincerely on his face.

Ahau sat resignedly against the tree from which he had first spied the three men and spoke to Tikal. "This is so hard to believe. Do you think he was telling the truth?"

Were those men really here to protect the nobleman? That question kept repeating itself in his mind. He had been so sure that they had been there for him. Something just didn't quite correspond. Kankin Mol was at the heart of it. *Why would someone as respectable as Ah Kaba use someone like Kankin Mol when he has his own warriors to choose from?* Apprehension turned Ahau's stomach into a hard knot. *Have I been duped? Have I let Ah Kaba convince me I am guilty when I am not?*

Tikal was still beside him, pressing cloth into the wound at his shoulder. The bleeding had almost stopped. The wound in his side,

179

high up on his rib cage, had already stopped flowing. His biggest concern now would be infection. In the forest, infection killed as easily as any predator. Later, he would have to make a poultice to bind into the wounds to prevent any further corruption.

Ahau searched his friend's face. He could read concern but nothing else.

"Tikal, I don't know what to do. I suppose it could be as Ah Kaba says, but it doesn't feel right. I was so sure...."

Tikal said nothing. Ahau stood up, brushing his friend's help away.

"It doesn't really matter, does it? Either way, I have no choice. My life is ruined. It would be suicide to go back to the village now. Ah Kaba was right about that. Exile is the only way out. You have to help me, Tikal. I have to see Jada first. If she will go with me, I will take her. Do you have a problem with that?"

"I was going to suggest the same thing, my friend. Of course I will help you. I think even Mother will understand. It will have to be later, though. Ah Kaba was also right about the village's reaction. The hunt for you will be intense. I will be right in the middle of things. They will know that I am with you now and will not trust any directions I give them. In fact, it would be better if I do not know where you go. This is what we will do."

***

Pochotl was indeed pleased with Ah Kaba's news. He agreed with the nobleman. Tikal would be useful a while longer yet. They could dispose of him later if it came to that.

The council was informed of Ahau's treachery, and the village was full of volunteers to help find the young man. Nothing like this had ever happened in most of their memories. Death was a common element in their lives, but not within these parameters. War, disease, accidents, and even ritual slayings they could understand. Ahau's actions, however, were the work of a mind gone mad. First Ah Tok, and now three others. His perversity was an affront to Itzamna and all the other gods. He would be found. Justice demanded it.

Within a very short time, twenty four warriors were on his trail, all anxious to be the one to find him. Ah Kaba had offered thirty pieces of jade for the one who did. Most had supplies for several days.

Each had their own hopes of finding the young man first. Reaching the bald, grassy knoll, the warriors found the three dead men. Curiously, none of them wanted to leave the chase to take the bodies home. After a lot of argument, they split up in several different sized groups, all smelling out the obvious signs going north, toward the river. In a frenzied clamor, they spread out, running to catch the priest's crazed apprentice. They couldn't believe their luck that Ahau would be so stupid. Once he reached the river, there was nowhere to go. The river at this time of the year would be impossible to cross. They each knew that in a short time Ahau would be spotted. Most did not care one way or another if the young man was guilty; thirty pieces of jade was more than enough reason to kill him. That much jade could change a man's life.

***

Ahau heard their yells of excitement dissipate in the distance. It had been a grave gamble, but it had paid off. High up in his blind, in the very tree most of the warriors had stood under, Ahau sighed with relief and let the nocked arrow relax in his bow. For several long moments he had not been sure if the warriors would follow his false trail heading north. One had even looked up into the tree. Tikal had made sure Ahau was invisible from below before he left, but it was unnerving just the same. The warrior had stared into the tree as if he could see something, turning his head to the side and looking right at the spot where Ahau sat for several terrifying heartbeats. Thanks to Itzamna, he had left with the others and now hunted his quarry toward the river.

Ahau eased himself down the tree and stayed low in the grass. He knew he had to move fast. Not all of them would be fooled for long. Tikal would be waiting for him in the forest on the other side of the village with supplies. There was no time to speak to Jada. That would have to come later. It would be night before he got to where he was going as it was. To make things worse, the rain once more started to patter the leaves overhead. Soon it would begin in earnest. Coupled with the growing darkness, the conditions were going to be hard to see in. Speed was imperative. He ran along the paths the warriors had taken for as long as possible, hiding his own passage, then circled wide, missing the village.

181

***

Pochotl made tea. Tea assuaged the soul and softened the day's troubles. He gulped in the freshness of the recently picked leaves and smacked his lips. The spearmint added just the right flavor. He downed the remainder of the cup and poured more steaming water into the container. Using the claw that hung around his neck, he stirred the water brown. Bela's claw. It reminded him that the warriors sent to kill the great beast had still never shown back at the village. It would not be long before other people started thinking about the men. Bela might be dead. They all might be dead. Who knew? As long as the demon stayed away from him and the village, he didn't really care. Maybe after the rains, they would send someone to see what had happened.

He took another substantial swallow and closed his eyes, enjoying the sensation of the tea and the relaxation it afforded. The tea also reminded him of another matter, something he meant to resolve very soon. Jada. In his possession were two plants that when mixed together would sedate all of the young woman's inhibitions. The tea would camouflage their tastes. Pochotl smiled, gurgling on a chuckle.

***

A large skin was wrapped amply around as many food supplies as Tikal could find. He added two knives, several chunks of obsidian, and seven bare arrow shafts Ahau had left behind. With sisal twine, he tied the skin tight and hung it over his back. He could only give Jada and his mother the briefest of explanations. Time was critical. He just hoped Ahau would be there when he arrived.

As carefully as he could, he left the village undetected and ran into the forest, skirting the maize fields. Agreeing to hide in the tree, Ahau had placed his life in his friend's hands. It had been Tikal's plan, and responsibility for it rested heavily on his mind. As he ran, he prayed to as many gods as he could think of who might help. It never hurt. They might be listening, though he doubted it. He had prayed before, only to be met with silence and cruel disappointment. Rain drops thumped him on his head as he ran. He cursed and ran a little faster.

CHAPTER 14
DANCING ON RED JEWELED PEBBLES

Bela twisted and yanked the leg bone from the socket, closing his cruel teeth around the flesh. He tore a huge chunk from the meat and chewed it viciously, sucking the juices from it before spitting it out. Gray and shapeless, the meat splattered the rock at his feet, adding to the mound already there. Beetles, flies, and an undaunted cockroach stuck their snouts into the guck and scurried off with what they could, unnoticed by the great beast. Bela threw the gnawed bone against the side of his cave's wall and stood, smacking his lips loudly. Errant juices ran in rivulets down his chin. He wiped them away with his forearm, deciding he was still hungry. The meat had been left over from the night before, and he wanted something fresher. Beetles squished under his feet like full, thin skinned eggs, emptying their yellow juices to the floor. Other beetles scrambled to taste their brothers. Bela left his cave in search of larger game.

After storming through the immediate forest a few nights ago, killing everything that moved, the wildlife was understandably hard to find. He moved farther west and out of his usual haunts. Without realizing it, he was looking for brownskins. Bela picked up their scent before he heard their noisy chatter. A group of three warriors, separated from the main group of those who hunted Ahau, had picked the wrong direction and definitely the wrong night to camp where they now were.

"Ooooruh!" Deep in the darkness of tangled vegetation, Bela's voice echoed through the snarled blackness of the forest beyond, cutting the stillness like an obsidian blade slicing through infant flesh. His voice, full of lonely anger, was thick and menacing. Creatures,

183

small and large, cringed and pushed themselves deeper into hiding, keenly aware that Bela was among them.

The brownskins were camped near the river about five-hundred strides from his current position. His senses picked them out as neatly as a viper's would mice. He rumbled pleasure deep in his throat and headed toward them. The moon was eclipsed by a ponderous, slow-moving cloud. The rain was only occasionally spitting at the forest, hardly noticeable after the pelting earlier. Bela moved closer on silent, padded feet. Saliva dripped through his curled lips, promising his digestive tract that soon blood would flow.

He could see the twinkling of the small fire now. He wanted all three of them. None would escape. A level swatch of dark green beckoned him…the heavy bushes would do just fine. They were close enough to the brownskins to serve his purpose. He knew from experience that he would be able to get very close to the puny creatures and they would never know. A strange sense of having done this before flowed like a warm breath through his mind. This was how it had been when he had first encountered the brownskins. He remembered. *Ahhuu! The young brownskin who got away!* Bela had not thought of the young man for a long time. Ahau's image ran through his mind as the young man had laid on his back, foul mud covering up strange wounds. He even remembered Ahau's taste. Maybe one of these three was he. He moved to the heavy bush. Bela's small fleshy nub that had once been a tail twitched rapidly. He was almost ready.

***

One of the brownskins saw the twin lamps of eyes, horribly intelligent and aware, staring through the shrubbery near his left side. They went out and then came back. A blink. Numbing disbelief shook his sanity as the bushes parted slightly, revealing a muzzle too full of impossibly sharp teeth. In the smallest part of a heartbeat, he registered light twinkling off the wet daggers and realized they were meant for him.

Abruptly, the stillness was broken. A scream rose in the closest man's throat, but the muscles contracted and only a cawing gurgle emerged. Thick curds of spit splattered on the man's face as Bela's teeth ripped his throat out. Black claws, each at least half a finger's length, shredded through the chest of the middle man, leaving him in a sundered heap at Bela's feet. Blood red mist sprayed through the air from several sources. Each drop was momentarily highlighted by the fire, like small jewels, before tumbling to the ground.

The last man slumped in utter desolation, knowing he was next and there was absolutely nothing he could do about it. His weapons were behind the beast. A scream vibrated his throat, sounding thin and pitiful. A daggered hand cut in and up through his stomach's lining. A thought coherently worked its way to the surface. *Bela!* Red curtains drew black across his consciousness. There was not time for the pain to express itself. He collapsed to the forest floor, eyes still open, as dead as the cooked piece of deer still partially lodged in his gullet.

***

Bela "Ooooruhed" to the forest and the sky that hooded above. Tonight, three brownskins had died. Soon, they would all know who really owned the forest. He gouged a hole out of the neck of the brownskin closest to him and pushed his mouth deep into the wound, chewing and sucking the meat. Bela cracked the bones of one of the men's neck between his teeth and tasted salty squirts of nourishment. Hot blood cascaded down his throat, nothing like the cold juices he had earlier tried to coax from meat left on the floor of his cave. He took his time. It was almost dawn when he finally retreated to his valley and the safety of his sanctuary.

***

North and west of the village, the forest had been decimated by a fire several months earlier. Rendezvousing there was dangerous. Flames had chased away or killed any benevolent spirits that might have been in the area. Ahau's people believed that until the forest reestablished itself, terrible beings called Kaaxen, who had an evil hunger for the living, lurked among the burnt remains of the trees. The people never invaded such places unless they had no other choice. Ahau and Tikal had picked this region for that very reason. Ahau's hunters would be fearful of entering the land.

The Kaaxen were the ghosts of dead men caught by past fires. They continuously smoldered from the blackened cracks of their skin. Gray tendrils of smoke circled their heads and spread the stench of death as they searched the land. These abysmal spirits hoped to trade their dead souls for those of the living. They haunted the blackened landscape at night, moving through the broken teeth of lifeless trees. Their reputation as terrible hunters was well known.

It was here that the two young men sought refuge. Tikal perceived that darkness had probably won the race. The two young men were not going to find each other in the short time remaining before absolute darkness closed in. Tikal made it to the burnt edges of the desolation, but saw no Ahau. Only a few fingers remained of daylight. The bordering trees screened the sun's remaining light with a barrier of crowded green. Either his friend had made it to the forsaken ground and was further in, or was close by, still in the thick of the forest. He refused to think about the other possibility. Tikal was acutely aware that if he did not find Ahau, then his plan had failed and his friend's body was being paraded into the village over the shoulders of warriors. Tikal timidly went in.

The trees were small and spread far apart in most cases. The sky actually touched the ground in well over half the area, even though the smaller plants were becoming well established. Scraggly stumps with jagged heads loomed everywhere in front of him. Even with all the recent rain, the air smelled dead. Dark, murky dust rose up in little eddies like burnt offerings with his every step into the fire blasted landscape. The stillness of air and sound was ominous in its portent. Tikal knew he must find shelter immediately. There were no rock outcroppings visible. He shuddered to think about being in the open during the night while hungry, malignant spirits walked the land.

His choices limited, Tikal crawled under heavy bushes spiked with sharp nettles, and backed up to the singed, black scab of a tree trunk, pulling Ahau's supplies and his weapons after him. It was meager shelter. Morning would be a long time in coming. Niggardly space between the tangled branches of the bushes allowed him almost no view of the area around him. Ahau could walk right by him and unless he heard him, he would never know. Tikal made holes in the tangled mat of vegetation with his knife, affording him a little more access to scrutinize his surroundings. It was still difficult to see, but it was better.

Night was closing in now on stampeding hooves. He hadn't much time. Tikal wiped charcoal over his face and chest, hoping to fool the lethal spirits. If he already appeared lifeless, maybe they would lose interest in him. He pulled small, hollow bones from his pouch and placed them in his mouth to disguise his breath with the odor of death. He placed an eagle feather within the snarled shrubbery in front of him. The feather embodied purity and would help ward off the evil that stalked the barren, stagnant earth between the borders of the living forest. His spear, bow, and arrows would be useless from this position. He pulled his knife and kept it in his hand.

He had been wrong…the cut spaces did not help. He could see nothing. The blackness of the night was complete. Even the sky gave no assurances of light. Cloud-swathed, the thin sliver of the moon was completely obscured. Tikal leaned back and tried to slow his breathing. He was beginning to panic. Since he was a little boy, he had been told about the dangers of such a place. If he had not felt so responsible for Ahau, he would never have entered. Horrible visages, with the grisly remains of their still living victims hanging from their mouths, plagued his imagination.

The night passed slowly. Tikal could hear the high pitched voices of the dead trees as the wind began to whistle through their hollowed innards. They creaked and groaned as gusts blustered against them. Tikal knew that the Kaaxen were at their boldest and shrewdest when people believed the dead sounds of the trees was only the wind. They hunted and communicated on small breezes sent by their rancid breath to search for the living. They would not fool him. He would stay awake and fastidiously stay on guard regardless of how tired he became. Pochotl had once told Tikal that the blackened husks of the once living spirits could peel venomous smoke from their skins and spiral it toward a living target. If the smoke was breathed, it could separate a man's soul from his body. A person could tell if the smoke was poison by the way it stung and nibbled at the nasal passages. Once the soul attached itself to the smoke, the Kaaxen would pull the soul back into the corrupt skin of the wraith-like shadows. Tikal controlled his breathing, keeping it slow and shallow, in case one of the dark shades directed a stream of fetid breath in his direction.

Except for sounds, the first half of the night passed uneventfully.

187

Sometime between then and dawn, the noises became more specific.

Tikal could hear them coming. He knew from the sound that there was more than one. Footfalls sounded heavy and close. He shrunk back tighter against the nub of the tree, holding his knife tightly. He wasn't sure it would be of any use, but it was all he had. The terrible sound of evil padded closer. Tikal tried to hold his breath. Fear, bright and glowing, roared in his head, devouring all else. He could see nothing. Loud snuffling rattled the edges of the bushes just to his right. Panic seized his heart. He tried to make himself even smaller.

Long, sustained sizzles trumpeted the ground from two directions, sending acrid smelling dust into his lungs. He tried again to hold his breath, breathing only small gasps between tight fingers pushed against his lips. Wetness muddied his thigh. The warm moisture seemed to burn his skin. This was more than his terrorized mind could stand. He burst out of the bushes, wielding his knife in stiff, narrow arcs as hard and fast as his arms could swing. There was a fast scudding of feet, but he could still see nothing in the dark. Sounds indicated that they had abruptly scattered as he burst from his hiding place and now were circling him. Low, wrathful growls reverberated menacingly under several pairs of yellow lights blinking malevolently in his direction. He quickly counted eight sets of the baleful, mysterious eyes.

Tikal was almost grateful for the darkness. The Kaaxen's grotesque organs of sight appeared to be made of liquid fire. He wasn't sure he could stomach seeing the rest of them. They were perversions of nature. Evil incarnate. Tikal was assailed by pure terror. The knife dropped from quivering fingers, the idea of defending himself long gone. His chest shuddered in spasms, threatening to hyperventilate. Tikal, consumed by hysteria, ran right at them, his arms flapping indifferently at his sides. He made whining noises that confirmed his all-consuming fright. A screech arose in his throat and built to a deafening roar that shattered the confidence of the liquid fire eyes. One by one, they blinked out and dissipated back into the darkness. Tikal continued his frenzied dash into the inky landscape until a low-lying bush and small stump brought him up short. He hit the ground and rolled painfully to a sitting position. His scream persisted, stopping only long enough to draw a breath and then starting again.

Abruptly he stopped, realizing he was still alive. The eyes were gone. He could no longer hear the shuffling of feet or smell the tart, bitter dust that had pervaded his nostrils earlier. He was alive! Tikal wobbled to his feet. New terror assaulted him. He could hear a voice calling. They knew his name! He turned back and forth, trying to get an idea from where it was coming. One of the dead, inhuman atrocities knowing his name could not be a good thing. He wanted to run, but in which direction? He listened closer.

"Tikal. Tikal, is that you? Where are you? Tikal...."

It took Tikal a few moments more to realize he knew the voice. It was Ahau, and he sounded close. Remembering the eyes, Tikal was reluctant to answer. Instead, he carefully picked his way toward the voice. A fragment of the moon emerged from behind the clouds, just enough to allow him to avoid the silhouettes of burnt, broken tree bottoms angling out of the ground like perilous teeth in the dark. Ahau was still calling. Tikal was almost to the voice when he discovered he had left all of his weapons and Ahau's supplies back in the darkness behind him. He also realized that he was not going back. If the Kaaxen wanted them, that was fine. He would check in the morning. Maybe.

***

The young men had arrived in the same area at different times, each unaware of the other. Ahau had wisely stayed in the thickness of the trees, not wanting to enter the desolate wasteland for the same reasons Tikal hid in them. He, too, had heard stories all of his life about the terrible beings who inhabited the blackened remains of a once living forest.

When Tikal screamed, Ahau had been asleep against the back of a large, flat rock rising out of the ground under the protective embrace of several branches. At first he was not sure what the sound had been. The piercing shriek seemed to come from the direction of the wasteland. He was sure some poor animal had been taken by the dead. The second half of the shrill wail sounded more human, more like...Tikal. Ahau had burst from his sitting position, spear in hand, to help his friend. Getting no answer to his call, he slowed his run to a

189

deliberate walk, not wanting to run into the unknown. Images of Bela burned bright in his mind as he remembered that night not so long ago when he had camped with his brother and uncle. A scream had sundered the night that time, too.

The emotional lines around Tikal's eyes and mouth worked overtime when he finally spied his friend coming through the thin vegetation. Ahau was equally relieved to see Tikal. Together, they found Ahau's rocky retreat, well back in the realm of the forest proper, where the only things they feared were living. Tikal immediately built a small fire. He kept breaking and piling small bits of dead wood until the flames illuminated the night around them. This close to the village such a fire was dangerous, but Ahau did not interfere. He could tell something had badly frightened his friend, and waited patiently until Tikal was ready to tell him.

It was nearly morning when Tikal finished telling his story. Ahau could only sympathize with his friend. Tikal's encounter was well outside of anything he had ever experienced. Light was filtering through the edges of the forest in earnest when Tikal and Ahau decided they must go back into the burnt regions of the Kaaxen. Sunshine should provide sufficient protection, as long as they avoided the deep shadows. The supplies and weapons Tikal abandoned last night were too important not to try and recover. Awash with the golden glow of sunrise, even tempered as it was through thinning clouds, the burnt ground did not appear so frightening. It was almost beautiful, but neither said as much. Both of them remembered what it had been like just a short time before.

As they walked, Tikal told Ahau how the news of the three dead men had been received. As expected, Pochotl and the council were enraged over the death of Ah Kaba's bodyguards. The whole village was after him. The news of the thirty jade pieces was a surprise, however. Ahau wondered about the real motivation behind that. It was no wonder so many warriors had shown up. It had worked to Ahau's advantage, though. A real hunting party may not have been fooled by the false trail long enough for him to escape. Greed had tempered their objectiveness, and they had seen only what they wanted to see...Ahau trapped against the river.

Grass, short and fiercely bright green, fought to reintroduce itself out of the blackened residue of the incinerated vegetation. Here and there, Tikal found his weaving footprints stuttering through the eerie landscape. Ahau suppressed a grin, as the trail looked like the meanderings of a serious drunk. Following the trail back to the nettle bushes, they found Tikal's knife. Closer in, up against the bushes, they found the prints of the Kaaxen. Ahau got down on his hands and knees to study them more closely. The information was jumbled. He tried to piece together in his mind what had happened last night from the blurred scratches in the dirt. If these were the marks left by evil entities, bent on ravaging the souls of the living, they were suspiciously familiar. The feet of the Kaaxen must look a lot like wolves' paws.

Ahau pushed his head into the bushes to see if the supplies and weapons were still there. The strong, bitterly caustic smell of urine assaulted him. He quickly jerked back, his eyes watering. Last night, he had smelt the same offending odor on Tikal, but hadn't recognized it until now. It made him wonder. He did not want to contradict Tikal's story and embarrass his friend. *Maybe the wolves came after the Kaxxen. Maybe spiritual beings don't leave prints. Maybe it doesn't really matter. The important thing is that the supplies and weapons are still here.* Ahau had much more serious trouble to think about than the Kaxxen.

The two men talked as they walked for most of the morning. It was decided that Tikal should go back to the village and behave as naturally as he could. In two nights, if things were right, Ahau would chance seeing Jada. Tikal would explain the situation and accompany his sister, if that was her wish. They picked a spot they both could find in the dark. One lone pine, only slightly scabbed by the fire and still within the forest's margins, stood taller than everything else around it. Here, they would meet. Solemnly shaking each other's wrist, they parted.

***

Still searching far to the southeast, the logical voices in the men's minds said it was time to quit. Almost to the man, however, they continued looking for Ahau, even though they knew he was not anywhere near where they originally thought he might be. They were still lured by the promise of jade. Only after the discovery of Bela's carnage did they head for home, and then in a hurry. The warriors who first happened upon the slaughter site called to the rest. Soon, all the remaining hunters were staring at the butchery. There was no doubt that Bela was responsible. A man could not have caused the bloodshed they discovered. Pieces of the men were found everywhere. Even a jaguar would not have left such a mess. It was difficult to establish identities from the remnants. Only the weapons, still leaning against a tree, identified the missing men, none of them Ahau.

The warriors came back to the village by the same route and recovered the bodies of Kankin Mol and his associates. They were fully alert to the dangers of Bela. Yesterday, the warriors had left the village yelling promises, and running to beat the person beside them. Now, they slumped dejectedly into the village, empty-hearted and empty-handed.

It was not long before the news of Bela's return to their part of the forest spread through the village. The people demanded that the council do something about it immediately. A frail, small woman claimed Kankin Mol's body. No one helped her as she rolled the body onto a large skin and dragged the remains home. A small boy, Kankin's son, helped his mother bury the body well behind their hut. They apparently did not care to have the spirit lying under the floor to remind them of the man it had once been. The other two bodies, ceremoniously wrapped in mantas and surrounded by prized possessions, were enshrined by their respective families in the hard mud floors of their homes.

***

Pochotl stayed out of it. The members of the council were frenzied, each with his own opinion as to what to do. The old priest watched his friend, Ah Kaba, wondering what the nobleman would do. If Ah Kaba really wanted to become head of the council, then here was his chance to assert himself. Most of the council was clamoring for some sort of retribution, but no one had a clear plan. Pochotl now privately thought that it was suicide to try and physically go up against the demon.

Ah Kaba demanded silence. Disappointingly, it was only to ask Pochotl what he thought they should do. They stopped their bickering and listened. The old priest shook his head and threw up his arms.

"I...I mean *we*," he corrected, "sent our best to destroy Bela. None of them returned. Why send more, if fourteen could not kill the beast? With the best interests of the village in mind, I also sent Besh Po and Tarnae to check on their progress. We can only presume their not returning is a sign Bela killed them also. No. It is clear what the gods demand of us, Itzamna in particular, since Bela is his demon."

Pochotl got down on one knee and pulled his knife from its scabbard to draw in the dirt. The council came closer and surrounded him so that they could see. The priest made marks indicating the river, the depression believed to be Bela's home, and the village.

"Look! The majority of the killings occurred in this area." He drew a lopsided circle to encompass the location of the last three men's deaths.

"This, I believe, is Itzamna's domain. Bela, as a guardian, kills any man who steps foot into it. It is true that he visited our village, but that was probably because of Ahau. Think about it for a moment. When Bela was first encountered, who escaped? Ahau! Bela came to the village for retribution. When he could not find Ahau, he killed indiscriminately. It did not make sense until now. If we stay away from that part of the forest, we are safe. We must respect Itzamna's wishes. I cannot tell you the reasons why we are not permitted there; I only know that it is true. Ahau has been an evil presence in our village from the first. Who died first at Bela's hands? His uncle and brother. Even they were sacrificed by the vileness that must possess Ahau."

Pochotl drew new lines in the dirt. "All of this...." He indicated below the river and west of the lopsided circle indicating Bela's territory. "Is ours. Too many of our people have died because of Ahau and Bela. We need to fortify and protect our village here." He stabbed the dirt, marking the spot.

"Let us worry only about our families and the welfare of each other. Finish the Sun Temple. Continue our efforts in building the life we sought when we left Kohunlich. Let us pay tribute to what we have and construct our buildings and raise our families. These are the things that are important. I suggest, at least for a while, that we stay close to home and fortify the edges of our village in case either Ahau or Bela make an appearance. I do not think that either will appear, but it will make our wives and children feel safer. It is for you to decide. I am only here because you graciously asked me to attend."

Pochotl poked the knife into the village and pushed himself up to a standing position. The air was hushed, everyone lost in his own thoughts, evaluating what the priest had said. Ah Kaba, always trying to please his master, broke the silence.

"I say we do as Pochotl suggests. He makes sense. Fortify the perimeters of our village and see what happens. I, too, think we have seen the last of Ahau and Bela."

The nobleman fairly beamed at Pochotl, looking pleased that he had seconded the priest's ideas. He was oblivious to Pochotl's real thoughts. After brief discussions, the council voted to do as the priest suggested. They would stay at home. Maybe it was time to think about something else besides Ahau and Bela. They still had a city to build.

As Pochotl walked by Ah Kaba, he whispered through clenched teeth, "Bring your worthless, gutless skin to me tonight!"

Small droplets of spittle splashed the nobleman's face, accenting the priest's displeasure.

Ah Kaba, his smile fading, nodded his obeisance.

Pochotl was infuriated that the nobleman had not recognized his chance to make the council aware of his intelligence and skills for decision making. He should have been the one to suggest they concentrate their efforts on the village and not Ahau or his pet demon. The two of them had discussed this very thing only a few hours before the council met. *Maybe the fool doesn't deserve to become Batabob, head of the council and second in command to me once I am Halach Uinic and the Ah Kin Mai.* Pochotl promised himself that he would make things very clear to Ah Kaba later tonight. He patted his knife, thinking of ways to inflict upon the nobleman's mind how precarious his position was.

***

Tikal, Ix Cuy, and Jada sat close to the fire and spoke of forbidden things. The situation had become more dangerous in one way, yet safer in another. Ix Cuy lacked the strength to prohibit her daughter from leaving with Tikal. She had been young once and remembered well how passion ruled over logic. Ahau's future was so uncertain it seemed suicidal for Jada to go with him. How would they survive? Where would they go? She loved her daughter obsessively. She did not want to see her make this mistake. Yet, she wanted Jada to be happy. She clenched and unclenched her hands as she rocked back and forth between the two of them, in anguish over a decision already made. Jada had said she was going regardless of the consequences, and that was that.

Ix Cuy finally gave her blessing, wondering if she would ever see her daughter again. Tikal had explained that tomorrow's night would be the time of their leaving. It was good news for Ahau that he was no longer hunted, except by those few who still had visions of the thirty pieces of jade. Pochotl had cleverly united Ahau's name with Bela's, however. The village would forever perceive them both as enemies of similar natures. Small children probably cringed at their names now.

***

Bela could be the other problem if the beast was anywhere nearby. Tikal flinched, thinking about his sister and Ahau meeting Bela in the forest inadvertently. He also could think of a thousand reasons why Jada should not go. The plans had been made, though, and he would do what he could to help them both. He hoped Ahau was safe and would be there when they arrived. Getting through the new village's security shouldn't be too difficult. They would be watching for Bela or Ahau to come into the village, not for someone trying to leave.

Tikal stood and approached the door, momentarily looking back at his mother and sister. Their pain was his. He wished, again, that events had not led them to these decisions. He left the house. It was time to report to Pochotl. The old priest had let up on him lately, not requiring nacom practice anymore. He guessed he had proven himself proficient enough to satisfy the old man. He saw Pochotl as the real evil that plagued the village, but did not know what to do about it or who to tell. He had trusted Ah Kaba and now did not know what to think. It was possible that the nobleman had asked those men to be his bodyguards. All three of the men, however, were of the lower classes and not of very good character. With Ah Kaba's wealth and contacts, he could have hired the very best. Tikal was beginning to think like Ahau. Maybe Ah Kaba and Pochotl were in this together. It

195

would bear remembering.

Through the rest of the day and late into the night, Pochotl kept his young apprentice working within the temple walls. Many of the tasks were menial. The priest used Tikal for the distasteful chores he himself did not want to do. It was only after Ah Kaba made an appearance that Tikal was dismissed.

***

The next morning....

A thin, breezy whisper blew in swirls across the village ground, picking up speed as it went, flicking a corner of Jada's cover and causing her to turn over in sleep. Her subconscious told her it was almost time. She promised herself she would wake up soon. There was much to do. The breeze splashed against her wall, dissipating. Remnants found their way back out the window, adding their separate energies to a new wind.

Jada's mind did as it promised. Images of Ahau's arms around her flickered behind closed eyelids. Her lips built the beginnings of a smile that never reached full promise. Recollections of her father's death and all that followed pulled Ahau's embrace from her thoughts and pushed her eyes open wide. A small whimper replaced the smile. She sat up, her hair hanging loose, falling in a thick, dark wealth to her hips. Her black eyes registered sadness, deep to the bone. This had been the last night she would sleep in this bed, ever. Tonight, Jada would flee with Ahau. To what, she did not know. Their plans were vague at best. Thoughts of her mother and brother came unbidden. The realization that after tonight she may not see them again tore at her heart. Beads of moisture pearled in the corners of her eyes. Their combined weight caused them to roll together and gently stream downwards. Jada swiped them away and willed them to stop. Nothing would change her decision now. By Ahau's side was where she belonged. She couldn't imagine living without him now.

Jada's bare feet pressed against the cold stone floor, balancing her weight as she stood. Stretching, with arms above her head, Jada glowed as sunlight through the window burnished her taut, bare skin. A strong sense of urgency compelled her to dress quickly. Jada knew the need to travel light limited what could be taken. She would have to choose wisely. There would be no coming back once she left. It would be almost impossible to say goodbye to her mother and brother. She dreaded the moment. Jada's long hair shielded her strained expression.

Spreading a blanket on the floor, Jada began piling a few belongings on it. Choosing what to keep and what to leave was arduous. Everything would have to be packed in one bundle. As the morning light grew, so did her pile. It quickly became obvious that most of her prized possessions were too numerous to comfortably carry.

***

Ix Cuy leaned against the entrance to Jada's room and tearfully watched her daughter pick through the ever-changing pile of possessions. She offered little advice. Whispering reverently to Itzamna, Ix Cuy prayed that Jada's decision to leave with Ahau would not prove a fateful one. It was still intensely difficult to believe that today would probably be the last time she would see her daughter's beautiful face. Remembered childhood images, made sweet by the passing of time, fluttered like butterflies momentarily grazing Ix Cuy's mind; Jada running to her father's knee, her small voice crying, or the puzzled look when for the first time her reflection stared back at her from the water's edge, or Jada's face excited by the great crowds at Kohunlich's Sun Temple. The scenes kept playing. They played right up to the terrible moment she woke up in her husband's blood, and Jada had rushed to her side. The tears flooded freely now. Ix Cuy went to her daughter's side.

***

Pochotl and Tikal were squalid with mud. The priest and his apprentice had spent the last third of the night digging up Kankin Mol and dragging him into the Sun Temple. The small dirt-feeding animals had protested when Kankin had been pulled from their grasp. Many of their brethren still crawled under the fetid chunks of rotten flesh clinging loosely to the bone.

Tikal had to fight his stomach. The smell was abominable. Pochotl seemed not to notice. The hymen worked quickly and efficiently, carving away unwanted meat and cracking off chunks of the skull with a fist-sized rock. Splinters of bone crushed and ground into smaller and smaller pieces under the twisting blows delivered by the priest. He had already selected a few of the disks from the top of the spine. These would eventually be pulverized into dust with the skull. The rest of the body would be reburied somewhere else later.

Kankin Mol had been an evil man, and it was this very virulence Pochotl coveted. All of the corruption and wickedness that marked a man's life was always concentrated in the remains. The core of Kankin's depravity would be intensified within the skull. Pochotl collected only the pieces he needed and shoved the rest to the floor.

"Tikal, take this disgusting mess out of here. Bury it deep somewhere in the forest. Make sure no one knows. We do not need anyone asking questions later. Slide it out on the same blanket we brought it in on. When you are done, clean up and come back here."

The drag was relatively light. Tikal was nauseated by the broken husk that had once been a man, but did as he was told. He had disliked Kankin Mol when he had been alive. Now, looking at what was left, he understood why. Sickened, Tikal retched over the top of the pitiful remains, adding to his distress.

Less than two hundred steps into the forest, Tikal began to dig. The morning people were already out doing their chores. The village was awake. He worked quickly. It did not take much of a hole. Water seeped in from the sides of the muddy gash and filled the bottom. He shoved the blanket and its contents in. From his knees, Tikal pushed the soggy earth back on top with his hands. He stood up and stamped a few times on the new grave and surveyed his work. If anyone chanced upon the spot in the next several days, they would be able to tell that someone had recently dug there. Tikal decided he didn't really care. *If they took the time to dig, what would they find?* Nothing could be connected to him.

Tikal left the grizzly site and headed for home. He couldn't wait to wash off the mud. The abhorrent thoughts of last night would be harder to rid himself of. He thought that they might be with him for a long time. Pochotl had explained the importance of collecting the corpse dust, but it still seemed wrong. The priest had said that the dust was the most important element in making dark magic against one's enemies. Evil in its purest form would visit anyone who ingested even the smallest part of the dust once it had been mixed with other ingredients that Tikal knew nothing about. Pochotl was indeed a powerful priest if he could work magic such as this. Tikal shuddered to think what else the old man might know. It would be very dangerous to be on the wrong side of such power.

Tikal stopped in his tracks as the implication suddenly became clear. *Just who is the dust for? Surely Pochotl would not make the evil concoction just to have around for emergencies. There has to be someone who is a target right now, but who?* Tikal continued on, still puzzling over the answer.

***

A smile sadistically curled one side of Pochotl's mouth, stretching the lip into a soft snarl that spoke volumes. He talked to himself in a low voice as he ground the chunks of bones into smaller and smaller pieces. Sweat curled around from high on his neck and dropped from his chin into the mix, unnoticed. A cloth rag covered his nose and mouth. His black eyes caught the light from the torches above him and gleamed maniacally. Bone dust covered his forearms and chest in a light, white patina. He was almost finished.

Sometime later, Pochotl tore the grimy rag from his nose and mouth and tossed it to the floor, then turned his head to the side and gathered in a clean breath. The musty, bitter smell still clung to his nostrils. The old man cut his thumb and pinched the blood into the dust, creating a pink paste. He added dark drops squeezed from a purple nightshade plant and entreated the gods from the underworld to help him. Each of these gods had several demon pets that occasionally could be coaxed from their guardian posts to do the bidding of priests if the need was great enough. These demons were attracted to the profane presence of corpse dust, and could sense its presence from a great distance once it was consumed by the innocent. Pochotl pulled Bela's claw from around his neck and used it to stir the mixture. Such a powerful talisman could only add to the dust's potency. He ground up plump, yellow beards from wolf lichen and added this to the mixture. Still grinding, he again implored the gods to send one of their pets. Pochotl recovered his nose and mouth and focused on his objective. His eyes smiled and then narrowed to tight slits.

***

Tikal washed off what he could at the village cistern, drawing

199

repulsive looks from the women washing clothes. He offered no explanation, hoping as Pochotl's apprentice no one would ask. Finally ridding himself of most of the filth, Tikal left the women's company with as much composure as he could muster. Less than twenty steps away, he could hear the women giggling. Each offered her own explanation for Tikal's strange and pungent appearance. He just couldn't bring himself to care. Tired, still dirty, and not at all sure what the consequences would be of his labors, Tikal entered his mother's home.

Jada and Ix Cuy were still sitting in the middle of the floor, surrounded by small piles of things. They were laughing now, their tears forgotten for the moment. Ix Cuy was lightly fingering the small scar near her daughter's right ankle, reminding Jada of the time when as a young girl, she had gotten lost in Kohunlich. The family had searched for her for most of the day, only to find her near the river trying to get a ride from a turtle only four hand spans across. Jada had been sitting on the turtle's back, slapping the poor thing, trying to get it to move. The turtle had finally had enough and twisted out from beneath her, biting a small chunk from Jada's ankle before scurrying to the water's edge and plopping out of sight.

Tikal leaned on the doorway and quietly watched the two of them, not wanting to interrupt. The two of them had precious little time together as it was. Not for the first time, Tikal wondered how things could have gone so wrong in such a short time. Sadness clamped tight around him. He went back outside before either noticed him.

***

Pochotl did indeed have a target. Two of them. If events went as planned, unique and dreadful accidents would soon befall at least two people. It was sometimes hard to contain evil once it was released, but Pochotl believed he had the power to exert considerable control over the demon's fury. How could he not? He was destined to be the Ah Kin Mai. He just hoped one of the demons of the underworld lent his help.

Tomorrow the old man would use the dust. It only needed a short time to cure. Ix Cuy and Tikal would soon be out of the priest's way, and no one would ever suspect his hand in it. Jada, as the sole

200

survivor of her father's fortune, would then be his for the taking. Anything was possible then. The old man gently slid his tongue between his teeth as he thought of the young girl. He closed his eyes and bit cautiously. A sharp sensation tingled through him. His left hand went into the pouch at his waist. He fondled Zac Kuk's torn, grisly trophies, and thought of Jada. *Tonight...yes, tonight. I've waited long enough. I will have her tonight.* His eyes closed tighter as he worked the decomposing flesh. A satisfying shudder struck him, causing him to momentarily lose his balance.

The old man stretched, working his neck this way and that, trying to relax. He tugged a bound package of weathered plants down from the shelves above his head and pulled at the knots binding them together. The dried, fragile heads were already beginning to crumble to the touch. Gathering the tops and crushing them in his fist, Pochotl brushed a pile of yellow, red, and black pieces into a flat, shallow clay bowl. The old priest was humming to himself now. His fingers flicked through several more bundles until he found the one he was looking for.

The old man beat small purple berries loose on the table and brushed these into the bowl as well. Using his knife, he sliced a twisted curl of brown root into thin slices. The exposed root oozed a red-brown. The smell was pungent, like the rot of the swamp. These too were added to the bowl.

A strong herbal tea was simmering over the small flames in the fireplace. Pochotl emptied the bowl's contents into the tea. Pieces floated to the top, and he stirred them back to the bottom. The aroma was heady. It would take a while for the tea to brew to its full potency. Pochotl dipped his finger in the turbid, sienna colored tea and sucked it for taste. Bitter. If the tea was going to have the desired effect on Jada, he would have to sweeten it considerably. He added a crushed handful of spearmint leaves and stirred. Again, he tasted. Better. He added more. The fire would have to do the rest. It would not do to burn it, though. He moved it adjacent to the heat...just enough to keep it tepid. The old man smiled with satisfaction. Tonight would be a good night. Jada was in for a pleasant surprise. He was sure she would thank him later.

Tikal walked in. "My priest, I am back. Kankin Mol's remains are once again buried. I'm sure no one saw me."

"It was a simple enough task. I hope you are right about no one seeing you. We don't want to cause any suspicion. It wouldn't take much for someone to figure out what we would be doing with the corpse of such a man as Kankin Mol. Corpse dust is as evil as it gets, my young friend. It could cause a real panic...and we don't want that do we, Tikal?" Pochotl moved closer as he spoke and draped a fatherly arm over the young man's shoulders. "I doubt very much that Kankin Mol's family will ever miss him. I didn't feel a lot of love when they buried him out behind their nasty little hovel," said the priest.

***

Tikal murmured a "no," and squirmed delicately out from beneath the sour smell of Pochotl's underarm. He did not want to give offense.

"I don't want to risk your anger, Your Holiness, but I am troubled and curious about why we need the dust." Tikal chose his words carefully. "As you have said, the dust is demonic. I don't mind admitting I am fearful."

"I have few secrets from you, Tikal. After all, you and I will be performing rituals side by side in the near future. Of course you may ask questions. You are to me as a son." Again the sweaty arm wrapped around Tikal's shoulder. With as much sincerity as his voice could muster he said, "What is it you would ask? I am at your service."

Tikal's inner alarms were screaming now. He could feel the priest's breath stir the small hairs on the side of his face by his ear. He couldn't bring himself to look Pochotl in the eyes, staring at the floor instead. Pochotl was never this condescending. Again, the young man formed his questions carefully. "Why did we make the corpse dust? Do we have enemies near at hand that can be only be overcome by such a vile means? I have no experience with the white powder. I really know only what I have heard whispered. Isn't it dangerous to even have around? Is it controllable?"

***

Pochotl's eyes had a fanatic's gleam, pulled from the black depths of his pitiless soul. He could almost feel the cleansing comfort that

202

would come from feeding the crumbly white grit to the witless boy. He fervently hoped whatever demon the dust called would linger over Tikal's death and make it a tortured agony, sure and final. Giving his adopted son a final fatherly squeeze, Pochotl stepped in front of Tikal and intently searched his face for any duplicity. *Is the boy really as naive as he acts?*

***

"Let me answer you in reverse order, Tikal. Yes, it is possible to control the effects of the powder. Very few people have the power." Pochotl drew himself up. "I am powerful enough to keep demons at bay and command them to my bidding as long as the evil dust is sealed. I am about to do exactly that."

Giving his words action, the priest used a large eagle feather to push the newly cured powder into a ceramic vial, stoppering it with a cotton rag stuffed deeply into the opening. Tikal noticed that considerable powder residue still coated the inside of the shallow bowl as Pochotl set it aside. He jerked his eyes away from it, afraid Pochotl would see his thoughts. The priest bonded a leather strip to the neck of the vial and tied it securely next to his favorite pouch around his waist. He wanted the powder next to him at all times. The feather he tossed into the fire. He resumed answering his apprentice.

"Enemies…of course we have enemies. They may not be in the village this very moment, or even make an appearance this season. But, make no mistake. Our people must be protected from those who would take what we have worked so hard to have. I'm talking about war, Tikal. Eventually another city will covet our feats and send warriors against us. It always happens. Even the mighty city of Kohunlich will be desirous of us eventually. They all will be." Pochotl was talking fast now and staring straight ahead, beckoning to the ceiling with his arms.

Tikal had seen the old man like this before. It was almost like he was in a spirit world, barely aware of his surroundings. His voice elevated to a louder pitch as if he were speaking to the whole village. Pochotl was in the middle of the room now, with his arms raised and in front of him, palms up. He was beseeching his audience to hear and understand him.

"…very possible that we will become the most important city in

203

the world under my leadership. I can see in my mind the sky-reaching pyramids, each gloriously exclaiming our worth. People will come from all directions to...."

Tikal was trembling, trying to steady his hands. He would never have a better chance to avenge his father's death, and he knew he had to act now. The eccentric old man might come out of his self-homage at any moment.

Tikal said a quick prayer and wiped the inside of the bowl with his fingers, covering them with the corpse powder residue. Still trembling and daring not to take his eyes off of Pochotl, Tikal fumbled on the table for the priest's drinking cup. He almost knocked it over but steadied it in time. Swiftly he brushed the dust into the bottom of the cup and stepped away from the table. His heart was truly in his throat now. Heat suffused his face and made his ears hot. He shuddered as he wiped his fingers clean on the edge of the table. He thought that if the priest looked at him right now, he would somehow know. Tikal swallowed hard and fought for control. His eyes darted to the cup. It was still standing. In his paranoia, he thought it might have toppled. He swallowed hard again and diverted his eyes back to the priest. He tried to pick up Pochotl's still rambling dialogue and look as if he were listening. Willing his heart to slow, Tikal sat down on the floor, crossed his legs, leaned forward, and let his chin rest on the palm of his hand, elbow on knee. He hoped he looked entranced with what the old man was saying.

"...are very lucky that Kankin Mol was the kind of man he was. His festering evil may finally serve us as nothing else can. We had to harvest the corpse when we did. The time was right. All of the corruption had collected in the meager remains of bone. If we have warning enough of other's intentions, then the powder can be used against them. As our little village grows to the city it will become, the people need to remember how I sacrificed to keep them safe. When I am proclaimed Ah Kin Mai, I can do more, so much more." Pochotl actually hugged himself. Almost immediately, he must have realized how silly he looked. He turned on his heels and found Tikal with his eyes. The answers were over.

"I hope that clears things up for you, my young apprentice. What we have done today may prove invaluable in the near future. Right now, I'm tired, and so are you. Tired men make mistakes. Leave. Go and rest. Who knows? Tomorrow could be a very special day for you."

The old man made a shooing motion at Tikal and turned his back on the young man. He walked to the table and picked up his cup. Tikal's heart again floated to his throat. Gaining his feet, he left quickly, afraid to say anything. Chancing one last look, he saw the priest pour drink from a small jug into the cup. Tikal left the temple. Outside, a smile built slowly, lighting his eyes. He had heard revenge was sweet; maybe now he would find out. Pochotl had killed his father. Of that, he was almost positive. *Who else could have? Maybe now my father's spirit can rest, knowing I have avenged him.* Tikal walked with new energy to his mother's house.

***

A shrill animal scream caused Ahau to swivel in the tree to his left and search the forest behind him. The shriek ended abruptly. Startled birds winged their way from trees in sheets of red, yellow, and brilliant blue, disturbed by the sound. Whatever had caused it made no other sounds he could hear. Some animal had died unexpectedly far behind him on the forest floor. The piercing wail sounded angrier about its demise than in pain. Ahau wondered what it had been, but felt no threat. He gripped his bow tighter, secure in the knowledge that he was safe in the tree.

Thin slices of deer meat lay drying in strips across the branches in front of him. There was enough to keep Jada and him traveling for maybe four days. He knew they could live off the forest as they went, but wanted to travel fast. Stopping to hunt took away precious time. He wasn't sure that anyone would follow them. There was the distinct possibility that none would care one way or the other about them. It was better to assume they might, though. If they could put a few days between them and the village, he would feel safer. Ahau shooed flies from the drying meat and continued to survey the forest.

Jada slipped unbidden into his thoughts and caressed his mind. Tonight, she would be with him. It was enough. There were many cities to the east and north that they would be welcomed in. Jada had relatives in Calakmal. They would try there first. Ahau absently pulled one of the not-quite-dry strips from the smooth bark and chewed off a piece of the red meat. It had a rich, straightforward taste that he took strength from. He felt stronger and more confident.

Mist still rose in pallid, thin rags from the cold forest floor. It was hard to see through the cloud banks, but Ahau thought it might be just after midday. Sunlight filtered through in patches, illuminating bits and pieces of the tree he sat in and those around him. He leaned back against the huge trunk and propped his feet on the ample bough on which he sat, and again let his thoughts drift towards Jada. Ahau closed his eyes and chewed small bites from the meat, contented and relaxed. It would be quite a while before nightfall and the need to start heading toward the point of rendezvous. Behind closed eyelids, Jada again danced before him, eyes only for him. Drowsy, Ahau walked into his dream and held her close. As his chin sluggishly slid onto his chest, the strip of meat tumbled from his limp hand and dropped to the forest floor. Ahau slept.

***

Ix Cuy was reluctant to let Jada loose from her arms. They had been sitting on Jada's bed now for quite some time, intermittently hugging each other and telling stories from precious memories. Jada pulled away from Ix Cuy just far enough to see into her mother's face. Tears still wet Ix Cuy's cheeks. Her mother pursed her lips in a tight smile and tried to briefly look away. Jada tenderly cradled the sides of Ix Cuy's face with her hands.

"Mother, I'm out of words. I hurt for both of us. It tears at me to have to leave you." Jada paused, fighting through her emotions. "Who knows? We may yet see each other again. I can't really believe that this goodbye is forever. You will always be in my heart and in my thoughts. Everything that I am is because of you, Mother. If there was any other choice, you know I would make it. I love you." Again they hugged, silent...agonizing...both trying to hold onto the moment.

Jada had finally collected all of the things she thought most necessary and tied them in a large blanket made of woven cotton with fur edging. All wrapped up, the bundle seemed small and inconsequential, considering a life was enveloped within. Ix Cuy had sewn several dozen pieces of jade into a leather belt that could be used as currency when and if the couple needed it. Jada hefted the brown belt, feeling for its weight. She thought it would be cumbersome carried around her waist day after day, and then wondered if it was heavy enough. The jade might be all that stood between them and disaster. The future was so questionable. *What if my relatives do not take us in? Will the people in Calakmal accept us?*

Jada pushed the negative thoughts out of her head. The time to leave would soon be upon her. Thin cloud banks gathered, restraining the fires of sunset and souring the sky a grieving gray. Looking out the window, Jada could see shadows lengthen and merge, losing their individual shapes, and creating darkness only the village fires would hold at bay. *Yes, it is almost time.*

***

Curled tight on a woven mat near the front door, Tikal lay sleeping. No qualms of conscience troubled his dreams. Pochotl deserved anything and everything he received in the way of retribution as far as Tikal was concerned. The old man may have considerable powers, including dominion over Tikal as an apprentice, but surely even he could not sway control over a demon provoked by Kankin Mol's corpse dust. Jada's brother's eyelids moved rapidly, his face serene, as he dreamed of his father before leaving Kohunlich. Everything had seemed right then...he had been happy. Remembered bits of his family's former life comforted him.

Outside, night had come. Clouds obscured the moon, making the darkness complete and utterly black except for the small places light from the evening fires reached. Jada gently shook her brother awake. Tikal sluggishly opened his eyes, reluctant to leave his dreams. After a few moments, the here and now asserted its sober presence and claimed all of Tikal's attention. Azure skied ribbons of dreams evaporated into wisps of nothingness. *Pochotl!* His first reaction was to check on the old man, wondering if the powder had worked its magic yet. If the stories he had heard growing up about the corpse dust were even partially true, then Pochotl was in real trouble. Tikal grinned, thinking about it. He would wait, though. Tomorrow would be soon enough to see what he would see. Tonight he needed to help his sister. Ahau was waiting.

After a quick meal, Tikal slipped out the door to see who was about. Jada and he had already decided on the most likely route out of the village. Guards still patrolled the perimeter, guarding against any

207

possible attack by Bela or incursion by Ahau. Fires could be seen seemingly everywhere. Paranoia was running high. Tikal walked along the northern edge of the encampment, nodding and voicing the occasional encouraging greeting to the guards. They stood in groups of two or three, most with their backs to the fires, looking outwards into the forest. Some were stationed high in the trees. They were the ones whom Tikal and Jada had to be most concerned with. From their vantage point, little would go unnoticed. Tikal chortled at the thought of how dangerous the village now thought Ahau had become. Pochotl, once again, had done his work well. The theory that the priest had planted about Ahau possibly being demon-possessed had spread quickly. *If the gods believe in justice, if the ancient ones truly watch over their children, then tonight Pochotl will come to an evil end.* Tikal mused about possible ways the old man might die. Each was violent and painful. He almost wished he could physically do it himself.

"You." A voice from above swiftly brought him out of his fantasy. "What are you doing here? You know this is no place to be after dark."

Tikal shaded his eyes from the glare of the fire and looked up into the trees, trying to find the face that belonged to the voice.

"Tikal, is that you? Sorry, you startled me. I had no idea anyone was there. I'm a little nervous up here. I don't mind telling you I'd rather be back in the village." A young man lithely jumped down from above, landing just in front of Tikal.

Tikal knew the young man well. Before he had been made a priest's apprentice, they had both been part of the hunting clan, *Ah Cacaw.* Tikal had not seen his friend for weeks. They shook each other's shoulders in greeting and spoke briefly about how long it had been since they had seen each other. The words seemed vacuous and stale. It became apparent quickly that both had moved on. Their interests had changed even though they had been close once. Now the young man's demeanor seemed somehow juvenile and immature to Tikal. Too many things had happened since they spoke last. Tikal guessed that it was he who had changed the most. He was more serious and solemn now and looked at things considerably different than he had before. They parted after promising to get together soon, both knowing that they probably wouldn't.

Tikal was irate with himself that he had not seen the young man in the tree. If he was going to help his sister leave tonight, then he had better start paying closer attention. The young man had not been in the trees the past few nights. Of that he was sure. *Why of all nights would he be there now?* This was the very spot he had hoped to take his sister through. Now, they would have to find another path to take. Tikal continued his walk around the village, looking for just the right place. The guards would be paying attention to what was coming into their circle, not what was going out. That was their edge. He just needed to find the most vulnerable place for them to sneak through.

***

After what seemed an eternity to Jada, Tikal came back. He had found a place. They would have to slip through one at a time. There were guards to contend with, but Tikal had a plan. He was going to distract them long enough for Jada to skirt them and enter the forest. Tikal would be close behind a little later. It was the only way he could think of.

They kissed their mother and left. Ix Cuy's eyes were dry as she gave each of them a final hug and wished them a godsend. All the words had been spoken. There was nothing left to say. She quietly shut the door behind them and watched from the darkness of the window.

Tikal grabbed his sister's hand and led her to the large cistern in the middle of the village where he had washed earlier. No one was about. The moon was still obscured by ponderous clouds, making the darkness almost complete. Tikal whispered once more for his sister to wait several moments before going. He needed time to get the guards' attention. He squeezed Jada's hand and left in a bent over crouch to the north. Jada sat on one of the benches near the cistern and tried to be patient. The bench was partially hidden by a snaggly old tree whose leafless branches hung low like the aged, ancient fingers of a long dead creature.

Tikal disappeared quickly in the dark. She tried to search his path but could not see more than twenty body lengths in any direction. Fires flickered ominously in several places in the distance before the forest began. Occasionally she could see the silhouettes of men walking around them. She watched the spot Tikal had indicated between two of the fires intently, trying to see her brother. She clenched her bundle tighter, wishing she knew exactly when to leave. If she left too late or too early, they would never get through. Both of them would be taken to the council in the morning and made to explain why they had been trying to leave the village. Again, she squeezed her eyes slightly tighter and tried to see farther into the blackness. Jada was almost convinced it was time. She would wait a few moments more.

A deep, timberous voice broke the silence just behind her left side. A hand compressed her shoulder, holding her down.

"Jada...how fortunate. I was just thinking of you. It must be Itzamna's intention that I find you here."

Jada was terrified. From the first syllable, she knew the source. Pochotl. Her heart thundered in her breast. She wanted to bolt, but the hand held her solidly in place. In the space of a heartbeat, questions raged through her mind. *Why is he here? What do I say? What if he asks me why I'm out? How do I get to Tikal? Why? Why? What does he want?*

***

Pochotl could feel the young girl trembling beneath his fingers. Even in this blackness he could see the panic in her eyes. He had not seen Tikal leave. The old man was just thirsty and had stopped for water. Pochotl had intended to see her a little later tonight in any event. The fact that she was here only made things easier. He had devised the perfect excuse to stop by Ah Tok's house and see his dead friend's beautiful daughter under the guise of having news of Ahau. Of course, that news could only be imparted to her in the Sun Temple. That's all he really needed. Getting her in the temple behind a closed door was crucial to his scheme. He thought quickly.

"Jada, my dear. How very fortunate that I have found you here. I have important news of Ahau for you. Good news, in fact."

He could still feel the trembling beneath his hand. He made little circles with his fingertips, rubbing her shoulder. He liked the little quivers she made. It made him feel powerful.

Jada pulled loose from the old man and stood, hoping it was dark enough to hide her foot kicking the bundle deeper underneath the bench where she had dropped it. She would never be able to explain it if the priest saw it. Pochotl stepped closer, trying to see her face

210

clearly.

"Did you hear me, my dear? I said I have news of Ahau."

Jada willed her voice steady. "That is good to hear. What...what did you want to tell me, Your Holiness?"

Pochotl smiled and pursed his lips. He could still feel her fear. It was almost malleable. He reached and grasped her hands in his, bringing them together.

"Jada, I think I know of a way to put all of this nonsense about Ahau being a murderer to rest. Information. New truths have come to my attention. As you know, I have always had Ahau's best interests at heart and have been searching for the facts that would clear him. I think I have found them."

***

Jada's hopes soared but only briefly. She knew too well how Pochotl lied. Her mother had warned her of the priest. She had said the old man was like a scorpion, only with a smaller stinger. The thought brought a brief bubble of laughter to her throat, but she kept it from escaping. Her instincts communicated there was extreme danger here. She willed her hands to still their quivering and tried to act sure of herself.

"I have always hoped that you would be the one to help Ahau. Only someone of your power and importance could discover the real truth. Tell me what you have learned." Jada pulled her hands ever so slightly. Pochotl's grip was firm. Afraid she would anger him, she relaxed them and waited for his answer, leaving them in his grasp.

"Unfortunately, I am old, my dear. The humidity in this cool air dampens my bones. Come with me to my lodging in the Sun Temple and we will continue this conversation. I even have hot tea to share while we talk." His hold on her hands increased as he led her away from the bench and toward the temple.

Jada's mind screamed to come up with an excuse not to go. Tikal would be waiting. She could think of nothing. Meekly, she allowed herself to be led, vowing to get away as quickly as she could at the first opportunity. She glanced back over her shoulder in the direction of the spot Tikal said would be her path into the forest. She could see nothing. To keep from stumbling in the dark, she moved up closer to the priest.

Pochotl shut the massive wooden door behind them, and indicated a place for the young girl to sit. Jada had never before been inside of a priest's living quarters and was assailed by the hundreds of sights and smells. None of them helped quiet the growing panic quaking her soul. The place smelled evil. A large fire, encased by three sides of stone, cast dancing shadows against the walls, shapes that constantly shifted and changed. Much in the room was hidden in the dark. Her imagination, much like her brother once had, brought images of festering, profane demons just out of reach of the light. The smell of something long dead, over ripe and rotten, permeated the air she breathed. She was almost nauseated. She made herself think of other things. She wondered if Tikal would come looking for her when she didn't show.

Pochotl busied himself with the tea, making small conversation about the weather and how the rains were almost at an end. Hiding his actions with his body, he poured Jada's cup to the brim with the special brew he had made earlier. In his cup, he poured four fingers of balche. The old man sat down near Jada and offered her the tea. She took it with both hands but did not immediately drink.

"You are right, Your Holiness. It is much warmer in here. I am honored that you have invited me to your home. My mother will be expecting me, though. I can't stay long. Please, tell me what you have found out," Jada said.

Pochotl made a smacking noise as he sipped his drink, exclaiming how good it tasted.

"Ah, how right you are, my dear. I will explain everything. But first, taste your tea. I made it fresh only this morning. Can you taste the spearmint?" Pochotl gently helped Jada's cup to her mouth. She drank a small portion.

The taste was heady, but good. Jada looked at the old man, waiting for him to continue. Pochotl began talking about how distressed he had been when Jada's father had been murdered and what a blow it had been for him to have such a good friend taken so violently from his life. Jada sipped more of the tea as the priest talked. Her mind felt warm. It was beginning to be hard to follow the priest's words. She drank more of the tea. Her scalp tingled at the roots. A warm, growing sensation filled her skull. Jada's mind soared. It skimmed through a bright light and like a falling feather, floated slowly downwards to the shadows. She felt herself slide beneath the darkness. The cup fell from her hand, the dredges spilling to the floor. The old man smiled and continued drinking his balche, humming to himself. Jada fell on her side, eyes closed.

CHAPTER 15

REPRISAL

Bela sat high up in a tree near the people's village, looking into the encampment, watching the pitiful brownskins sit by their fires with their little spears and weak knives. He detested them. It had taken two nights to get here, but now he would kill them all. Brown saliva ran down his chin as he thought about gorging from their ripped throats. But first, the old man.

He had seen Pochotl lead the female into the stone enclosure. The large tapetums at the back of his black pupils glowed angrily from the available light. The twin lamps blinked and then were gone. Bela slipped from the tree and made his way to the temple. Stone stairs, going up the back of the building and ending on the second level, provided him access. A black cavity at the top of the stairs showed him the way inside. The great beast silently, on padded feet, started down.

***

Tikal didn't see Jada leave the village, but assumed she had. There had been no trouble deflecting the guards from their posts. Everyone loved a good story and he had told them one. Afterwards, he had simply slipped into the forest unnoticed by any of them. The three guards were still in a bunch, each trying to outdo the other with a story. Tikal rubbed his face and raked fingers through his hair. *Where is she, though?* Jada wasn't at the rendezvous place. *Maybe for some reason she moved further in.* Tikal searched again. He was too close to the village to call her name. He just hoped the silly girl had not gone on without him. He knew she was anxious to be with Ahau, but

215

the night forest was no place for a girl to be alone.

Tikal gripped his spear a little tighter and made for the thickest part of the forest. Much later, a tingling, numbing worry ran through Tikal. He was at least halfway to Ahau and still had not found his sister. A torch was in his free hand, lighting his way, allowing him to search through the litter on the forest's floor for tracks. He cursed himself for not being with her. *How did we miss each other?* Tikal was sure she had not been back at the cistern. Before he left, he had gotten close enough to look. He was sure that he had made good enough time to cut her trail by now.

He called softly again. "Jadaaaa. Jadaaa, where are you?"

No answering call came back to him. Small animals scuttling out of his way were the only responses he received. Tikal now had to decide. It was just as far to go back as it was to go on. *Ahau will be waiting. Maybe together, we can find her.* Again, he cursed himself. *It all should have been so simple. How did I go wrong? Where is she?*

"Jaaada. Jaaada, where are you?"

Tikal repeatedly reviewed those last moments at the village in his mind. He could come up with no explanations. He dispensed with calling her name and looked for tracks. Tikal moved as fast as the light from his torch would allow him to go. If Jada was in trouble because of his stupidity, he would never forgive himself. There was the slim chance that he might find Jada with Ahau, but he doubted it. She did not have a torch with her when they had parted. If she had one, she would have had to make it. He wasn't sure she even knew how. The more he thought about it, the surer he was that she was in trouble. He had to get to Ahau.

***

Strange, powerful odors bathed Bela's face after the first five steps down. The great beast slowed his descent, trying to puzzle through the smells. Death and decay were easily separated from the rest. Plant scents he could also recognize and see the foliation clearly in his mind. There were others, though, that required more thought. He cautiously continued down, rubbing the side wall with one hand. His nails left little snicks of sound trailing behind him. Firelight from below flickered against the stone as he rounded the corner. Pochotl and the female were somewhere close below him. Bela could smell them both. He moved slower. At the bottom of the next landing, he crouched in the corner shadow. He could see most of the room now, hidden in the dark where the light from the fire did not penetrate.

The female was bare and apparently unconscious, tied to a table, feet on the floor and chest against the rough wood. Her legs were roped to the table legs and her hands outstretched and tied strong to the opposite legs. Bela lifted his snout in her direction and gathered in more of the available odors. Strange hormonal stirrings quickened within him. The old man was brushing the back of his fingers down her back, making small sounds of pleasure in his throat. Bela's eyes narrowed as he watched. Instinct almost made him lunge, but reasoning made him wait. *What is the old man doing?* In the two hundred years of his life, Bela had seen almost every animal in the forest mate, but this was different. The female was asleep. Something didn't feel right.

Pochotl's backside was lush with sweat as he moved in position behind the female. Bela sensed urgency in the old man's movements. Pochotl seemed displeased about something. The old priest snarled a curse and slapped the female's backside again and again. He was working feverously now and Bela could see the old man's back muscles shuddering. Pochotl closed his eyes and lifted his head high in the air. He made whimpering noises and continued to beat the female in earnest.

The great beast searched the room for other avenues of escape other than the one he sat on. There were none that the priest could reach in time. The huge wooden door was shut with another heavy table pushed against it. Bela guessed the walls to be as thick as a large tree's trunk. Sounds would not penetrate to the outside. He could take his time.

Bela stood, still cloaked in the darkness at the landing's corner. In a deep, soft purr he said the old man's name. "Pochooootl."

The priest froze in mid crouch, his hands still under his flap. Again, he heard his name called softly from somewhere above.

"Pochooootl."

***

The old man slowly swiveled his head, trying to peer into the darkness above. His first reaction of guilt was swiftly replaced by a

217

growing dread. He had not imagined it. Someone was up there. The voice sounded deep, and decidedly male. *One of the demons from the underworld…maybe it is here to help me after all.* Pochotl turned completely and took a step closer to the sound, trying to pierce the gloom with his eyes. Twin flickers of lights beamed momentarily out of the darkness like eyes, and then nothing. It was too dark to see.

"Who's there?" Pochotl demanded, trying to sound confident. "This is a holy place and off limits to you. Speak up! Who is up there? Step into the light."

Pochotl was met with silence. He moved a little closer. He was almost at the bottom of the steps, but could still see nothing. The darkness was complete, swallowing the voice's source.

"Ooooooruh! Meee seee youuu, Pochooootl." The great beast made a wet, spitting sound with his tongue on the last syllable and stepped into view.

Pochotl's eyes widened in abject fear. He fell to his knees, groaning in pitiful hitches of half breaths. His hands waved in front of him as if he could erase the horrible visage. He knew exactly who it was. Bela. A warm stream of urine rolled down his legs, puddling the stone beneath him.

There was no mistaking the beast's intent. The old man tried to stand, but his legs refused to respond. He tried to speak, but only a gurgle sounded. The muscles in his throat constricted in horror. He had trouble breathing.

***

Bela filled the steps, flowing like black, blown smoke down the stairs. Menacingly, he moved to the old man and stood above him. Bela wanted to rip and slash the old man's chest then and there; push his mouth into the steaming guts and drink from spurting arteries. But, he found patience and stayed his hand. There were questions to ask; things he wanted to know. He wrapped his long, thick fingers around the top of the old man's head and pulled the priest to the center of the room, closer to the table where Jada still lay, unconscious. Pochotl whimpered in pain, squirming along on his knees, trying to keep up.

Bela remembered Chan Chel. The hunter's broken leg had kept him from getting away. Such a thing would work with the priest. He took Pochotl's left leg in his hands and snapped the bone backwards at the knee. The old man howled in agony and fell hard against the stone floor. Bela knew his screams could not be heard outside the temple. Pochotl tried to push away from Bela with his good leg. It was a mistake. Bela grabbed that leg and pulled the priest to him. He broke it at the ankle, twisting it until it snapped and hung with the toes pointing backwards. Splintered bone broke the surface. Pochotl's screams pitched higher, but the thick stone walls still muffled his shrieks. No one heard, not even Jada, who was still cheek down on the table facing them. Only the ropes kept her from slumping to the floor.

Bela enjoyed hearing the old brownskin sob his pain and grab at his broken body. He could smell the fear. It was tantalizing. The great beast stooped over the priest and pushed him onto his back. Then he saw the finger...his finger. Hanging from the old man's neck was the burnt, severed trophy taken from the small cave.

Bela's right hand flashed downwards in a killing stroke that ended just before the sharp claws pierced the flesh. *Not yet!* Instead, he delicately seized the mutilated piece of flesh and pulled it from Pochotl's neck, tearing the leather strip where it tied in a knot. He held it close to his face and studied it. Disgust wrinkled his snout and a small whining sound burbled from his throat. This had been his finger. He remembered the pain and humiliation. More reasons to kill this trembling, dirty little brownskin right now where he lay. But patience reasserted itself. Bela had come here for more than just that. He wanted to know the answers to many questions...questions that this old man would provide the answers to.

Bela took the burnt finger and traced the tattoos of gods that circled Pochotl's chest with its sharp claw. He would start with these. *What are they?* He made a shallow incision around the outside border of the first image of thirteen. Blood beaded up like iridescent pearls, marking the path of the knife-like claw. Bela licked the red line smooth. New pearls immediately bubbled up; red round pledges of the pain to come.

"Whaaat is thiiis, Pochoootl? Telll meee. I waaant tooo knooow."

***

The old priest was beginning to go into shock. The pain was

219

settling into agony that surrounded him and became his whole world from edge to edge. Pochotl's skin trembled, but not from pleasure like before. Through gritted teeth, the old man spit the names of the thirteen upper world gods and their role in life, one at a time. With each answer, Bela made the incision longer. Pochotl clenched his fists, furious that this could be happening to him. He vowed not to give into the pain. It was a hollow promise. By the time Bela reached the eighth image, Pochotl was screaming to Itzamna and any other god who would listen to release him. He squirmed and fought to be out from under the great beast, but Bela held him firm. The thirteenth answer connected the incision's finish to the start, completing a bloody circle that bathed Pochotl's chest in a sheet of trembling scarlet.

Bela did not completely understand who the gods were. *How can the unseen exist?*

Bela was just getting started.

"Pochoootl, telll meee why yoou heeere? Yooou cooome from wheeere? Arrre yoou moore?"

Pochotl ignored the beast, trying to reconcile himself to the pain, but Bela would not be denied. He grabbed the priest's left hand and started pulling slowly but steadily on the index finger. The knuckle joint started to separate, then popped free. Thin connecting layers of muscle, cartilage, and flesh parted, releasing the finger into Bela's grasp. He had the priest's attention now.

"You finger liike miine." He held his dead claw and the priest's finger together side by side. Blood spurted in gluts of hot red from Pochotl's hand. Bela put the wound to his mouth and sucked. Amazingly, the old man stopped screaming. Devastating pain caused most of his body to quiver in spasms. Again Bela asked his questions, taking the injured hand from his mouth but not releasing it. This time the priest answered quickly, his voice trembling violently. Bela had trouble understanding the words, but not the intent. Pichotl's underworld demon of death had come after all.

Bela thumped his chest with the back of his hand. "Ooooooruh! Nooo! Thiss iiis Belaaa's treees. Meee liiive heeere looong tiiime. Yooou alll die. Nooo mooore cooome!"

Spittle from Bela's seething words flecked Pochotl's uncaring face. The old man's eyes were glassing over, the shock and loss of blood taking their toll. Bela crunched another finger off with his teeth and sucked it end over end in his mouth, drinking the juices from it as he thought. Again he held up the first finger severed from the priest beside his own. The pale, pinkish-brown finger looked insignificant beside his. He decided he would keep it as a souvenir. He spit out the second.

Bela prodded the old man in the chest, trying to get his attention. Pochotl did not respond, except with a weak intake of breath. Bela pushed the tips of his claws under the incision around the priest's tattoos. He pushed a little harder, working his fingers underneath the skin. With both hands, he slowly tore the circle of tattooed flesh from Pochotl's chest. The ripping hide came away whole. Pochotl only groaned weakly, having lost consciousness. Bela licked the underside of his trophy clean and wrapped the severed finger up in it. Nothing else of the old man did he touch. Other thoughts pushed their way into his mind. *The female.*

Bela moved to her, standing directly over the female's still body. He sifted pungent aromas from the air that distinctly belonged to her. They excited him. His lust for blood succumbed to the newness of arousal. Bela placed his mouth near her ear and purred a deep rumble. The female did not respond. He traced a bloody claw lightly down the middle of her back, as he had seen Pochotl do, ending at her buttocks.

He hated all that was brownskin, but this was somehow different. Bela examined the sisal rope that held her to the table. He cautiously pulled on one of the ties. The binding held to the female's wrist, giving no ground. She was not going anywhere.

Bela left her for the moment and inspected the rest of the room. The walls, tables, and floor were covered with clutter. Many strange things captured his attention. He lifted his head slightly with an intake of breath. Most of the strangest odors were coming from the littered table and shelf to his left. He began ripping the stops from the many different ceramic containers and pouring their contents onto the table's surface and floor. Each, he sniffed. Some he recognized, most he did not. The emptied vessels smashed against the stone where he dropped them one by one. His great hands swept the shelf empty, spreading Pochotl's myriad of holy things across the room.

His foot blundered against leather bunching lying just under the table's leg. They were the old man's pouches, left there in a heap where he had hurriedly discarded them. Bela picked them up and held them close to his nostrils. The smell was one of death and decay. Using one of his claws, he ripped through the thin hides, tumbling their contents to the table. Shriveled, gristly pieces of rotten meat piled upon themselves. Corpse dust followed, covering them white. Bela stirred the small heap with an index finger, puzzled as to its meaning. Bringing the powdered finger to his nose, he snorted. He touched the white to his tongue, still trying to puzzle out the meaning. The taste was disgusting. Bela made several hacking noises in his throat, trying to rid himself of the taste, and shoved the offensive mound to the floor. *Enough!*

Bela went back to the female. Instinct told him to take her. She was not like the other brownskins and definitely was not a threat. She might prove useful later. He cut through the bindings with the sharp edge of his claw and hoisted her easily over a shoulder. The female's unconsciousness reminded him of picking up a clumsy Chan Chel after he had fallen from the cliff. Her body heat against his chest, however, suggested that she could be of a much different use. Bela grabbed the rolled, tattooed hide, stuffed it under Jada, and went back up through the stairwell and into the night. At the top of the landing he overlooked the village. Like holes in the darkness, the fires surrounding the encampment blazed their lights, giving false comfort to the guards that stood around them. Bela's hatred for the puny brownskins returned full blown. He still wanted the female, but ached to shed more blood. If he was careful, he thought he could do both. He picked his path... straight through the middle, toward the same fire Tikal had left by earlier.

***

The first guard never knew Bela was there. He died with his back to the village, looking out toward the forest, protecting his people. Bela's claws plowed deep channels through his neck and back with a single blow that crumpled the guard without a sound other than his falling. He did not die unnoticed, however. Tikal's friend, from high in the tree, perceived the motion of the falling warrior from the corner

222

of his peripheral vision. He jerked his eyes to the fallen warrior and watched in horror as Bela stepped over the body into full view. The fire clearly illuminated the great beast and the baggage over his shoulder.

The young man responded immediately. He began yelling and banging his spear against the trunk of the tree. Bela also reacted immediately. Three guards, several strides to his left, turned and ran toward the commotion. Bela cleaved through the closest one. The other two only had time to get their spears up before they, too, died gurgling from grave wounds through their chests.

Bela turned in the direction of the young man in the tree, eyes blazing hatred and assurance that his turn was next. The beast rapidly sprinted to the base of the guard's tree. He shrugged the female off his shoulder and started up. The terrified young man ineffectively threw his spear and started climbing, yelling for help at the top of his lungs. Warriors came from all directions, spears bristling in their hands, taking courage from their numbers. Some of them reached the tree quickly.

***

Bela had to make a fast decision. He still wanted the female. He "Ooooruhed" his loathing and sprang onto the two brownskins standing below. One of their spears ripped a painful furrow through his left shoulder before breaking from the force of his jump. Bela paid the wound no heed, slashing through them with terrible claws, his teeth gnashing black breaches in their throats. They fell sundered and bleeding at his feet. He grabbed up the female and the trophy roll of flesh, and sprinted into the darkness of the forest.

***

None of the warriors followed. They yelled their defiance and some even ineptly threw their spears in the general direction Bela had gone, but held their ground. Each was glad that no one gave chase; then they all would be obliged to follow. The illumination from the fire deftly delineated the boundaries of their courage.

***

Tikal found Ahau right where he expected him to be. After a quick explanation of why he did not have Jada with him, the two friends hurried back toward the village. They were within hearing

223

distance and could make out some of the words, and they picked up their pace. Scant torch light hindered their pace. The thought that Bela was in the village pushed them to breakneck speed through the darkness. When they arrived at the outskirts, they could see what appeared to be the entire male population standing just inside the firelight near the skirt of the forest.

Ahau remained in his place, sending Tikal to find out what had happened. Tikal came back moments later, his face ashen. He explained to Ahau what he could. The information was jumbled. Everyone was talking at once, each with his own version. One thing was certain. Bela had been there and several people had died. One of the guards swore the beast had a female hung over his shoulder when he left.

"That has to be wrong. Why would Bela take a hostage? To feed on later?" Ahau's eyes were large and his throat dry. "What if it is true, though? It just can't be Jada. It just can't."

The two men ran unchallenged to the cistern, where Tikal had left his sister. No one was there. Panic constricted their chests. Ahau found the bundle underneath the bench…Jada's bundle. They looked at each other, both reading the other's thoughts. They ran to Ix Cuy, hoping against what they knew was probably true that she would be there.

Ix Cuy was standing in the doorway, trying to discern what all of the commotion was about. She was sure that Jada and Tikal had been caught. Her heart thundered when she saw Ahau and Tikal running toward her. She tried to see beyond them. Was anyone chasing them? Where was Jada? Ix Cuy moved aside, hurrying them inside before anyone saw them. Tikal grabbed her hands in his and faced her close before she could ask.

"Mother, we cannot find Jada. Did she come back here?"

Ix Cuy shook her head no.

Ahau echoed the question once more. "Are you sure? We found her bundle by the cistern." He paused. "Bela's been in the village."

Ix Cuy started trembling, and her legs went weak. Only Tikal being so close kept her from falling. He tenderly went to the floor with her, cradling her in his arms.

"Mother…we don't know that Bela even saw Jada. She could be

hiding somewhere." Tikal left out that someone had seen the beast carrying a female from the encampment. There was no reason to alarm his mother further with guesswork. If it was true, he refused to believe that it was his sister, anyway. "Mother, we have to go. We do not have much time. We have to find her quickly and leave before the village recovers and sets new guards. Have you seen Pochotl? Has he been around? It is strange that I did not see him with the other men."

Ix Cuy again shook her head and squeezed her son's hands, whispering weakly, "Find her, Tikal...find her. She has to be close by. I think I would sense it, if she were...dead. Hurry! She's probably hiding somewhere near the cistern."

Both young men left quickly. Urgent screams answered each other from different locations. The village was still in an uproar. Tikal suggested they check the temple. It was the largest building in the village and it wasn't far from the well. She could be hiding near it. Both of them hunched over and ran toward the cistern and the looming black building beyond. After circling the temple and not seeing Jada, they cautiously went up the back way and down into Pochotl's housing.

At the same landing Bela had earlier watched the old man from, they hesitated. They could sense the wrongness. The rank, coppery smell of blood flowed up at them. They could only see part of the room, but what they saw was enough to convince them that something terrible indeed had happened. By dying firelight, they could see jumbled rubble everywhere. Ceramic shards from pots, vials, and bowls littered the floor, their contents strewn. Bundles of plants, roots, and seed were torn apart and scattered. Colored powders covered almost everything. Most of the wreckage lay in shadow, the feeble firelight only hinting at what was there. Dank odors, like long spoiled fruit, assailed them.

They moved slowly down the stairs and into the room, each ready to bolt at the slightest sound. Neither said a word, each thinking the same. *Bela has been here.* They stayed close together and searched the room. Tikal pulled one of the torches from the wall and lit it in the dying embers. Ahau did the same. They soon found the table with the severed rope hanging, but could make no sense of it. One of them gently prodded a pile of clothing under the table.

Tikal instantly recognized it. "This is Jada's! She was wearing this tonight. Look, there at the bottom of the pile...hand me that leather belt." Ahau did as he was told, handing the brown, sewn leather to Tikal.

"Yes. I know this was Jada's. Mother filled this with jade for the two of you. Look!" Tikal used his knife to pick through the stitching, revealing the green stones. "She was here."

Both of them raised their torches and moved on. It was then that they found Pochotl. The old man was lying on his back, his eyes open. Both of them jumped back. The sight of the ruined priest was unnerving. Neither of them had any doubts about his being dead. They could see the black, runny wound where his chest had been. One of his legs was twisted at an impossible angle, the foot from the other broken and laying perpendicular to the joint. Tikal spoke first.

"Well, Pochotl, it doesn't look like you will be anyone's Ah Kin Mai." He spat into the old man's open eyes, and kicked him in the ribs. The blow made a satisfying thunk. "I'm glad you insisted we make the corpse dust, old man." Again he booted the old man, this time in the face.

Ahau stared disbelieving at his friend's actions. He had no love for the priest, but certainly didn't expect Tikal to react this way. He grabbed him by the arm and pulled him back.

"What are you doing? Have you gone mad?"

Tikal jerked away from Ahau but said nothing. He pushed the hair back off his face and glared at the old man. "I'll tell you all about it later. Right now we have to find Jada. I just hope Pochotl didn't get her killed. Bela's been here. Look at those wounds. Nothing else could have done this. We also know Jada was here. From the reports, Bela left carrying a female. It has to be her. I can only guess why she was nude." Again, he kicked the priest in the face. "Come on. Let's move. We may not have much time."

***

A weak breeze brushed over Pochotl's dying fire, causing the charcoaled embers to wink like dozens of angry red eyes. They crackled and popped in annoyance for some time before finally winking out for good, leaving the room shrouded in dead darkness.

***

Tikal and Ahau experienced no trouble leaving the village. Once in the forest, they circled to where Bela had left, hoping to pick up his trail. They moved fast. The morning was still some time off, but enough light squeezed over the horizon to see by. It was Ahau that declared Bela's intentions.

"He's going home. He has to be going back to the depression where I saw him first. My instincts tell me that is his home. He will go nowhere else. If Jada's still alive, we will find her there."

Both young men hardened their resolve now that they had a destination. They would find the beast and confront it. Ahau strung his bow and pulled his best arrow from the quiver. Grim determination flowed through his veins, scalding his need to kill the beast. Nothing would stay his hand now. There was no fear, no thought for his own safety. Bela had chosen the wrong female to take. Jada *was* still alive, he could feel it. Ahau *would* find them.

***

Ah Kaba shoved against the door to the temple. The huge wooden table pushing back from the other side finally began to slide away. A crack appeared between the door and its stop. Ah Kaba put his face against it and tried to see in, but it was too dark. He called out to Pochotl, but there was no answer. Bracing his feet in the soft earth, he levered once again at the door, pushing with all of his strength. The crack widened. He hammered at the door with his shoulder in short bursts, widening the entrance. It was enough. Ah Kaba squeezed in, and again he called.

"Pochotl, it's me, Ah Kaba. Are you here?" From the door, a thin shaft of young sunlight revealed broken shards of pottery. Ah Kaba stepped carefully. "Pochotl. Pochotl. Where are you?"

The nobleman pulled the table completely away and opened the door wide. The room was a disaster. The priest's torn hand lay in the light. Ah Kaba rushed to the body, squatting to his knees beside his mentor. Pochotl was cold and rigid to the touch. Ah Kaba bowed his head. Tears began to flow for what could have been. The priest had represented his one chance to be someone important. Now, that was all gone.

Pochotl's occluded eyes stared accusingly at the nobleman. The pallid face looked considerably older in death, but none the less imposing. Pochotl's lips were parted, giving credence to Ah Kaba's imagination that the priest was speaking to him, arraigning him somehow for his death.

Ah Kaba stood, shaking his mind loose from the frightening grip of his subconscious. He shivered involuntarily. Looking around the rest of the room, he spied the table with the tattered rope bindings. He knew immediately what they had been for. Pochotl had once allowed him to watch from hiding. Using his knife, he severed the rope and tossed it well away from the table. It would not do to have Pochotl's death connected with such perversities.

It was time to let the rest of the village know of the priest's death. Ah Kaba stepped back outside the temple and called for help. After the Council of Elders made their usual speeches, war was declared against Bela. By mid-morning, over one hundred men followed the beast's back trail. Ah Kaba was with them. Opportunities might still be available.

***

Bela kept going through the night, and thought he was nearing the halfway mark. The sun, though, would soon end his travel. He chose a familiar area in which to hole up. The female was still unconscious, only occasionally moaning feebly. Bela pushed Jada into the small enclosure and crawled in tightly beside her. The beast had scanned with his senses behind him several times during his flight. No one followed him that he could discern. He was safe for the time being.

Bela lifted the female onto her back and sniffed her face, detecting her breath. She was still alive. Hunger fought with his newly awakened desires. The smell of her hot blood pulsating just beneath the fragile skin of her throat made him lick the artery, savoring the salty taste of her sweat. His pebbled fingers brushed the smooth skin of her face. Bela thought she was unattractive, even a little repulsive with such uniformly flat features. Still, she was female, and the nearest to his species he had discovered. Desire held dominion. Bela moved over her.

***

Ahau and Tikal were exhausted. They had traveled far and fast but were still a long way from Bela's lair. Ahau well remembered the

228

way. It seemed like a lifetime ago, coming back from his uncle and brother's death, searching for the rest of his people. An azure halo grew in the east, defining the horizon's canopy. A faint red line moored its base to the trees. Stars began to retreat one by one. The coming of day gave them hope.

Ahau instinctively knew that Bela was a night animal. Almost all of the beast's killings were at night. Pochotl had said Bela was a demon…maybe he was. It didn't matter. If the beast only traveled at night, then they had a chance of catching it. They pushed on, resting only a few moments by a stream. High winds pulled dark, ponderous clouds behind them from the west, their bellies distended, threatening to burst.

***

Rain skittled down from leaf to leaf, finally plopping in puddles on the floor of Bela's nest. Hooded eyelids unsheathed dark slits as Bela prodded the immediate area with his senses. No animal was near him. The rain was a nuisance. It was hard to sleep with its incessant rattling of the foliage. Bela tenderly patted the still unconscious female and came to his feet. Rain always meant heavy clouds this time of the year. The sunlight would be held at bay. Bela moved to the opening of his hide and brushed the leafage back. The light was muted, but still uncomfortably bright by Bela's standards. He could move, nevertheless.

Bela was curiously anxious to get the female back to his cave. He wasn't sure why, he just felt that he needed to. Bela dragged the female out by her feet and draped her over his shoulder. He tucked the rolled skin back under her stomach and worked his way into the thickest part of the forest, where the light was most scarce. He did not stop until he reached the depression. It was the first time he had ever covered the distance between the brownskins' village and his home so quickly. Usually it took two nights of travel.

It was good to be home. As usual, he stopped at his slide and checked the area first for any unwanted presences. He detected none and slid down. He carefully laid Jada on her back on the cave floor and brought her water as he had Chan Chel. Bela tried to pour the water into her mouth but only succeeded in pooling it around her head, so he gave up. Hunger told him it was time to eat and night was almost here. He patted the side of her face and left.

***

Ahau and Tikal had also sloshed through the day, nearing the depression by nightfall. Ah Kaba and his men, to their credit, were not far behind. Neither group knew of the other.

Ahau suggested to Tikal that they stop for a short while before going on. Both were spent. A huge fallen tree provided a trunk to lie upon. The ground was miserably wet. Like the dead, the two young men lay for some time before they found the energy to move. Ahau got up first, sluggishly stretching, trying to revitalize exhausted limbs. Anger and fear had gotten them this far, this quickly. Now, they needed a plan. The depression was near. If Bela's lair was where Ahau thought it might be, then they would do Jada no service by rushing in and getting themselves killed. The two men put their heads together and schemed.

To their luck, Bela had gone in the opposite direction for food. Ahau and Tikal worked themselves down into the depression as quietly as they could, moving slowly, carefully. Even so, they made more noise than they would have liked. They were on full alert. In the dark, the forest seemed almost impassible, but they did not dare light a torch.

Sometime, just after what they guessed was the middle of the night, they almost stumbled into the cenote, as had Chan Chel before them. Their hearts thundered in their ears. This was the place. If Bela had a lair anywhere in the area it would be here. Ahau pushed himself to the edge on his stomach and tried to see down, but it was no use. The darkness was impenetrable. The only sounds were those stirred by the wind, high up in the canopy. No animals, small or large, seemed to be present. The usual chatter of the night was missing...more proof that Bela was probably somewhere below. In whispers, they decided to stay right where they were until the first glimpse of the morning light. Then they would see what they would see.

***

Bela came back to his cave just before morning. He brought a portion of meat to share with the female, but she was still unconscious. He rolled her over on her stomach and then rolled her

230

back. The young female was still insensate. Bela mewed and purred over her, playfully nipping her buttocks with his teeth. She remained incognizant of her surroundings. Her breathing had dangerously slowed and her body heat was depleting itself rapidly. Bela knew none of this. He only wanted her to wake up.

Bela went to the front of the cave and peered out on his kingdom. He did not sense the two young men lying in the damp leaves at the edge of his underworld. At almost any other time, he would have known they were there by smell alone, but tonight he was thinking of the female. He felt dirty. Bela jumped into his private pool, swollen from all of the recent rains, and swam to the bottom.

***

Ahau and Tikal instantly became alert. The splash had been somewhere below them. It sounded as if a large animal had made it. They again tried to pierce the gloom but could see nothing. They continued to wait for the light.

***

Bela swam back to the surface, swatting at the bubbles that accompanied him. He pulled himself out of the water and began his cleaning ritual. The water had awakened the wound on his shoulder, causing it to itch and throb. Bela rubbed it tenderly, flexing the shoulder in different directions. No serious damage had been done, but it angered him to think that the brownskins had wounded him twice now. He "Oooooruhed" his displeasure.

***

The warriors moved rapidly at first light. Noise from their passing created a tremor of fear that rippled well out into the forest ahead of them, pushing animals small and large. Ah Kaba struggled to keep up. He guessed they were about a quarter of a day's march from the depression.

***

Tikal and Ahau almost jumped out of their skins. The roar had sounded near…too near, in this blackness. They stayed motionless, shaking slightly from cold fear.

A while later, faint sunlight trickled through the heavy canopy above. Ahau whispered in Tikal's ear. "Look. I can see my hands. Morning must be near. Can you see anything below?"

231

Tikal scooted to the edge and looked down. Ahau did the same. Ambiguous forms began to take shape. They could see the darker maw of the cave and the inky blackness of the pool. Large rocks, broken at the bottom, hid most of the ground's surface in their shadows. But they could see Bela nowhere. They pulled back to wait for more light to filter through before trying to go down.

***

Bela arched his back and slid the palms of his hands on the stone until he was stretched out from a kneeling position. He yawned, smacking his lips. He had been napping with one arm thrown protectively over his female, inadvertently keeping her warm. She moaned slightly and shifted her weight. It was the first sign Bela had seen indicating she might be waking up. He rumbled in his throat and licked her face. Jada, however, did not respond. After a time, Bela got up and went to the cave's entrance. His addiction to the orange fungi was not all-compelling, but it was strong when the need came upon him. He felt the desire assert itself.

***

Tikal nudged Ahau and pointed at the spot where he thought he saw movement. It was Bela! They lost him momentarily beneath the darkness, but picked him out again, negotiating up near the cave's outer wall. It was impossible to tell what he was doing. Ahau thought it was his imagination when he saw a brief flash of iridescent orange, then it was gone. Bela climbed back down and went into his lair. Jada was nowhere to be seen. They assumed she was somewhere further in the cave.

The light was getting stronger, but it was far from actual sunlight. The massive trees all along the perimeter of the cenote were overgrown, one into another. Their enormous number of limbs and leaves covered over the top, hiding the jagged, rocky hole beneath. It was an anomaly of nature. Daytime was a myth here. This was Bela's world.

***

The bitter-sweet softness of the fungi melted on Bela's tongue, generating the euphoria he craved. The great beast went back into the cave and lay back down near his female, caressing her with his arm, licking her neck, breasts, and stomach. Contentedly, he placed his head on her chest and napped. His warmth pulled life back into her comatose young body. She shuddered pleasurably as the heat sought her core.

***

Ahau and Tikal knew there was no easy way. The distance to the bottom of the cenote was too great for a killing shot from Ahau's bow. They would have to be at ground level near the cave to cause any serious injury to the beast. They circled the deep hole, trying to find a way down as far from the entrance to the cavern as they could get.

Then they found Bela's slide. It was fairly close to Bela's den, but obviously the easiest, quietest way down. Ahau sat down and went first, the bow in his hand. Tikal followed with both spears. They used their heels to slow their descent, taking their time, watching the cave's entrance for any sign of movement. Once at the bottom, they circled to the side and prepared themselves.

***

Bela dreamed within the orange world of the fungi. His senses picked up the two brownskins, but in his drugged lethargy they became Chan Chel, coming back to visit him. The hunter looked well, no longer the broken plaything Bela remembered. Chan Chel bellowed a challenge for the great beast to come out and play. "Bela, come out. We know you are in there. Come out. Come and get us."

Bela's snout wrinkled in indignation. This is not the way Chan Chel spoke to him. Something was wrong. Instinct wrenched him emphatically from his dream. Something really was wrong. Awake, he instantly sensed the two brownskins. One of them even smelled moderately familiar.

"Ahhuuu." Bela's voice was mucous thick from the fungi. He snorted and came to his feet.

Bela could see Ahau and the other brownskin clearly now. They were straight across from the cave, on the other side of the pool, standing defiantly. "Ahhuuu, meee knooow yooou. Yooou stilll aliiiive?" Bela raised his guttural voice at the end of the statement, framing it into a question.

***

Ahau was rocked to his heels to hear his name issued from the beast's lips. It was unequivocally terrifying to hear the beast-demon

233

speak, and especially distressing to discover that Bela knew his name. Gravel scritched as he dug in. The bow was in his hand and the arrow nocked. As was their plan, Tikal stood to the side, one spear stuck in the ground, the other raised in his hand in a half throwing position. The throw was too far from here, but it was comforting to have a spear in his fist, and another close for the grabbing. For the thousandth time, he wished he had brought his bow.

Bela came out, standing on the lip of his cave just above the water. He felt no reason to fear the two young brownskins. They were in his world now. He began to skirt the pool from his side, coming at them in no hurry. Both men watched him warily. When Bela rounded the corner, still maddeningly slow, Ahau locked his shaking knees and pulled the feathered shaft to the side of his chin. He tried to still his trembling hands, but it was next to impossible. Face to face with the beast, Ahau's fury was dissolving into the fearful suspicion that he may have made a fatal mistake in assuming his little wooden bow was a match for Bela. It seemed ridiculous, in fact.

Bela was almost in range. If he didn't shoot soon, he would lose what little resolve was left. He took a deep breath, aimed, and opened his fingers, releasing the arrow. It thwacked the sand three lengths from Bela's feet. Ahau had misjudged the distance. He fought the panic bubbling up his throat and grabbed for another shaft.

***

Bela watched the strange stick penetrate the sand just in front of him, confused as to how it had gotten there. Its flight was too fast to follow. He stopped his advance momentarily and prodded the stick with his foot. Its presence, stuck there in his sand, angered him. Blood lust propelled him. He began covering the distance between Ahau and himself with a sudden burst of speed that was unnaturally quick.

***

Ahau was truly trembling now as he pulled the hawk feather to rest against his face. The beast was almost upon him. In less then twenty strides, he would be. Ahau released the second arrow. It pierced the thick hide of Bela's chest, two hand spans below his neck. The force of the shaft ended the beast's charge instantly. Bela skidded to a stop in twin furrows on his knees. A look of bewilderment came over him as he looked down at the feathered stick protruding from his chest. Blood bubbled from the corner of his mouth. The arrow had pierced a lung at the least.

Bela began to choke and briefly fell to his side, but was back up immediately. Anger seemed to launch him forward. Bela's face was screwed up into a contemptuous look that was eerily human. Ahau could only stand his ground, frozen in fear. There was not time for another shot.

Tikal ran past Ahau with his spear in both hands. With his entire weight, Tikal thrust the flint spear into Bela's belly. The spear's back end shoved into the sand. The weight of Bela's forward momentum pushed the point through his body. He howled in pain and disbelief.

Tikal's impetus carried him into Bela's outstretched arms, pushing them both over into the water, where they sank from view. Turbulence boiled to the surface, but Ahau could see nothing. He screamed his friend's name until the water stilled. The green pond scum swirled and then was quiet, but Tikal never emerged. Ahau sank to his knees, crying in anguish. His friend had sacrificed his life to save him. Bela most certainly would have reached him if Tikal had not interfered. He looked up to the dark green canopy and wailed his grief. He was answered.

Warriors lined one end of the cenote, looking down at Ahau. They had seen the entire thing, and stood hushed high up along the rim. They were dumfounded that Ahau's arrow had done such damage, and overwhelmed with the bravery of Tikal's sacrifice. It was Ah Kaba who shouted down Ahau's name. Ahau looked up, incredulous that help had arrived and instantly saddened that it was too late. Tikal was dead.

In moments they were down the slide and next to the young man. Several entered the cave with their weapons ready. One of the warriors reappeared at the cave's entrance with Jada in his arms. Ahau burst through the tight knot of men that surrounded him and ran to her, yelling her name. She was alive!

Ahau gently took Jada from the warrior's arms and laid her on the stone floor of the cave. Her naked body was limp and cold, bruises beginning to show in several places. Someone brought a blanket. Ahau covered her with it, tears streaming down his face. He delicately kissed her lips and eyelids, holding her tight. He could feel her warm breath on his neck. If there were injuries, they must be internal; he had seen no open wounds. He pulled her onto his lap and rocked back and forth, shamelessly crying her name. The men stood a polite distance away.

***

Most of the warriors prodded the pool, looking for any evidence of Bela or Tikal. None of them jumped in to confirm the bodies.

They found Chan Chel's upright body pushed into a rock crevice. He stared back at them through empty eye sockets and slivers of rotting flesh. It was obvious that he had been dead for quite a while. They could only guess his story. They left him where he was. If the demon had placed him there, it was not in their best interests to interfere.

Convinced that the beast was dead and nothing more could be done for Tikal, they left the cenote and headed back toward the village. Jada was showing signs of waking up. She mumbled incoherently, drank water, and thrashed about. They carted her in a makeshift litter made of blankets and thick poles.

Still suspicious of Ahau, a tight group of warriors flanked the young man as they traveled. Ah Kaba took possession of Ahau's bow and arrows. Even under guard, Ahau would let none care for Jada but himself, administering to her the entire way. A little afraid of the young girl, the guards were happy to allow him to do so. Being under the influences of Bela for as long as she had been might mean her unconsciousness was a form of possession. They were a superstitious and fearful lot.

It took two full days to reach their home. It seemed like half the village rushed out to meet the men as they came close to the village. As good news had a way of doing, word of Bela's death had spread ahead of the main body of warriors. Tikal's hand to hand combat with the beast-demon made him an instant martyr and the topic of conversation. Ahau's part in Bela's death was vexing. They weren't sure what to make of it. Wasn't the young man still accused of heinous crimes?

Jada's condition soon became spectacular fodder for gossip and speculation for all of the old women in the village. Ix Cuy, of course, was exhilarated to see her daughter safely back home. The tears for her son were heavy, but tempered by the bravery he had shown in saving Ahau's life. Everyone said it was the most fearless thing they had ever seen. His legend was assured.

As soon as could be arranged, the Council of Elders met to try and sort through the truth of all that had happened in the last few days. Everyone seemed to have their own opinions and skewed set of facts. The biggest questions were: *Was it safe to continue living here, now that Bela was dead? What of Pochotl? Would Ahau be executed for the death of Ah Kaba's body guards and the death of Ah Tok?* For most of the day and well into the night, the old men sat talking around their fire. They were left to it. No one ventured near, as was the custom in such matters. The people had complete faith in the council, and would do and even believe as they were told.

***

Ah Kaba saw this as an opportunity to make his position within the council a little more important. He was the only one of the council who had gone with the warriors in search of Bela. This alone should be of some worth. He arose, with as much dignity as a plump old man could muster, and took his turn speaking. The others wanted to hear a firsthand account of Bela's death. Ah Kaba could not lie. Too many warriors had seen the same sight, and if the truth were really known, he had missed much of it. The out of breath old man had been struggling up to the rim of the cenote, well behind the rest of the men, and had missed Ahau's bow shots. He had arrived just in time to see Tikal hurl himself at Bela and topple into the water with the beast-demon wrapped around him. His version of the skirmish mentioned Ahau's part, as he had heard, but focused on Tikal's selfless act of heroism.

Ah Kaba, while he had the floor, talked about the great Pochotl. The priest's death at Bela's hands was a sore blow to the people. His guidance and influence would be missed. The other men nodded their heads in agreement and murmured to themselves how exalted Pochotl's presence had been. Without him to guide the religious soul of the village, there was a tremendous breach in their foundation. It was agreed that Pochotl would be forever remembered in their hearts, prayers, and eventually in stone. His name would figure prominently on the outside stone reliefs of the Sun Temple once it was completed.

Ah Kaba picked this moment, while they were thinking so reverently about the priest, to unveil his plan. "Noblemen, I have heard you tonight speak your hearts about a great man we all will miss. I know we were waiting until the village became more complete before naming it, but perhaps now is the time. I propose we name our new city Pochotl."

Complete silence met his words. Ah Kaba was almost ready to sit back down, embarrassed by the stillness, when another spoke up. "He is right! What better tribute could we give to a man we owe so much too? It was Pochotl who came to each one of us in the beginning, asking us to join him. It was he who led us to this new land where our families owe only to ourselves. Pochotl would be proud to be the source for the naming of our city. Ah Kaba shows us the way. Let us do as he requests. Pochotl. I like the sound of it."

After little discussion, the growing city had a new name. Pochotl. The rest each had their turn to speak on the subject, but one by one they agreed. No one wanted to stand out as the lone dissenter. They moved on to the concerns of Ahau.

Again Ah Kaba asked for silence, his confidence growing. He spoke quietly, reverently. "Pochotl made it clear for all of us. Ahau killed Ah Tok. It is that simple. He also killed the three men who were my bodyguards. I was there. I saw him do it. It is true that Ahau had a hand in killing Bela, and for that we are grateful, but we cannot forgive the rest. If we as a council do not act justly in this matter, then we lose the respect of the people. It is my opinion that we shou—"

At that precise moment, Ix Cuy burst into the midst of the council, yelling in anger. "I've been standing just outside the firelight for some time listening to you old fools. Before all of you convince yourselves that everything Ah Kaba says is true, or that even everything Pochotl ever said was true, you had better listen." Ix Cuy vehemently spit out the name of the priest, like she was describing the disgusting splat of a spider under her foot. "Ah Tok was my husband. When he was murdered, I lay right beside him. At first I couldn't remember. I was coming out of a deep sleep when I sensed a presence in the room. My mind hid from me what my eyes saw that night. I think I just refused to believe it. Now, I'm sure. I'm as certain as I am that there was a sun above our heads today. It was Pochotl. Your precious priest killed Ah Tok, not Ahau. I can prove it."

The men roared their protest, many of them grabbing the woman to usher her out of the circle. How dare she, a woman, break into their meeting, shouting absurdities? One of the noblemen came to her rescue. He had been a friend of Ah Tok and would hear what she had to say. He yelled for them to unhand her and went to her side. "Please, Ix Cuy, continue. How would you prove such a thing?"

Ix Cuy turned and called into the darkness. A woman and her small boy stepped forward into the light. Ix Cuy offered her hand to the woman and pulled her into the circle. "Don't be afraid. They will cause you no harm. Just tell them what you told me."

The woman was Kankin Mol's widow, the boy his son. It was obvious that the poor woman was terrified out of her wits. She nervously looked at the ground, rolling her hands one on top of the other. She would not look at any of the men and spoke in a small voice that the noblemen strained to hear. "You know who I am. I have worked in most of your households at one time or another. I am just a poor woman who has no business here in the midst of such great men as you. Ix Cuy," the woman nodded in her direction, "asked me here after I came to her two days ago. I could not hide my shame any longer. I should have come forward sooner, I know, but I am nobody and try to mind my own affairs and stay out of things that do not concern me."

The old woman was very convincing. No one in the circle believed she could lie. They did all know her. That she was too scared to lie was obvious. As one, they leaned forward to better hear her soft words.

"The night Ah Tok was killed I was looking for a place to sleep. It was very late, and no one else was about. As you know, my husband sometimes beat me. I'm sure I deserved it, but my son did not." She motioned for the timid boy to come to her. She wrapped a protective arm around him. "I was taking him to a safe place when I saw Pochotl come out of the Sun Temple. I wasn't spying, truthfully...." Her voice cracked a little at the suggestion. "Sometimes there are eyes where there shouldn't be. Pochotl entered Ah Tok's house through the window. I could clearly see the knife in his hand. Sometime later, I saw him leave the same way. The next morning, when I heard of Ah

Tok's death, I knew he had done it, but was too frightened to speak up. Please forgive me."

The men all started speaking at once, not sure what to believe. Ix Cuy went to Kankin Mol's widow and led her out of the circle. After only a few moments, she reentered, shouting for them to still their tongues. She had more to say. "I, too, saw Pochotl that night in my mind's eye. I was too afraid to acknowledge it then. I think I thought I was suffering through the horror of a bad dream. It wasn't until I awakened that I realized my dream was reality. Only recently, with Pochotl's own death, did the image of the presence in my room become clear. I'm telling you that our priest, for whatever reasons he had, killed my husband that night. Ahau had nothing to do with it. It is also interesting that Tikal told me Ah Kaba's bodyguards threatened Ahau first. Which one of you would not have done the same as he?"

Ix Cuy locked eyes with each of the noblemen, daring them to accuse her of lying or just being a woman. "I'm also telling you that with Tikal gone, Jada and I are the wealthiest people in the village. We affect more families in this community than the rest of you combined. You can take from that what you will. I'll leave you, now, to do the right thing."

Ix Cuy walked away from the council. As she passed Kankin Mol's widow, she pulled from her waist a small leather pouch filled with jade and pressed it into the woman's hands, whispering her thanks.

It did not take long for the council to change their minds about Ahau. They entirely believed the two women. There was no reason for them to lie. They had no idea why Pochotl had killed Ah Tok, though. That remained a mystery. Only Ah Kaba really knew the answer, and he kept his silence. The growing city would have to wait a little longer before it received a name. Naming it Pochotl was probably not the best choice.

***

Jada was placed in her own bed. The whole village seemed to check on her in the days that followed. Ix Cuy eventually had to post guards to turn the well-wishers away. When her daughter finally opened her eyes, Ahau was beside her.

Jada blinked several times, trying to adjust her vision. Licking her dry lips, she asked in barely audible murmurs, "Where am I?" Focusing her eyes on Ahau, she smiled and said, "Mmmmn, Ahau, is that you? Is it really you?" She hugged him tightly.

It was sometime later in the morning when the memories began flooding back. She could only remember Pochotl and the tea. Everything else was a blank. Ahau filled in what he could, but Jada had trouble believing him until others in the village substantiated his story. Many days passed before the young girl was her old self physically. Nightmares still plagued her dreams. She had difficulty believing that she had actually been in Bela's cave and Tikal and Ahau had rescued her. She cried incessantly, thinking about her brother's death. Even Ahau's comforting arms could not curb the hurt.

The days passed. The rains ended. Without a priest to perform Chac's end-of-the-rain ceremony, the people celebrated for the first time in their lives without a young virginal sacrifice. Adding to the festivities, the Council of Elders used their power to proclaim the marriage of Jada and Ahau sacred and complete.

The settlement, for the first time in its short existence, began to experience the hopes, joys, promises, and safety of a new home.

Postscript

Bela's chest exploded with pain. The impact from the wooden shaft literally stopped him cold. He fell to his knees and clutched at the wound. He could see the feathers sprouting from his chest. Bela brushed his fingers against their wispy edges. Even that light touch sent thrums of agony spinning through him, and he fell to his side.

The realization that this runty little brownskin had done real damage infuriated him. Bela felt weak, hurt to his very core, but he was determined to finish killing Ahau before he went down. He tripoded back to his feet and rushed his antagonist, bloody resolve twisting his features into absolute hatred. Bela could see the understanding in Ahau's eyes. The young brownskin had only moments to live. Then something slammed into Bela's stomach. *The other brownskin.* He had forgotten about him. The impact of the spear anchored against the ground was excruciating. Bela grabbed Tikal, falling into the water as he did so.

Even as the water closed over them, Bela ripped through the young man's face, throat, and most of his chest in a killing frenzy. As they tumbled through the depths, Bela, in his anger, kept digging at the young man's vitals until his own wounds asserted themselves. The two of them hit the bottom, wound together like spent lovers. Their collision with the sand and silt rolled them over, sending whirling, spinning clouds of bottom debris to the top.

Bela could not breathe. Frothy, red bubbles leaked from his collapsed chest around the feathered shaft, adding their substance to the rubbish already swirling in the water. Bela's mind began to grow dark. It was hard to think with the terrible ache for air insisting he get to the surface. His limbs would not obey his thoughts. Darkness was enveloping him.

Instinct made him half-crawl, half-swim to the underwater embankment that led up into a cavity in the rock just below Ahau's feet. The beast dragged himself into the small space, gagging out clouts of blood and water from lungs barely responding to his needs. This was his secret place; a place he had found many years ago while swimming in the pool. He rarely came here anymore. The bones from his mother rested here, rescued from the embrace of the tree long ago and placed reverently in a pile near the back. He swallowed the dank air in large gulps, each breath sending red spasms of new pain through his chest. But, he was alive. It was all he could do just to lie there. Bela's claws grabbed for purchase. He pulled himself a little further out of the water and slid over to his back. The arrow was still lodged deeply in his chest. On his back he could feel the point near his spine.

Above him, Bela could hear the brownskins celebrating. He was beyond caring. *Mother, I'm with you now.* He felt blindly for her bones. Darkness closed over him. In a coma, he laid for several days, his miraculous body trying to heal itself.

***

Ahau and his new bride could not have been happier. The council persuaded Ahau to become the new priest. He was the only one in the community that had any experience. Ahau readily agreed, but refused to live in Pochotl's old housing. The village was convinced to build new quarters on the other side of the temple. Pochotl's room was sealed off forever. His evil spirit was condemned to the darkness. In the meantime, they stayed with Ix Cuy, who was grateful for the company.

Within a few months, it became apparent that Jada was with child. Everyone was ecstatic. She grew abnormally large quickly. Their child was going to be a warrior for sure. Life was good. Laughter had been missing from the village for a long time. Now, it was frequent. Everyone was happy. The corn crop was the best they had ever seen, thanks to the fertile bottom land in their new home.

Ahau was pleased. As the new priest, it was his responsibility to keep the village safe and out of harm's way. He performed all of the rituals with growing confidence. The gods were smiling on the

244

people.

***

Between her knees, Jada stared at the wrinkled blanket and breathed with rapid, shallow jerks, preparing herself for the next contraction. She screamed, clutched her mother's hand, and rocked back and forth, tears staining her face. Only seven cycles had passed since she had missed her first moon's blood. Something had to be wrong.

This was her second day of birthing. Her strength was flagging. She wasn't sure how much more she could take. Jada bit her already swollen and bleeding lip as the next contraction chewed her womb. Blood began to run in trickles down her legs. She squeezed harder on her mother's hand, fingernails digging into the flesh, fighting through the agony.

Several of the women had to support the young woman now. Her strength was ebbing. Blood continued to pour from her poor, pain wracked body, despite the women's efforts to staunch its flow. A white globe of flesh slid out onto the piled, soft receiving blankets. The umbilical cord trailed down, pulsating darkly just under its pale, rubbery surface. The women rushed to pull the thin, transparent sheet of mucous membrane from the child's face, clearing its breathing passages.

A shrill wail of panic came from each of their throats almost at once. The child was an albino male. A child of the gods. Others were known about, obscured in the legends of a distant past, but this was the first in their living history. As one, they muttered a prayer to Itzamna for his blessing. Ix Cuy pushed the women aside and finished cleaning the child. She cut and tied off the cord, the whole while glaring at the women, who seemed paralyzed with fear. They were in a tight knot, clutching at each other, afraid of what they had just witnessed. A child touched by Itzamna.

Jada slumped down on the blankets, her face almost as white as the baby. Shallow breaths barely raised her sternum. She asked through closed eyes, "Is it male?" She had to gather another breath to go on. "Is it whole?"

The women did not answer, each looking at the other. Ix Cuy kneeled at her daughter's side. She could see the massive blood loss

245

was past probable survival. She fought back the hot sting in her eyes and tried to make her voice even.

"The child is whole. We are blessed with a male, my daughter." Ix Cuy's voice was soothing. She carefully stroked the sweat-matted hair from Jada's forehead. "He has been touched by Itzamna. Your son has the prophesied color. See for yourself." Ix Cuy gently laid the child in Jada's arms. "He's beautiful, my daughter. Hold him near your face so that he may know you."

Jada pulled the young male to her so she could see him. She extended her legs to ease the muscles. A smile widened her face. "Oh, Mother, he is beautiful."

Jada's voice was weak. The child squirmed up tighter, next to his mother's neck and chin. Jada closed her eyes. Tears streamed freely now from Ix Cuy's eyes. She quietly told one of the women to get Ahau quickly.

***

Ahau entered the birthing chamber and immediately saw, within the pale hollowness of Jada's eyes, her life trickling away. Hastily, he lowered his eyes and blanched at all of the blood that pooled at his feet. He knelt beside his wife and child and tenderly kissed her brow. His trembling fingers felt the moist skin of her face. He could barely hear her breathing. Jada's eyes closed slowly, the hint of a smile playing contentedly. Ahau looked at Ix Cuy, who sadly shook her head. Tears stung his eyes as he kissed his young wife and whispered in her ear.

"Oh, my dearest Jada, we still have so much to do. We have a whole life to live together. Our child badly needs you; I need you." A shiver of dread passed through him as he realized the truth. His fingers lingered against her neck. "Just relax, my love. The hard part is over."

Quiet sobs racked his body as he held Jada and the child close. The young woman's face had a strangely slack look, the skin waxen and unresponsive. Jada's eyes fluttered open. "Ahau, it's a male. A beautiful boy. I just wish…." Her voice trailed off.

Several moments later Jada's eyes again slowly opened. She peered into her child's dark pink eyes, noticing the gold and green flecks that floated there. She stroked his white hair and gently kissed his forehead, telling him who she was. She died with him against her bosom, her gaze fixed upon some distant place only she could see.

Ahau was heart stricken. His soul felt rent, torn beyond repair. Jada's death was the hardest thing he ever had to endure. It was two days before he could forgive his son enough to see him. He had not even noticed the child was albino until someone told him. The child had caused his beloved Jada to die. That was all the child meant to him. It did not matter that the white child had been touched by the gods and would bless his village forever. The boy had ripped Jada from his life, and that he could not forgive.

***

At first Ahau only endured the child. Ix Cuy became his surrogate mother. The boy lived with her and was only visited occasionally by Ahau. Even at only a few months, it was easy to see that the young boy was going to be large. Everything about him seemed to develop faster than the normal child of his age. With help and advice from the village elders, Ahau named him Dios Del Oeste El Primer, First Man from West Deity. There were those within the elders who still believed in Pochotl's prophecy. Their Halach Uinic, supreme ruler, would be a child with Itzamna's essence of spirit. This unusual child could very well be the promised one. The whiteness of his skin was proof that he was special.

Dios Del Oeste El Primer, however, developed his own nickname by the peculiar habit of constantly making the sound "Bahhga" at three months old. It didn't matter if he was hungry, or just pointing at something he wanted, the response was the same. "Bahhga." Everyone began calling him Bog. The young child seemed to enjoy the name and would mimic it over and over when called.

***

Four years later...

Bog towered over the other children. At four years, he was already eight hand spans tall. The average adult was only ten. The differences did not end there. More muscular and faster than children three times his age, he owned the village playgrounds. He was always careful, however, not to hurt his playmates. Bog was loved and revered by the whole village. Even Ahau began to spend more and more time with him, eventually forgiving the boy for the death of his mother. It was obvious that the growing town was blessed. Bog was special. It wasn't until age twelve that people started noticing the increasing strangeness.

When Bog got angry, his skin pebbled just beneath the surface. Like a newly born sparrow, the thin skin covering his graceful hands showed traces of his blue-black veins. The nails thickened abnormally. At nine hand spans, he frightened some of the children and gave the adults pause. It was more than just aberrant that a child of twelve years should be so large, so white, so...different. If he was a child of Itzamna, he was a dangerous one. It wasn't that Bog ever hurt anyone. He didn't have to. People gave him whatever he wanted, whenever he wanted it. Only his father could refuse him, and even then by small degrees. Out of Bog's presence, however, many of the village spoke their worries to each other that the boy might be too different. They were leery and watched him closely.

His strength and size at age fifteen were enormous. Bog's voice was soft, husky, and full of menace whenever he spoke. Angry, his voice boomed in deep bass tones that commanded attention. His eyes would snap furiously when even slightly denied. His pebbled skin became more pronounced, even when he wasn't angry. Ahau cautiously watched his son. He loved him as his own, but increasingly began to have small doubts nag the back of his mind.

Bog towered over the rest of the town. Over fourteen hand spans, the young man was surely the largest man that had ever lived. The men treated young Bog as at least an equal. It wasn't long before they began to defer to him, asking for his opinions about almost everything. The young women in the village offered themselves, but Bog always declined. He was maturing, but not interested in female flesh as yet. He was also becoming the adult his father hoped he would be. The welfare of the people came first in Bog's mind. As his father's apprentice, he grew in the arts of the priesthood and assisted in many of the lesser rituals. Ahau's doubts about Bog's holy lineage, as foretold by Pochotl, seemed for the moment inconsequential. The boy was as he was and that was enough.

At age twenty, his white hair flowed well below his shoulders. Bog's musculature and bearing were god-like. Bog was very cognizant of his great physical superiority, but through the years, found that just natural strength was not enough. He began to envy the people of the village for their intelligence and their ability to solve problems. He learned. Ahau and the other elders shared many things. They taught him the importance of family. They taught him the significance of being just and fair when dealing with others. He learned the value of having the trust of the people in all things.

The people began to think of Bog as the embodiment of everything they held sacred. Everyone agreed that it was only a matter of time before they proclaimed him the Halach Unic, supreme ruler; the one true man. There was no one else in the small town that could or would rival him.

***

Ahau wished that Ix Cuy had lived long enough to see what a fine man Bog was becoming. Before succumbing to old age, she had taken great pleasure in watching her grandson grow, and had known in her heart of hearts that Bog would be exceptional. She would have been especially proud that he was following Ahau into the priesthood. Ahau thought often of the old woman lately. She and he had become fast friends after Tikal's and Jada's deaths. The old lady helped raise Bog as her own. Like a surrogate mother, Ix Cuy had lent her support every time Ahau needed it. Before she died, she let it be known that all of her wealth would go to Ahau, to use as he saw fit for the benefit of the people.

As he was sitting on the new fourth landing of the Sun Temple with the golden rays of a new day washing over him, Ahau's thoughts drifted back to the village's beginnings. A strange mixture of pride in their accomplishments and the question of whether they had lost too much along the way rolled in his mind. He missed Jada and Tikal terribly. They were still part of the roots that held the soil of this special place. Their names and deeds would become part of the stories that were their heritage. The worth of their lives could still be felt.

It was then, almost twenty one years after Tikal's death, that Ahau privately decided to make a secret trek back to the depression…back to the cenote and the green-black pool that marked his friend's grave. None of the people had ever been back. The area was avoided at all costs. The people believed that the cave was an entrance to the underworld, and that even with Bela dead, other

249

demons might still guard its boundaries. Ahau scoffed inwardly at such thoughts, but publicly supported them wholeheartedly. Still, Tikal deserved a ceremony that celebrated the ultimate sacrifice he had made for his sister and friend. The time was right. The number twenty one held special holy meaning for the people, and even though Ahau couldn't be sure of the exact date, he would leave in the morning. He began to prepare.

Two days later, Ahau found Bela's old slide. The forest had reclaimed most of it, but enough was still there to make it the easiest way down. The cenote was just as he remembered it. The canopy still kept most of the sunlight at bay, and it was hard to see in the dark gloom. Ahau squatted at the spot Bela and Tikal had fallen into the water. He could see nothing that evidenced it ever happening. There were no visible marks in the sandy soil. All of the footprints had been forever erased.

Ahau sat on his haunches and sighed. He could remember the details like they had just happened. He twisted off a piece of grass and tossed it into the murky pool. It floated in the brown swirls, never sinking, momentarily drawing the attention of a silvery minnow that flashed toward it. The small fish inadvertently bumped a reed where a dragonfly nymph shed its skin for the last time, drying in the minuscule breeze. The minnow frightened it into flight before it had been ready. In a jerky, erratic pattern it hovered over the reed before flitting to another one. He wondered if Tikal's spirit knew he was there.

Ahau spread his ceremonial blanket on the sand over the spot he last saw his friend alive and pulled his obsidian knives from wrapped, leather pouches. He chanted with his eyes closed and drew one of the knives over his forearm, collecting the trickle of blood in a ceramic bowl. Ahau genuinely felt he was close to his friend and slipped into a semi-trance while he prayed to Itzamna for guidance. For long moments, he lay back on the blanket and spoke to his old friend. Tikal looked as he had remembered…the young man had not aged. Tikal already seemed to know about his sister, mother, and Bog. They laughed together in Ahau's mind about how Pochotl had so fooled the people. It was a laugh of pain, but good for their souls. Ahau reverently thanked Tikal for his life.

When Ahau finally said his goodbyes and opened his eyes, it had grown dark. He did not feel frightened at being in such a place at night. He was at ease. A kind of peace enveloped him. Small silvers of moonlight made it possible for Ahau to catch momentary glimpses of himself in the thin bands of liquid silver. Swirling wind rippled his image, the darker water erasing portions of his face. Ahau felt the hot chill of blame coil tightly around his heart. Tikal was dead. Imagination sometimes enhanced old memories. His friend's face stared from the cold, dark depths of the pond.

Ahau once again saw Tikal's suicidal charge at Bela in his mind's eye. The beast had snarled something obscene just before the two of them toppled into the water, each grappling with the other. Tikal's spear had bitten deep. The great beast's claws had bitten deeper. That much Ahau remembered vividly. Great gouts of their mingled blood had churned up to the surface, coloring the water in dark sheets of swirling scarlet. Neither had returned to the surface.

Ahau turned from the pond and built a fire in the sand. He sent his blood, mingled with copal resin, to the sky. The night wrapped warm memories of Jada and Tikal around him as he pulled the blanket tighter across his shoulders. Ahau tossed another stick on the fire. The night's blackness swallowed all but the thin light that came from it. He watched it smoke, and then begin to blaze red, snapping sparks in a shower that swirled upwards.

***

Inside the cave, up high behind the rocks, shadowy eyes watched the brownskin's ceremony. Terrified that one of the hated brownskins had come back, he huddled behind a corner where the cave veered to the sides. Thick scabs and open sores, some of them oozing pus, covered his body. His body weight was less than half of what it had been twenty one years ago, and his strength even less. Every time Bela breathed, a sucking sound came from the hole in his chest. It had never closed. The tissue around it had healed, but the hole itself still went to lung tissue. For years now he had subsisted on the blood of snakes, rats, and other small creatures when he could catch them. He hid from the larger animals, knowing they might kill him if he approached them. His scales no longer shined, but looked dull and ragged where rock had worn them down. He no longer had the ability

251

to regenerate new ones.

Bela peered out at the brownskin, trying to remember. His mind told him he knew him, but he couldn't concentrate long enough to come up with the answer. He made a pitiful mewing sound and moved back farther into the cave. Bela hoped the brownskin would soon leave...he was thirsty.

When the brownskin cut his arm and the blood smell entered the cave, Bela longed for a taste but never moved. He whined quietly and held his head. It hurt from trying to remember things he didn't really want to know. Bela tried to sleep but kept waking up, afraid that the brownskin might come into the cave. It was a long, sleepless night for one who had once owned the darkness.

***

The next morning, a conscience cleaned Ahau woke up with a crick in his neck and back, his legs vehemently protesting around the knees. It had been a long time since he had slept on the lap of the forest. He was used to the soft comfort of his feathered bed. He pushed himself up, groaning all the while. It felt like morning, but down here it was hard to say. The air seemed to have a dark brown tinge, just short of black, to it. With his hands on the back of his hips, he raised his face to the canopy and pushed his groin forward and his shoulders back, stretching as much as he dared. He twisted his neck first one way, then another, trying to rid himself of the crick.

From near the entrance of the cave, a soft glow of orange just on the edge of his periphery vision caught his attention. Ahau jerked quickly to his right to see what it had been, instantly wishing he hadn't. The crick turned into a fierce pain that made him stumble forward and bring both hands to his neck. He winced and went to his knees, briefly closing his eyes and rubbing the soreness that radiated from the left side of the back of his neck across the shoulder.

After a few moments of cursing, Ahau, slowly this time, turned to his right to find the orange glow again. He could see nothing. Memory flooded back from his time on the top edge of the cenote watching Bela come out of the cave so long ago. There had been a quick flash of orange then, too. Tikal and he had not known what it had been, but they had both seen it.

Ahau turned his head carefully once more in the same direction he had seen it last. Looking forward, he searched along the right side of his edge of vision. He raised his head a little. There! It was like a phantom light. If he looked at it directly, it was gone. It was almost as if it was hidden by something from this angle. Ahau walked toward the spot where he had seen it. Up against the side of the cave's entrance, there seemed to be something. He skirted the pond and began climbing up the rocks. The closer he got to the cave, the surer he was that it was from here that the strange, soft glow of orange came from.

Climbing up to an area almost even with the cave's entrance, Ahau found the orange fungi. It was nestled among ancient tree roots that firmly clutched the stone face of a large boulder. It didn't actually glow, but captured the little available light and stored it almost like the wings of a morpho butterfly. He had never seen anything quite like it. It covered about an area equal to his chest. Roots surrounded little pockets of the fungi. None of it grew directly on the roots, but it thrived between their embrace. Outside of the root system, none grew.

Ahau instantly recognized that the tree somehow was a partner with the peculiar orange growth. He got closer. Partially healed furrows streaked through some of the larger patches, almost as if.... *Bela! This is what Bela had been doing that day as Tikal and I watched from the rim. These dug-out areas are from his claws. He probably ate the stuff.*

Ahau slowly and deliberately reached out an index finger and touched the orange growth. It felt almost like soft fur. Criss-crossed everywhere were indentions that had grown over but were still discernable. He trailed his finger across them, feeling their alien texture.

Ahau took his knife and scraped a little off into his hand. Bringing it to his nose, he smelled first gently, then more powerfully. The stuff was similar in smell to mildew but had an underlying tint of sweet decay. He flicked a meager amount with the tip of his tongue. The taste was tangy, a little like the aroma but encouraging. He tried more, emptying the contents of his hand onto his tongue.

As a priest, Ahau almost immediately recognized the effects of a drug. He sat down on a nearby rock and closed his eyes, analyzing the consequences of the orange growth. Heat suffused his chest, arms, and neck, swelling to his face. Pleasant warmth played behind his eyes. Colors blossomed beneath the darkness of his eyelids, exploding into random patterns that disappeared almost as soon as they were born. He could not hold onto any of them. They made him feel at peace. When he opened his eyes, little residues of pale, colored light seemed to sparkle just outside the corners of his vision. He felt very calm. He waited to see what other effects the orange drug might have. Except for the exceptional clearness in thought he was experiencing, there seemed to be none. Ahau closed his eyes again to see if the lights still played behind his eyelids. They were only a ghost of what they had earlier been.

Ahau repeatedly ran his fingertips over the furry orange surface. He gently tugged some of it loose from the stone and tucked it into his waist pouch for later. Again he tasted a small amount, this time swallowing a piece about the size of his thumbnail. Still enjoying the soft feel of the orange texture, his fingers found three parallel grooves that seemed much fresher. Too fresh. New growth barely covered the deep scratches that went all the way to the rock. Alarm tried to insinuate itself into Ahau's mind, but the warm tingle of the fungi was already pushing the significance of the scratches away.

Sitting comfortably back against the rocks, Ahau looked down in the direction he had camped the night before. A feeling of unequivocal euphoria settled around his shoulders, and wrapped him tightly in peaceful contentment. Ahau glanced around himself, going from far left to right. Slowly at first, then more vividly, colors seemed to dance from the surfaces of all he could see. The browns, grays, and blacks of the rocks and sand shimmered like they were alive. New colors insinuated themselves in between and around the drab colors of reality. Ahau felt like he was seeing things as they really were for the first time in his life. Colors, shapes, even the aggregate edges of the stones seemed more distinct than ever before. Every surface appeared to him in minute detail that seemed to subtly change as he stared at them. Color cunningly shifted and vibrated like it was alive, exposing purposes and designs he was never before aware of.

Ahau looked up to the canopy. Very little light penetrated the heavy covering. What light that did traveled rapidly in shafts of pink and golds that seemed to splash against the sand, turning each small pebble into a softly glowing sphere that competed with its neighbors for attention. The small particles of sand conversed with each other with infinitesimal bursts of soft glittering light. Ahau felt like a divine being contentedly watching his children play far below him. Glimmers of twinkling small lives worshiped him in their eagerness to outshine their neighbors.

Ahau noticed a growing perception just behind his eyes. Diminutive crackles, one on top of another, broiled in his head. He could feel the sensation more than hear it. The feeling was not unpleasant. It lasted only a short while but was intense while it did. Ahau felt like he had transcended to a newer, higher level of consciousness.

He swiveled his god vision to his left and observed the entrance to the cave. The blackness invited him to enter its embrace. A flurry of quick movements seized his attention. He cocked his head, not understanding what he was seeing. He watched complacently. There was no feel of alarm. Danger was out of place in this new world. Ahau sensed the cautious movement within the cave more than he actually saw it. Darkness sufficiently cloaked any real detail, even with his heightened senses.

Ahau settled back more comfortably against the stones and watched the entrance with his hands loosely clasped and draped over his stomach. Twin orbs of pale light momentarily gleamed from far back in the cave and then went out. There. Once again from a different position. Ahau was mesmerized. More entertained than curious, he giggled quietly to himself.

***

Bela watched the brownskin climb up from the sand, coming closer to the entrance to his cave. He pulled his hands up tight against his chest and rolled them together in anguish. A thin whine of apprehension burbled from his cracked lips. The brownskin was coming closer. Bela rocked sideways on the balls of his feet. Fear squeezed his lungs, making it difficult to breathe. The ragged, wet breaths from his wound bubbled faster. Hot urine ran freely down his legs. Bela crouched farther down behind the broken rock and moaned. His legs were quivering from the panic, making him go to his knees. He tried to keep the brownskin in sight, but the man had

255

climbed out of his line of vision.

Bela tried not to shake. If the brownskin came into the cave, his only chance was to stay perfectly still and stay hidden where he was. Small whimpers still sounded from his clenched lips even though he tried to still them. He closed his eyes and strained to be quiet.

Eventually, Bela's shaking stilled and his breathing became more regular. His whimpering subsided to a barely audible sound. More than enough time for the brownskin to enter the cave had passed, yet he was still alone in the dark. Bela chanced a furtive glance at the entrance. The brownskin was nowhere to be seen. Calmed by this, Bela relaxed a little more. He tried to sense the brownskin's presence, but his diminished capacity only gave him a hint that the man might be somewhere to the right of the cave. Anxiety made Bela mewl his discomfort. In the hope of getting a better feel of where the brownskin was, Bela came guardedly closer to the entrance. He moved as far left as the cave's walls would permit, and risked a quick look to the right of the cave.

Ahau's back was to Bela, only about forty strides away, rubbing his fingers against the orange fungi. His fungi. Emotions clashed. Anger fought with his fear of the brownskin, creating a new panic all of its own. That was his most private sustenance. He needed the precious orange rock flesh to survive. It grew nowhere else in the forest, and it was his. It had always been his. A soft "Ooooruh" whispered out from between clenched lips.

Bela hunkered down in the darkness and watched the brownskin eat from his cherished cache of rock food. Anger grew, watering down the terror that had possessed him so tightly earlier. For the first time in years, Bela began to feel a purpose. A reason for living. The anger was like a soothing balm that rubbed a thin veil of comfort over all of the old fears. For years he had hid in his cenote, rarely venturing far past its borders, content to forage for food close within the perceived safety of his cave.

His mind was still jumbled and confused. Most memories were only faintly remembered or gone completely. It was hard to think. When he tried to add details to the few half memories he had, Bela usually failed. Maddening frustration made him quit trying most of the time. The brownskin outside of his cave was such a memory. He felt like it was important he remembered, but could not. He gently fingered the small, partially healed hole in his chest, feeling the raised, round, hard scar that still pained him when he breathed.

***

Bela was blissfully unaware that only his miraculous genetics and the accumulated orange fungi in his body had brought him back from death twenty-one years before. For a full day, Bela had lain lifeless on the small rock shelf near his mother's bones under the water. On the second day, a small spark of life ignited itself deep within his brainstem, giving ethereal birth to other sparks. Several more days passed before his body twitched slightly and changed positions. Internally, sparks coaxed life back on the lowest levels, feeding and healing the inert tissues from within.

Eventually, Bela awoke to an intense pain that seemed to be everywhere at once. He spasmed, clawed hands jerking in the air, and fell back into the dark peace of death. Again the orange sparks roused life where before there was none. Faster now, the body healed to an awakening state. Bela screamed with dry lungs and throat, drawing a breath that finally blossomed into new life. Pain shuddered his body.

Bela tried to sit up, but the movement made the pain crescendo to new thresholds. His mind was black. He could not remember even the simplest of things. He knew not where he was or what he was; only the pain and darkness were experienced. Bela lay on his back for two more days, alternating between consciousness and the blessed relief of nothingness. Instinctively he cupped his hand and drank from the water that lapped at his side, falling back beneath the darkness of near death from the increased pain even the smallest of movements caused. Time passed slowly for Bela. Each day, he was a little more aware, but always confused. The torment of his body became accepted as the only reality. He knew or remembered nothing else but the suffering and misery his torn flesh gave him.

Instinctively, he finally crawled out of his stony tomb and slid into the soothing dark waters. Intuitively knowing the air he needed was above, he broke the surface of his pond and paddled to the shore. There he lay for a while on his back, pulling in the clean air that racked his chest with every intake, but reveling in the taste and smell of fresher surroundings. Bela still remembered nothing, but the fresh air was helping.

Slowly, shards of old memories came back to him. Bela recognized an image of a brownskin that flitted across his synapsis as being a dangerous enemy. Other animals and his place in the forest flashed in his mind, but he was still terribly confused.

Bela slightly turned his head and thought he recognized at least where he was. The canopy over his head felt right, and the cave was vaguely familiar. He felt his chest where the pain seemed to be most centered. A jagged piece of Ahau's wooden shaft still poked just above the flesh where it had broken off. Bela rubbed his finger across the tip, feeling the depth of the shaft move in his lung. He used his claws and pinched what he could of the shaft and pulled with all of his strength. There was a sucking sound as the shaft broke away from the flint tip and pulled to the surface. Blood welled to the edges of the black hole and bubbled. Bela fought through the pain and pushed against the wound with the palm of his hand to staunch the flow of blood. He could still feel the foreign piece of stone deep within his lung, but could do nothing more now. He closed his eyes and slept half out of the water, with his head cradled in the sand.

***

Now, an old familiar enemy was once again invading his private domain. Bela lifted his muzzle and tried to catch the brownskin's odor. His diminished senses could only capture the feather of a breath that held the brownskin's scent. It was enough, however, to tell him that somewhere in the past, he had met this creature. Images of Chan Chel making fire in his cave brushed his thoughts and then were dismissed. It was the first time he had been able to put a name to the old skeleton that was squeezed into the rocks of his cave. Other memories of Chan Chel trickled through his concentration, but he knew this brownskin in front of him was not the same. There was something just at the edge of his perceptions. He reached for it but it was gone, like squeezed water in his hand.

Bela fingered the hole in his chest out of habit as he thought about the man sitting a short distance away. He stood and moved to the darkest shadows, becoming one himself. His every breath was a labor that he no longer thought about, just accepted as part of life. His foot stumbled against Chan Chel's old broken spear, long forgotten in the dust near the wall. Bela picked it up and turned it over and over in his hands, trying to make sense of it. Sudden comprehension burst through his mind like lightning unzipping a cloud.

"Speeeer," he whispered. Now he could see the brownskin clearly in his mind. "Ahauuu."

Bela could piecemeal the past enough to remember the younger version of the brownskin as he made the strange sticks fly through the air. Like it was moments before, Bela felt the feathered shaft strike him in the chest. He groaned and twisted as the phantom arrow once again pierced his scaled hide and bit deep into his lung. New anger flared, flashing in his eyes as his hands twitched with his claws extended. Then he remembered the other brownskin...the one with the spear that he had run into. The great wooden shaft had been anchored in the sand at an angle that pierced through his stomach, almost pushing through to the other side. He remembered grabbing the brownskin as the momentum carried them both into the water. The spear had dislodged and tumbled to the bottom of the pool, but the damage had already been done.

Bela razed the air in front of him as he remembered tearing through the brownskin's body before they hit the bottom and everything went black. He felt the long, raised ridge of scar tissue across his abdomen. Then he remembered the all-consuming pain that had reawakened him after the blackness. Involuntarily, he whimpered, all of his thoughts of confronting Ahau forgotten. It was easy to fall back into the old emotion of fear. He had lived with it for so long, it was like an old friend.

Bela pulled the old fears around him like a second skin, slipped farther back into the cave, and waited.

***

Ahau sluggishly pulled himself out of the drug induced perspective. The colors that had so fascinated him moments before snapped back to the old, drab ones he so readily knew. Sadness engulfed him. Tears washed freely from his eyes at the loss of so much beauty. He had truly felt godlike. Now, the world was the same dreary, dismal place it had always been. He just had not recognized the failings before. In fact, everywhere was darker. The day had moved on, nearly at the midpoint now, Ahau realized. Scratching the

259

bridge of his nose, Ahau noticed dingy, black stains on his hands. *Where did that come from?*

Ahau turned his hands over and saw some of the same stain on the back sides of his fingertips. *The orange fungus.* Only instead of orange, now it was a greasy dark smear. He wiped the residue on his wrap. Turning his attention to the fungi, Ahau saw that it still burned orange against the rock face of the boulder in between the thick fingers of roots. He again saw the old furrows, probably left by Bela so long ago, but the smaller, new ones triggered alarm. Ahau turned swiftly toward the cave, the crick in his neck and shoulder long gone. He remembered the twin orbs of light, a slightly whiter shade of pale that had pulsed at him within the cave. *Could it be?*

Ahau climbed back down from his position to where he had left his bow and spear. He chose the spear because of the tightness of the cave, and bounded back up the rocks, easing toward the entrance. The depth of the powerful urge to enter the cavern was only partly realized. As a priest, he was well aware that such cenote cavities were said to be cracks into the underworld where only the dead were privy to go. Trespassing here was more than just dangerous. It was forbidden.

Ahau fought his fear, forcefully ingrained since birth, and crossed the cave's threshold. If Bela was still alive, he wanted to know. Dregs of the rock-root drug made him reckless, feeling like he could meet any danger and still prevail.

Inside, the darkness was almost complete. Barely visible by the wall near the entrance was a large clutter of small dry sticks. Ahau used his knife to cut away a swath of his loin wrap. Gathering several of the sticks into a bunched group, he twined the red cotton cloth around them. He tried striking his spear's point against the darker swirls of rock on the floor until he got a spark. After several attempts, Ahau saw the edge of the cloth blacken and smoke. Moments later, the cloth caught and a small flame blazed. He bundled the remaining sticks on the floor and set them to fire also. He left them burning by the entrance, in case the hand torch burned out and he needed to find his way back. The darkness receded a short distance, as if chastised by the light. Ahau thought it was enough. Holding the light high in his left hand and the spear out in front of him in his right, he proceeded into the cave.

Almost immediately, a wave of rot washed over him. The odor of decay was cloying. Ahau moved his feet in small steps, careful not to stumble in the unknown terrain of the cave's uneven floor. Against one side he moved until a shelf of rock made him move more to the center of the floor. Ahau played the torch's light across the shelf. Large skulls, like trophies, were assembled in a row, the empty eye sockets seemingly guarding against unwanted intrusion into their black sanctuary. Ahau could not mentally put flesh on them in a recognizable way. They were just too large to be from any animal he had ever experienced. Unaccountably, a small mouse's skeleton lay in the dust beside them. He moved on.

Other, smaller skulls sat back farther on the rock shelf. Ahau pressed the light closer to see. They were human. He shuddered, images of all of the people in the village who had died at Bela's hands coming unbidden to his mind. He could recognize none of the skulls, but felt the sadness and pity of losing a friend to such an end. It was obvious that this shelf was at one time a well-kept hoard of trophies. The dust, dirt, and general feel of disuse made Ahau think that it had been some time since the skulls had been last fondled or looked at.

The torch was burning fast. He navigated farther into the cave. Stuck into a tight crevice of stone, Ahau found Chan Chel. He was sure it was the hunter because of the design along the edges of the loin cloth. Small, hand painted black jaguars ran in single file along the borders. He did not have time to give the hunter proper homage now, but silently said a quick prayer.

Bones, small and large, littered the floor. Many of the smaller bones still had meat decaying on them. This was the source of the rot he had smelled when first entering the cave. Ahau waved the torch high while slowly turning in a circle. Whatever animal had made the kills could very well be near at hand. He clenched the spear a little tighter and went on.

The cave came to a T, veering left and right. Dislodged pebbles noisily clattered to the cave's floor from his left. Ahau hunched over and turned in the direction of the sound, holding the light well out in front of him. He could not see far in front of him and had no clear idea how far the cave deviated in this direction. He was beginning to wonder how intelligent it had been to come in here alone without even a decent torch. Maybe this was a crack to the underworld. Maybe it was inhabited by demons that guarded the entrance. Maybe he needed to be somewhere else. Anywhere else.

Just as he was about to talk himself into turning back, a pitiful mewing moan sounded close by. The sound seemed to come from above him and a little to his right. The pathetic sound could not have come from anything threatening. It sounded wretched and terrified. It came again, only stronger this time. Ahau lifted the torch and spear in unison toward the sound and shuffled closer. He could see the cave ended much faster than he had earlier thought. The walls curved to a close in a jumble of tumbled rocks. The ceiling climbed a bit higher. It was from there, somewhere behind the larger rocks, that the grievous cries had come.

Ahau, never taking his eyes off the rocks near the ceiling, bent down and grabbed a few small stones, holding the spear against his side with his torch hand's elbow. He chucked them in the direction of the ceiling. Again the cries sounded, this time stronger with an even more terrified edge to them. Ahau threw more in hopes of the animal revealing itself.

***

Bela squirmed tighter against the light's intrusion. He literally quivered in fear, trying to hold still and keep silent. The brownskin was near. He could feel him. *Ahauuu!* There was nowhere else to go; nowhere else to hide. The glare of the torch danced shadows against the roof of the cave as Ahau came closer. Bela could not stop the whimpers that escaped from his clenched lips. Small rocks landed near him, startling him even more. *The brownskin knows where I am.*

Bela peered between the edges of the two large rocks that hid him. He could see the blaze of the torch and Ahau silhouetted behind it. Out of desperation, he tossed rocks back at the brownskin. "Gooo. Thisss meee plaaace. Gooo. Leeeave, Ahauuu."

***

Startled, Ahau almost dropped the low burning torch in his eagerness to get the spear back out in front of him. The rocks had not hit him but landed near enough. *That voice. I know that voice. How can it be? Bela is still alive.*

262

Ahau felt empowered by rage. Images of Jada and Tikal suffering at the hands of the great beast controlled him now. "Come out. I know you are there. We have unfinished business, you and I. I will come up if I have to."

Bela's voice, soft and low, answered. "Gooo awaaay. Thisss plaaace mine."

Ahau started up the rocks, scrabbling for purchase. He could see that his hated enemy could go nowhere else. The cave's walls were directly behind him, with only the rocks separating them. Ahau knew that it was foolhardy to corner a dangerous animal, but didn't care. This time he would make sure Bela died. The torch could be a problem, though. It was almost finished. Whatever he did would have to be fast.

***

Bela could hear Ahau coming up. A fierce struggle of emotions fought for dominance. Fear, anger, and resentment battled with each other. Fear won out. He jumped from his hiding place and tried to make a dash to freedom, bowling the brownskin over. Ahau went down painfully on his side, trying to protect his spear and torch. Bela streaked past him into the main of the cave. Ahau struggled up and gave chase. The torch was now only burning red embers, close to his hand. Ahau tossed it. Impossible to move fast now, Ahau felt for the wall and let it and his memory guide him. Reaching the junction, the light improved considerably. His eyes now being accustomed to the darkness, coupled with the entrance and small fire burning beside it, allowed Ahau to see reasonably well. Droplets of hot spit landed on his head. He turned his face upwards. Bela was just above him, crouched on a large boulder, waiting for him. The beast's hands twitched, claws extended, mouth chewing at the air. Ahau slowly backed away with the spear in both hands, pointed at the beast.

***

Bela's tortured lung wheezed its pain as he squatted above the brownskin. Indecision delayed his movements. Anger and terror struggled for control over his emotions. He was deathly afraid of the brownskin, but an unyielding recollection of pride made him furious that he was being hunted in his own cave. Memories of Ahau eating from his orange rock tipped the balance.

263

"Ooooruh!" He lunged for the brownskin.

***

Bela's uncertainty had given Ahau time to get back. It saved his life. The beast's charge fell unexpectedly short. In that brief moment, Ahau saw that Bela was terribly injured. A reek of nauseating rot washed over him. He jabbed his spear with all of his strength at the great beast's gut. He could feel it hit just below Bela's sternum and sink several inches into the flesh. Ahau tried to push it further.

***

Bela's reaction was immediate. He broke the spear's shaft in a single stroke and howled his rage. His damaged and weakened hide had allowed the spear to enter where before such a thrust would have skittered off. Luckily, it still retained hardness enough to keep the wound from being fatal. Leaping forward, his right hand slashed Ahau's arm, the claws tearing the flesh to the bone. Ahau rolled to his right but could not get up before Bela was on him. He reached for his knife. Again red hot pain exploded. This time Bela opened four diagonal furrows across his chest. His weight was terrifying. Ahau savagely tried to plunge his knife into the beast's eye, but Bela ducked to the side. The blade skittered against the side of his head. Insane with fury, Bela savagely bit Ahau's shoulder, sinking his teeth into bone. Ahau screamed his agony and thrashed furiously against Bela's size and strength, but to no avail. The great beast had him at his mercy.

Bela recognized his advantage and old memories of his former life came unbidden to him. He remembered when he was the single most dominant force in the forest. He remembered how all other animals in his world had panicked with terror when he approached them. He remembered the brownskin below him so many years ago. Bela brought his head closer to Ahau's face. Warm sputum dripped from his huge muzzle, slathering Ahau's face. The young priest turned his head to the side and closed his eyes. He recognized his own death was close.

Bela felt a searing pleasure that he had not felt in many years. He almost felt like his old self. He chew-sucked the priest's shoulder, taking his time and thoroughly enjoying the brownskin's screams. Bela wiped his mouth with his hand, splattering blood against the floor of his cave. He again brought his warm breath close to the priest's face. He tried to look into the priest's eyes to see the terror he was causing and to gloat his dominance, but Ahau had lost consciousness. He lay quietly under the beast, not moving. Bela pierced the young man's chest with one of his claws and drew a small line, trying to get a response. Ahau only slightly quivered and then was again quiet.

Bela, in an almost tender voice, said, "Ahauu...doon't die yet. I waant to plaay moore."

He thought of Chan Chel. He too had passed out from the games they had played together. Bela moved off the young priest and stood up. His damaged lung made it hard to breathe with all of this exertion. He sat down beside Ahau and waited, once in a while slightly kicking the sleeping form.

***

Ahau was beginning to come to. He hurt terribly from his wounds. Bela could be heard beside him, muttering weird sounds, some of them words. Ahau kept his eyes closed as he tried to assess the situation. After a few moments, he could feel the shattered wood shaft from the spear beneath him. He could not tell if it was the handle end or the head of the spear. As stealthily as he could, he shifted his weight enough that he could feel under his self. He edged the broken spear out from under his back. It was the handle end.

Ahau shifted his attention to Bela. The beast demon was still mumbling weird sounds with the occasional words. It was almost like he was having a conversation with himself that only he could understand. There was a sharp kick to Ahau's side, and he involuntarily groaned. Bela was again on him, demanding, "Ahauu, yoou plaay now."

Ahau felt for a better grip on the handle, hoping the broken end was forward. He thrust the ruined spear into Bela's face. The shattered wood pierced just below Bela's eye socket, the wooden shard piercing his brain. Bela shuddered and fell on top of him. Ahau tried to push him off but his body wouldn't respond. Blackness enveloped him. Orange sparks danced around the edges.

Ahau awoke, not knowing where he was. Feeling Bela's weight on top of him quickly brought his memory back. The stench from the great beast was sickening. He pushed, squirmed, and slid his way out from under the carcass. He had no idea how long he had been unconscious. The entrance to the cave showed dim light from a new day, but what day? The fire near the opening was long dead.

Ahau pushed himself to a standing position. He remembered his wounds and carefully checked himself. He didn't think he should even be alive. A chill ran down his spine. Both wounds were terribly sore, but felt as if they had been healing for a month. The flesh had knitted back together in rough ropes of tender scar tissue on both his chest and across his arms. Ahau had been sure when he received the wounds that his life had ended. *What is going on here?* He pushed Bela onto his back. The beast was cold to the touch. Ahau's broken spear was still embedded in Bela's left eye. Rigor mortis had slackened, meaning that at least a day had passed. Ahau pulled the beast's body to the opening of the cave.

Tenderly, cradling his injured arm and moving slowly, Ahau went down to the sand below. He gathered as much loose, dry wood as he could and took it back to the cave, then piled it high around the beast demon. It took several trips. His chest, arm, and shoulder throbbed their soreness. Ahau reverently pulled Chan Chel from the cave's stony embrace and slid the bones into the deep water of the pond, giving Chan Chel release from Bela's imprisonment and access to the underworld and the glory beyond. The shelved, blanched skulls of the warriors, whose identities Ahau could only guess at, were also given to the water. He wished he could do more. At least they were no longer forgotten trophies, shelved in a cave for the enjoyment of a beast that should never have lived.

Ahau put sparks to dry moss from the water's edge and fired Bela's pyre. For long moments Ahau watched the great billows of black smoke surge and roll to the cave's roof, spreading outwards and up from the opening's edge. The priest sat on his blanket and watched until the smoke swirled in only thin brown and white wisps, Bela's body a blackened husk that would forever guard the entrance.

Sitting there watching the great beast's body burn and thinking about the events that had led to this moment made Ahau realize maybe there truly were gods. Privately, he always had his misgivings, especially since Jada's death. But now he could see a purpose. Perhaps

Bela really was Itzamna's way of testing the people's worthiness, as Pochotl had suggested so long ago.

An epiphany came to him. It was a thought that had been denied until now. Bog, which he had always thought of as his own son and a gift from the gods, was in reality a result of Bela. The beast demon had captured and taken Jada to his cave. It was a thought that he knew was fact. Bog was Bela's offspring. He fought with this new knowledge, conscious that he loved Bog as his own. He decided the village would never know. Unofficially, he was sure there were some who suspected the truth but would never give voice to it publicly. Bog would someday become the Halach Unic, the one true man, ultimate leader and king of all that he surveyed. If the people thought he was directly touched by Itzamna, then so be it. They need never know that Bela had been his father.

There was still the matter of how his wounds had healed. Ahau thought he knew, but needed to make sure. He tore off more of the orange rockroot and came back to his blanket. Using the edge of clamshell from his waist pouch, the priest dragged a serious cut down the length of his leg. He quickly ingested the orange rockroot and lay back, closing his eyes. Again, a plethora of colors gloriously danced behind his eyelids. This time, however, the patterns gave way to iridescent images of Jada, Tikal, and Ix Cuy, who spoke to him at length about all manner of things. They told him of the future and the past, explaining his part in the scheme of things, and how he would always be revered by the people.

When he awoke, the night had passed and midday of the new sun had come. Ahau felt along his leg and found the tender, pink scar he knew would be there. Somehow, the orange rockroot had the power to heal. This had been Bela's secret. Itzamna had led him here to discover it and bring its power back to the people. All the resentment and bitterness Ahau had felt were cleansed by the drug's passing. He solemnly asked the gods' forgiveness for all the difficulties he had charged them. Ahau felt inner peace, content that all was as it had been promised so long ago.

Join our Newsletter & Receive Release Day Announcements, News, and Special Sales!

Before You Go...

HELP AN AUTHOR
write a review
THANK YOU!

Share your voice and help guide other readers to these wonderful books. Even if it's only a line or two your reviews help readers discover the author's books so they can continue creating stories that you'll love. Login to your favorite retailer and leave a review. Thank you.

About the Author

Archie Oliver is a retired teacher of art who paints when he can and writes when he can't.

He has always had an interest in telling a good story and stretching the truth. He began his adult life as a basketball coach for a small high school. It was the kids in the classroom, though, that made him stay for 43 years. Now, as a retired baby boomer, he has the time he has always needed for his artistic endeavors. He now lives in the same small town in Southwest Kansas where he was born. In a way, the circle is complete and life is good.

www.ingramcontent.com/pod-product-compliance
Lightning Source LLC
Chambersburg PA
CBHW030242200626
46816CB00002BA/470